SEA OF TR...

Marrimian shivered and looked desperately at the sea of sneering, hate-filled faces and the forest of iron spikes and spears raised against her and the circle of mudbeasts. "I . . . I . . . I command you to lay down your weapons," she cried, but her voice was lost in the roar of the crowds as they surged forward.

A piercing shriek suddenly cut through the marshmen's shouts. It was Pinvey, her voice making the marshmen fall silent as they turned, craning their necks to see where she struggled in the crowd at the edge of the hall. Pinvey was shouting and screaming, sneering and mocking Marrimian in a voice that boiled with hatred. "They'll never take you as their queen. You'll never rule!"

Also by Mike Jefferies

LOREMASTERS OF ELUNDIUM:

1. The Road to Underfall
2. Palace of Kings
3. Shadowlight

THE HEIRS TO GNARLSMYRE:

1. Glitterspike Hall

Published by
HarperPaperbacks

HALL OF WHISPERS

MIKE JEFFERIES

BOOK TWO OF THE HEIRS TO GNARLESMYRE

HarperPaperbacks
A Division of HarperCollins*Publishers*

This is a work of fiction. The characters, incidents, and dialogues are products of the author's imagination and are not to be construed as real. Any resemblance to actual events or persons, living or dead, is entirely coincidental.

HarperPaperbacks   *A Division of* HarperCollins*Publishers*
10 East 53rd Street, New York, N.Y. 10022

This book was published in 1990
in Great Britain by Fontana Paperbacks.

Cover art by Geoff Taylor

First HarperPaperbacks printing: June 1992

Printed in the United States of America

HarperPaperbacks and colophon are trademarks of HarperCollins*Publishers*

10 9 8 7 6 5 4 3 2 1

*To Helen, Katie and Emily,
three wonderful daughters.*

1

Touching the Glitterspike

"**Y**OU have touched the Glitterspike! You have touched the heartstone of your father's power. Now the throne, all the swamps and marshes and all the lands that you call Gnarlsmyre are yours to rule. But be quick. Now you have triumphed beyond your wildest dreams you must show these marshlords and their waders and hunters who trample and swarm all around us that you have the strength and determination to rule over them. They are gathering around us now to snatch it all from you."

Krann was shouting to Marrimian, Lord Miresnare's daughter, as she stood in the center of the bellowing, roaring circle of mudbeasts with her hand placed triumphantly upon the Glitterspike. The beasts roared and plunged, grinding up showers of stone dust and broken bone splinters, their close-shackled hairy flanks rubbing and chafing together as they defended the Glitterspike against the surging hordes of marshlords who choked the hall.

The marshlords saw Marrimian snatch the throne from beneath their very eyes and they surged forward, their shouts of hatred swelling up across the frost-sharp walls of the great hall to vanish in thundering echoes amongst the darkened rafters high above their heads.

"Be quick! Shout out your right to rule Gnarlsmyre," Krann yelled again, stumbling over Naul the master mumbler who lay, a sprawling heap of rags and bones, where Lord Miresnare had tried to murder him, upon the dais of the throne. Krann's boots crunched through the shattered pieces of the mumbler's pine-oil lamp as he struggled to reach the throne and defend it against the swarming marshmen.

Naul wept and cried out, scrabbling with bloody fingers to gather up the broken fragments of his foresight from where they had scattered across the floor. "Marrimian had the right to joust for the throne," he shouted into the writhing mass of angry marshmen's faces. "She drank from the crystal cup at the Allbeast Feast. She has fulfilled the joust by passing between the mudbeasts to touch the Glitterspike."

A new wave of hatred swelled up on the heels of the mumbler's words in thundering echoes amongst the tall fluted columns of the hall, to swamp the high throne and crash against the glittering finger of crystal where Marrimian clung, making her stumble for a moment in her purpose.

One single shout and oath of rage rose above the others: "You are a woman, nothing more than a woman. You can never rule us!"

The marshlords knew the truth in the mumbler's

words but Marrimian *was* only a woman. They would destroy her. They surged forward in one rush and crowded each other in their desire to slaughter the mudbeasts and overrun the throne.

"No woman is strong enough to rule us," sneered a marshman close to the dais of the throne. "Kill her! Hurl your spears and iron spikes at the mudbeasts!"

"Take her! Take her!" thundered a chant as the horde pressed forward, their weapons thrust out toward the circle of mudbeasts.

The chained beasts snarled as the marshmen surged against them. They humped their spines and sent rippling shivers up across their hides as they pushed and barged against each other, tightening their circle to defend Marrimian and the Glitterspike. Yaloor, champion beast of the hall, who had worn thin his oiled chains in defense of Marrimian, lowered his horns and raked them across the floorstones, ploughing up clouds of stone dust and maggoty strips of carcass that littered the mudbeast circle as he flexed his claws and arched his back.

Marrimian shivered and looked desperately at the sea of sneering, hate-filled faces and the forest of iron spikes and spears raised against her and the circle of mudbeasts. "I . . . I . . . I command you to lay down your weapons," she cried, but her voice was lost in the roar of the crowds as they surged forward.

She looked between the shifting mudbeasts toward the high dais of the throne where Krann was fighting beside Ansel and Treasel in an effort to keep the marshmen back. "What can I do?" she shouted helplessly.

"Call to your father's archers who overwatch from the gallery. Call them, tell them to clear the hall."

A piercing shriek suddenly cut through the marshmen's shouts. "No! No, you shall not rule anything!" It was Pinvey, her voice overpowering Krann's and making the marshmen fall silent as they turned, craning their necks to see where she struggled in the crowd at the edge of the hall.

Marrimian snatched her fingers away from the Glitterspike and looked up into the galleries. She cried out to the archers, ordering them to clear the hall, but they hesitated. "Your father Lord Miresnare is dead, murdered by those mudbeasts that surround you," spoke one. "We dare not obey you, firstborn, you are only a woman and a woman cannot rule Gnarlsmyre." He turned away and one by one they all lowered their bows and withdrew from the balustrades of the galleries.

Pinvey shrieked with laughter which echoed through the hall. She was shouting and screaming, sneering and mocking Marrimian in a voice that boiled with hatred. "They'll never take you as their queen. You'll never rule!"

"Who would you have—that treacherous marshlord Mertzork?" called Marrimian, her eyes searching the shadows beneath the galleries for her sister. She caught sight of her balanced awkwardly on an upturned broth boiler's cauldron, her wrist still bound to Mertzork's by the sharpwire of their mistrust. Alea and Syrenea were beside her, helping her to stay upright on her slippery perch.

"You shall not claim the throne, nor will you rule over one miserable mudslapped hovel in all Gnarlsmyre while I live," Pinvey hissed, her face bleached white with hatred, her hair flying out in writhing, raven-black streamers as she quivered and shook with rage, stabbing her clenched knuckles toward Marrimian.

In a moment of silence Marrimian opened her mouth to call on the archers again and command them to obey her but as she glanced up into the galleries she saw that they had all vanished. She shuddered as the marshmen began to surge restlessly forward again toward the circle of mudbeasts, their cries fueled by Pinvey's hatred.

Pinvey laughed again, her voice swelling in wild shrieks. "No one will obey you, sister; the marshmen and all this city will turn against you!"

"The throne is mine by right—I touched the Glitterspike," cried Marrimian, shrinking back against the finger of crystal as the hordes of hostile leering faces closed in about the circle of mudbeasts.

"Miresnare is dead!" shouted a dozen voices. "His laws are worthless, the hall—the city—everything is ours!"

Their voices rose into a thunderous roar chanting for the mudbeasts' deaths. Cruel barbed spears and heavy razor-sharp iron spikes were hurled high into the air above the circle of beasts.

"Let the beasts help us—release them," cried Treasel. Marrimian spun round at the sound of the marshgirl's voice.

"Yes, mistress, give them their freedom; they'll drive these marshscum back into the quickmires," shouted Ansel, her voice sounding quite close to Treasel's, somewhere in the middle of the crush of writhing marshmen who had thrown themselves against the throne in the final rush to seize power.

"How can I break their shackles without a striker?" cried Marrimian in desperation as she caught sight of Krann's dagger blade in the press of bodies on the dais of the throne.

"Search in the bone litter around the base of the Glitterspike!" called out the master mumbler as he fought at Krann's side.

"Where will I find a striker in all this mess and rubbish?" Marrimian wept to herself, her lips trembling with hopelessness. She had to jump and scramble over the knots and loops of the heavy iron chains which snaked and clattered, rubbing up plumes of sparks between her feet as the mudbeasts charged backwards and forwards across the circle.

The marshmen were hurling their spears at the mudbeasts and howling for Marrimian's blood, driven on by Pinvey's wild cursing. They were sneering and taunting her to be quick and find the key to the beasts' shackles before they speared them all to death. Marrimian climbed frantically over the huge iron rings, deaf to their shouts, scrabbling between the thick wedge-shaped locking bolts that the hall wardens had driven through the chain links, searching for something to loosen them.

A spear rose shrieking high into the air before it dipped and struck the floor beside her, sending up a brittle cloud of stone splinters as the blade buried itself in the floor. She cried out and threw herself against Yaloor's flank, stumbling and falling sideways as the marshmen's laughter and sneers of hatred rose into a thundering roar. Yaloor bellowed and reared up, covering her with his shadow, and Gallengab, the sandbeast chained beside him, charged through the circle to defend her as the air grew thick with the sharp rain of falling spear blades.

"I *must* find a striker," Marrimian cried, gritting her teeth as the tortured screams of the mudbeasts on the outer edges of the circle reached her ears.

She hurried now between the iron rings around the base of the Glitterspike and snagged her toe on the remains of a maggot-riddled carcass, claw-torn and crushed amongst the heaps of chains. Shuddering, she jumped backwards but caught the carcass with her heel and dragged it back with her. She gagged on the stench as the rotting flesh and bones crumbled apart, but lying there long forgotten beneath the splintered bones and ribbons of corrupted flesh she saw the smooth bloodsmeared wooden handle of a forging hammer.

"By all the mumblers' magic . . ." she whispered, reaching down with both hands and pulling the hammer clear.

Straightening her back and gritting her teeth, she

swung the heavy hammer at the closest bolt and
sent up a plume of bright sparks as the head struck
the tapered point of the pin.

"I will set the beasts against you, I will . . . ." she
shouted angrily, tottering forward under the
weight of the hammer. She struck bolt after bolt
until her arms grew numb and her head spun and
ached from the thunderous roars of the mudbeasts
as she stumbled blindly in amongst them, ducking
and weaving between their restless claws as she
moved from ring to ring.

As she dragged the heavy hammer behind her she
cursed her own weakness each time the burred
blunt head snagged or trapped itself between the
uuraveling, clattering chains that she had already
broken free. "I must release you all," she cried,
hurrying in an everwidening circle and giving a
shout of triumph each time she knocked out one of
the locking bolts and a mudbeast lurched forward,
its chain sending up a blaze of sparks as it clattered
through the iron ring.

The marshmen's shouts were growing fainter.
She snatched a glance across her shoulder and
would have laughed and shaken her fist at the retreating hordes who were scattering in terror and
fighting each other to escape the advancing mudbeasts, but a freed chain snaked toward her, caught
against her ankles and wound itself on to the head
of the hammer, snatching it from her hands and
making her topple on to her knees. She threw out
her hands and caught hold of the long smooth handle, wrenching it free from the last unwinding

links of the chain as it swept past the hems of her skirts in a grinding clatter.

"How many more?" she gasped wearily as she slowly rose to her feet and searched for breath. She shook her head, blinking, and rubbed a dirty sweat-streaked arm across her forehead as she looked at the rows of empty iron rings that marched away around the Glitterspike, casting long shadows across the ruined, bone-littered floorstones. "By mumblers' magic I have freed them all!" she whispered, twisting and turning to stare out across the empty circle at the great towering beasts who were taking their revenge on the marshmen, spreading chaos and panic wherever they trod throughout the length and breadth of the hall. Only one chain still loosened and tightened around the Glitterspike, drawing Marrimian's eyes. She twisted around and looked up to see that Yaloor was still protecting her, his age-scarred, tangled hide wet with blood from where the marshmen's spears had pierced it.

"Yaloor," Marrimian called quietly, feeling hot tears wet the corners of her eyes as she caught sight of the oozing gashes in his back and flanks. Her lips thinned into a white, bloodless line of anger at the marshmen as she gripped the long handle of the hammer and moved close to the Glitterspike to free Yaloor. She struck at his locking pin to break it free but time had burred the edges. Looking desperately at the heavy iron chain, she chose a place where her champion had worn it thin as he protected her from the marshmen who had come to claim her in each season's joust.

"Of all the beasts in Gnarlsmyre you should have your freedom," she cried, planting her feet wide apart on either side of the chain, and locking her fingers around the handle of the hammer, she swung it up high above her head. She cried out as she tottered backwards for half a step, arching her spine and knotting her muscles, then gathered the last shreds of her strength and hurled the hammer downwards, throwing her head back and crying out every snatch of magic that she could remember to give the blunt forging hammer the power to snap Yaloor's chain. The hammer sang through the air. The fleeing marshmen turned in terror at the flash of sunlight reflecting from the flat striking face of the hammer as it swept toward the chain. The hammer struck in a blinding spark, the chain split into jagged pieces and the long handle shivered, numbing Marrimian's fingers as it shattered into a haze of splinters. The hard granite floorstone beneath the links fractured, crazing into countless mosaic pieces as white-hot sparks flew up to sting her face.

"Yaloor, Yaloor, you are free," Marrimian shouted, laughing and crying as she smudged the blackened spark marks across her cheeks.

Krann gave a shout of triumph from the dais and Ansel laughed and struck out with new strength at the scattering marshmen as Yaloor slowly lowered his head and gently scented his mistress. The huge mudbeast brushed his broken horn against the weave of her skirt and clawed deep scrapes in the floorstones before he began to turn and sweep his pitiless gaze after the fleeing marshmen.

"You are free," whispered Marrimian, "free to go where you please in all Gnarlsmyre." She reached out and touched the tangles of his hide and firmly pushed him away from the broken links of his chain.

Yaloor snarled, sending a ripple up across his hide at her soft touch, and he lumbered slowly forward, crushing a path through the litter of blood and bone that spoiled the outer edges of the circle. He gathered speed in lengthening strides and swept his horns from left to right at the last of the fleeing marshmen, crushing them under claw or tossing them high into the air. As he drew level with Gallengab he slowed and pressed his flank against the huge sandbeast's flank and the two most fearsome beasts ever snared in the marshes of Gnarlsmyre began to charge through the hall together.

Suddenly Pinvey's voice cut across the hall, making Marrimian spin round and search for her beneath the galleries. White-faced and gaunt with hatred, she shook her fists at Marrimian. "You may have driven us off with your filthy, marshbound beasts but we will return and tear this hall down stone by stone," she cursed, hurling the words across the empty space toward her sister. "Erek the healing woman will curse you and blacken everything that you think you have won and she will destroy everything you try to do within this wretched hall."

Marrimian opened her mouth to call out to Pinvey, to beg her to put her hatred aside, to tell her that she would forgive all her treachery, but Mertzork snarled at her and leapt forward, only to jerk to a halt as the sharpwire that bound Pinvey to him tightened on his wrist.

He glanced up and down the hall and suddenly laughed, curling his lips back cruelly over his teeth and whispered down to Pinvey. "Your sister and those cursed followers of hers know nothing of hunting mudbeasts. Quickly, run for the nearest low archway, where the beasts cannot follow us. They'll turn on your precious sister when they have destroyed the last of the escaping marshmen. Watch. Watch and enjoy seeing her death."

Mertzork stumbled backwards and gave a brutal pull on the sharpwire as he searched desperately over his shoulder for the nearest low archway for their escape.

But Pinvey crouched, clinging to one of the greasy, soot-blackened legs of the cauldron, using all of her strength to resist the biting cut of the sharpwire around her wrist. "You are afraid," she sneered, holding his gaze. "You—the champion that I chose out of all the marshmen flocking to my father's hall—you who would try to steal my father's throne—you are afraid."

She paused and spat, curling back her brightly painted lips to expose her teeth in a snarl. "You are afraid of the handful of hide-scarred beasts that my sister has loosed against this rabble."

Mertzork blinked in surprise that she had dared to answer him so and he flexed his arm and dragged her roughly from the cauldron. "Fool!" he hissed, pulling her up from her knees and sweeping his free hand across the pandemonium that the rampaging beasts were spreading wherever they trampled. "You understand nothing, woman, if you cannot see that spears and iron spikes are useless against these beasts."

"But my sister . . ." muttered Pinvey, then broke off, reaching out and grasping Alea's wrist as Mertzork dragged her and Syrenea toward a low archway where a crush of marshmen were fighting their way through.

Mertzork paused and stabbed his hand back at the huge lumbering beasts that had now reached the far end of the hall and were beginning to turn toward them. "You know nothing of hunting beasts. It would take an army of marshhunters spread throughout the rafter beams of this hall with iron woven nets to ensnare these rampaging beasts," he snarled.

"But my sister went amongst them with nothing," whispered Pinvey bitterly. Her dark eyes flashed with anger still at the thought that Mertzork was trying to run away and she wished that she had chosen better as she scratched at the tight knot in the sharpwire that bound them so closely together.

"Magic!" Mertzork hissed, turning his back on the hall. "She must be using that stranger's magic to pass amongst the beasts, the one who helped her reach the Glitterspike, but, mark my words, nothing will save her or keep safe any of those who help her once the mudbeasts have sniffed at every low archway on both sides of the hall and realize that the marshlords have escaped. Look at them, Pinvey, they have been made ragged by the shower of spear blades and bloodied by those they have crushed. Now, run for that archway over there before the closest beast tramples on our heels. We must find Erek the healing woman and those black hags she calls her gathering of crones. Their magic will slaughter these rampaging beasts and help us to snatch back everything that your cursed sister has stolen from us."

Mertzork shouted out and struck at the milling crush of marshmen who were trying to squeeze through the archway at the same moment. He snarled as he knocked the closest aside and he swung his iron spike at those directly in his path and forced a way for Alea and Syrenea to slip beneath the arch. Reaching back, he gave the sharpwire a brutal tug and made Pinvey stumble in after him. She stopped and clutched at the rough stonework, turning her head back toward the great hall, and stifled a cry of pain as the sharpwire cut into her wrist.

"A moment! A moment!" she hissed, looking toward the throne where the fat scullion, the marshgirl and the mumbler were all raising their hands in triumph. A breath of hatred escaped from between her lips and her face became pinched and taut with defeat. Slowly she began to curse Marrimian. Then the shadow of the huge mudbeast that had scented them turned toward their archway and spoiled her view of the hall as its tangled, armored hide smothered the opening. Pinvey cried out in rage as the beast reared up, "We will return and tear this hall down stone by stone!"

Mertzork screamed at her to follow him into the low corridor, pulling her back from the beast that tore at the archway, bellowing and snarling, drowning out her curses, as it gouged deep claw-scrapes in the keystones of the arch.

"We must go to the Shambles and find Erek. She will help us to destroy the mudbeasts with her magic. The hall will be ours before nightfall if we hurry," he hissed, pulling Pinvey after him.

Pinvey stared, for a moment full of hatred, at the nape of Mertzork's dirty neck as he turned from her and forced a path through the crush in the narrow corridor. "All I wanted was one moment to watch the beast turn on Marrimian," she muttered, scraping the back of her hand on the low brick roof as the crowd carried her forward away from the hall. Rising on tiptoe, she caught the briefest glimpse, past the beast, of Marrimian standing alone beside the Glitterspike, resting her hand upon the sheer finger of glittering crystal.

"You will not keep any of it, sister," she hissed as the crowd took her around a sharp twist in the corridor and the great hall vanished from her sight.

2

The Mudbeasts Rampage

"IT is your victory, mistress, everything that you strove to win!" shouted Ansel with relief and laughter in her voice and a dozen dimpled smiles creased her plump, oven-bright cheeks. She sighed, thankful that the fighting was over, and tried to shut out the roaring, bellowing cries of the mudbeasts that were rampaging through the hall, sniffing at all the low archways that they could reach beneath the galleries. She wiped her broad, blunt hands on the tails of her dirty, crumpled apron before she placed them firmly on her hips and cast her frowning gaze over the mess and rubbish that fouled the floorstones of the hall.

"It will take an army of underscullions and scuttles to clear this up," she muttered to herself. She looked to where her mistress stood alone amongst the broken chains and huge iron rings in the shadow of the Glitterspike.

"Everything! Is that what I have won?" whispered Marrimian, shivering, her spine tingling as she remembered the tail-end of hatred in Pinvey's voice as her sister fled beneath the low archway.

Slowly she shook her head as if to try and scatter the echo of those words and shake off the growing feeling of despair that was spoiling the moment of her triumph. She turned to move toward the throne and opened her mouth to call to Krann when she stopped mid-stride, her breath catching in her throat as she saw her father's cloak half-hidden beneath the loops and twists of the broken chains. She remembered how he had tried to stop her, how he had been seized with madness to keep what had been his and how he had fallen headlong on her heels into the circle of beasts.

"Father!" she cried, running to where he lay among the litter of rotting carcasses, broken spears and twisted iron spikes. She fell to her knees beside him, blinking back the hot tears of despair that burned her eyes, and threw aside the heavy links of chain that lay across his body. It all came flooding back to her: the echo of his hatred of her womanhood, the blind, glazed look of madness in his eyes and the yellow flecks of spittle that foamed in his mouth as he had tried to stop her entering the circle of mudbeasts. She remembered clearly his last words as she had broken free of him.

"Run! Run for the Glitterspike, my daughter," he had sneered, his face bloated with triumph. "But you shall not pass between the mudbeasts, no matter how many rumors of beast-riding you have seeded to snare and trick these gullible marshscum. You are a mere woman, a worthless nothing, and the beasts will destroy you if you try to slip between their armored flanks. Run, child, hurry to your death, treacherous daughter; the mudbeasts are eager to tear you bone from bone. Remember, daughter, as you reach out to embrace the beast Yaloor that it was I who snared him while you were still cradle-wet. Remember that he is my champion and he will not let anyone past to touch the Glitterspike and steal my throne!"

Marrimian shivered; she remembered his screams as he had fallen amongst the mudbeasts and they had borne down on him, snarling and clawing, rending his cloak and tearing through his gown.

"This is not the victory I wished for," she wept, reaching out to turn him over and gather him up into her arms, but she shuddered as the torn and bloodied cloak fell apart at her touch. She cried out and let his body sink back amongst the broken chains, snatching her hands away from the splintered bone ends that had broken through his flesh, and the bruised and blackened face that stared up at her so accusingly.

"I did not want this," she gasped, shrinking away from the blind stare. "I only wanted . . ." Her voice trailed away as the bile rose in her throat and choked her into silence.

"Mistress Marrimian, quickly, we must escape while there is still time," urged a familiar high-pitched voice from behind her, making her rise and stumble backwards away from the place where the mudbeasts had crushed and trampled her father to death.

She turned toward the throne and saw Naul, the master mumbler, pointing wildly up and down the length of the hall, the windbells in the hem of his saffron gown singing with shrill music.

"The mudbeasts have driven all the marshmen out of the hall. Look, they will turn back toward us, they will trample and crush us just . . ."

"Quickly, crouch down behind us women and keep very still. They won't hurt women," hissed Treasel the marshgirl to Krann and Naul. She beckoned Marrimian and urged her to join them on the dais of the throne before the mudbeasts turned and charged back toward them.

Gripping Ansel by the wrist, Treasel pulled her close and whispered that she must spread her apron tails as wide as they would stretch. The mudbeasts had chased the fleeing marshmen beneath the galleries, goring them and trampling them under claw as they fought each other to escape into the low archways. Now they were tiring of clawing at the empty spaces and they reared up, splintering the joist beams of the galleries, then charged heavily through the rows of supporting columns and brought the galleries crashing down around them.

Marrimian took one hurried glance across her shoulder as she ran for the dais of the throne and gave a startled cry as she saw the galleries collapse in a roar of falling masonry and splitting timber. The noise of it echoed through the hall and the giant beasts vanished in a billowing cloud of fine stone dust.

Stumbling and scrambling, Marrimian grasped hold of Treasel and Ansel's outstretched hands and leapt up on to the dais. "What are we to do?" she cried, casting another glance over her shoulder, only to see the first of the mudbeasts emerge bellowing and snarling from the cloud of dust.

One by one the huge beasts began to cross the hall, sending ripples up across their tangled hides to dislodge the splintered beams and flakes of masonry that clung between their spines. They bellowed softly and stretched their necks, raking their horns through the litter of dead marshmen. Lifting their heads, they wrinkled their noses, their jaws gulping, opening and closing. It was a nerve-chilling sight to see so many rows of teeth; it looked as though they were trying to drink in the air of the hall in huge swallowing movements. Yaloor and Gallengab were a pace before the other mudbeasts, their small cold unblinking eyes fixed upon the dais of the throne.

"Stay very still, they must not see whom we hide," whispered Treasel, her lips hardly moving as she spoke. "They are scenting us. If they come any closer we must sing and let them hear our women's voices."

Marrimian nodded without answering. She felt weak, as if all courage had melted, and she tightened her grip on Ansel and Treasel's fingers and sensed the damp, sweet smell of her fear mix with theirs.

Yaloor roared and took a step toward them, and Marrimian, her nerves stretched tighter than a sharpwire, lifted her head and sang those same half-forgotten snatches of hall talk that she had sung when they had ridden the wild mudbeast through the marshes. Her voice rose clearly, as pure as beaten silver, echoing through the empty hall, and beside her, deep and guttural, Ansel's voice began to chant, awkwardly at first but growing stronger with each rising note. Treasel smiled at the scullion and sang with her and one by one the great beasts slowed, lowered their horns and let them sway as the haunting chant flowed all around them. Gradually the mudbeasts became restless, shifting from claw to claw, and crowded closer to the throne, trampling through the litter of broken bodies, their cold eyes following every movement and each shallow terror-drawn breath the three women took. They had lumbered past the Glitterspike and now only a dozen clawscrapes separated them from the dais of the throne.

"Sing! Sing!" gasped Treasel, her jaw aching, her throat raw and burning.

The great beasts were now level with the gloomy, high-arched entrance to the hall and, soothed by the singing, their snarling voices fell silent and they lowered their heads, tilting and turning them to catch the fading sound of running footsteps as the marshmen sought the quickest way through the maze of passageways and alleyways that would lead them into the main corridor and to the outer doors of the hall.

Gallengab bellowed and turned toward the high entrance, drawn by the marshmen's voices, but mixed with the fading shouts and curses he could scent the bulrush stems and rank grasses that grew across the endless swamps and mangle groves, far away beyond the Hurlers' Gate. As he lumbered away the other beasts followed on his heels, barging and bumping, humping their backs and locking their horns. Now the cold marsh wind blew and whistled its way through the winding corridors and into the hall and ruffled the coarse, tangled hair that hung down across their flanks.

"Sing—chant as you have never done before," hissed Marrimian between breaths as the two mud-beasts closest to Gallengab charged beneath the keystones of the archway, their horns clashing, their claws sending up a thunderous echo as they vanished from sight.

The whole herd of mudbeasts began to crowd the entrance, bellowing and clawing deep gouges in the floorstones, impatient for the rank odors and wet mud of the quickmarshes. Yaloor reared up as if searching, looking for Marrimian, as the heaving press of beasts took him with them beneath the archway. His broken horn cast a long shadow over the other beasts as they surged all around him.

Marrimian took a step toward the entrance and raised her hand, her lips numb from the desperate chanting, and she formed silent words of thanks to the champion from her childhood, but Yaloor was gone, swept away from the hall before she could find her voice to cry out her farewells.

"Well then, better gone, and good riddance to every one of them," muttered Ansel with a sigh of relief as the last beast charged beneath the archway, and she sat down heavily on the edge of the dais and with the tails of her apron dabbed at the trickles of sweat that had run down into the corners of her eyes.

Krann and Naul rose slowly to their feet, flexing cramped fingers and stiff joints as they gazed around the empty hall.

"You have a powerful magic," whispered Naul as he kneeled before Marrimian and held out his pine-oil-stained fingers to her in a salute.

Marrimian shook her head and laughed uneasily as she looked down at the mumbler's shaven head. Slowly he raised it and held her gaze with his piercing eyes that seemed to strip away Marrimian's defences and see into every secret. She shivered and blinked to break the mumbler's gaze and dispel her childhood fears of these magic mumbling men. She could never imagine anything dimming her sense of panic at the merest whisper of the windbells that were sewn on to the hems of their saffron robes or the sweet smell of the pine-oil lampsmoke that clung in every secret fold of their cloaks. Even now, as the master mumbler kneeled before her, she imagined she could hear the tramp of the other, lesser, mumblers' dancing feet and for a moment she held her breath, expecting to look across the hall and see their dance, an unbroken circle around the Glitterspike, vanishing in and out of the fog of lampsmoke that billowed from their lamps.

Marrimian tried to overcome her uneasiness and laughed again. "Our power over the mudbeasts was nothing, nothing more than . . ."

She stopped abruptly, the words trapped in her throat as a thunderous roar suddenly filled the hall, shattering the empty silence, and made her clutch the armrests of the throne.

The ground shifted beneath her feet and the Glitterspike trembled from where it rose out of the bones of the earth to where it vanished amongst the smoke-blackened rafters high overhead. The gemstones and ghosted veins of molten silver sparkled and shimmered as the skirts of hoarfrost crackled into a thousand new feathered patterns. Puffs of stone dust and flakes of dried-up polish from the rag bindings that clothed the ragmen's feet billowed and burst up all along the cracks where the floorstones lay edge to edge.

"What was that?" Marrimian cried, the mumbler before her forgotten as she twisted and turned from left to right, following the echoes and rumbles as they swept across the hall.

Ansel had clenched her fists in terror and leapt down from the dais ready to defend her mistress when a second thunderous roar and the sharp sound of splintering crystal swallowed up the dying echoes of the first noise.

"Mistress," she gasped, staggering back against the dais.

Treasel, who had been born beneath an open sky and feared the dark roof overhead and the dark, narrow closeness of the warren of passageways that had brought them into the hall, wept and crouched at Marrimian's feet, her head buried in the hem of her mistress's skirt.

Naul spun around, his eyes narrowing as he followed the thunderous sound. "The mudbeasts must be rampaging through the city," he hissed, turning toward the tall window arches above the ruined gallery.

"I will look," cried Krann, jumping down from the dais and running the shortest route through the mounds of rubbish that littered the floor until he stood in the shadows of the ruined galleries.

He caught his breath as he climbed on to a splintered beam that protruded from the gallery and pulled himself up amongst the broken floorboards, carefully working his way through the ruined beams until he reached the nearest crystal window. Balancing as best he could, his fingers clutching the icy stone window-sill, he pressed his cheek against the glass and looked down. He saw the broken, jagged edges of stone archways and sheets of crystal that must have clung to the outer walls of the hall just below the sill. Beyond the ruins he could just see the steep maze of winding lanes and alleyways that spread out beneath the hall, dark, shadowy, echoing places that fell away toward the Hurlers' Gate and the endless quickmarshes that lay beyond. A blinding flash of sunlight reflecting from the uppermost broken sheet of crystal just beyond the window-sill dazzled him as the crumbling structure swayed and the crystal began fracturing wildly into a thousand brilliant patterns as it struck the stone window-sill. It was followed by the sudden rumbling thunder of falling masonry that shook the wall and made Krann press himself tightly to the balustrade as he craned his neck and peered downwards over the sill.

"I can see the whole city!" he shouted as the rail he was balancing on trembled and fine cracks crazed their way across the clear sheet of crystal he was looking through. "It's those tall glass houses, the ones that we could see reflecting the sunlight as we crossed the marshes toward the city, the ones you called the crystal houses. They are collapsing one by one."

Krann's voice trailed away into silence as he reached up and took a finger-hold on the lace-fine stonework that graced the window arch. Slowly he edged himself upright and spread his feet along the narrow sill, curling his toes for a better grip.

"Take care, please take care," Marrimian called anxiously as she reached up with empty hands outstretched toward him and moved to the edge of the dais of the throne.

Krann shifted his weight to the balls of his feet and took a firmer hold on the stonework of the arch as he looked downwards. He let his breath whistle through his teeth as he saw the heaps of shattered crystal and the wreckage of broken stone columns and window arches piled up and strewn along the base of the sheer wall below him. The mudbeasts were rampaging amongst the wreckage, crushing the broken crystal beneath their claws and tossing the slender, fluted columns high into the air with their horns as they fought one another to reach and eat the sweetest of the hanging vines that had grown around the columns and crisscrossed the narrow glass houses. Everything was being trampled underclaw as they moved through the crystal houses.

"The mudbeasts," Krann shouted without daring to turn his head. "They are smashing down the slender stone columns that support the crystal houses. They are rearing up to graze on the hanging vines. Look out, another crystal house is about to collapse!"

Krann pressed himself against the stonework of the window frame and gritted his teeth while he watched the tall house of glass shiver and sag as the lower latticework of the slender columns and archways was snapped as easily as stalks of summer grasses by the mudbeasts' horns. For a moment he held his breath while the sunlight flickered on the swaying sheets of crystal, a maze of cracks ran silently across the glass as it broke free from the wall of the hall. A dull rumble rose to a thunderous roar that shook the hall as the crystal house vanished, folding inwards upon itself in a shower of stone dust and glittering splinters of crystal that cascaded down on the rampaging mudbeasts' backs.

"They have been starved of mangletree roots and marsh grasses, that is why they have entered the crystal houses," cried Treasel as the thundering roar of falling masonry echoed and died away through the hall.

"Crystal houses," muttered Ansel to herself, a frown crumpling her forehead as she turned her head to follow the fading echo of shattering crystal vanishing beneath the ruined galleries. Anxiously she turned to Marrimian and tugged at her sleeve.

"We will starve, mistress, if they destroy all the crystal houses. There will be nothing to eat in the wet seasons when the marshes flood."

Marrimian stared at the scullion as she tried to grasp the meaning in Ansel's mutterings.

"Why will we starve?" she shouted against the roaring echo of falling masonry that drowned out her voice as another of the tall glass houses collapsed, making the floorstones of the hall tremble beneath their feet.

Ansel frowned and shrugged her shoulders. She spread her empty hands and stabbed her broad kitchen fingers across the hall to where the slender glass houses had once leaned their backs against the sheer walls. "Because," she began, struggling for words, "because the frozen nights never crept beneath the sheets of crystal. No . . ." She stopped and shook her head. "It is more than that. That is where everything that we ate during the wet seasons was grown. All the sweet vines, herbs, fruit and vegetables . . . everything except the meats and the fish, which were always brought up from the smoke houses before the rains began, but there won't be any meat either now, since Yaloor didn't slay any of the other mudbeasts in the joust."

Marrimian listened to the scullion's voice and her words seemed to echo shrilly in Marrimian's head long after they had faded from the hall. The terrible meaning that they held seemed to fall as a lengthening shadow of despair across her triumph as the rumbling crash of the collapsing crystal houses once again soared around them.

"Everything that we ate?" she asked in a whisper. Ansel let out a long sigh, folded her arms and slowly nodded her head. "There will be nothing to feed the people of this city once the rains begin and everything beyond the Hurlers' Gate is flooded. We will all starve, mistress."

"That is why your father had so much power," whispered Naul from where he crouched beside the throne. "The crystal houses and the smoke houses fed the city during the wet seasons and he controlled them with an iron hand, measuring out each morsel of food so meanly that it forced the people to submit to his every whim, and if they spoke against him then he starved them and forced them to tighten their belts until the wet seasons had passed and the harvesters and gatherers could bring the fruits of the marshes once more into the lower markets of the city."

"But I did not know . . . I never gave a thought to where the food that I ate came from or to how we came by the feasts that I overwatched. I did know that the sweetmeats were gathered in the crystal houses, but I never understood their importance," Marrimian muttered, sinking down on the dais of the throne and letting her head fall forwards into her hands as she realized that it was all her fault that the beasts had rampaged through the crystal houses, that it was because she was a woman the joust had been changed and because of that the city now lay in ruins and the smoke houses were empty of meats to cure for the wet seasons.

Marrimian looked between her outspread fingers

at the crushed and crumpled remains of her father amongst the loops of chains and wept. "It is all my fault. If only I had been born a boy . . ." Her voice faltered as large teardrops of despair trickled between her fingers.

Ansel whispered softly and reached out to comfort her but Naul stopped her hand with a piercing gaze and the slightest shake of his head that set the windbells in his robes singing with soft music.

"Leave her," he whispered. "She is our Queen. I foresaw it in the lampsmoke and she touched the Glitterspike to make my foresight into truth, but now she must grow her own strengths out of her despair if she is to hold on to what she has won and rule the lands of Gnarlsmyre. Leave her be."

Krann was oblivious of Marrimian's despair while he pressed his nose against the window pane and watched the last of the glass houses waver, sway and then slowly break away from the sheer wall of the hall as its columns snapped. It seemed for a moment to hesitate, suspended, trembling in the wind, and then the gap widened and it gradually over-balanced while the wafer-thin sheets of crystal fractured into thousands of brittle, glittering splinters that scattered across the city as it fell.

Krann sighed and shifted his weight to ease the tingling cramp in his fingers and toes and let his eyes sweep over the ruins of the narrow, twisting lanes and alleyways that spread out below him. He realized that now the crystal houses had collapsed he could see every roof and chimney pot, and everywhere through the drifting haze of smoke, groups

of fleeing marshmen running beneath the overhanging galleries or disappearing in and out of the
narrow shadows that filled the gaps between the
houses as they fought and elbowed each other for
the fastest road down to the Hurlers' Gate. He
could hear anxious shouts and saw wild eyes glance
over shoulders as the running throng watched for
the rampaging mudbeasts who, new-gorged from
their grazing through the crystal houses, had
caught the marshmen's scent and were following
them, charging down the narrow alleyways, bellowing and roaring. Their horns sent up ribbons of
bright sparks as they gouged and struck at the walls
of the closely crowded houses.

Krann smiled, watching the leading beast close
on the heels of the marshmen and then he let his
gaze travel past the Hurlers' Gate and far, far across
the endless wastes of mud and swamp. He looked
on past the mangle groves and the banks of tall
bulrush reeds to where, on the very edges of sight,
beneath a vault of blue he could just glimpse the
bright indigo, the soft yellow, green and blue
splashes of color where Rainbows' End, his gateway home, was painted in shimmering archways
across the sky.

"Elundium," he whispered with longing and he
rested his forehead on the back of his hand as he
remembered the rolling grasslands and silent
wooded valleys. He closed his eyes and he could see
so clearly the high arched trees that grew beside the
Greenway's edges and faintly and far, far away he
imagined that he could hear the sound of hooves

galloping across the whispering grasslands toward the setting sun. "Elundium!" he called again and the smile that had begun to crease the corners of his mouth trembled and disappeared as the memory of what had driven him to flee his home and led to him being here, crouched in this high window arch of Glitterspike Hall, came flooding back and he shivered at the jumble of dark images that rose up to haunt him.

The darkness filled Krann's mind as he recalled growing to manhood in the Granite City, surrounded by whispering lies, half-truths and uneasy silences about his beginnings. He recalled how events had led to him taking that secret ride which Fairlight, his one true friend, had urged on him so that he could watch the Shadowtreading ceremony on the Rising, and which had led to the nightmare realization that his beginnings were shrouded in dark shadows, that he was a part of that hideous mummers' dance trodden in the fresh-raked snow. He shivered again and caught an echo of the voices and the vision of the nightbeast creatures that had driven him to flee everything that he had known and search out the truth of his beginnings beyond the edges of Elundium. The voices had taken him deep into the Shadowlands and the swirling fog banks before abandoning him and leaving him to find an inner strength to choose his own path through the quicksands and the dreary wastes of mud and mire into the land of Gnarlsmyre.

Krann suddenly blinked and opened his eyes. Marrimian's rush to touch the Glitterspike amid the roars of the mudbeasts and the shouts and curses of the marshmen had driven it all out of his mind and made him forget. He smiled. Laughter was on his lips as he remembered how fate had crossed his path with Marrimian's, how through their touching, as he had helped her, she had lifted the edges of the dark curtain that had clouded his memory and shown him clearly that he was not all bad, that there was more to him than shadows in the darkness.

"There are so many questions! I must go back now," he whispered to himself. He shifted awkwardly in the window arch and turned his head to call down to Marrimian but the laughter died on his lips as he looked down and saw her despair as she sat alone and weeping on the dais of the throne. And one fleeting glance at the ruin and desolation that surrounded her told him that he had to remain at her side until the people of this wretched land of Gnarlsmyre had accepted her as their Queen.

Krann turned back and stared out across the quickmarshes. He swallowed that moment of happiness, letting it and the sweet scent of pine needles that drifted through the faraway forests of Elundium slowly fade from his mind. "One day I will return, I know I will, I believe it," he whispered, forcing himself to look away from the view of Rainbows' End.

3

Weaving Webs
of Lies

WILD screams and shouts of terror echoed
in every dark lane and narrow alleyway of
the city as the marshmen poured out of
Glitterspike Hall and fled from the enraged mudbeasts that Marrimian had set free. Desperate to
reach the Hurlers' Gate and the marshes beyond,
they barged and fought one another and trampled
and crushed anyone who blocked their path.

Erek heard the thunder of their footsteps and
threw open her door within the Shambles. "There
is fear and terror in the air, I can almost taste it,"
she hissed, frowning at the sudden commotion and
snapping her fingers at her haggle of crones, commanding them to follow her as she hurried toward
the entrance to the Shambles.

"Who or what are you fleeing?" she hissed,
snatching at one of the running marshmen who had
stumbled near the entrance and become entangled
in the shroud of webs that hung across it.

The marshman fought against her, screaming as
he saw the swarms of spiders scuttling down across
the canopy of webs toward him. "Marrimian, the

Beast Lady, has touched the Glitterspike and claimed the throne. She has freed the mudbeasts and they are joining her against us!" he cried, tearing himself free of Erek's grip and throwing himself back into the mass of marshmen who were rushing past the entrance.

"Fools, useless fools! You should have killed those beasts while they were still shackled instead of letting them chase you out of the hall. Where was Mertzork? He should have known what to do," hissed Erek, spitting venom on the heels of the fleeing marshman and staining the darkened cobbles beyond the entrance of the Shambles as she sprang through the hanging shrouds of thread into the narrow alleyway. Staring up toward the hall, she caught sight of Mertzork and Pinvey in the headlong rush for the Hurlers' Gate.

"You have wasted all the magic that I put at your fingertips," she shrieked and scattered the crush of fleeing marshmen who crowded outside her entrance to the Shambles with a handful of her most venomous spiders cast between their marshbound feet. Seeing Alea and Syrenea trying to slip past her, she snapped her crooked fingers and caught them. She pinched them cruelly with her fingernails and forced them into the entrance to the Shambles.

"Dance, dance," she hissed, calling to her sisters, the ancient crones, and setting them to leap and sway in an unbroken circle. As they swayed they sent their black skirts flying up to hide Mertzork and Pinvey's scents from the pursuing mudbeasts, as they reached the Shambles, pushing through the crowds.

Erek caught Mertzork and Pinvey's wrists, breaking the sharpwire that bound them together, and pulled them both deep into the mouth of the alleyway, making them kneel while she thrust her searching mirror against their lips. Moving it backwards and forwards, she watched the truth of their defeat within the hall form in the tiny beads of moisture that wet the glass. Her eyes narrowed beneath their hoods of cracking skin and her thin, bloodless lips trembled with rage as she watched Marrimian thwart her revenge.

"What of Naul? What of the mumbler that Miresnare stole from me?" she whispered, her narrow beak of a nose smearing the mirror as she tried to see his fate.

"Mumbler? Who cares for that bundle of wasted rags and bones wrapped in his saffron robes?" sneered Pinvey, snatching her head away from Erek's rancid breath. "My father threw him to the ground and smashed his lamp into a thousand pieces and trod him into the floorstones of the hall as he chased Marrimian into the circle of beasts."

For a moment Erek and Pinvey's eyes met above the searching mirror in a withering stare and neither flinched or blinked or looked away. The gloomy, airless entrance to the Shambles seemed to darken beneath the crisscrossed, sagging spiders' webs, and the bellowing roar of the mudbeasts together with the shouts of the fleeing bands of marshmen seemed to fade. For a moment Erek's eyes flickered and bitter tears of sadness brimmed there. "Naul—my child," she whispered, wringing her gnarled hands, but the tears dried in a hot wave of hatred for the Miresnares that seemed to muffle the noise of the city into nothing as she held Pinvey's unblinking gaze.

Pinvey was a Miresnare but Erek must not let that spoil her revenge. She knew that she must use it, but she sensed a raw and dangerous power in Pinvey and knew that she must tread with care if she was to twist her to her own advantage. "Queen! You shall be Mertzork's queen and together you will rule all Gnarlsmyre," whispered Erek, swallowing the disaster of her son's defeat and letting her shoulders sag a little and her eyes hood and narrow with hidden cunning.

Erek was far too clever to let Pinvey see how the loss of Naul had hurt her or to show a moment's weakness. She was not going to waste precious time when there was a throne and revenge to snatch. She cracked her knuckles, then smiled and stroked the rich fabric of Pinvey's soiled gown.

Pinvey drew back from the healing woman's touch, sensing danger and treachery. She let her gaze sweep over the mean Shambles, the airless alleyway strung with countless loops and tails of fine gossamer threads, beyond where Mertzork kneeled to where her sisters huddled in terror of the spiders that crowded a fingerspan from the hems of their skirts.

"If you have the power to make me Queen why don't you turn these fleeing marshscum that crowd every lane and alleyway back toward the hall and make them tear it stone from stone?" she demanded, her fists clenched in great anger and her voice edged with bitterness and hatred.

"Yes, why don't you use your magic to kill these mudbeasts?" snarled Mertzork, leaping to his feet, a sharpwire stretched between his hands, its razor edge gleaming in the gloomy half-light. "Use your magic to help us destroy the hall!"

"I cannot kill all these mudbeasts, even with my most venomous spiders." Erek shook her head, shrieking with dry laughter from dribbling lips. "But even if I could, you have a greater enemy. Hundreds of simple marshmen from beyond the city have been gathering at the Hurlers' Gate, drawn by the rumor of the Beast Lady whom they want to serve. If you try to reenter the hall and kill Marrimian they will kill you both. We have to find another way." Erek snapped her mouth shut as her cunning mind began to work. Slowly she wiped her searching mirror clean of their defeat with a twist of gossamer web, turning a sharp ear to her dancing crones. As she slipped the mirror beneath her cloak, she carelessly shook loose a swarm of hidden spiders from the darker folds of her sleeves. "Listen to the crones; they have the answer," she hissed, sweeping her crooked fingers toward the blur of ancient hags that leapt and spun past the entrance, their riddle of rags hiding them from the pursuing mudbeasts. "Listen to the secrets that they have harvested beyond the Hurlers' Gate. Look at the splashes of quickmarsh that spoil their boots. Listen to what they stole!"

Pinvey hesitated, clutching on to her hatred, and leaned toward the entrance, but all she could hear were shrieks of madness, wild chanting and the rush of boots while each crone's face leered in at her as it sped past.

"Nothing? You hear nothing!" shrieked Erek, her voice tight with impatience as she drew Pinvey and Mertzork further into the Shambles.

Pinvey shook her head and Mertzork cursed and muttered under his breath as the healing woman stared at them. "You heard nothing of the rumors of this Beast Lady? You heard nothing of how the marshmen have followed the rumor across the length and breadth of Gnarlsmyre to serve her?"

"Nothing! I heard nothing!" Pinvey muttered, impatient to be free of this dried-up hag whose skin crawled with all manner of creeping things.

"Then listen again," hissed Erek, sensing that Pinvey's hatred for Marrimian had dulled and blinded her to everything else. She smiled at Pinvey, her face softening into a maze of wrinkles. Now she had seen the girl's raw hatred she could easily use it to stir up the people of the marshes against Marrimian. "Listen to what the crones have discovered beyond the Hurlers' Gate," she whispered, drawing both of them into a huddle. "I sent your sister, Marrimian, as a prisoner in Vetchim's safekeeping to be locked away in Mertzork's marshery, but she must have escaped because when you were merely footsteps from touching the Glitterspike she returned, triumphant, out of the marshes as the Queen of Beasts and ever since she entered the city marshmen have been gathering beyond the Hurlers" Gate to await her. Those are the bones of the rumor that is being whispered throughout the city, but now I will tell you what the crones learned and how you must use it to destroy your sister."

Erek sucked in a shallow breath of air and clutched at each of them as she whispered, "There is a power in the quickmarshes that Marrimian stirred in the marshmen's hearts. They followed the rumor of the woman who tamed and rode upon the beast from Rainbows' End to the very gates of the city and they await her, armed and ready to do battle in her name, but the secret is that most of them know only of the *rumor* of your sister's beast-riding—few have seen her. Now, you must go down to the Hurlers' Gate and seize that power she holds over the marshmen and ride triumphant to Mertzork's marshery. Tell them, Pinvey, that *you* are the Beast Lady and make them follow you and then poison their hearts against everyone in the hall."

Erek paused for breath and turned her gaze toward Mertzork, touching the sharpwire with her fingernail as she cackled. "And you can strangle all those who doubt Pinvey's right to be your queen and drown them when the marshes flood."

"No!" hissed Pinvey, stamping her foot and scattering the swarms of spiders that had silently crept close to the hems of her skirt. "I will not flee the city to rot in some hovel in the marshes while the cursed first-born struts freely through Glitterspike Hall!"

Erek threw back her head and her shrieks of laughter shook the hanging canopy of spiders' threads just above their heads. "Did the mudbeasts destroy the crystal houses, as was clear to see in the mirror?"

Pinvey nodded, tight-lipped.

"Then she will not strut in that cage for long for two reasons that anyone can see. First, she is a woman and as such she cannot rule alone. Second, the power that your father held in his iron grip over the city has gone; it vanished in the shattering crystal and the rumbling crash of falling masonry as the mudbeasts plundered the crystal houses. All that she thinks she has achieved will slip through her fingers when the wet seasons flood the marshes and the people of the city begin to starve. Wait patiently and all that she has cheated from you will melt as easily as the marshcrust thaws when the hot sun burns upon its surface."

Pinvey looked from Mertzork to the wrinkled hag, doubting and undecided, her anger and her hatred torn in two. She reached out and almost touched the dry parchment skin of the healing woman's rough hands. "No, I shall claim to be the Beast Lady and lead the marshmen up to the gates of the hall!"

"And what will you ride, you fool? What if Marrimian has kept even one beast to sit upon? Who would the marshmen follow then?"

Pinvey hesitated as she saw a glimmer of truth in the healing woman's words. Reluctantly she nodded but, "What of these others?" she asked, her voice trembling with defeat as she threw out her hand and stabbed a sharp fingernail to where Alea and Syrenea cowered. "What of them and my other sisters still lost somewhere in the rambling corridors and passageways of the hall? Surely they will steal the throne the moment I have passed through the Hurlers' Gate?"

Erek slowly turned her head and watched Alea and Syrenea for a moment, her hooded eyelids flickering, her thin lips twitching. She felt beneath her skirts and brought out two large black spiders and cupped them in the palm of her hand. "No one will take what is yours," she cackled, brushing her lips over the spiders' furry backs. "These two sisters will be your handmaidens. My watchers will guard their tongues while I weave webs and traps with every drop of rain that swells the wet season to ruin everything your sister does to keep the throne that she has stolen from you and Mertzork."

With that Erek whispered over each of the spiders. She drew out a strand of silken thread from beneath their swollen bellies and bound them around Alea and Syrenea's necks, tying them together as she chanted a spell over the invisible knot, then slipped the spiders inside the lace-trimmed edges of their gowns.

Both sisters screamed in terror, twisting and turning against Erek's restraining fingers, their skin crawling as they felt the cold touch of the spiders which scuffled down between the tears in their gowns.

Alea shuddered, waves of dizziness sweeping over her. She staggered and sank down against the cold, damp, mud-slapped walls of the Shambles. She strangled the screams in her throat and sobbed in despair, but she kept her teeth clamped together to rob Pinvey of the pleasure of seeing her terror of the spiders. She turned her face from the entrance of the Shambles and stared blindly into the airless shadows of the alleyway to hide the hatred that blazed in her eyes. It blazed against Mertzork for all that he had done to her. It also burned in her heart against this foul hag of a healing woman with her swarms of spiders, but most of all she hid her blazing hate for Pinvey, wishing with every fiber of her helplessness that she had never left the safety of the daughtery to follow her whisperings of excitement and adventure with the marshlords. Alea felt someone slump down beside her and quickly turned her head to see Syrenea's tear-streaked face, her wild, terror-filled eyes and her mouth stretched wide in silent screams. She sought her hand in the shadows and gripped it tightly.

"One day," she hissed through clenched teeth. "One day we'll kill them all . . ."

"Be still," Erek shrieked, prodding Alea sharply with her toe and making her cry out. The healing woman cracked her knuckles and made both sisters look up into her hooded, narrow, cunning eyes.

Erek carefully explained to them both that their lives now depended on how they served Pinvey and that they must now call her their Queen and boast to the marshmen of her skills in taming the wild mudbeasts and how she rode upon them. "Speak well of her or die by the spiders' bite," she whispered.

"Now I am your Queen!" Pinvey gloated as she sneered down at her sisters. She threw back her head and distorted her cruel, raven-headed beauty with a shriek of laughter at their wretchedness. She goaded them on to their feet to dance and curtsey and then to crawl on their hands and knees to kiss her feet.

Erek suddenly turned her back on the sisters' misery with a rusty-dry swish of her skirts and ran to the entrance of the Shambles, pulling Mertzork and Pinvey with her. "Listen, listen," she hissed, stopping the leaping, chanting crones with a crack of her knuckles.

"I hear nothing but the roar of the mudbeasts somewhere close by," muttered Mertzork, parting the long gossamer threads, leaning out of the entrance between the stilled crones and looking from left to right, up and down the steep, winding alleyways.

"It is the silence that tells us we have wasted too much time," cried Erek. "The marshmen that fled with you from the hall have passed us by. They have by now reached the lower alleyways of the city and they are closing in upon the Hurlers' Gate. Quickly, we must reach the gate before they do!"

But Erek hesitated for a moment and selected three of the crones. She burdened them with a swarm of venomous spiders and bade them enter the hall secretly and spin and dance through the mumblers' cells and kill every one of the lesser mumblers and break their lamps to deny this cursed firstborn the benefit of their magic. And this was the beginning of her revenge. She gathered the remaining crones tightly around her until their riddle of rags and cloaks had blended into one mass of shifting, whispering shadows. She bent her head amongst their hawklike beaks and urged them to offer up the secrets of each of the narrow streets that they had ever walked upon and show Mertzork and Pinvey the fastest road down to the Hurlers' Gate.

"Use a hedgehog bound with spiders' thread," cried Mertzork. "Just like the one you gave me to find a way up into Glitterspike Hall."

"No time! No time!" shrieked Erek, impatiently pushing Mertzork, Pinvey and her two sisters in amongst the crones and following, herself, as they began to spin and weave their way out of the entrance of the Shambles.

"Hold on tightly to their cloaks!" she cried as the crones gathered speed, their rags flapping and snapping in the whirlwind they stirred up.

Pinvey laughed and shouted. The sheer excitement of their downward flight through the city bubbled in her veins. She was to be Queen and she couldn't resist thrusting her hands through the flying rags and cloak tails that had blown up and wound themselves around her, to brush and touch all the glittering, echoing, shadowy shapes of the mud-slapped hovels or the sheer walls of flints that crowded in and rushed past on either side. The city folk had locked their doors in fear of the marshmen and the rampaging beasts and they quaked in terror at the shrieking wind that the crones stirred up as they descended through the city.

"Hold on tightly to the crones' cloaks or you will slip and fall," cried Erek, throwing her words back over her shoulder above the shrieks of the spinning crones. Pinvey snatched her hands back into the safety of the riddle of rags moments before the crones darted to the left down a steep alleyway, slipping through the merest shadowy crack between two leaning hovels. As they did so they shrieked to them to duck their heads or lose them on the overhanging galleries.

Darkness swallowed them up; their racing footsteps thundered and echoed as they plunged giddily downwards, their feet slipping on ancient, time-worn steps. Door arches opened on either side and blacker, bottomless chasms and tall, narrow window niches flashed past in a blur of sharp, bone-cracking edges.

"Slip or fall," gasped Syrenea to herself as she caught the tail-ends of the healing woman's warning words and she saw in them the smallest chance of escape. She gave half a thought to the spider hiding beneath her skirts and gritted her teeth and let go of the cold, sticky riddle of rags and stumbled, her feet slipping on the sheer steps as she threw herself at one of the passing door arches.

The crones' rags tore through her fingers as she flung her arms free of the scratching cloth that clung to her while she fell. Somewhere above and behind her she heard Mertzork's voice curse her and she felt his strong fingers clutch at her arm, but the riddle of rags had made her skin damp and sticky with the spiders' spit that the crones had woven into their cloaks and she slipped through his fingers. She fell headlong out of the stairway and into the door arch, tumbling over and over, her head hitting the sharp edge of the doorstone. A black wave of silence washed over her.

Mertzork stumbled against the spinning crones, cursing Syrenea as she slipped through his fingers. He would have stopped and searched the black door arches for her and beat her for trying to escape but Erek shouted at him, "No time! No time to waste on such folly, leave her to the spider's bites!" and then the crones bore him away, taking them down through the last maze of crowded, gloomy and airless alleyways in huge, breathless leaps and bounds toward the marshmen who crowded together in the muddy lanes and walkways of the beasting pits beyond the Hurlers' Gate.

Erek raised herself on tiptoe, her hooded eyes flickering with satisfaction as she surveyed the empty cobbles that lay between the first crowded row of hovels of the city and the high archway of the Hurlers' Gate. "We are not too late," she cackled, rubbing her hands together. She slowed the crones and made them fan out to fill the alleyway. Their webs of leaping shadows fell across the warm cobbles to touch the Hurlers' Gate.

"Chant! Chant and fill the waiting marshmen with joy that their Queen has returned triumphant from Glitterspike Hall. Sow the seeds with your whisperings of Pinvey's success and tell how she has come back amongst them to claim the marsheries."

The crones trod forward, spreading out across the cobbles, their boots clattering and scraping as their voices rose in praise of Mertzork's victory and his taking of Pinvey, the Queen of the Beasts, to share in his triumph. Slowly, as they advanced, passing under the first high archway of the Hurlers' Gate, their riddle of rags began to unravel the webs of threads and shadows that they had woven about Mertzork and Pinvey to keep them safe on their descent through the city, and as the ties melted, leaving them plain to see, untouched and unruffled by their downward flight, the waiting crowds of marshmen began to whisper and mutter.

Angry shouts mixed with a rush of marshmen's footsteps and the roaring bellows of the pursuing mudbeasts sounded in every alleyway, lane and dark opening between the crowded houses that lay behind them.

Mertzork half turned, his hand on his iron spike, but Erek pushed him forward. "Go through, go through the gates, proclaim your victory and name Pinvey as your Queen. Go, go!"

Mertzork laughed, his face splitting into a cruel sneer as he snatched Pinvey's wrist and pulled her after him through the archway. "It will be my victory, not yours!" he hissed, the words echoing painfully in her ear as he pushed his lips against her cheek and ignored her startled glare of betrayal.

Mertzork turned toward the shifting throngs of marshmen who lined and crowded the upper edges of the beasting pits. "There are no more Glitterspikes to touch!" he shouted, thrusting Pinvey's hand up into the air, his knuckles whitening as his grip upon her wrist tightened. "No more games or jousts for the throne or the dry lands of Gnarlsmyre. Lord Miresnare is dead, and I, as victor in the game, have claimed all, and I have taken his daughter, Pinvey, who has tamed and ridden the wild mudbeasts, as my Queen!"

The crowds of marshmen stirred uneasily and uncertain whispering ran backwards and forwards through their ranks like the dry crackle of a changing wind amongst the tall banks of bulrush stems that grew wild across the quickmarshes.

Their voices rose in doubting murmurs and suddenly the crowd shifted and broke apart as Vetchim, the marshman who had first led Marrimian out into the marshes, forced his way through. "She is not the lady who tamed the mudbeast," he cried, pointing a finger at Pinvey. "I was there when our Queen climbed . . ."

Erek spun toward Vetchim, a stream of evil spells pouring through her lips, and she struck him dumb, tying his tongue in an endless knot of torment.

Mertzork sneered, loosening his iron spike from his belt, and swept his eyes across the crowds. "Who else will challenge me? I am the champion of Glitterspike Hall. Who will deny this or say that Pinvey is not the Beast Lady or your Queen? And who amongst you is foolish enough to challenge the healing woman's magic?"

The crowd surged forward a pace and then hesitated, anxious eyes on the healing woman and her gathering of crones.

"Who will dare?" sneered Mertzork, stabbing a finger toward the helpless marshhunter, Vetchim, who had fallen on to his knees, clutching at his throat, his mouth opening and closing soundlessly, his eyes wide and wild with terror.

Behind them the rush of footsteps echoed on the cobbles and the marshmen who had fled the hall with Mertzork spilled through the Hurlers' Gate. Seeing him, they added their voices to the swelling shout against him.

"Beware the mudbeasts that my Queen has freed to run on your heels, marshscum," Mertzork laughed, snapping his fingers at those behind him before turning back toward the crowds that thronged the beasting pits, knowing that it was they who blocked his way to the freedom of the quickmarsh and the safety of his marshery.

"You are no better than a common murderer!" shouted a familiar voice in the crowd, making Mertzork turn his head and stare at the sea of hostile faces.

"Andzey?" he snarled, recognizing his half-brother and pushing Pinvey behind him as Andzey elbowed his way through the crowd until he stood a dozen paces from him.

Andzey trembled and pointed an accusing finger at Mertzork as he told the crowds how Mertzork had murdered their father to steal his knowledge of the marshes and had stolen the beast Gallengab for himself. "Murderer! Common murderer!" he screamed, his eyes blazing with anger.

"Murderer! Murderer!" the crowd began to chant. Andzey stepped forward, his hands stretched out, his fingers twitching in rhythm to encourage their rising voices.

Mertzork laughed, curling his lips back across his teeth as he beckoned his half-brother to come to him, but his eyes were narrow and glittered with cunning as he bent his knees and took his weight on the balls of his feet. "Come, then, come to me," he goaded and sprang lightly away, sneering at Andzey's clumsiness as he grabbed only his beastskin cloak.

"Gasp your last, brother," he gloated, the laughter and the cunning sneer hardening into a killing snarl as he leapt behind his brother, dropped the hidden sharpwire looped between his fists down over Andzey's head and flexed the muscles in his arms to tighten and strangle.

"Do not kill him, use him!" Erek hissed, suddenly appearing at Mertzork's shoulder, her crooked fingers on the tightening sharpwire while the crones gathered around. "Pinvey is the Beast Lady without a beast to ride; let her use him as her mount."

Pinvey caught Erek's whisper and looked past Mertzork at the crowding marshmen. Their chants had fallen away to angry murmurings as they hesitated with fear and doubt in their eyes. She swallowed her hatred of Mertzork and seized the moment of uncertainty. She leapt forward on to Andzey's back, clawing at his face with her talon-sharp fingernails. "I am your Queen and I ride upon all beasts that roam across the quickmarsh, especially those who doubt me or call my Lord Mertzork a murderer! I have freed the mudbeasts who helped us to claim the throne and I have given them the city to roam in during the wet seasons."

Erek cackled with delight at Pinvey's speed. She crammed a gossamer cloth into Andzey's mouth to silence him and whispered a swarm of spiders out of the folds of her cloak to bind his hands and arms tightly behind his back.

"Pinvey is your Queen—your Queen who will tame any who mutter against her," she hissed, advancing menacingly toward the crush of marsh-men. Then she placed a silken bridle and two woven gossamer reins that the spiders had spun across Andzey's lips into Pinvey's hands so that she could ride him in triumph wherever she chose across the marshes.

Pinvey laughed harshly, and turning Mertzork's helpless half-brother, she goaded him with the sharp edges of her shoes toward the road that led down to the beasting pits. "Who dares to challenge us?" she sneered, tossing her head to spread her raven-black hair out in the wind behind her. She held the marshmen with her cruel, pitiless gaze and they silently parted to let her pass between them.

Mertzork frowned, his eyes narrowing, as he watched Pinvey ride his brother down into the beasting pits. He saw a glimpse of her ruthlessness and realized that she had almost stolen his power over the marshmen. Her strength made him uneasy but he knew that he must use it to make the marshmen fear her and obey him and he laughed and shrugged off his worries, knowing that the marshmen must not see his concern as a weakness. Roughly, he pushed Alea to follow in Andzey's footsteps, snarling at the now silent marshmen on either side. Suddenly Erek touched his shoulder, bringing her lips to his ear, warning him to watch Pinvey closely. She slipped a web full of venomous spiders into his hands, some to place on Andzey's shoulders or on to Alea's gown, and some to use against any who rose against him or his Queen, making sure that the marshmen saw her gift.

The mudbeasts' roar came closer and Erek urged, "I can only hold the mudbeasts for a short while. Go quickly before they break through the threads the crones are spinning across the Hurlers' Gate. Return in the first days of the next dry season. By then Glitterspike Hall and everything that Marrimian stole from you shall truly be yours."

Mertzork laughed and swept up the heavy web of venomous spiders high above his head. He saw the fear that it cast amongst the silent ranks of marshmen crowding the edges of the beasting pits. "Who would whisper one word against us now?" he sneered, thrusting the web out at arm's length, making those closest to him cry out in terror and scramble and fight one another to retreat from his reach. "Follow me and chant out my name as the new Lord of Gnarlsmyre and Pinvey as my

Queen," he ordered, snapping his fingers in their faces and turning on his heel to take the road down through the beasting pits. The marshmen reluctantly followed him, their uncertain chants swelling from a mere grumbling whisper to a thunderous shout.

Pinvey clung on to Andzey's shoulders, gripping his strong neck between her thighs, and the power that she now held over him made her tingle and her blood ran hotly through her veins. "Faster—faster," she hissed at her mount, reaching out with her foot to prod Alea between her shoulder blades, making her sister stumble and tear the hem of her skirts on the rough descent. "I'll ride you too if you won't keep up," she sneered spitefully. She turned her head and picked out the healing woman on the uppermost ledge of the beasting pit and waved her hand in thanks for giving her such a proud beast to ride across the marshes.

Erek watched her for a moment and frowned, worrying and doubting her own wisdom. Perhaps she should have killed her and nipped all that power in the bud before it had the chance to take root out there in the marshes. Perhaps it would flower into something that Mertzork could not control. Erek sighed. She touched the searching mirror beneath her cloak and whispered Naul's name, wondering if in those last moments as Lord Miresnare had smashed his magic pine-oil lamp and trampled on him whether he had felt a grain of hatred for his master.

"The mudbeasts are almost at the gate," chanted

the crones, making Erek blink and shut out her sorrow at the destruction of her child's magic. She turned back toward the Hurlers' Gate, only to trip and almost fall over Vetchim where he lay in choking silence.

"You are a curse on all my magic," she hissed, kicking him savagely in the small of his back and making him roll over and down the steep descent. He fell headlong over the upper ledge of the beasting pit into an empty, evil-smelling cage. Without a second thought for the marshhunter's fate Erek called the crones into a spinning, leaping circle around her, each one shaking out the spiders that spun their webs in the secret folds of their riddle of rags. Round and round, faster and faster they spun, clearing a path through the last of the fleeing marshmen who were streaming out beneath the high archways of the gate to escape the grinding claws and gouging horns of the beasts that ran on their heels.

The ancient hags swayed from side to side, slowing as they passed into the shadows of the gate. They lifted their hands high above their heads and spun countless gossamer threads from the spiders that clung to their fingertips. The spiders' webs shimmered and trembled in the cold wind that blew in from the marshes as they crisscrossed the gateway, clinging to the ancient stone archway and the heavy, age-worn door posts, woven into a solid sparkling curtain of sticky threads

The mudbeasts were lumbering beneath the first archway but they slowed and clawed at the cobbles as they prodded their horns against the curtain of threads. The first two beasts barged into each other, roaring and bellowing as their horns tore through the spiders' threads. The other mudbeasts retreated, shaking their heads to dislodge the sticky, ragged tatter of threads that clung to their horns. But the more they tossed their heads the more the webs clung, blinding them as they stuck to their eyelashes. Slowly the herd of beasts passed beneath the archways, blindly following the scent of the wild marshes that lay before them.

Erek smiled and brought her fingers to her lips. She led the crones on tiptoe between the blinded, wandering mudbeasts, ducking and weaving underneath their horns. Then she and the crones slipped back into the city through the Hurlers' Gate and vanished in a rustle of rags and cloaks into the airless silence of the Shambles.

4

Beneath the Kitchen Archway

*A*S Krann began to pick his way slowly across the splinters of broken rafter beams toward Marrimian he hesitated and frowned. He thought he had glimpsed something in the shadows below where the last narrow alleyway of crowded hovels met the wide sweep of cobbles leading toward the high archway of the Hurlers' Gate. He retraced his steps and clung once more to the stone windowsill and pressed his nose against the pane of broken crystal.

"Crones!" he muttered and was filled with disquiet at the sight of those black, ragged hags who had shadowed their path up through the city and showered them with foul poisonous spiders. He shuddered as he watched the crones' spinning, swirling riddle of black rags break away from the dark entrance of the alleyway and cross the cobbles to disappear beneath the archway of the Hurlers' Gate.

"Good riddance . . ." Krann began, only to fall silent as he saw them reappear on the rough ground beyond the city, above the beasting pits. The spinning crones were slowing and breaking apart, to reveal three other figures within their circle. Others were emerging from the beasting pits.

Krann narrowed his eyes and drew a sharp breath as he watched the distant figures through the smoke and fumes of the unchecked fires that drifted across the city. "There's treachery beyond the gates, I'm sure of it," he cried with alarm. "Those crones must be spinning webs of dark magic over the marshmen who pledged themselves to Marrimian." He rose on tiptoe as the billowing smoke obscured his sight. Gradually it cleared and Krann blinked and rubbed his eyes. The space before the gates was empty. The marshmen had vanished. When his gaze traveled he saw rampaging mud-beasts crowding the lanes and alleyways just inside the city. Gradually they lumbered down through the gates. He could just hear them bellowing and snarling as they streamed through the beasting pits and into the stinking mud on the edges of the marshes, sending up huge plumes of sludge and slime as they plunged their way out of sight through the thick banks of tall bulrush stems and clumps of marshoak that grew across the bleak wilderness.

"It looks as though everyone, even the marshmen who had gathered at the gates for her, has deserted Marrimian now," Krann muttered to himself as he turned thoughtfully away from the window and cast his gaze across the ruined rafter beams and broken floorboards of the gallery that should have been crowded with her father's archer guard.

Moving quickly, he crossed the gallery and scrambled down into the hall. He smiled to himself as he overheard the master mumbler urging Ansel and Treasel to search for the hall folk who had hidden from the marauding marshmen.

"Go, go," Naul was urging softly, with a flick of his wrist. "It will bring more comfort to your mistress to look up from her despair and see the hall bustling and to hear the clatter of brooms and brushes than to dwell upon this gloomy, echoing emptiness. Go, both of you; run as quickly as you can and search every dark nook and hidey hole. Gather all the people of the hall that you can find."

Ansel hesitated and clenched her huge fists as she half turned to where Marrimian sat, deaf to them all, hunched in her own despair. "But my mistress weeps. She needs me. I should stay close to her side, just as I did in the marshes."

"No," answered the mumbler firmly, shaking his windbells at the two of them and holding Ansel's eyes with his own piercing gaze. "You are Ansel the overscullion. The hall folk will know and trust your voice. Go and call out in every corridor and passageway for the underscullions, dusters, lamp-wicks, fetchers and carriers to assemble before their Queen."

Ansel opened her mouth to answer the mumbler but fear of his magic made her think better of it and she snapped it shut again. She turned on her heel and hurried through the mounds of rubbish, pulling Treasel after her.

Marrimian shivered and looked up as Krann

reached the dais. She half rose from where she had slumped on the edge of the throne, wiping at the tear stains that had scarred her cheeks and rubbing at her red-rimmed eyes with the back of her hand. She blinked and tried to smile, reaching out for his hand, clutching it as though only he could save her from sinking further into the quicksand of her despair.

"Where is the joy? Where is the triumph of my victory?" she wept, Krann's face blurring in her sight as new tears brimmed in her eyes and coursed down her cheeks. "All I have succeeded in doing is killing my father and turning my sisters against me. All I have created by demanding the right to joust for the throne is these piles of decay. Oh yes, I have touched the Glitterspike—and won a fool's victory!"

Krann shook his head. "No, your father was seized with a madness to keep his throne. He would never have yielded it, not even to the bravest marshlord if his hand had touched the Glitterspike before yours."

Marrimian screwed up her eyes and clenched her fists, her body wracked and trembling. "I care nothing—nothing—for who is the bravest, or the best, or the quickest. For all his faults I loved my father and I cannot shut out his piercing death shout as I claimed the throne. Just look all around us at the heaps of uncounted dead that my womanhood has caused. Look! Look at the ruin and destruction that now fills this hollow, echoing hall of death!"

Marrimian's voice faltered into strangled sobs

and her head fell forward as she whispered, "Everyone has turned against me: the archers in the high gallery. Pinvey. And even the mudbeasts: look how they repay me for their freedom by destroying the crystal houses. Now everything lies in ruins, everything."

Krann frowned and silently shook his head. He slipped his hand beneath her tear-stained chin and gently lifted her head until their eyes met. "You have suffered much and you overburden yourself with hatred for being a woman," he whispered, forcefully holding her gaze. "What you have done today, that great rush across the hall, defying every hand that was set against you, touching the Glitterspike, the heartstone of your father's power, and claiming the throne, all this heralds the dawn of a new Gnarlsmyre where no man will ever again dare to trample on a woman simply because of her womanhood. It is a glorious beginning and the litter of battle that lies heaped all around us is little of your doing. You did not invite the marshmen to crowd your father's hall; their greed brought them here. No, you merely proved your worth by chasing them out."

Marrimian frowned and bit her lip. "But I am all alone, everyone has deserted me."

Krann laughed softly and tried to smother her fears and give her courage. "No, not everyone," he answered. "Ansel and Treasel are still with you and Naul the master mumbler. He was here beside the throne a moment ago." They looked round but Naul had vanished.

And as the sunlight streamed across the hall he knew that he must keep secret for as long as he possibly could what he feared he had seen beyond the Hurlers' Gate.

"Where are Ansel and Treasel?" Marrimian suddenly asked, looking all about the gloomy hall.

"Do not fill your mind with fears." He smiled, choosing his words carefully. "Ansel and Treasel will not be far away. They are searching for the hall folk. Rest now and sit here upon the throne, put your head on my shoulder and gather your strength. Give your frightened people time to savor the silence that you have won for them. I am sure that by tomorrow everyone who is hiding will be crowded into the hall. Be patient, Marrimian, your triumph has wearied you and made you see shadows looming in every patch of sunlight."

Marrimian frowned and shook her head. She would have pulled away from his strong arms, but Krann held her gaze, his pale blue eyes willing her to rest, and they spoke without words. Krann's voice seemed to soothe away her anger and melt the burden of despair that had cast a shadow over her heart. Wearily she smiled and brushed at a strand of hair that had fallen across her face. The drying tear stains itched and glittered on her cheeks.

"You are a great comfort," she whispered, drawing closer to him, her fingers tingling as their hands entwined for the first time since she had touched the Glitterspike. For the briefest moment she could almost imagine that here in her father's hall she felt the warm sun on her back and smelled the rank marsh odors of the water meadows that stretched out in endless pools and narrow channels between the tall banks of bulrush stems. She could sense the whispering windbell flowers beyond Rainbows' End and she felt her lips draw into a smile as she remembered rushing forward to warn the dancing stranger of the dangerous quicksand where he wandered. Yet it had been she who floundered when the soft earth bank she was standing on collapsed and he had been the one to do the rescuing. And then, as now, he had seen all her despair. He had stripped her secrets bare at a glance with his power of second sight and he had given her comfort and strength to follow her destiny.

"I cannot rest with so much to do," she whispered, looking up at him. "I must go to the marshmen, I must go to Vetchim and all those who wait in the shadows of the Hurlers' Gate. My little sister, Treyster, is hiding in the stitchers' cubbyhole, I must find her, we made her promise to stay hidden until it was safe. And there are my other sisters, perhaps still hidden in the daughtery, we must go and look for them. And then there are the ragmen, the dusters, the servers, they must all be gathered . . ." Marrimian's voice trailed away into silence, her failing words echoing between the piles of litter and moldy rubbish that spoiled the hall as she realized what a task lay before her. She yawned and tried to shake the weight of weariness from her shoulders.

Light, running footsteps suddenly sounded on the far side of the hall, mingling with the fading, whispering music of the windbells sewn into the hems of the master mumbler's saffron robes. "Mir . . . Mar . . . Marrimian," an anxious voice stuttered through the gloomy sunlight.

The sound made Marrimian turn her head and half rise, smiling, from the throne. "Treyster . . . it is Treyster!" she laughed and reached out to clasp her sister's hand as she ran breathlessly on to the dais of the throne.

Treyster gathered up the torn and dirty hems of her gown. She threw her arms around Marrimian's neck, then greeted Krann. "I know . . . I know I promised to stay hidden but I am so worried about Cetrinea and the other two, who locked themselves in the daughtery. I just couldn't wait a moment longer. The silence that fell following the mudbeasts' snarls and roars was so deafening, I had to risk creeping out of that hole and . . . and . . . then I caught the sound of Ansel's voice. She was calling for her scullions to come out of their hiding places. I knew then it must be safe."

Treyster stopped for breath. Her words had poured out in such a rush that they had bumped and stumbled over one another.

"Where are all the marshmen? How did you drive them out of the hall?" she gasped, her eyes round and full of wonder as she twisted and turned and tried to look everywhere at once, but Marrimian's thoughts had drifted.

"I heard windbells. Was the mumbler with you?" Marrimian frowned as she looked over Treyster's shoulder.

"Oh yes," Treyster explained as her gaze settled for a moment on the entrance to which he had led her. "Naul found me wandering through the heaps of rubbish that littered the stitchers' corridor and he brought me to the hall. He told me that you had claimed the right to rule all Gnarlsmyre. Is it true? Did our father give his throne to you? What of the madness that seized him throughout the joust? He seemed to grow wild with the thought of keeping the throne to himself, fierce with hatred, especially against us, his daughters. Surely he would have rather died than see you, his firstborn, snatch the throne away from him. What of Pinvey and that murderous marshman, Mertzork?" Her voice grew deep with fear and hatred as she thought of them.

Marrimian shivered, her lips pinched tightly with the bitterness of her triumph, and in fits and starts, glancing constantly around the empty hall, she answered Treyster's flood of questions. It both angered and relieved her to talk about those last frantic moments and new tears sprang up as she told Treyster of their father's death, but these tears glittered with rage in the sunlight. She wrung her hands helplessly when she spoke of Pinvey's curses and shrieks as she and Mertzork fled from the hall.

"She is so set against me," Marrimian whispered. "She is so full of wild hatred, and . . ." She lowered her voice and looked cautiously into the gloomy emptiness of the hall, trying to stifle the echo as she spoke. "And I know that Mertzork and Pinvey were aided in their treachery by Erek, the healing woman. It is her evil magic and that gathering of ragbound crones who do her bidding that we must watch for." Marrimian paused for breath. "And we must tread carefully with Naul, father's master mumbler, because he is Erek's child. I found out that secret in the Shambles, in Erek's lair, the very center of all the webs and the hatred and malice that the healing woman has woven against this House of Miresnare."

"No, no," Krann interrupted her quickly, shaking his head. "You judge him over-hastily, giving him no time to utter one mouthful of words in his own defense. You have quickly forgotten how he leapt to your defense and cried out your right to claim the throne, risking his life in the face of your father's madness."

"He led me safely into the hall," interrupted Treyster from where she perched on the edge of the dais of the throne close to Marrimian. "He could have quite easily bundled me into any one of those dark cubbyholes that open out on either side of the stitchers' corridor and strangled the life out of me."

Marrimian frowned and looked from Krann to Treyster. "Well, I still fear him," she whispered, sweeping her gaze across the hall and frowning as she caught sight of two figures between the mounds of rubbish at the far end. She paused to stare up at the Glitterspike, following the moving veins of molten silver that lay as faint, ghostly patterns beneath the heavy, clinging skirts of frost.

"Ansel? Ansel is that you?" she cried as the larger of the figures paused beneath a low archway and turned.

"I'm searching, mistress, searching for the hall folk." Ansel's deep voice boomed across the echoing hall.

"Treyster's with me," Marrimian called back. "We will make our way to the daughtery and see if any of our sisters are still there."

Ansel waved to her and vanished beneath the low arch. Marrimian rose to her feet. She cast her gaze across the deep clawscrapes in the floorstones and the loops and twists of the heavy iron chains that had once bound her champion to the base of the Glitterspike. Shivering, she turned to Krann. "Where is Naul?" she hissed angrily, "The mumbler has slunk away without a word. Perhaps he is visiting the Shambles and hatching new treacheries with the one who spawned him!"

"Once you trusted my foresight," Krann snapped angrily as he turned to follow her, "and you did not hesitate to use it to claim the throne. Why now am I so wrong about the mumbler's innocence?"

"The healing woman's crones fooled you while we were finding a path through the city. Perhaps he has clouded your foresight with his magic."

Treyster suddenly laughed, her voice cutting between them as she interrupted. "He . . . he . . . he was not plotting, he was muttering to himself, muttering something about being on the Queen's business."

"Business? What business?" Marrimian cried, clutching her sister's arm and turning on her.

Treyster shrugged her shoulders helplessly. "I

didn't catch anything else. He said he was in a hurry, turned away from me and vanished into that maze of passageways beyond the stitchers' corridor. There his voice was lost in the shrill clatter of his windbells."

Krann sighed and stepped down from the dais of the throne. "Well it doesn't matter where or who the mumbler is or what he is up to. All we can do is keep an eye open for him on our way to the daughtery."

Marrimian nodded silently and led the way toward an archway on the far side of the hall. "It's blocked!" she cried, scrabbling at the heaps of cold gray stone that filled the passageway to the daughtery. "How shall we ever clear this? Our sisters are trapped alive!"

"Where are all the hall folk hiding? Ansel hissed grimly, her eyes widening as her words vanished in muttering echoes in the dark, gloomy corridor. Cursing under her breath, she kicked aside a mess of maggoty gnawed bones, refuse and scattered debris of the joust that the marshmen had trampled into the uneven flagstones of the corridor as they fled from the hall.

"Underscullions!" she muttered. "That is what is needed to set the hall and all this warren of passageways to rights!"

Treasel's fear of the dark corridors made her head dizzy and her breath come in short gasps as she tried to keep up with Ansel. She frowned when she looked down at the piles of rubbish. "It looks no worse than a marshery after a busy season of hunting and fleshing. Why should you wish to clear it away? These mounds are just ripe and ready for gleaning."

Ansel shuddered at the thought of what foulness squirmed and crawled through the marshmen's maggoty refuse and she pulled Treasel away into a cleaner, narrower corridor. There she found them a place to squat for a moment where the damp flagstones were only scuffed and spoiled by dirty marshmen's feet.

"This is a terrible state," Ansel whispered fiercely, stabbing her broad hands back at the mess behind them. "And it stinks!" she added grimly, wrinkling her nose in disgust. "Why, in better days there was not a speck of dust or a single scuff throughout these narrow corridors. Nothing marred the beauty of Glitterspike Hall. Everything was neat and tidy and in its place. Everything gleamed in the lamplight, reflecting the awesome power of Lord Miresnare. This great hall bustled with underscullions fetching and carrying, scrubbing and honing to prepare for the thick layers of polish. The silent ragmen buffed the polished floorstones into a mirror of glittering reflections and they glided effortlessly backwards and forwards on the rags, crisp with wax, bound around their feet. These passageways were constantly dusted and swept. And everywhere smelled of beeswax mixed with the heady scent of black ebony trees."

Ansel sighed softly and drew a deep breath, her nostrils twitching as if she were searching for those forgotten scents amongst the rancid decay that lay all around them.

"Underscullions—ragmen—whoever will you tell me of next?" exclaimed Treasel, turning to the scullion.

Ansel shrugged her shoulders and muttered almost to herself, "Oh there were dusters, dressers, servers . . ." but her voice trailed away into silence. She realized that the hall would never be quite like that again no matter how much of the rubbish and litter was swept away. She realized that no amount of elbow grease would grind out the deep claw-scrapes that the mudbeasts had gouged in the floor-stones of the hall. Shivering, she leaned forward and climbed awkwardly to her feet, puffing out her cheeks as she waited for Treasel to join her.

"Well it doesn't matter now what went on before—we are all going to starve once the rains begin," Ansel grumbled, looking at the marshgirl. "Now that the beasts have destroyed the crystal houses we will die here and become just another pile of dusty bones."

"No!" whispered Treasel, touching her hand. "There is plenty to eat in the hall and in this maze of corridors if you know where to look for it. I have already told you that these mounds of rubbish are ready to offer up a rich harvest."

Ansel shuddered and pulled away from the marshgirl staring at her in horror. "I suppose you would eat the flesh of those dead marshmen that litter the hall?" she gasped, her red, dimpled cheeks draining of color. The thought of squatting on any of those mounds of rubbish and picking them over bone by bone, squashing the wriggling maggots and scraping off the mold! She shuddered and felt her stomach tighten into a knot as she realized what must have been bubbling in the boiling broth cauldrons which gave off that vile odor that had clung in every crease and fold of her dirty apron when she had led Marrimian and the others secretly to steal their first look at the crowded chaos that filled the hall.

Treasel laughed quietly and shrugged her shoulders. "There were no crystal houses in the marshery. We ate everything that grew or crawled or we would have starved to death when the wet seasons came and the marshes flooded."

"No," whispered Ansel, looking desperately at the mounds of rubbish and imagining that she could see all manner of foul creeping things wriggling through them, making them sway and tremble. "We must find another way to gather food. Perhaps if we searched every corner and rescued what we could from the crystal houses . . ." she muttered. "Krann will know what to do, he will help us to find food."

Somewhere ahead of them a door creaked and Ansel fell silent. She frowned and turned her head. "Listen!" she hissed. "There's someone there."

Treasel leaned forward and looked past Ansel. She turned her ear to each of the dark, arched corridors that branched out before them and tilted her head as she listened for the slightest echo of what Ansel had heard.

"Yes, it's there," she whispered, pointing a trembling finger toward the corridor that led to a courtyard to their right.

"That's beyond the hoemasters' quarters," Ansel grumbled, tugging firmly at Treasel's sleeve to keep her by her side as she began to move forward.

Treasel hung back, "I . . . I . . . I'm afraid of these dark passageways. They are so airless, I feel as though they are swallowing me alive."

Ansel reached out and gripped her hand. Her cheeks puffed into a smile. There was so much difference between them and yet she had never had a friend as close as Treasel. "Follow in my footsteps," she whispered gently. "Follow me just as I followed you through the treacherous marshes." They set off down the corridor.

"Where are you? Where are you hiding?" Ansel muttered impatiently to herself as she wrenched open door after door on either side of the passageway. Suddenly Treasel stopped and made them both retrace their steps. She stood, turning her marsh-sharp ears from side to side, in the entrance of the widest of the passageways they had passed. "There are noises in this dark tunnel," she whispered. "I can hear the scrape of rusty hinges and hesitant footsteps."

Ansel looked up at the low-vaulted archway and felt the rough stone walls on either side before she turned to the marshgirl and muttered in disgust, "It's that mumbler's fault. He's blocked off passage-

ways and made these corridors into a maze to stop
the marshmen reaching the hall. It's made us search
in a circle. This was the main kitchen passageway;
reedlamps used to flicker in those rusty iron brack-
ets and cast leaping, bustling shadows. I knew there
was something familiar about it. It was always full
of rush and clatter. Look how the floorstones have
been worn away by the constant tread of the servers' feet as they carried the steaming bowls of food
and hot trenchards into the hall for the feasts."

Somewhere ahead of them in the gloom a door
creaked open and the sound of whispering voices
echoed and grew louder, filling the corridor.

"Listen! I can hear the bustle of feet beneath the
kitchen archways," Ansel cried, the color flushing
through the broken veins of her cheeks as they
puffed and sweated into a broad grin. "Yes! I can
almost smell the fish cooks, almost see the bakers,
scullions, underscullions, and the grimy, soot-
covered scuttles," she sighed, gulping in a deep
breath. She cupped her hand to her mouth and
shouted out her name against the rising echoes,
then gathered up her apron tails, fussing and brushing at the layers of marsh grime that had spoiled the
apron, and set off as fast as her fat legs would carry
her toward the kitchens. "Follow me," she called
back carelessly over her shoulder toward the
marshgirl.

Treasel tried to take a step but Ansel had already
vanished from sight before she could gather up the
courage to follow and face these scullions and scuttles from the hall. She sank down against the cold,

damp wall of the passageway, shivering and afraid. She wished that she were out in the endless wildness of the marshes rather than huddled in this airless warren of stone passageways. The whispering sound of windbells, no louder than the murmur of wildflowers brushing together in the hot marsh breezes, their brittle, silver gray flower heads gently touching, made Treasel cry out. She spun around to see Naul the master mumbler standing just behind her.

"New things are never easy," he whispered, moving his empty hands as if to swing the pine-oil lamp that his master, Lord Miresnare, had smashed into a thousand pieces.

"I . . . I . . . I am not afraid," Treasel stuttered, trying to mask her terror of the echoing corridors and the low-vaulted passageways that opened out on every side. "I am watching—keeping guard for Ansel," she whispered, catching her breath. She stepped back a pace deeper into the kitchen passageway to escape the mumbler's piercing eyes that seemed to glow in the hollow, shadowy eye sockets and strip her naked to the bone as they revealed her every weakness.

Suddenly, from behind her, the noisy babble of kitchen voices fell silent and just Ansel's voice echoed clearly in the passageway, calling out her name.

"There is much to do and countless new things to learn," smiled the mumbler, stepping forward, his hawk-sharp eyes softening as he pointed with a dry, twig-thin finger past her shoulder and into the gloomy, litter-choked passageway that led to the kitchens.

Treasel saw the mumbler's windbells sway and heard their soft music as he stepped toward her and she scrambled backwards, grazing her knuckles on the rough stone walls as she turned, tearing her eyes away from his gaze. She had heard rumors in the marshery of these magic men and their spells and her heart threatened to stop beating. Suddenly she turned and ran as fast as she could, following the scullion's voice around the twisting bends of the passageway.

"Treasel, we are here, Treasel!" Ansel's strong voice was full of laughter as she stopped the marsh-girl's flight by catching hold of her wrist and pulling her beneath the kitchen archway, where she was met by a sea of strange faces.

Treasel hesitated on the threshold stone and half turned her head as the mumbler's voice floated past her—"Search and find. Mend and scrub. Gather and glean and make like new." Treasel shivered as the voice broke into easy laughter and faded into a swish of echoing windbells.

"Those magic men see too clearly and the master mumbler used to spin that pine-oil lamp of his and look straight through you and use you simply as a window into tomorrow. It's almost as bad as that healing woman's searching mirror, the one that she thrusts beneath your nose to search and pry into all your secrets," Ansel muttered, pulling the marshgirl firmly over the threshold stone into the kitchens.

"It was his eyes! The way he looks at you!" Treasel answered in a whisper, her voice dying away into nothing as she turned and swept her gaze over the gloomy vastness of the kitchens. She blinked and forgot the mumbler and Ansel as she tried to look at everything that crammed that treasure house. Her eyes darted between the forest of smoothly fluted stone columns that rose out of the uneven floorstones like so many petrified tree trunks to spread their spider-fine upper branches across the low, soot-smeared, vaulted ceilings. In the dim light that filtered down through the narrow, dirty window slits she could see huge, empty baking ovens, their doors hanging wide open to reveal cavernous iron racks and stone shelves. Cold, cinder-choked fire pits littered with rusty iron roasting spits and upturned cauldrons crowded the hearths and the chimney corners while on all the table tops gutting slabs, cutting blocks and pastry boards were piled high, spilling over with broken pots and pans, scraps and half-chewed rinds mixed with moldy, stale trenchards. Underfoot the once polished floorstones were begrimed and greasy beneath an oily carpet of sticky fish heads and rotten broken bone endings.

Treasel's eyes shone with the wonder of it all and she took in a deep breath and savored every hidden scent as she made to step forward, but she felt fingers touching her arms, pinching at the coarse weave of her clothes. She blinked again and looked about her to find that the kitchen folk had silently closed in all around while she had been gazing spellbound at the bake ovens and the gutting slabs and all the other wonders of the kitchens.

"Ansel! Ansel!" she cried, scratching at the hands and trying to break free of their grasp.

Ansel had followed the marshgirl's gaze through the ruined shambles of the kitchen and she shuddered as she saw how much filth now spoiled it. She frowned at the marshgirl's cry and turned, clapping her broad hands to drive the scullions, underscullions and scuttles away from her.

"Have you no manners?" she demanded, fixing the whispering crowd with a withering stare. "Is this how you would treat someone who helped your mistress, Marrimian, to be the new Queen of all Gnarlsmyre? Lord Miresnare is dead, you know, and Marrimian touched the Glitterspike to claim his throne before she drove the marshmen from the hall, while you all ran away and hid yourselves in every dark crack and corner that you could find!"

"The marshmen were torturing all the hall folk they could catch, trying to find a way through the mumbler's mazes into the hall. We had to hide," wailed a dozen voices.

"We only wished to feel the weave of her coat," called out one of the underscullions. "We meant no harm, but she is so different from us."

Ansel's face softened and she placed her hands on her broad hips as she slowly looked at each of their anxious, staring, pale faces. "This is Treasel, my friend from the quickmarsh," she said proudly and she took Treasel's hand and led her forward.

In that moment, as the scullions and the scuttles

and all those who had been hiding from the marshmen's murderous wrath crept nearer for a closer look at the marshgirl, Ansel saw how much stronger she had grown in their eyes, how they hung on her words and shrank back at the slightest hint of displeasure in her face. It seemed as though the hurtful taunts and spiteful kitchen whispers that had once plagued her every waking hour were gone, banished by her mistress's triumph or perhaps by her own courage in fighting against the marshmen. Now, if she turned or strode toward the scullions or any of the other kitchen folk they stepped back respectfully and offered her their help almost before she could ask for it. She sighed softly, suddenly remembering that even Vetchim, the marshhunter, had pledged his troth to her at the Hurlers' Gate, and she brought her thoughts back to Treasel.

"Tell them of Rainbows' End and the Beastweir marshery." She laughed easily, her dimpled cheeks flushing with pleasure as she beckoned the eager crowd forward around Treasel. At the same time she felt impatient with them as she thought how they had left their mistress, Marrimian, hunched and weeping with despair, on the dais of the throne.

Moving away from the eager chorus of questions and Treasel's hesitant and breathless answers about the world beyond the Hurlers' Gate, Ansel picked her way between the chimneys and lifted up a rusty roasting spit to riddle the cold cinders of the central hearth. She wondered how she could begin to turn all this ruin and chaos back to the order there had been before the marshmen had rampaged through the hall. The sharp cinders in the hearth crumbled apart as she prodded them and sent a thin spiral of soot and ashes drifting up the chimney, and for a moment she imagined the fires kindling.

"A feast," Ansel cried suddenly as she saw the beginnings of an idea in the spiral of soot and ashes. She clapped her hands and brought the babble of kitchen questions around Treasel to a halt. "This is what we must do. First we must clear the refuse from the hall and build a pyre of all the dead marshmen beyond the doors. And then, when everything is set as fair as we can make it, we will prepare a feast for our mistress to celebrate her triumph over the marshlords. Yes, that is what will bring a smile to her lips!"

Ansel snapped her fingers and set the scuttles to find brooms, shovels and brushes and then she divided everyone into small groups which she sent into every corner of the hall to begin to clear away the mounds of rubbish. Some she kept in the kitchens to scrub the pots and pans, some to sweep, some to fetch and carry, yet others were sent to scour through the larders and salting houses to search for every scrap of meat or bundle of dried vegetables and herbs that the marshmen had not stolen or spoiled in their plundering. She gathered the fish cooks around her in a huddle and told them of the ruin and destruction in the city and warned them to tread with care as they journeyed down to the fish moats with every net that they could find and as many empty fish kettles as they could carry. Calling out for the glazers, basters and gutters, she sent them to sift through the wreckage of the crystal houses for every morsel of food that the mudbeasts had not crushed or trodden underclaw.

"And make your way down to the smoke houses to see if anything can be rescued," she called after them as they hurried beneath the kitchen archway.

Turning back, Ansel stared at the cold fire pits and muttered anxiously, "We will need a lampwick to kindle the flames in the hearth and the ovens," and she strutted into the center of the dusty kitchen, watching the scuttles noisily attacking the mounds of rubbish, absently rubbing her chin as she wondered where all the lampwicks, ragmen, dusters, hoemasters and servers had found to hide from the marshmen.

"Who are those over there?" asked Treasel, breaking into Ansel's thoughts and tugging at her sleeve. Ansel turned to look where the marshgirl was pointing, toward the furthest gloomy corners of the kitchens, beyond the huge black bake ovens and gutting slabs. "They have been slipping into the kitchens as quietly as shadows ever since you called out the scullions and set them to work," whispered Treasel anxiously as she moved closer to Ansel.

"Drawn out by the kitchen clatter no doubt," muttered Ansel, grimly biting her lip as she stared into the gloomy reaches of the kitchens. "Those are the ragmen—the tall, stooping figures with their feet bound up in bundles of rags—and there in amongst them I can see servers, dusters and . . ."

Ansel hesitated as she caught a glimpse of a soot-smudged lampwick. The silent watchers shifted uneasily and whispered together.

"Why are they just standing there? Why don't they come forward?" asked Treasel, her lips barely moving.

"I'm not sure," frowned Ansel, slowly folding back her marsh-soiled cuffs as she not only searched for words to explain her fears to the marshgirl but also tried to grasp at the heart of the worry that had been gnawing away at her. It had begun after Lord Miresnare had tried to follow Marrimian amongst the mudbeasts to stop her claiming his throne and the beasts had trampled him to death. It had been that moment which had troubled her most, the moment when everyone had turned against her mistress. She had seen clearly the archer guard that Lord Miresnare had set in the high gallery to overwatch the joust and protect the eventual champion, had watched them crowd forward as her mistress touched the Glitterspike and seen them shake their heads and draw back and disappear, leaving Marrimian at the mercy of the rabble of marshmen who were swarming through the hall. Every man except Krann and the master mumbler had seemed to surge against her and she knew that Marrimian would have been trampled to death if she had not set loose the mudbeasts to rampage through the hall. Ansel shivered. She worried whether the men of the hall would ever take Marrimian as their Queen or whether they would seek out Lord Miresnare's archers and guards and gang together with them in secret groups and try to seize the throne for themselves now that the marshmen were gone. She stared helplessly at Treasel. How could she expect her to understand when she came from such a different world, where most women did not even have a name and everyone lived from hand to mouth scavenging in the marshes.

Ansel drew breath and realized that she must try to make the marshgirl see the danger they were in. "I think they will not help because we are women. Because men have always ruled in Glitterspike Hall they will not touch a woman's work nor bend to take a woman's orders," she whispered grimly. "And I fear that they will gang together and try to seize the throne from our mistress rather than serve her."

Treasel's eyes narrowed and she clenched her hands until her knuckles blanched. "Mistress rescued me and gave me a name; they will never take that from me," she hissed; showing such anger that it gave Ansel courage. She snapped her fingers threateningly at the whispering crowd and called the lampwick to come forward, telling him to light the hearths and ovens.

Reluctantly the lampwick shuffled toward the fire pit that the scuttles had piled with kindling and fidgeted with his fire tools. Then he stopped and shouted, "You have no right to call for fire. Your place is to cook and scrub and fetch, only the master server can call for fire."

Ansel threw her head back and let out a great shout of laughter loud enough to rattle the piles of pots and pans, to stop the kitchen bustle and turn every head toward her. "Talk to me of rights when your belt buckle touches your backbone with hunger, for without your fire you will eat nothing from my kitchen!" she thundered at the startled man, her face blackening with anger, her jaw thrust out. "And mark my word, all of you, Lord Miresnare, your master, is dead and his firstborn Marrimian is now the Queen in Glitterspike Hall. Yes, Marrimian!" she cried as the startled crowd of ragmen, dusters and servers gasped. "Yes, she was the only one brave enough to pass through the mudbeasts chained around the Glitterspike and claim her father's throne. Then she set free the beasts to chase out that rabble of marshscum from whom you fled to hide in all the dark cubbyholes for fear of losing your lives. She won't take to your talk over-kindly." As she shouted she advanced in huge threatening strides and snatched the startled lampwick's fire tools from his hand.

"Marrimian is our Queen?" cried another lampwick.

"A Queen has driven out the marshlords!" ran a dozen whispers through the crowd, stirring them to shuffle forward. The kitchen people had heard whispers, wild rumors of a woman who had tamed and ridden a beast across the quickmarshes, but none of them had believed a word of it.

Ansel glared triumphantly at the shifting crowd she would have shrunk from in Lord Miresnare's day. She slipped the lampwick's fire tools into her voluminous apron pocket and placed her hands on her ample hips. "Yes. Marrimian is the new ruler of this hall. And you had better run as fast as your legs will carry you to kneel before her and pledge yourselves to serve her. And then you can begin to clear . . ."

A voice from within the crowd laughed and cut the scullion short. A hoemaster forced his way to the front. "You say this Queen of yours freed the mudbeasts?" he demanded, stabbing a leathery, earth-stained finger at Ansel.

"Yes! Yes! She broke their shackles and then drove the marshscum out." Ansel's voice hesitated and she sought the courage to hold her ground as the hoemaster advanced toward her.

"Then she's a Queen of fools!" muttered the hoemaster, rubbing his hands together, the dry scrape of his leathery skin rasping in the gloomy silence. "It was the mudbeasts that I heard rampaging through my courtyards!" he cried, turning toward the kitchen folk, who had edged closer to listen to him. "I first thought it was more of those marshlords in their armored boots wreaking havoc but there was no disguising the thunder of mudbeasts' claws or the sound of shattering crystal as they plundered and trampled their way through the crystal houses. Your Queen Marrimian will have starved us all to death when the wet seasons begin by recklessly freeing those beasts, for they have trampled and destroyed everything that we might have eaten. I heard the destruction through the door crack of my secret cubbyhole."

"Everything is destroyed!" "Everything has been

ruined!" rose the angry frightened whispers among the ragmen.

"What will we eat then?" demanded a gilder, crackling a thin sheet of finest gold leaf that was used to gild the roast pindafall birds, its crinkled surface shimmering in the half light.

"There'll be nothing served up to you but these moldy bone endings and rotten fish heads!" Ansel cried, fiercely shaking her fist at the shifting crowds as they began to move toward the kitchen entrance. "Nothing, I tell you, if you don't go straight into the hall and pledge yourselves."

"We will see this Queen for ourselves. We need none of your orders, scullion," shouted one of the ragmen over his shoulder in anger as he turned and followed the hurrying crowd into the corridor which led to the great hall.

"Wait! Wait!" cried Ansel, still shaking her fist at the milling crowd of men as they surged angrily around her, bumping and barging her as they hurried under the kitchen archway toward the hall. "This is a new beginning for all of us. Now that Lord Miresnare is dead we can clear away the marshmen's rubbish together and . . ."

Ansel's words fell on deaf ears. She reached out in despair and tried to clutch at the last of the departing ragmen but they glided and swayed around her, staring fixedly ahead, their hands clasped firmly behind their backs, their long thin necks and sharp angular chins thrust forward as they vanished beneath the kitchen archway. Behind them the scullions and scuttles stirred uneasily and frightened whispers passed back and forth. Suddenly they pushed aside the piles of pots and pans and they too began to move toward the kitchen entrance.

"No!" cried Ansel, her eyes blazing with anger, her fists clenched so tight that her fingernails dug painfully into the palms of her hands. "No, you shall not follow that rebellious rabble," she ordered, grimly striding across the kitchen, blocking the entrance with her ample bulk.

The kitchen folk slowed and glanced at one another and their whisperings rose into angry mutterings.

Treasel caught the scent of danger in their voices. She unsheathed her dagger and quickly filled the gap beside Ansel. "I'll gut anyone who takes another step," she hissed, baring her teeth.

Ansel frowned and gently shook her head. She put her hand on Treasel's arm and pushed the dagger down. "There'll be no bloodshed in my kitchens. But there'll be no woman amongst you who will not take your mistress, Marrimian, as your Queen."

The kitchen folk hesitated and whispered, huddled together.

"But who else in Gnarlsmyre will ever take Marrimian as their Queen?" rose a voice.

"She'll find a way to feed us now that the mudbeasts have destroyed the crystal houses, I know she will," called another, her voice silencing the anxious doubts in the kitchen clamor.

Gradually, one by one, the kitchen women cried

out against the ragmen and their like who had slipped from the kitchen. "Perhaps they'll try and steal the throne! We must go to Marrimian and protect her," shouted a dozen voices.

"Yes," cried Ansel, turning and ducking beneath the kitchen archway. "Help the master mumbler and Krann protect her."

"The master mumbler was wandering in the corridor. He spoke to me," interrupted Treasel.

"Then we must run as though we had wings on our heels," urged Ansel.

Treasel suddenly stopped and gripped Ansel's arm. "You have forgotten. There is the army of marshmen, hunters and waders who have already pledged themselves to our mistress. Remember? She made them wait for her in the shadows of the Hurlers' Gate. Can't we somehow lead them up into the hall?"

"There is no one at the Hurlers' Gate!" called out a grimy scuttle, who, on a scullion's orders, had clambered up on to the soot-smeared ledges to scrub above the cold bake ovens and who now peered down through the dirty window slits. "There is nothing moving beyond the beasting pits, nothing except the bulrush stems bending in the wind on the endless quickmarsh. There are no marshmen anywhere to be seen."

"But where is Vetchim? Where have those treacherous marshmen vanished to?" Ansel muttered, her face darkening into a frown as she turned anxiously toward Treasel.

Treasel shrugged her shoulders hopelessly and

whispered that they must have betrayed their pledge and followed the marshmen who had left the hall and fled back into the marsheries. Ansel felt a cold shiver run up her spine, and an ominous tingle of dread knotted the pit of her stomach.

"We must keep their treachery a secret," she whispered bitterly, trying to shut out the picture of Vetchim's face as she brushed her lips against the marshgirl's ear. She smoothed the dirty creases in her apron and tried to swallow her despair. She searched her mind for the words that would assure the kitchen folk that the marshmen were loyal to Marrimian.

Slowly she turned and forced a smile on her blackened face. "Of course," she cried, making to slap her forehead with the palm of her hand as though she had forgotten something that any fool should have remembered. "I am such a silly scullion. The marshmen at the gates pledged to hunt down and kill anyone who would not take Marrimian as their Queen. That is why the gates are deserted: the loyal marshmen are hunting on the heels of those who fled the great hall. Now, come on, be quick, before that rabble of ragmen threatens our Queen."

"But there are no dead marshmen littering the gates," called out the scuttle perched on the top of the bake oven, but her words were lost in the rush of footsteps beneath the low archway.

Ansel's eyes brimmed with tears at Vetchim's treachery, but she took a deep breath and swept her gaze across the anxious sea of faces that crowded around her as they ran toward the hall. Only Treasel saw the hot tears of despair that ran down her cheeks to splutter on to her dirty apron collar as she whispered Vetchim's name over and over again.

5

A Cold Throne
for Comfort

*K*RANN heard the rush of footsteps echo suddenly in every low archway and corridor that flanked the hall and he spun around, throwing aside the heavy slab of gray stone that he had been clearing from the threshold of the corridor leading to the daughtery. "Quick! Arm yourselves with iron spikes. The marshmen have returned," he shouted to Marrimian and Treyster where they crouched above him tearing at the mound of rubble.

Marrimian jumped lightly to the ground and took a step into the hall. The footsteps stopped abruptly. Krann frowned and swept his gaze across the rows of gloomy archways. There were shadowy figures there, indistinct shapes, hovering, watching, and there were voices, muttering and whispering on every side, closing in all around them. The great hall had become a hall of whispers.

Krann drew his dagger as Treyster jumped down from the mound of rubble and pressed against his arm. "We must escape," Krann hissed. "There are too many of them. They will overcome us in moments."

"Wait! Wait!" breathed Treyster, turning her head from side to side and listening to the rising whispers. After a short while she laughed softly. "There is nothing to fear in what you hear. It is not the rush of marshmen's feet; no, it is the hall folk we hear creeping through every door crack and passageway toward the hall. Ansel and Treasel must have found them and called them out."

Krann frowned anxiously and moved closer to Marrimian. "There is a harshness in their whispers."

"We have nothing to fear from them," Marrimian answered quickly. "They are the ragmen, dusters, scullions and scuttles. They would not dare to raise a hand against me. I'll call them forward to help us clear the corridor to the daughtery."

"No," hissed Krann. "Don't step into the rays of sunlight that flood the hall, just in case those archers from the high galleries are amongst the crowd."

"There is nothing to fear," she murmured again. "There isn't a hint of a scrape of armored boots amongst the shufflings of the hall folk. My father's guards have fled; these people have come to me."

"But what if they don't accept you as their Queen? What if they have come to snatch the throne from you? Step carefully," Krann warned as Marrimian moved away from him into the shafts of sunlight.

"Come. Come forward, my people," Marrimian cried as she crossed the hall and climbed up on to the dais of the throne. "It is I, Marrimian, the first-born daughter of this hall," she called out, conscious of the sudden silence that filled every archway. "My father, Lord Miresnare, lies dead, crushed by the mudbeasts that he set to guard the Glitterspike, but I passed through the circle of beasts to touch the Glitterspike and by the lore of the last joust my father set, I claim his throne and the right to rule all of Gnarlsmyre as your Queen."

"They doubt her," hissed Treyster, gripping Krann's arm. "I can hear it in their silence. Quickly, we must go to her."

Figures were emerging from the gloomy archways. Crowds were forming on the edges of the hall, filling every space beneath the splintered rafter beams of the ruined galleries. Some tall, angular figures, some short and swarthy ones were beginning to shuffle between the mounds of refuse that littered the hall and come toward the dais of the throne.

Marrimian swept her gaze across their faces and saw in their rigid, unblinking stares a tide of doubt. She realized that they had become deaf to her words. "Krann, where are you?" she hissed anxiously. She stepped back until her foot snagged against the throne.

"We are here," he answered quietly, appearing beside her and touching the sleeve of her gown.

"They . . . they doubt me. What shall I say? How shall I convince them? What words shall I use?" she whispered, clutching at his hand. She begged him to tell her how the great ladies of Elundium addressed their people. At the same time she realized that the people of the hall, her father's people, were turning against her, just as his guards had done.

Krann frowned. "The words of Elundium are based on history. Whole books of lore govern what is said, and set the manners of my people. But here in Gnarlsmyre this moment is raw and new. This is *your* moment, Marrimian, and no one, not even the wisest loremaster of Elundium, can tell you how best to use it."

"But the future of Gnarlsmyre hangs on every word I utter. Please help me," she implored, the color blanching from her face.

Krann glanced at the grim, silent faces of the hall folk pressing ever closer to the dais. "My counsel here in the shadow of your throne would be no different to the one I gave when fate crossed our paths in the water meadows beyond Rainbows' End."

"What counsel?" she hissed. "I have forgotten your words of wisdom—tell me again!"

Krann turned toward her and smiled sadly, holding her gaze. "You have learned nothing and understood little of what I tried to teach you as we trod together through the marshes if you cannot reach back now and remember. This moment is the true test of your queenship. You must sway your people and make them want to follow you and believe that you are worthy of being their Queen. You cannot rule them with force; they can easily overwhelm us."

Marrimian frowned and bit her lip as she tried to

catch the words he had uttered across the ribbons of dancing sparks from their camp fire. "You talked of my being determined and you counseled me not to despise my womanhood and . . . and there were so many things," she muttered angrily with half an eye on the crowds who were edging forward.

"I called you brittle and counselled you against boiling with anger too easily!" he whispered. "But most of all I counseled you to be yourself. That is your greatest strength. Now use your strength wisely."

Marrimian nodded and whispered, "Stay close to me."

Krann frowned as he caught a glimpse of the dark, desperate days that lay ahead for Marrimian and he remembered watching the crones spin and weave their spells over the marshmen who had pledged themselves to her. He drew her close until his lips were almost brushing against her ear. "You have so much doubt to talk away. So much to change in these people. Expect little from them and yet temper your judgment of them and be patient; you will only change them slowly, as you teach them to love and follow you. Remember, trust no one until you have knowledge of the color of the lining of their cloaks. Count your friends carefully and do not forget those who helped you touch the Glitterspike."

"You sense danger. You think they will rise against me; I can hear it in your voice."

Krann smiled grimly. "You have snatched a great prize, Marrimian. If the people of the hall do not follow you there is danger waiting to trip you in every untrodden shadow."

"Then I will meet it head on," she muttered grimly, stepping away from the throne and moving toward the edge of the dais, but she stopped mid-stride and turned toward the kitchen entrance. The crowds who had been shuffling silently nearer through the shafts of sunlight suddenly hesitated, then split apart.

"Ansel! Treasel!" cried Marrimian, her face breaking into a smile. With a sudden rush and clatter of footsteps the scullion and the marshgirl burst into the hall through the kitchen archway. Behind them streamed a long procession of grim-faced scullions, fish cooks and scuttles. Angry whispers began to ripple through the watching crowds. "Kitchen women are not allowed into the hall," muttered a server.

"Scuttles, wheelbarrows and turfers are forbidden to tread beyond the kitchen passageway. They spoil the floorstones of the hall with their dirty footprints," grumbled one of the ragmen in the crowd, his voice disappearing beneath the tramp of scuttles' feet.

"Marrimian is our Queen!" thundered Ansel, forcing and barging her way through the crowds until she had reached the dais of the throne. Turning, she glared at the shifting crowd, her huge hands planted firmly on her hips. The closest gaggle of ragmen retreated a step beneath her withering gaze as the rest of the kitchen women surrounded the dais of the throne.

"That's right, stare as much as you like," Ansel continued a little breathlessly, "but my mistress, Queen Marrimian, touched that Glitterspike just as I told you in the kitchens, and the throne is hers; the mumbler said it was, so you had better pledge yourselves to her and be quick."

"Queen Marrimian? How can we have her as our Queen? We have never had a woman to rule over us," cried out a voice from the back of the crowd beneath the galleries.

Other voices began speaking of the rumors and the wild tales that Ansel had spun beneath the kitchen archway and amongst the grumblings and the mutterings there grew a realization that there must have been some truth in all of them.

"That *is* Lord Miresnare's firstborn on the dais of the throne," called out a ragman, standing on tiptoe and shading his eyes against the rays of blinding sunlight streaming across the hall.

"But she is dead! I saw her father cast her out at the Allbeast Feast," called a bewildered duster, craning his short neck for a better view of the throne.

"It is Lord Miresnare who is dead," cried Ansel. "He lies there, amongst those rusty iron chains. Look for yourselves."

The crowd shifted, pushing and shoving, edging toward the litter of broken bodies amongst the heaps of iron chains.

"Look, look, I can see the bloodied hems of his gown," cried a voice from the crowd.

"Dead!" Our lord and master is dead!" wailed a dozen voices.

Suddenly the mob began to shout angrily.

"Send these scullions back into the kitchens where they belong, then we'll get a new lord of our own," grumbled the ragmen on the far side of the hall.

"Yes—and call for the master mumbler; he set down every one of our master's laws. He will soon settle all doubts on who can claim the throne and where these wretched kitchen scum can trespass," shouted a disgruntled server.

"And what of *him?*" demanded a hoemaster, pointing an accusing finger up at Krann, and for a moment the clamor of voices fell silent.

"Perhaps that stranger was really the one to touch the Glitterspike. Perhaps he can put an end to these wild claims from the firstborn about her right to the throne."

"Yes. He must have won the joust," cried one of the hoemasters. "He's the one who should have the throne. He's a man and he's strong enough to rule over us."

Krann felt his face tighten with anger as the hall folk sneered at Marrimian's triumphs and swept her claim to the throne aside simply because she was a woman. Moving closer to her, he pressed his spark secretly into her hand. "Blind them with some magic. Make them fear you and respect you," he hissed, stepping quickly away from her.

"Perhaps the stranger will claim Marrimian as his prettier. Perhaps . . ." sneered the leader of a tight knot of dusters, leering and elbowing his way through the crowd toward the dais.

"Prettier? I am no man's prettier!" cried Marrimian, cracking the spark alight between her fingers and sweeping the blazing light out against the surging crowd.

The crowd's sneers and shouts turned into one great startled gasp of terror as the blinding spark-light burned into their eyes. Barging and pushing, they turned to flee, only to stumble and trip over their own shadows which the bright light between Marrimian's fingertips had set to dance and leap amongst them. Tall, stick-thin, angular ragmen skidded on their ragbound feet while swarthy dusters tripped over their neatly bound brooms and twig bundles and pushed into the hoemasters, who cursed and fought to be the first to reach the safety of the maze of gloomy archways that flanked the hall.

Krann could have laughed out loud at their blind panic but he smothered the impulse and touched Marrimian's arm, whispering, "Enough, the magic will burn your fingers. Now make them understand that not only did you have the right to joust but that you are strong enough and determined enough to succeed and rule."

Marrimian let the spark splutter and go out and she laughed harshly, her voice cutting through the shouts and cries of the frightened crowd.

"You dare to question that I had the right to joust," she snapped, her eyes blazing with anger as her father's servants stopped and slowly turned back toward her and she fought to hold on to the edges of her temper as she spoke to them. "My father proclaimed that anyone who drank from the jousting cup, man or woman, had the right to quest for his throne. Which of you doubters had even enough courage to stand shoulder to shoulder with the marshmen at the Allbeast Feast and wet your lips on that cup? Which of you were there beside me when I fought my way across the hall? Who amongst you was brave enough to take just one step in amongst that circle of shackled beasts?" Marrimian paused for breath and unsheathed her dagger and the long, thin blade reflected the rays of morning sunlight across their startled faces.

"Find the master mumbler, if you can," she hissed, "for he knows all the lore of the joust. He will tell you clearly that I had the right and if that is not enough and you still cry out against my womanhood I will fight you one by one to keep what I have won!"

"Marrimian is the Queen of Gnarlsmyre and she does not stand alone!" cried Krann, loosing his dagger as he saw the people of the hall hesitate, unsure of what they should do or think.

Marrimian lifted the spark again and ragmen, dusters, hoemasters and servers alike cried out in terror as the searing flame burned their eyes. Lampwicks cowered, overawed by the power of her magic, and the panic caused by her anger spread in widening waves whichever way she turned.

"Who will challenge me now?" she shouted, thrusting the spark this way and that, and the crowds of hall folk scrambled and barged into one another in an effort to escape her fury.

Marrimian could feel the white-hot core of the spark blistering her fingers but the more it burned the more it fired her anger and the harder she thrust it at the fleeing crowd.

Ansel could see the pain etched on her mistress's face as the spark glowed between her fingers and she knew that she must do something quickly.

"Get out there on either side of your Queen. Protect her with your gutting knives, basting spoons, cleavers—use anything that comes to hand," she hissed, hurrying the scullions and scuttles out around either side of the dais of the throne. In a dozen huge strides she and Treasel closed in beside Marrimian, their daggers in their hands.

"Run!" Ansel sneered at the mob. "Flee for the safety of your hiding holes just as you did when the marshmen overran this hall. Our Queen's not afraid of the likes of you; she's got us to defend her."

"She's not afraid of anybody," shouted Treasel. "Not after rubbing shoulders with the marshmen and riding through the marshes to Rainbows' End on the backs of mudbeasts."

Ansel glared at the crowds. "And you will all go hungry until you accept her as your Queen. You'll get nothing from the kitchens, not even the crumbs that we throw to the pindafalls!"

Marrimian suddenly dropped the spark into her other hand and juggled it back and forth, cooling it as quickly as her anger. She had glimpsed in Ansel's words the beginning of a way that might make the people of the hall accept her and take her as their Queen.

"Ragmen, dusters, lampwicks," she called, springing up to stand upon the throne. The fleeing crowds hesitated and turned to watch her with suspicious eyes as she held up her spark. "The crystal houses lie in ruins, the smoke houses are empty, but by my power of fire I will feed everyone who bows to me as their Queen, the rightful ruler of Gnarlsmyre."

Ansel spun round at her mistress's wild promises, and behind her, harsh laughter broke out across the hall. "How will you fill our bellies with empty promises? There will be nothing for anyone to eat when the wet seasons begin," cried out a dozen voices.

"There will be food enough for those who will follow me, but there will be none for those who do not sit at my table," she answered quietly, sweeping her hand across the sea of heads.

The crowds shifted and formed tight huddles as each man clung to others who belonged to his guild or craft and their voices rose in urgent whispers. They had seen the power of the fire; perhaps she could conjure up food with the same magic? Marrimian saw their hesitation and heard the beginnings of hope in their whisperings.

"Will everything change?" called out an anxious ragman. "Will women be allowed into the hall?"

"That much my mistress promised out in the marshes," muttered Ansel loudly.

Marrimian laughed and cast her gaze slowly

across the crowds before pointing to the Glitter-spike. "Nothing can ever be the same again, and I would not wish it so," she answered quietly as her eyes picked out the bloodied hems of her father's cloak amongst the jumble of iron chains. "But I will promise you this," she cried fiercely. Her voice hardened as she looked across the destruction that her father's madness had wrought on the hall. "I promise you there will be no more jousts for this throne, nor will there be any marauding marshmen or mudbeasts rampaging through Glitterspike Hall. No, we will barter with the marshmen for the flesh of the beasts, by the ancient rules, at the turn of the fourth season. We will barter on the broad sweep of the cobbles in the shadow of the Hurlers' Gate, just above the beasting pits." Marrimian paused for breath and looked down to catch Ansel's eye.

"Yes, truly, much will change," she went on, breaking into a smile and looking out again at the sea of listening people. "There will be no dishonor in being born a woman. This hall and a seat at my table will be here for everyone who barters their skills and secret crafts to help me rebuild this city and restore this great hall to its former beauty."

"Barter? You will have us live by the ancient rules of barter?" cried a hoemaster in disbelief as he rubbed his leathery hands across his face. "But we haven't bartered for seasons beyond counting. Where would we start? How would we begin?"

Ansel laughed and slapped her huge hands together. "You will labor in the high terraces of the great ridge of Gnarlsmyre to harvest the wheat-corns and in return we will bake your bread." Turning, she pointed a finger at a gaggle of lamp-wicks who crowded near the far side of the dais. "And in return for light during the frozen hours and fire in the roasting pits there will be fresh marshfish baked with wild flower seeds and crushed almond flakes upon your plates, and . . ." The scullion hesitated. She knew that her words made perfect sense but she also knew that the larders would be completely bare since the handful of scullions she had left preparing the feast for Marrimian's victory had finished. There would never be enough to feed everyone now that the fish moats were empty and everything in the crystal houses lay in ruins. "That is how the barter will unfold; surely any fool, even a harvester, can see that!" she finished crossly, anxious that she had let her tongue run away with her.

"There are mounds of rubbish to be cleared from the hall and crystal houses to rebuild. There is work for everyone and you can start now by helping us to clear the corridor that leads to the daughtery," cried Marrimian, clapping her hands together as the crowd began to whisper again. "And there will always be places at my table for those who bend their backs in labor!"

Marrimian tried to laugh and talk easily with Krann but she could not ignore the people of the hall and her eyes strayed constantly to the shifting crowds who were whispering and muttering, some being for her laws of barter and some against.

Groups of ragmen were picking their way through the mounds of litter shaking their heads in despair at the deep clawscrapes that the mudbeasts had gouged in the once smooth and polished floorstones of the hall. Dusters threw their hands up in horror at the broken benches, the rich beastskin covers ripped and torn beyond repair, while the servers and the lampwicks searched in vain for any trace of the tables and chairs or the reedlamp holders that were the hallmarks of their crafts.

Marrimian turned her head and caught whispers of despair from every side. The ragmen were muttering that there was too much ruin, that the corridor to the daughtery was blocked with more broken masonry than they could move in a whole season. The clawscrapes were too deep for them ever to buff out. They would never be able to return the hall to its former glory for all the barter in Gnarlsmyre. The hoemasters were grumbling that every courtyard had been trampled into a wilderness. They insisted that they were growers and harvesters, pruners and trimmers; none of them had the tools to break new ground or the skill it would take to rebuild the crystal houses.

"She asks too much," whispered a huddle of dusters.

"This Queen would have us all tied to the scullions' apron tails," muttered a knot of lampwicks as they moved across the hall toward the low archway that their guild always used to make its way down into the city.

One of the lampwicks paused beneath the arch-stone and whispered to a group of ragmen bent by the deepest clawscrapes close to the Glitterspike. "There is nothing in the barter for us. We are going down into the city to trade our skills with the city folk for a better price."

The lampwick's whisper spread across the hall faster than a windblown flame would travel through a summer reedbank.

"There must be courtyards that need hoeing," whispered a hoemaster.

"Or benches to dust that the marshmen haven't destroyed," muttered one of a huddle of dusters.

"And there will be tables to serve," cried a server, quickening his pace to join the rush of bodies that crowded every archway.

Marrimian opened her mouth to command them to stop but Krann gripped her arm. "Let those who wish to, go," he whispered. "Let them see for themselves what the marshmen have done to their city. We must get those who have stayed to help us clear a passageway to the daughtery."

"They'll be back, mistress," grumbled Ansel as her eyes followed the last of the ragmen with a withering glare. "I'll lay a kettle of marshfish that they'll come crawling back begging for the crumbs from your table."

Marrimian looked past the scullion toward the empty, gloomy archways, her face bleached and pinched with worry. "It will take so long to clear a way to the doors of the daughtery even with the help of all those who have stayed. We'll never reach it by nightfall."

"Now, don't you go worrying yourself, mistress," fussed Ansel, hurrying to Marrimian's side. "Every scullion and more scuttles than I care to count, all the needlewomen and washwomen from the hall who have dared to come out from their hidden holes are with you, and we are bound to find more of them when we search through the maze of corridors beyond Threadneedle passageway and the daughtery."

Krann frowned as he listened to the scullion and he let his eyes wander through the shafts of sunlight and the deep shadows beneath the broken galleries. There was something strange, something unnatural, about the people of the hall, something he couldn't quite put his finger on. It had nagged and troubled him from the first moment when they had passed through the Hurlers' Gate to make their way up through the city to Glitterspike Hall.

There were no children in the city of Glor. It was children's voices and quick shadows darting in and out of the alleyways that he had missed as they found a way up through the city. He had thought then that the city folk had hidden them from the marauding marshmen but the marshmen were now gone, there was no danger, and he wondered where the children were.

Turning toward Marrimian, Krann smiled. "We must organize those who have stayed in the hall to rescue your sisters," he urged her quietly. "We must free them and all the children of the hall and find food for them before night falls."

Marrimian put a hand to her mouth. A look of

fear crossed her face and she frowned and glanced uneasily into the furthest corners of the hall and repeated his words, "Children?" Her voice echoed around, unnaturally loud.

The excited hall talk that had begun to grow again fell to nothing. The crowds shifted and drew together as if a hand of dread had touched a raw nerve in each one of them and prodded at some dark secret that they kept well hidden beneath their cloaks.

Krann looked from face to face but all the older ragmen, dusters and scullions shuffled and looked away from him. The scuttles merely glanced fearfully over their shoulders and whispered together. Krann felt a shiver of real fear pass through the hall. "What is it? We must bring the children out from where you have hidden them. The marshmen have gone; surely you will not leave them locked up?"

The crowd stared at him silently. Their uneasiness unnerved him; he had grown up amongst silences such as this and he would not be a part of them here in Gnarlsmyre. They must tell him now what they feared or strove to hide from him.

"It is forbidden to talk of the children of the hall," Marrimian cried, rushing to him and pressing her fingers over his lips to silence his questions. She glanced anxiously over her shoulder into the high-arched doorway that had led to her father's chambers as if she half expected to hear the rasp and grate of his boots upon the stairs.

"Forbidden? By whose law?" laughed Krann,

pulling away from her, yet his eyes glittered with hardness and his lips trembled as he sensed that the shadows of her father's madness still held the hall and all its people in a terrible grip. "Your father, Lord Miresnare, is dead," he hissed, spinning her around and making her look at the place where he lay amongst the heaps of iron chains. "The days of his madness are over; he cannot harm you now, Marrimian. Tell me, where are the children hidden?"

Marrimian frowned and shook her head. The color had drained from her face and she was trembling from head to foot. "Forbidden, it is forbidden," she mumbled over and over again as she struggled against Krann's restraining hands.

"She does not know," cried a voice from behind Krann, making him release Marrimian and turn sharply to face an ancient scullion whose wrinkled face was barely visible above the starched ribbons and bunches of bows woven under her chin.

"What do you know of these children and the terror that Lord Miresnare spread throughout this hall?" Krann demanded, advancing on the old lady.

A whisper spread through the hall. "It's mad Susis," people repeated. "What does she know of where the children are hidden?"

The scullion quailed and shrank back from Krann's anger. She would have fallen had she not stumbled against those who crowded behind her. They cursed her and pushed her back toward Krann.

Krann smiled and bent to offer his hand to the old

woman and helped her steady herself, begging her forgiveness for his raw temper. He glared the crowd into silence before he asked her again in a softer voice to tell him who she was and what she knew of the children of the hall.

"Susis. I am Susis, and I was the overscullion in the days of Lord Miresnare's youth, before any of these hall folk were out of their birth rags, and they should certainly show more respect for me now," she muttered at the uneasy crowd. She placed her frail, bone-thin fingers into Krann's hand and showed him a mouth of empty gums as she smiled. For a moment she hesitated and fear clouded her eyes as she glanced at the edges of her master's robes amongst the heaps of iron chains.

"He is dead, he cannot harm you, and none of those gathered here in this hall will raise a hand against you, you have my word on it," Krann whispered, coaxing her to speak.

Susis drew in a shallow breath and it rattled softly in her ancient throat as she began. "In those early seasons the hall was alive with laughter and the shouts of children's voices. Lord Miresnare encouraged all the children born to his hall folk to play around him, but . . ." The old scullion paused for breath, her forehead wrinkling into a frown as she let her mind run back. "But when he failed to sire an heir he grew jealous. At first he banished all the male children from entering this hall but with the passing of the seasons and the spawning of more and more daughters he forbade all children save his daughters from entering Glitterspike Hall. Later he forbade women to birth anywhere in the city beyond the doors of the chambers of the birthing houses that he had set aside for such purpose. To disobey the law was punishable by death beneath Yaloor's claws."

Krann stared at the scullion. "Who gave him the counsel to make such laws? Who sowed this seed of madness in him?"

Susis threw back her head, her eyes reflecting all those seasons of terror, and she clamped her thin fingers over her ears as if to shut out the screams of the children and the crunch of Yaloor's jaws from her memory. "The mumblers—they foretold the birthing houses," she whispered.

"Then they began the madness," Krann interrupted.

"Oh, no," cried Marrimian, cutting across his words. "The mumblers sowed seeds of great wisdom and they saved countless children from my father's rages." She stopped abruptly and buried her head in her hands. The scullion's words had awoken raw memories, so many childhood memories that her father's murderous rages had blotted out.

Susis stared at Marrimian for a moment and then nodded gravely. "Yes, you have touched on the real truth of it, my Queen," whispered the wizened scullion. Now she remembered how as Lord Miresnare's mad desire to sire an heir overcame everything else, the mumblers had foretold the birth houses, for it had become his custom to snatch up any of the hall children that he thought might threaten one day to steal his throne and hurl them beneath Yaloor's claws.

"But to have imprisoned them? To have gathered them all together . . . surely it was to kill them?" Krann's voice died away in horror as he realized fully how he had stumbled on the awful truth of the childless city, the explanation of the emptiness that he had felt.

"No, he never ventured near the birthing houses," Susis added quickly, seeing the look of horror in Krann's eyes as she sucked in shallow breaths. "The mumblers forewarned him against it, no matter how much his jealousy burned in him. It was the children that the birthing houses and chambers protected, not our Lord Miresnare."

Krann frowned. "But I do not understand. How could a mumbler's warning keep such a madman as Lord Miresnare from sacking the birthing houses? I have heard that once he sacked the Shambles and drove all the healing women out into the quick-marshes to perish. Surely it would have taken less than a whim for him to . . ."

Susis shook her head fiercely. "The mumblers sapped his anger and turned his rage and hatred against the marshmen. The joust was born and that turned his mind away from the children of the hall."

"I do remember my father's hatred of the sound of children's voices," Marrimian cried.

The old scullion threw up her hands helplessly and then swept her bony arms across the rows of gloomy archways that opened out on either side of the hall. "It was impossible, my Queen. We banished and beat and scolded them and forbade them to tread beyond any of these doorstones, but all our threats merely spurred them on to seek what had been denied them. They saw nothing of the danger in your father's madness. It became a game to rush across the room and touch the Glitterspike, an adventure to dodge in amongst the long-spined hunting dogs and scrape away a handful of hoarfrost. It was something to be dared, and later, beneath the kitchen archways, they boasted of their daring in the flickering firelight. It was nothing in those early seasons before the just began to see twenty or perhaps even thirty shrieking children ducking and squeezing between the gliding ragmen's feet, sending them sprawling across the polished floorstones. Or they would creep up as dusk fell and upset the lampwicks' bundles of reeds, or as the dawn broke across the frozen marshes they would loose all havoc amongst the servers who were setting up the long eating boards for morning foods. In many ways they fueled our master's madness and I am sure that he would have murdered every one of them if the mumblers had not danced around the Glitterspike and foretold the birthing houses in the billowing pine-oil lampsmoke that fogged this hall."

Marrimian laughed bitterly at how little her late father must have realized that those childish games of touch heralded and foretold his own death.

"But if he hated those children so much surely his guards could have put them to the sword?" insisted Krann, breaking into Marrimian's thoughts and making her look back at the scullion.

Susis shook her head, a dribble of laughter wetting her shrunken gums. "The mumblers forewarned him against venturing across the doorstone of any birth house. I know, because I saw the mumblers' dance. Although it was forbidden for a woman to enter the hall I had hidden in the shadows of that archway over there, the one beyond the Glitterspike, the one that leads into the kitchen passageway. I heard the wild clatter of their windbells and the rising shouts as they stepped into the swirling lampsmoke. Their fingers glowed with the magic they had conjured up and they pointed at the throne as with one voice they told Lord Miresnare that he would ill-luck the heir of the Glitterspike and break the line of the Miresnares for ever if he so much as let his shadow once touch the liftlatch of a birth door." The ancient scullion fell silent and fiddled with the knots and ribbons tied beneath her chin.

"Mumblers and their magic! I will have none of them in my hall," cried Marrimian angrily. "They have brought nothing but misery and death and desperation." And she stabbed a quivering finger at where her father's body lay, cursing the madness that they had woven around him, forcing him to hang on to their every word.

"You must not fear the mumblers, my Queen. They were but a window on all our fates, they could not twist their visions of tomorrow to their own advantage, not even if they had wanted to."

Susis fell silent and glanced up fearfully at Marrimian, measuring her anger before she ventured on. "For without that first dance of foresight that told of the birth houses and the joust perhaps your life would have followed a different path than the one which led by many twists and turns to becoming our champion and the first Queen of Gnarlsmyre."

Marrimian glared at the old scullion, but she knew deep down that the old woman's words had a ring of truth in them. At the same time she could not believe that Naul had not in some way used the power of foresight to betray her father or spent some time meddling in treachery with the healing woman who was his mother. "Naul, the master mumbler, cannot be trusted. I will not have his magic in this hall. His beginnings were in the healing woman's birth webs and she sought to destroy this place."

The murmurs rose in the crowd. Heads nodded in approval of their Queen's outburst.

"That scullion's a foolish old hag," a ragman cried. "She's so wound up in her wild tales that she would not recognize the truth if it bumped into her and spilt across her apron."

"Our Queen should not listen to her rambling. There may be birth houses somewhere in this city but there are none here in the hall. They were forbidden an age ago," muttered one of the youngest scullions.

"No, no," cried a large scrub woman, forcing her way to the front of the crowd and staring gravely down at the old woman who had shrunk away from the press of bodies. "For all her rambling there is a thread of truth in what Susis has said. There were birth houses, somewhere here in the hall, but they were so well hidden that Lord Miresnare could not find them. And there were such houses in the lower circles of the city before the marshmen overran the place. I saw their red doorways once when I lost my way."

"Yes, there are still birth chambers in the hall although we are forbidden to know of them," called out a needlewoman. "One of my tasks long before the marshmen drove us all into hiding was to needle up the hems of the blood aprons for the birth women."

"Blood aprons? What are blood aprons?" muttered Krann, turning puzzled eyes toward the needlewoman.

Marrimian gave a sudden cry and gripped Krann's sleeve. The needlewoman's talk of blood aprons had touched her memory. "I saw those birthwomen once many seasons ago . . ." and then in hushed tones she told them all how she had once chanced upon these women in the warren of gloomy, little-used passageways beyond the daughtery.

"They were there before me, filling the corridor. For a moment I called out, asking them who they were, but they vanished in a rustle of scarlet apron tails. Rustling footsteps and the slam and rattle of a liftlatch and then they were gone. I thought I heard a muffled cry, but it faded into nothing."

"It would have been death for them if you had told your father that they had trespassed beyond a birth door," whispered the needlewoman. "They scratched their wants upon the doorstone and all they needed was gathered up and delivered to them in the frozen hours of darkness. Only when a child became of age did he or she leave the birth house and enter the guilds or crafts that had been chosen for them."

"What happened to the mothers of these children? There are no families. Where do you foster love here in this wilderness of Gnarlsmyre?" Krann cried in horror, searching the faces of the crowd.

"Your guild is your family," answered an angry scullion. "Motherhood is a woman's secret, a pain best forgotten and left in the birth houses once the birth is finished."

"Then you know of these birth houses and the chambers within the hall! Can you lead us to them?" asked Krann, shutting out the coldness in the scullion's words.

But she and many of the women in the crowd laughed harshly. "We who serve the hall do not birth our children here. The birth chambers within the hall were for the women that the mumblers chose for Lord Miresnare to lie with. To bear a child, for us, is not a time of joy. When our time draws near we are blindfolded and led by secret ways to the lesser birth houses. We trod in fear and terror that our path should cross that of Lord Miresnare, for he hated others having their chances of birthing a male child as much as he hated his own disappointments."

"I could show you a quicker path to the daughtery that bypasses that corridor of broken rubble and lead you to where the birth chambers lie," called out a hesitant voice on the edge of the crowd and heads turned. Whispers no louder than the soft touching of windflower heads in a summer breeze spread across the hall.

"Who are you?" Marrimian frowned, stepping back a pace as a ragged figure approached through the parting crowd. She gazed through half-closed eyes and shook her head. "No, you cannot be real, you are a part of the scullions' fireside tales," she whispered, looking from the figure's gaunt face, as pale as rime ice, framed with spikes and knots of wild hair, down to the long coat of faded ochre that swept across the ground, rows of huge empty pockets flapping open, and down further to the coarse, woven leggings and rush boots that creaked and sighed with every stride.

Susis stared at the figure for a moment and then whispered, "Garteret—it is Garteret the gatherer." The old scullion laughed and clapped her hands and then pointed at the fine trail of dust that trickled from his pockets as he crossed the floorstones of the hall. "Yes, you are so old, Garteret, that all your gatherings have turned to dust. Come! Come forward and meet your Queen, the first Queen of Gnarlsmyre."

Susis hurried the gatherer before Marrimian, her voice stumbling over itself with excitement. "He

was a master gatherer in your father, Lord Miresnare's youth. He was then the swiftest and the
most silent and he knew every footstep, every twist
and turn, every secret of the corridors and passageways of this great hall. None heard his comings and
goings but many found their wantings piled high
upon their doorstones in the breaking dawn."

"Master gatherer?" Marrimian whispered, speaking the words slowly and reaching out a hesitant
hand to touch the rows of empty pockets in the
gatherer's long, sweeping coat. "I thought you were
part rumor, part magic. Someone to whom we
called out our wantings as the hours of frozen darkness swept across the quick-marshes. I had always
thought the scullions or the servers listened for our
voices and gathered up and piled our wantings outside the daughtery. But you must have moved very
quietly and quicker than a shadow for I never saw
hair or thread of you, or heard a single rattle from
all the wantings you must have crammed into those
huge pockets."

Garteret bowed to Marrimian and spoke softly,
the sound whistling around the sparse stumps of
the teeth that still clung loosely in his gums. "I
knew you well, mistress, and I watched you grow
from a child. I always delivered your wantings first
as you were the eldest of my master's daughters, but
if you had seen or heard the master gatherer it
would have spoiled the wanting."

"But we believed you were just a rumor, formed
of idle hall talk. I should have probed more deeply
and then I would have known about the birth

houses and all the other secrets." Marrimian frowned.

Garteret shook his head. "Our guild was shrouded with secrets, mistress. It was safer if only a few knew of us."

"Do you really know a quicker way to reach the daughtery? Surely these passageways and corridors are carved through solid rock?" interrupted Krann, staring at the strange figure.

Garteret laughed, scattering dust from his pockets. "How could I forget any of the paths that I trod through those seasons of terror as Lord Miresnare sought desperately to sire an heir? He would scream and rant for the gatherers whenever the birth bell rang and demand to be shown the way to the chamber. He would have cast aside the mumblers' counsel so that he might take an heir and hold him. He would stalk the empty corridors, a frightened lampwick at his elbow, and search for a sign of us. But only we knew the truth of each and every secret path and for all the days of his madness we were less than shadows and with the passing seasons we vanished amongst the idle hall talk for all but those who watched over the daughters of the hall. Although my pockets have long been empty and others have trodden the paths that I first waymarked, I could never, never forget."

"Lead us first to the daughtery," worried Marrimian. "I would have my sisters freed before we follow you to those birth chambers."

Garteret nodded. "There is a secret opening less than two paces from the daughtery that will lead us directly to the birth chambers, my Queen, but from what I have gleaned and overheard amongst the younger gatherers who served the wantings of the hall before the marshmen drove them into hiding there is now only one chamber that the birth-women use and that lies beyond the vine-hung courtyards and the lace panels."

Garteret bowed stiffly and turned on his heel. He vanished silently into a little-used archway beside the stone-choked passageway. Treyster cried out anxiously as Marrimian led the hall folk after him. "The doors of the daughtery may be bolted and barred against us. My sisters thrust me out to search for food as I was the youngest and Cetrinea shouted to me through the closing door that they would jam the liftlatch shut until I returned with enough food for all."

"How many days were you wandering before we found you in the stitchers' cubbyhole?" asked Marrimian, turning sharply on Treyster.

The youngest of the sisters threw up her hands and hastily looked away. "Hunger blurred the days together. What with hiding from the marshmen and finding no more than a handful of crumbs, I never gathered enough to feed all of us." Treyster's voice trailed away and she blushed with shame.

"Axes! You had better bring axes, quickly," Krann ordered, turning to a group of hoemasters who were walking close on his heels. "And gather up some of the iron spikes that the marshmen left as they fled. They may be useful," he called to a line of dusters who were hurriedly following them, threading their way through the rubbish that still littered the hall. Marrimian and the others went on ahead. When Krann turned back the archway seemed to lead to a dead end. He could find no sign of the path that Marrimian and her followers had taken.

Suddenly a hand appeared out of the darkness. "Here is the way," laughed one of the scuttles, her voice bubbling with excitement. "Our Queen sent me back to show you. Squeeze past me and follow the rough stone wall with your left hand. This narrow passage is only a dozen paces long."

Krann shivered and his eyes widened in the cold darkness. He felt his way through the tiny gap. There was light ahead and he could see Marrimian. She was hammering on two huge, ornately carved doors of black ebony. Treyster was kneeling, and pressing her ear hard against the doors.

"No one is answering us. There hasn't been a single sound, no matter how many of us bang on the doors or how loudly we shout their names," Marrimian called anxiously as she touched Treyster's shoulder to draw her away.

"Please let me try again," wept Treyster. She opened her mouth to shout but Marrimian firmly shook her head.

"No. It's time we broke the doors down."

Treyster allowed Marrimian to lead her away and she sank down against the mound of broken rubble that blocked the corridor a dozen paces from the daughtery, her shoulders trembling with despair. "This is all my fault," she whispered through her tears. "They are probably all dead. If only I had returned. If only I had brought back those crumbs that I had gleaned."

"No! The mantle of blame you have cast about your shoulders is not yours to wear," Krann soothed as he motioned the hoemasters to come forward with their axes, and he gently touched her arm and made her look up at the deep gouges riven and torn through the ornate carvings of the black ebony muntins. "These doors would never have opened no matter how much you tried to lift the latch."

"The marshmen must have attacked the daughtery again and again after Cetrinea pushed you out," whispered Marrimian, trying to comfort Treyster. But Treyster was imagining the terror her sisters must have felt with every hammer thud and splintering blow that had buckled and twisted the heavy, ornate doors and jammed the thick stiles so tightly together that they would never open smoothly again.

"They have scratched with their daggers at every knot and thunder crack for a way in, mistress," muttered Treasel, pointing to the mass of savage knife cuts that spoiled the dark, grained wood.

"We will axe them down. Stand back," cried Krann, taking one of the axes that the hoemasters had brought from the courtyards. He gripped the long handle firmly in both hands and swung it up above his shoulders. Throwing all his weight behind the blow, he sent splinters of black ebony showering. The doors quivered and the axe head grated in the hard, black wood as he struggled to pull it free. Seeing the doors move a fraction at Krann's second blow, two hoemasters quickly joined him and wielded their axes on either side.

Marrimian gathered Ansel and Treasel to her and drew them to a safe distance from the doors as the axe heads tore through the wood and sent splintering echoes through the anxious crowds now choking the passageway on each side of the daughtery. A crack of light appeared where the stiles of the door were jammed together as Krann's axe head broke through the wood. He twisted the long handle of the axe and pulled the blade free, then rubbed with his sleeve at the trickles of sweat that dampened his brow.

"Come, one more strike at the liftlatch," he cried breathlessly and he and the two hoemasters swung their axes back over their shoulders and brought them down as one. The sharp axe heads sheared through the buckled iron latches and sent up showers of sparks as they flew apart. The doors moved and creaked as their stiles ground against one another. Krann lifted his boot and kicked hard, and slowly, grating on their twisted hinges, the heavy doors swung inwards and the evening sunlight flooding through the tall mullioned windows of the daughtery poured across the doorstone of the passageway.

Krann let the axe fall from his hands and swept his gaze over the scene that lay before him. Marrimian and the others filled the doorway in silence. Then Marrimian cried out, the color draining from her face, and she brought her hands up to cover her mouth. Treyster pushed past and stumbled over the doorstone in her haste to beg forgiveness from her sisters for not returning to share the meager scraps of food that she had foraged. She lost her balance and fell headlong amongst the tangle of gowns and upturned furniture that littered the floor. Her mouth opened and closed, her stuttering words strangling in her throat, as her eyes recognized what they saw. Nothing but the hum and drone of insects broke the dry, dusty silence in the daughtery, and not the slightest breath swelled the shriveled breasts of the three gaunt, bone-thin figures that sat huddled together, pressed into the recess beneath the windowsill. They were staring toward the doorway, their last gasp of terror frozen on their lips. They were clutching each other, the yellowing skin stretched so tightly that it showed every ridge and hollow of the bones it had once so amply covered. Treyster wanted to scream, to scramble to her feet and run away from the horror, but those blind, dead eyes held her and the gaping mouths accused her with silent shouts of betrayal.

"I . . . I . . . I could not . . ." she wept, finding her voice at last and reaching out pleading fingers toward the huddled corpses. "I lost my way in the mazes the mumblers set in the passagewars around the hall to thwart the marshmen . . . I . . . I . . ." Strong, gentle hands were suddenly helping her to her feet; Marrimian was beside her, and Ansel and the marshgirl had clasped her hands.

"You were the youngest," Marrimian whispered

softly, drawing Treyster close to her, but she had her head turned toward the skeletal figures and her eyes were hooded as she spoke. "They cast you out to fend for yourself, to forage for food for them to eat, when they should have protected you and shared their last mouthful equally. Now let us leave this chamber of misery behind and break open the birth chamber and see if tragedy awaits us there as well."

Krann shuddered as he looked away from the wasted bundles of bones that seemed to be held together by their yellowing skin and the richly embroidered gowns that hung from their shoulders. His gaze took in the upturned tables and chairs that showed endless rows of teeth marks. Starvation must have forced the women in those last desperate days to gnaw on anything in an attempt to stay alive.

"Their greed and selfishness forced you to tread a better path. Don't weep for them," muttered Krann, hurriedly turning away from the sickly, dry smell of death that scented the room.

Treyster looked up and blinked her tear-swollen eyes, wondering at what he had said, and as Ansel led her from the chamber, she looked over her shoulder to where her sisters' shriveled corpses huddled. She saw that there was enough space for her body to have huddled under that window-sill with her sisters had fate been crueler—or had they been kinder.

Marrimian paused on the doorstone for a moment and looked down, unblinking, without pity,

her lips tightening with anger. "There is nothing in Gnarlsmyre, not even this throne and all the power it controls, that I would not have shared with you, but you showed the seeds of our father's uncaring meanness all too clearly, and you would not even share your food with helpless little Treyster. Your deaths are not payment enough for such selfishness: there will be no funerals to honor you, your bones will mingle with the bones of the marshmen who lie dead in the hall. You will burn on their pyres and your ashes will be scattered over the quick-marshes and quickly forgotten."

She stepped back through the doorway, her anger melting away, and sighed as she signaled to the two servers who were waiting to slam shut the doors. She barely paused before following in Garteret's footsteps and passing through the silent crowds toward the birth chambers without a backward glance. Behind her many heads in the crowd nodded agreement as ragmen, dusters, scullions and scuttles alike thought on her judgment of her sisters.

Garteret turned away from the hall, leaving the stone-choked part of the corridor behind him as he led the way toward the birth chambers. Turning from left to right, he followed a path he clearly knew well through the warren of dusty, unused passageways that opened out before them. Marrimian thought that she had known every corridor around the daughtery in her youth and now she frowned and wondered where these birth chambers could be hidden. Suddenly and without warning the gatherer vanished into thin air just as he had done when he led them through the secret way to the daughtery. Marrimian stopped and stared about her. The crowds behind her shuffled to a halt.

"Follow! Follow!" echoed the gatherer's voice and his head reappeared immediately in front of Marrimians making her jump and cry out. "Follow, my Queen," he laughed before he disappeared again.

Marrimian felt carefully along the rough passageway with her fingertips until she came to a narrow crack. It was no more than three hands wide and barely tall enough to scramble through. "This cannot be the way," she called out uncertainly, her voice echoing in the gloom beyond the crack. "This is a bottomless fault in the walls of the hall. I have stood here before and listened to the bones of the earth grinding together far below the city."

Garteret laughed and his hand appeared out of the darkness. "You are standing on one of the threshold stones that lead to all the secret corridors we gatherers use. Come, step beneath our wide archway," he beckoned.

Marrimian hesitated. "But what of the grinding sounds—the darkness?"

"Merely footsteps and their echoes, my Queen, sounding endlessly backwards and forwards; but fear not, the way becomes lighter once you have entered the corridor."

Marrimian took a deep breath and, ducking, squeezed through the gap. Treasel cried out in terror of the darkness but Krann took her hand and led her through.

"Follow each other closely or you will become lost. The path is longer and more difficult to follow than the one that led to the daughtery," Garteret called as the hall folk whispered and muttered to each other before filing through the crack.

The gatherer now seemed more at ease. He laughed softly, his eyes twinkled in the dark. He turned on his heel and led them on without another moment's hesitation. Great shafts of evening sunlight broke up the gloom, glinting down through tall window slits hewn in the roof high above their heads. Deep-set door arches lay on either side, heavily barred, and huge iron bolts were driven into the stonework, locking them shut.

"Keep to the path that I take," Garteret called over his shoulder as their corridor branched into three forks.

The one Garteret led them down became narrower and Treasel clung to Krann's sleeve, her eyes tightly shut, as the high, arched roof sank lower with every stride until she could reach up and touch the rough bricks with the back of her hand. The way narrowed until they had to walk in single file and the walls scraped against their shoulders. Thick dust muffled their footsteps and made them cough and splutter if they stumbled. The gatherer whispered something to himself and slowed, then slipped through a small opening into a wider corridor. He called to those who were following to duck very low and to keep quiet.

Marrimian scrambled through and stared up and down the long, winding passageway that opened out before them. "What place is this?" she whispered, bringing her hand up to her mouth as she choked on the stale air, heavy with the stench of decay.

Garteret muttered to himself as if he were trying to remember something and he brought his finger up to his lips. "These are the birth chambers," he whispered, pointing and waving his long, thin, dusty fingers at the row of doorways on the other side of the passageway. Some of them had stout wooden doors with locks and bars while others were broken and hung from rusty hinges.

Treyster shuddered as she heard the gatherer's whisper. She clasped hold of Marrimian's hand and drew close to her, terrified of what they might see next. Slowly the gatherer moved from door to door, fidgeting with his empty pockets, scattering dust on each doorstone, as if he were searching for something.

"What are you looking for?" Marrimian asked in a whisper, hurrying to catch up with him.

Garteret turned, startled by her voice, and flung a handful of dust at the nearest of the broken doorways. "These that are open hold nothing for us," he hissed, "nothing but forgotten memories and broken dreams, barely visible beneath the lace-fine shrouds of dust and gossamer that time has drawn over them. But these doors which are closed . . ."

"How will any of us know which are still being used?" Marrimian asked just as the gatherer clapped his hands together and pointed to a series of scratch marks roughly cut into a doorpost close to his shoulder. "That is a gatherer's mark! That is what I was searching for. Look, there are countless other scratchings, on the door, on the post, on the archway. Yes, yes, this must be the birth chamber," he muttered, his voice quickening as he scraped aside the thin layer of dust on the doorstone with his rush-woven boots.

"I have seen marks like these on the wall near the daughtery, but I thought they were Pinvey's idle scratchings," exclaimed Marrimian, touching the doorpost and running her fingertips over the sharp gouges.

The gatherer hushed her into silence, his eyes widening in alarm. "I could tell you many of Pinvey's secrets and explain the code in her scratchings but our voices will set panic afire in the birth chambers. Only the gatherers know of this corridor. They will think that Lord Miresnare's guards have found the door."

Marrimian frowned. "How do you know if there is anyone alive in there?"

Garteret smiled and drew her away from the doorstone. "There are signs in the dust. It was thinner on the doorstone; there are many footprints that spoil the entrance; there are many scratchings; the bolts are drawn and the liftlatch has been worn smooth with constant use." He paused and beckoned to Krann, Treyster and Ansel, making them crowd closely around Marrimian before he continued. "And there is the smell of life behind this door. Can you not sense it?"

Ansel sniffed and made a face. "There is a stench worse than death."

"It's worse than the daughtery!" Treyster gasped, covering her nose.

Krann swallowed and looked at the heavy door, knowing that someone had to open it. He reached out his hand toward the liftlatch.

"No! No!" hissed Garteret. "I must remember and give the signal before we open the door. The birthwomen and their children do not fear the gatherers."

"Can you tell when the last gatherer brought their wantings?" Krann asked as Garteret slowly tapped with the knuckles of his left hand. Twice he knocked just above the doorstone, once beside either doorpost at shoulder height and twice underneath the liftlatch before he gripped it with his right hand.

"That's hard to say," he muttered, frowning at the freshest scratchings on the doorpost. "But by the dust that has gathered in these marks their wantings were delivered long before the Eve of the Allbeast Feast that heralded the last joust. But there may be nothing in my guessing; there is nothing you can tell for certain."

"Would they know anything of my father's death? Would they know of the ending of the joust and my triumph over the marshmen?" Marrimian asked quickly, making the gatherer hesitate as he pressed on the liftlatch.

He shrugged his shoulders as he clicked open the latch. "Who can say, mistress? Who can tell how rumors travel or what they feed on? I heard whispers of your triumph beyond the west tower of the hall; their fading echoes drew me into the great hall to find the truth of it." His voice fell silent and he gave the heavy door a gentle push, letting it creak open on its rusty iron hinges.

Treyster cried out and staggered backwards, overpowered by the stench that billowed out through the doorway. "That reek is a hundred times worse than the daughtery," she gasped, covering her mouth with her hand, the color draining out of her face as the terror of what they might find across the doorstone flooded through her. Ansel clutched at Treyster as she staggered and pulled her away from the chamber.

"I will help you, mistress," Treasel called bravely, overcoming her fear of the airless corridors that crowded around her. She unsheathed her dagger and moved to Marrimian's side.

"I will go first," whispered Krann, edging past the women until he stood at Garteret's elbow.

The door creaked on its hinges. Weak evening sunlight from high, narrow window slits on the far side of the chamber flooded across the doorstone, making Krann blink, then shield his eyes as he craned forward and peered into the room.

"By all the colors in the rainbow cloak . . ." he hissed, half stepping backwards and catching his heel upon the doorstone. He would have fallen against Marrimian but the gatherer and Treasel caught him between them and steadied him.

"What? What is it you see?" Marrimian asked in an anxious whisper as she pushed forward and pressed against his shoulder to look. He felt her gasp, shudder and catch her breath as she stared down at the huddle of thin, naked and filthy children who had been drawn to the door by the sound of voices.

"Look . . . look at their wild, frightened eyes and the dirty knots of hair that hang down their backs," she whispered, horrified, "and look at the way they scramble away from us."

"They are no better than animals," muttered Treasel grimly as she watched the children scuttle away on their hands and knees through the mess and litter that choked the chamber.

The children crawled toward a raised dais beneath the window slits, but every now and then they stopped and scrabbled on the ground, scooping up something which they put in their mouths. On the dais sat three figures in ornately carved chairs. They wore highwinged scarlet caps and dark red aprons.

To Marrimian there was something familiar in this chamber, something that drew her forward over the threshold. "Who are they?" she whispered.

"Those are the birthwomen. You can tell them by their blood aprons and the high caps that they wear," whispered Garteret proudly. "They rule everything in the . . ."

"Don't take another step!" hissed Treyster, the

panic in her voice cutting across the gatherer's words. She had crept back into the doorway, knowing that she must overcome her terror of what might lie hidden inside the chamber, but what she had glimpsed over Marrimian's shoulder made her grip her sister's arm and pull her stumbling back into the passageway.

"What is it?" frowned Marrimian, searching Treyster's frightened eyes and trembling lips. "We must go to these children, they are our sisters."

Treyster shook her head desperately. "There's something wrong with this place, I can feel it. It makes my bones ache with an awful dread, it is in the smell, the . . ." She hesitated, searching for the words to describe her feeling of impending doom, and sweeping her eyes across the vileness that crowded the chamber, she cried, "Look at the floor." She pointed down between the scattered piles of rubbish. "Look, there where the children paused as they scuttled away from us. I'm sure the floor is moving."

"And look over there: the children are fighting for a place on the lap of the woman who sits in the center chair," whispered Krann, making the others look across the room. The children on her lap were burrowing beneath her voluminous scarlet apron tails.

"They are hiding from us," muttered Ansel, peering over Krann's shoulder and looking into the filthy birth chamber. She frowned and thrust out her chin. "Look, those who cannot find a place on the center chair are scattering to either side of it and scrambling up on to the other two women."

"They do not lift a hand to soothe or comfort the children who are clambering upon their laps," frowned Marrimian. "They sit too still, as if they are unaware of them. They merely rock their chairs slowly backward and forward and stare unblinkingly at us."

Krann watched the birthwomen for a moment and shivered. "Treyster is right, there is something horribly wrong in this chamber and I'm sure it is those birthwomen. I think they are dead."

"Dead!" gasped Marrimian as she started forward for a closer look.

Treyster grasped her arm and hissed. "Look there, beyond the women, one of the children is scraping some of that oozing slime off the wall and putting it into her mouth."

Treasel watched for a moment and then laughed softly as she whispered, "Slimetouch! She is eating slimetouch! It must grow here just as it grows on the marshoaks near our marshery." Quickly the marshgirl stepped over the threshold and picked her way through the stinking refuse that spoilt the floor and went to the spot where the children had paused. Bending, she scooped something up and returned to the others in the doorway.

"The children were merely foraging for food as they fled from us, just as the children of the marsheries grub amongst the stilts of our dwellings for sweetmeats," she smiled and opened her fist, showing the mass of fat, wriggling insects that ran to the edges of her hand and fell back on to the floor to burrow and vanish amongst the piles of rubbish.

Marrimian and Treyster cried out and shrank back from Treasel while Ansel cursed the marshgirl under her breath for touching such filth. The gatherer, who had stepped into the chamber to give the others space to crowd the doorway, looked from the marshgirl's hand down to the wriggling centipedes and black-shelled beetles that had swarmed silently over his rush-woven boots. He gave a cry of horror, hastily stamped his feet and hurried back over the threshold.

"I cannot go in," gasped Marrimian, shrinking back from the doorway. "There is a foulness that infects this chamber. The floor runs with vermin and there is the putrid stench of death in the air. No, I cannot enter."

The center chair on the far side of the chamber creaked and jarred forward. A frail hand stabbed at the doorway, casting a long, thin shadow from the setting sun across Marrimian's face, making her gasp and clutch at Krann's hand as the figure spoke. "How dare you call our food vermin or utter one word against these dead comforters who sit on either side of me. These children are less fortunate than you, Marrimian; they were born to leaner times and they know of no one to snuggle up against in the frozen hours of darkness save these withered, shriveled birthwomen."

"Who are you?" whispered Marrimian.

The woman rocked her chair forward again fiercely and announced her name as Ankana, matron of the chamber. Her eyes blazed with hurt and anger that Marrimian had seen nothing of her ingenuity or the strength of her determination to keep the children alive through the endless days which had stretched into the whole seasons of their abandonment.

"You are truly Lord Miresnare's daughter to judge this chamber so harshly," she cried, making the children who clung to her apron tails scream with panic as her voice rose.

Marrimian forced her lips to stop trembling and clung on to Krann as she answered, "But I can only judge what I see, I knew nothing of you before this sun rose. Why do you live in such squalor? Surely the gatherers provided for all your wantings? Surely they . . . ?" She frowned and tried not to look at the small child stretching up to scrape handfuls of oozing slimetouch from the far wall.

Ankana threw back her head and let out a shriek of humorless laughter. "Gatherers!" she hissed. "We would have starved to death long ago if we had waited for the rattle of their knuckles on our door. We are a place of secrets that became all too easily forgotten with the birth of each new daughter."

"But to eat beetles and wriggling grubs—to swallow that oozing slime . . . Why didn't you bring the children back into the hall while my father slept? Surely the scullions would have hidden you? I would have helped you."

Ankana sighed and sagged wearily in her chair but her eyes hardened as she looked past her and saw the gatherer. "They could have shown us the

way," she muttered, pointing an accusing finger at the gatherer. "But they were always gone quicker than a shadow from our doorstone on their rare visits to these chambers. They would rub out their footprints with their longtailed coats so that we could not follow."

"It was forbidden," Garteret cried. "By the lore of the hall children were forbidden. We dared not take you back into the hall."

Ankana shrugged the gatherer's words away and smiled down at one of the small children on her lap as she took the offering of a small, black-winged beetle from her hand and crunched it slowly between her toothless gums before swallowing it in one gulp. "We survived despite being forgotten," she cried, fiercely, sweeping her hand across the chamber. "We survived by living as you find us, on the creatures that breed on our refuse, and by licking at the slimetouch that trickles down through that fissure in the wall."

Ankana paused for breath and frowned at her own anger. She plucked at the rucks and wrinkles that the children's feet had trodden across her scarlet blood apron and, sitting upright, shook off her resentment against the gatherers and put aside all the bitterness that could spoil this moment. She smiled at Marrimian and stretched her hand toward the open doorway.

"It was you, child, you who made all things possible. As you grew into womanhood and your strength and purpose flowered it gave us the will to

survive each lengthening day and passing season of
our solitude."

Marrimian stared open-mouthed at the frail
birthwoman. "How could you have known of me or
sensed strengths in me of which I was ignorant? I
knew nothing of these chambers until today. My
earliest memories are of the mumblers' chants
while I played with broken bone endings between
Yaloor's claws."

Ankana laughed softly and brought her finger to
her lips. "Listen," she whispered.

Marrimian strained her ears against the silence
and far away she caught the echo of the scrape of
footsteps in the kitchens and the rattle of pots and
pans. Faintly amongst the distant sounds she heard
the scullions' excited voices as they prepared the
feast of triumph to celebrate her victory. They
were laughing and chattering and spinning a thousand exaggerations about her beast-riding and de-
scribing how many marshmen she had killed alone
and bare-handed to reach the Glitterspike.

"You live in a hall of whispers, my Queen, where
nothing is a secret from us. We were powerless to
help you as we listened to each cruel word of ridi-
cule your father heaped upon your shoulders for
being born a woman, and yet those same bitter
words that bent and blackened Pinvey and
thwarted little Treyster and all your other sisters
grew the seeds of strength within you."

Marrimian smiled at the birthwoman and steeled
her courage, knowing that she must cross the chamber to where the woman sat.

"There were never doubts here in the birth chamber," Ankana whispered, reaching for her two knobbly walking sticks that hung on the arm of her chair. "No doubts at all. We knew that one day you would find a way through the gatherers' corridors and throw open that door and set us free. We knew that for all your father's wild ranting and his hatred of his daughters he had seeded the first queen who would rule Gnarlsmyre."

Marrimian stepped across the threshold and shuddered as she felt the crunch of countless beetles and grubs beneath her feet. She threaded her way through the mounds of vile rubbish toward the birthwoman and rested her hand on Ankana's arm as she began to struggle to her feet, grasping both of her walking sticks firmly in her trembling hands.

"Sit. Sit and rest your weary bones," Marrimian smiled. "Call out all the children from where they are hiding so that Garteret may lead them into the hall, for there is a feast to share, a feast of triumph that Ansel has prepared in secret. Two of the strongest hoemasters will carry you down in your chair."

Ansel blushed and wrung her hands together and opened her mouth to speak but Ankana cut her short. "No, I will walk and lead the little ones who cling to my apron tails. So many strangers will only frighten them more. My bones are not weary, mistress, merely weak from lack of use and from being kept prisoner in this cramped chamber."

Marrimian gripped Ankana's sleeve, her forehead creased into a frown. "Wait," she whispered, stopping the birthwoman from calling out the children who had hidden themselves amongst the dry flesh and bones of the two dead women and were cowering beneath their blood aprons. "You must have more magic foresight than the mumblers. To have been able to foresee that I would be Queen and to have survived so long in this secret place—tell me, please, use that foresight to look ahead and riddle out how I can feed the people without the crystal houses and make them accept me as their Queen."

Ankana laughed softly, her face creasing into a maze of dry wrinkles. She lifted her gnarled hand and pointed toward the open doorway crowded with peering faces, moving her fingers slightly to where Krann, Ansel and Treasel had ventured a few paces over the threshold stone and stood amongst the piles of broken furniture. "You already have wiser counsel than you will find in these moldering chambers. Listen to those who helped you touch the Glitterspike. But as to your queenship, that is your burden, Marrimian, yours alone. It will be tested by the quality of your judgments and the fairness of your laws."

"But how will I rule? I feel so helpless, so alone."

Ankana smiled and clasped Marrimian's hand. "You have always been alone, child. Even amongst your sisters only you played between Yaloor's claws and only you overwatched the noisy bustle of the kitchens and took the brunt of your father's anger for being a woman at the grand feast in the great hall. You are the firstborn, the one whom the hall folk have always set apart and in many ways looked up to. My counsel is to be as you always have been. Do not change yourself and the people will follow you."

The birthwoman paused for breath and pulled at Marrimian's hand, making her bend closer. "Look how many of the hall folk followed you through the gatherer's secret passages. Look how they crowd my door. They are just the beginning. The rumors of how you rule in Glitterspike Hall will spread down through the city and far beyond the Hurlers' Gate and into every corner of Gnarlsmyre."

Marrimian straightened her back as the birthwoman released her hand. She knew there was wisdom and knowledge in Ankana's words but they hadn't given her any idea of how they were going to survive or of where they were to find food.

"Listen to the wisdom of the stranger, Krann, and the marshgirl. Remember, the marshpeople survive the wet seasons without crystal houses," Ankana whispered as she rose shakily to her feet and began to usher the dozen or so children out from beneath her blood apron and from the aprons of the two dead birthwomen and told them to stand before Marrimian, their Queen.

Marrimian swallowed her repulsion and forced herself to smile and take the grubs and wriggling beetles they shyly offered her. She asked their names and their ages, though they did not answer, and tried to brush the filthy, matted locks of hair from their faces, though swarms of tiny insects stung her fingertips. Ankana saw the horror on Marrimian's face and realized how desperately she was trying to hide it from the children, so she clapped her hands and cried to the infants, "Follow the gatherer into the hall. Let him lead the way quickly into the scrub houses and the linen chambers so that these new daughters of the hall may be properly attired before their naming ceremony and the grand feast of triumph that Ansel's scullions have prepared for you."

"They have no names? But some of them must be ten or more seasons old," gasped Marrimian.

Ankana smiled as she hobbled slowly forward. "Lord Miresnare always chose the names of his children; it was the custom. We feared that he would kill this last handful of his daughters if he ever came to know of them. We muffled the birth bell and eventually, as the seasons passed, he thought his seed had failed him. He forgot the birth chambers and abandoned all hope of a male heir. We feared that it would ill-luck the children if we named them."

Marrimian paused on the doorstone and looked back at the two mummified birthwomen in their scarlet caps and aprons on the far side of the chamber. The setting sun cast deep shadows across their blind eyes. "You shall burn on an honor pyre set between the tallest towers of the hall and as the ribbons of sparks float over the city the children will chant and sing and tell the people of all the days that you cared for them. I will not forget you," Marrimian whispered.

Ankana smiled at Marrimian and knew that all the days and seasons of their wait had not been in vain.

6

Naul Vanishes

AFTER Naul had directed Treyster's footsteps toward the great hall and urged the frightened marshgirl to follow the fat scullion into the kitchens he hurried on toward the mumblers' cells through the maze of passageways and corridors that sprawled in every direction. He feared that the hall folk might turn against Marrimian and he was anxious to gather his mumblers in an unbroken dancing circle around the Glitterspike, to use their pine-oil lampsmoke to foretell how she should rule and to give her the wisdom of the morrow. Yet as he hurried he knocked on every bolted door that he passed until his knuckles were worn red raw and he shouted at every dark crack and secret cubbyhole of Marrimian's triumph and urged the hall folk to hurry into the great hall until his voice had faded into a dry whisper.

He drew further and further away from the hall and crossed the open courtyards and the shadow of his flying saffron robes with the shrill windbells grew longer and longer as the sun dropped toward evening time. He knew that he must hurry. The hall folk would grow more restless with each passing hour that trickled through the glass without the wisdom of the mumblers' foresight.

He paused for breath at the top of the steep age-smoothed steps that led down between the mumblers' narrow cells. He blinked and his eyes widened against the darkness, then he frowned and leant forwards, turning his head from side to side, listening for the whispering chants of the mumblers and the gentle clatter of their windbells.

Something was wrong. The silence lay too heavily in each gloomy doorcrack and he clutched with his bony fingers at the windbells sewn into the hems of his own saffron robes to stifle their music. He smelled the stale damp air and caught the odor of corruption. He should have been able to smell the sweet scent of the pine-oil lamps. Cautiously he began to descend the stone steps, letting his fingers slide over the slimetouch that grew on the rough stone walls on either side of him. He reached a twist in the steps and suddenly stopped. There were tears in the slippery fungus; bright orange sap had bled and trickled in sticky loops, and clinging to each glistening tentacle were black wisps of gossamer thread that wound itself round his fingertips when he touched it.

"The crones have been here," he hissed, hunching his shoulders and wondering what black treachery had brought them down into the cells where the mumblers lived beneath the great hall. Carefully he descended the last flight of stone steps, afraid of what he might find, and pulled open the first of the doors, which stood slightly ajar.

Naul cried out in terror, gagging and choking at the bitter stench of death that billowed out of the cell, and snatched up the hems of his robes and stamped his sandled feet at the swarm of black spiders that spilled through the open doorway. As he retreated from the small cell he glimpsed the mumbler he had known as Chant sprawled across his bed, his saffron robes bound in a tight tangle of gossamer webs, his shattered pine-oil lamp still clutched in his dead hand.

Naul scrambled up on to the third step. He turned and stared down at the living carpet of venomous spiders that were spilling silently out of every one of the mumblers' cells. He shuddered as he watched them climb on to the first step and began to feel his way backwards up the steep flight as fast as he could, knowing that he dare not take his eyes off them until he could run like the wind that rose in the marshes. He felt the twist in the steps and the heavy oak door frame with the heel of his sandals and then he gathered up his robes and turned and fled, slamming and bolting the door behind him. He did not stop running until he had reached the outer archway of the great doors of the hall and he could see the glittering ice stars in the dark night sky high above his head.

Slowly the pounding of his heart and the rasping cackle of his breath eased and he brushed the hems of his robes anxiously and shook out each dark fold to make sure that none of the black spiders had clung there. As he looked out across the dark ruins of the city he wondered what he should do now. He whispered and muttered to himself, worrying the windbells through his fingers one by one. He believed that Marrimian had every right to claim the throne. His tasks, beyond the one of foresight, had been to write down and recite all his master's lores, and Lord Miresnare had clearly proclaimed that anyone, not just a lord or a marshman, but anyone who touched the Glitterspike, had the right to claim the throne. Lord Miresnare had smashed his lamp. He could do nothing to help Marrimian on his own; that was why he had hurried back to gather together all the mumbling men. But now they were dead and bound in shrouds of gossamer thread. Now his foresight would be blind and ignorant without the unbroken circle of dancing mumblers. He had nothing to offer Marrimian now.

Naul left the shelter of the archway and paced across the cobbles. He shivered as the cold marsh winds rattled the windbells and he wound the saffron cloth more tightly about his narrow, bony shoulders. He stared down bleakly across the steep sprawl of night-dark lanes and alleyways that clung in the shadows of the hall. "Why, oh why did you murder the mumbling men?" he whispered over and over again as his eyes sought out the Shambles, that secret place where none but the healing woman, Erek, and her gathering of crones trod beneath the silent canopy of gossamer threads shimmering in the starlight.

Then he remembered something he had heard

and he crushed the fragments of black sticky threads from the crones' riddle of rags between his bony fingers. He remembered the whispered secrets of the crones his archer guard had caught as the women spun lies and rumors through the outer corridors of the hall. The words came flooding back to him. He had almost forgotten. Marrimian's wild rush to touch the Glitterspike and the rampaging mudbeasts had all but driven them from his mind, but now as the frozen night winds gnawed at his bones he heard again the whispers of that ancient hag as she told him that he was Erek's child cruelly snatched from his birth webs because the healing woman could not weave enough magic for Lord Miresnare to sire a son and heir.

Naul laughed bitterly, the sound strangling in his throat and changing to a broken sob as he realized that it must have been Erek, his mother, who had sent the crones into the mumblers' cells to punish him because he would not join her to vent his anger and take revenge upon Lord Miresnare. He shook his head sadly at the depths of her hatred as he saw how it had blackened and poisoned her heart and he knew in one frozen moment, standing there on the rim of the highest level of the city, that no matter what blood might flow between them he could never be a part of her plots and hatred against the house of Miresnare. He had grown up in the search for the truth of tomorrow and he could never use his gift of foresight or the mumblers' dance to serve her treacheries.

Naul suddenly caught his breath, threw his head

back and cursed the healing woman and all her crones. His voice howled in anger and despair across the dark city as he saw the measure of his mother's revenge against him: how by killing all the mumbling men and shattering their pine-oil lamps she had destroyed his power of foresight and stripped him naked of his magic. Now that there was none to join with him to make his dancing circle he had nothing but his wits to offer to this new Queen of Gnarlsmyre.

Naul sank down on the cobbles, his shoulders hunched and trembling, and he wept. He wrung his hands together. Without his magic he felt helpless and alone. Slowly, as the frozen hours passed, his lips tightened and his eyes narrowed at the thought of Marrimian and all the others the healing woman and her crones had used, and his mouth hardened into a grim line as he remembered how the crone had urged him in secret whispers to aid Mertzork touch the Glitterspike and then stand back while Erek murdered him so that he, her son, could take the throne.

"No! You shall take nothing that easily with your plots and treacheries," he hissed, knowing that he must help Marrimian in every way he could to thwart Erek and wipe away the stain of her blood that flowed through his veins. He cracked his bony knuckles and reached for the pine-oil lamp which used to hang at his belt as he rose to his feet. He laughed helplessly, without a trace of humor, as he remembered that the lamp was gone for ever.

"I must muffle these windbells and put the days

of magic behind me," he muttered grimly, knowing that the windbells shouted louder than the noonday clapper as they told of each tread he took through the city.

He strengthened his resolve and turned his back on the sheer, frost-glittering walls of the hall but he could not find the courage to cast aside the precious windbells that measured each season of his magic, though he plucked them from the hems of his gown. Smiling bitterly at his own weakness, he hid them carefully, one by one, in the flowing saffron folds of his sleeves and the secret inner lining of his shadowy hood. With each creaking, sandaled step he slipped silently through the cramped maze of ruined lanes, picking the fastest path down over the mounds of rubble that clogged the winding alleyways. With each hurried footstep he was closer to the entrance of the Shambles.

Naul was unsure what he could do to wipe away the healing woman's treacheries once he had reached the entrance to her lair and the more he tried to glimpse the future the more his foresight clouded over and his mind became riddled with black visions of his mother's hatred. He shook his head and slapped his forehead savagely with the flat of his hand but nothing would dislodge her festering evil. He reached the last steep flight of narrow, winding stone steps that rose above the Shambles and paused to catch his breath. He swept his piercing gaze down across the shimmering tangle of gossamer shrouds that Erek's hatred had woven over the alleyways and hovels of her domain in an attempt to hide her secrets.

As he hesitated and watched the sagging webs tremble and sway in the frozen night winds it came to him: an idea to help Marrimian. He must creep into the very heart of Erek's lair. He must spy and listen to every whispered plot and evil treachery that she and her gathering of crones wove beneath these stifling spiders' webs. He must bring the truth of what he overheard up into Glitterspike Hall. But he shuddered at the thought of the countless swarms of venomous spiders that must have spun those gossamer canopies and he wished he had the sweet scent of his pine-oil lamp to mask his terror. How he mourned the loss of his cloak of magic that would have taken him unnoticed through the tangles they had spun across the entrance of the Shambles. But then he laughed softly to himself as he set his foot on the first step of the winding stairway and felt the raw fingernail scars on the palms of his hands when he touched the rough, mud-slapped walls. The scars marked the first moment of self-knowledge when he had searched his mind for answers in the last hours of the joust for his master's throne, and he had learnt them without the magic of his pine-oil lamp. The dense shadows of the stairwell swallowed him up and he cautiously felt his way down until he was crouching opposite the entrance to the Shambles, a double handspan from the tangle of webs.

"Now!" he hissed through clenched teeth. "I must cross now and shed my terror." But as he half

rose on to the balls of his feet some instinct froze
him. Some hidden, watchful eye laid buried deep
inside him from the moment of his birth began to
warn him of a secret danger. Its strength had made
him master mumbler and it was more powerful
than all the shriveled magic he had learned in the
mumblers' cells. The fear clawed at the pit of his
stomach and made him shrink backwards to watch
and wait before he tried to dash across the alleyway
or creep beneath the hanging webs. In that moment
as he sucked in another shallow breath he saw the
silent spider guardians blink open their pale green,
red-veined eyes and search the alleyway as they
slowly crossed and re-crossed the entrance, spinning new sticky webs to snare anyone who dared to
try to enter beneath their dangling threads.

"How could anything slip past them?" Naul
barely whispered as he watched them blink and
turn and scuttle toward the slightest sound, the
tiniest crackle in the frozen silence.

Somewhere beyond the mumbler's sight, further
down the steep, twisting maze of alleyways, a sudden noise cut through the darkness, a startled cry
and a stumbling footscrape as though a hurrying
traveler had sprawled across the slippery, uneven
cobbles. The canopy of webs quivered. The tangle
of threads stretched and sagged beneath the weight
of the spiders that scuttled and crawled over one
another, appearing in the blink of an eye from
every black crack and secret cranny to form a seething mass of wriggling bodies, dark against the pale
starlight.

Naul watched the spiders, a whispering breath of terror escaping from between his lips. He leaned forward, his beak-sharp nose cutting through the inky shadows of the stairwell as he saw a way to slip through the entrance. Carefully he counted the moments, brief moments, that it took the swarming spiders to untangle their hairy legs and pressing bodies and to vanish back into the hidden corners of the entrance to the Shambles. He stroked his chin thoughtfully with a long, bony finger. Clearly there had been a moment when all the guardians had crowded toward the unexpected noise and had left a narrow gap on one side of the sagging canopy. Naul frowned, his high forehead creasing into a maze of furrows. The spiders had seemed to blink at the instant the sound echoed through the alleyway. Perhaps there was a moment when they were blind as they turned toward each unfamiliar noise carried on the night wind that blew across the city.

More footsteps sounded. Hesitant and faltering, they scraped across the cobblestones. They were different from the first sounds that had broken the silence and they made the mumbler turn his head and anxiously search the darkness. He worried his fingers together as he wondered how many pairs of prying eyes might see him slip into the Shambles and then how many mouths would sow the seeds of careless gossip that would tell Erek and her gathering of crones that he was spying on them. He knew he must be quick and cross the alleyway unnoticed before the footsteps drew any closer. But how? He eased his cramped limbs and leaned against the cold, mud-slapped wall of the stairwell. As he did so two of his hidden windbells grated against one another and the fragile clappers began to sing softly in the dark, secret folds of his saffron robes.

"Yes!" he gasped as he watched the spiders blink at the sound of the windbells before he stifled them. "The music of Glitterspike Hall will draw you away and deafen you with a measure of its magic while I slip beneath your webs!"

Crouching forward, Naul carefully tossed up first one and then the other of the precious windbells that he had taken from his sleeves. They arched high into the night air and he watched the frozen marsh wind catch them and lift them twisting and turning as they drifted in the starlight, their soft music singing of mumblers' magic as they flew over the shimmering tangles of gossamer. Naul held his breath.

The canopy trembled and came alive with the black, scuttling shapes of spiders following the music of the windbells just as he had hoped they would. The bells touched the sagging tangle of threads and rolled over and over, their clappers striking wild music. Faster and faster they tumbled as they were drawn down by the writhing mass of spiders across the tented canopy toward the furthest dark corner of the entrance.

"Never or now!" Naul whispered to himself as he gathered his robes and his courage into a tight knot. The swarms of spiders overran the bells and curled their hairy legs around them, trapping and strangling their music and wrapping them in shrouds of gossamer silence.

Suddenly he hurled another precious measure of his magic high up above the canopy and as the spiders swarmed after its haunting music he sprang forwards. He crossed the dark alleyway in two leaping strides, ducked and scrambled on to his hands and knees, and crawled unseen and unsensed by his mother's guardians beneath the lowest tangle of their threads. Dry-mouthed with terror, he grazed his knuckles and knees and tore his mumbling robes on every blind twist in the smothering silence of the Shambles. He hurried on, leaving the low, sagging canopy crisscrossing the entrance behind him. He reached a narrow junction where four alleyways met and was forced to stop. He glanced over his shoulder and allowed his breath to escape in a soft hiss of relief. The canopy was empty: none of the watching spiders had followed him. Only the pale, icy stars, blurred by the tangle of gossamer, showed overhead. Naul stared a little foolishly into each of the dark, silent alleyways, undecided as to which of them led to Erek's doorstone. He hesitated, searching the muffled, airless silence for one waymark or hidden clue, perhaps even a scrap of crones' riddle of black rags clinging on to the rough walls, but there was nothing to mar the hanging webs. He shivered, feeling helpless and naked without his pine-oil lamp. One spinning twist and a glance into the billowing smoke and he would have known which blind alleyway to take. He sighed as the knot of despair tightened in his stomach. He knew, no matter how much he yearned for it, he would never again feel the warmth of the lamp against his skin or blink in the heady, stinging smoke of foresight. He was as blind and weak as any other man who stumbled through the darkness. He bowed his head as he remembered that it had been his task as master of the joust to use his gift of foresight and know every lane, alleyway, secret stairway and gutter drain and use that knowledge to set false mazes against everyone. He laughed bitterly and mocked his own weak memory, for he was already forgetting the most common thoroughfares through the city; and here he was, trying to find a way through the Shambles, a place he had always steered well clear of because deep down he had known that there was magic here that could thwart anything the mumblers had taught him. He had never needed to set his mazes in the Shambles because no one, not even the most reckless marshman, was foolish enough to set a foot inside Erek's domain.

Naul forgot his caution and threw his hands into the air in despair, his fingertips brushing the tangle of webs. He snatched them back and smoothed his flowing sleeves in panic, making the hidden windbells sigh out their soft music. The gossamer threads trembled in the canopy overhead and danced in the starlight at the merest whisper of the sound. Naul shrank down and held his breath. His eyes narrowed as he watched for the spiders, but in that moment of breathless terror the magic that Erek had seeded during his birth flowered in the stifling darkness and that hidden eye that had waited through these many seasons of mumblers' dancing and blinding pine-oil smoke opened within him and he saw the loops and tangles of gossamer for what they really were—broad avenues and well-trodden highways that the spiders had spun from the center of his mother's hatred to the outer edges of the Shambles. He looked again at the shimmering threads and counted each and every one of them as they radiated from the narrow crossroads, and he saw clearly that the layers of threads came from the passageway to his left. That must be the way that led to Erek's doorstone.

Gathering his saffron robes more tightly about him, he slipped into the dark entrance and crept forward. The cobbles felt different beneath his feet and he realized that they must have been worn by Erek's treacheries. The loops and twists of gossamer thread were growing ever denser and the air became stifling as he reached the heart of her domain. Spiders were crossing the canopy over his head and blotting out the stars, but they seemed blind to him as they scuttled about the healing woman's evil purpose. Now he could hear muffled voices ahead of him; shrieks and wild chanting came from behind a heavy wooden doorway in the center of the alleyway. Naul made to hurry forward and press his ear against the grainy wood but his inner eye held him and he shrank back, pressing himself against the cold walls. Moments later the door creaked open and an ancient hag swept past him, cackling and rubbing her gnarled hands together, delighted at some black treachery that she had helped to hatch. Her flapping riddle of rags with its cold, sticky threads touched his face as she flew past him. Naul held his breath. Flickering firelight from Erek's hearthstone was lighting the alleyway; the crone began to turn toward him, wrinkling her nose and pulling aside the heavy hood that cloaked her face.

"Hurry, begin the whispering—hurry, hurry," shrieked Erek's voice calling across her doorstone and her crooked shadow leapt and danced impatiently in the firelight. The crone hissed and muttered and wrapped her hood more tightly about her face as she turned crossly away from Naul.

"Sow the seeds of doubt against that cursed firstborn, Marrimian; whisper false rumors everywhere," urged Erek and then she slammed the door to her hovel and turned the liftlatch with a snap. The alleyway was once more plunged into darkness.

Naul breathed a sigh of relief but he waited until the dry scrape of the crone's footsteps had faded into nothing before he eased himself away from the wall.

The crones' voices once again began to chant and shriek behind the door. He strained to catch their meaning and tiptoed forward to listen, but for all its age and its cracks the door muffled and blurred their words and he knew he dared go no closer. He stood rock still and let his gaze drift over the dark, narrow alleyway and the swarms of spiders shifting overhead. He allowed his inner sight to search for a crack or peephole where he could listen and spy on the crones' treacheries. Slowly his eyes were drawn up across the rough walls of Erek's hovel toward a broken gutter where only the rag ends of long-forgotten webs drifted in the frozen night winds and his secret sight clearly showed him that beyond the guttering, hidden from the alleyway and set high in the wall, there was a narrow window slit, its once sparkling crystal now grimed and grayed with countless seasons of revenge, dirtied with Erek's hatred. Climbing awkwardly along the guttering, Naul found a finger-ledge to cling to between the healing woman's hovel and the sheer, high, overhanging flint wall that crowded next to it. For a moment he stared at the maze of rooftops that marched away beneath, a petrified sea of gabled shadows, wrapped and shrouded in the silence of her revenge.

"Trample every seed that the mudbeasts did not destroy. Tear down the hanging vines that still flower above the lanes," rose Erek's voice through the dirty window, making Naul lean toward the gap to press his nose against the crystal. "I will spread rumors that the real Queen of Gnarlsmyre is in the marsheries taming the beasts and that she and Mertzork, the new lord, shall rule Glitterspike Hall and come triumphant into the city once the wet seasons have passed."

Erek stilled another of the crones who was spinning toward her hearthstone and pointed toward the human cocoons hanging from her chimney beam. "Spread whispers that we will feed all those

who will take Mertzork as their new lord on every
day of the wet seasons. Tell them that sweetmeats
and all manner of wholesome treats shall be there
for the taking at the entrance to the Shambles."

The crone ran her crooked fingers over the dangling carcasses and shrieked with laughter as she set
them twisting and turning in the smoke. "Who
would have thought that those who stumbled in
amongst your webs of hatred would ripen with the
passing seasons into wholesome treats to sour the
peoples' minds against Marrimian?" she cried as
she spun toward the doorstone.

Naul shuddered and almost toppled from his pre-
carious perch as he realized that this evil hag who
dared to call herself his mother was plotting with
her gathering of crones to feed the cured flesh of
those helpless wretches that dangled and spun from
her chimney beam to the people of the city.

Naul's lips thinned into an angry line. "Well at
least you haven't snared enough poor wretches to
feed more than a handful of the city folk with your
tainted meats," he muttered grimly as Erek darted
amongst the crones, spinning them faster and faster
as she whispered them out across her doorstone.

Naul knew that he must warn Marrimian as
quickly as he could and he turned awkwardly on
the undersill, searching with his toes for the broken
guttering. His foot slipped on the rag ends of gossamer thread and he fell and clutched at the window
slit in the rough flint wall, his fingers smashing
through the dirty crystal pane and gripping on to
the inside ledge. Blood ran between his fingers

from a jagged cut but he stifled a cry and hauled himself slowly back up on to the sill and stared down into the darkened room. His breath rose choking in his throat at the smoky stench that billowed through the broken window and as his eyes grew accustomed to the darkness he saw more cocoons than he could count. They hung from every beam and rafter hook and they shimmered in the starlight, twisting and turning in the thin wreaths of smoke that fogged the stale air. Horrified, Naul eased his cut hand through the broken crystal and finding the guttering with his trembling feet, he scrambled clumsily down into the alleyway. He stood staring bleakly at the blank flint and mud-slapped hovels that crowded all about him, wondering just how many of them were curing houses for the healing woman's revenge. In that moment he realized that the peoples' terror of the Shambles was not born of idle gossip.

He rose to find his way back to the entrance of the Shambles but light fingers clutched at his saffron robes. Spiders were scuffling over his shoulders, binding him in their silken threads, and a voice cackled and whispered in his ear, "Welcome, child, child of my loins."

Syrenea slowly surfaced from her faint and found herself slumped against a darkened door arch above the spiral stairway that led down to the Hurlers' Gate. She blinked and reached up to touch gingerly the raw, throbbing gash on her forehead. The bleeding had stopped and the oozing blood had crusted into a sticky ridge. She shivered and remembered the foul spider that the healing woman had slipped beneath her bodice to keep her Pinvey's prisoner. She held her breath while she felt for it with her fingertips and a sense of light-headed relief flooded over her as she found it crushed in a tangle of legs in a fold of her dress, just below her left breast. It must have tried to bite her as she tumbled helplessly away from the riddle of crones but its jaws had closed viciously instead on the heavy embroidery of her gown and it had injected its venomous poison into the cloth. She shuddered at the ice-cold touch of the venom on her skin and tore at the spider's lifeless body, hurling it out into the darkness.

"I must warn Marrimian, I must . . . I must . . ." she cried through chattering teeth as she clambered unsteadily out of the deep recess, her head still spinning from the fall. She hesitated and listened. She could hear only the far-off roars of mudbeasts that had found their way into the marshes. She held her breath, terrified that the crones would suddenly reappear and overrun her and wrap her up in their clinging riddles of black rags. But there was nothing else to break the silence and she turned. She took a step and then stopped as she realized that she did not know the way back up through the city. No matter how much she tried to gather her courage the tentacles of her panic spread before her up every winding step of the stairway, slowing her faltering feet until she stopped and crouched, staring at the maze of narrow lanes and alleyways.

Suddenly, behind her, she heard rasping footsteps on the stairway. Half turning, she stole a frightened glance over her shoulder and fled into the closest alleyway to escape her pursuer, losing herself hopelessly in the gloomy, airless lanes below the Shambles. She wandered, helplessly, hammering on every bolted door that she could find, scratching at every barred or shuttered window. But no one answered. The city folk were hiding in terror of the marshlords and the mudbeasts that they thought were still roaming through the city. The shadows lengthened and darkness fell across the city. Syrenea sank down in despair, weary and beyond caring what befell her. She shivered as the icy wind began to rise across the marshes and chill her to the bone. Movement in the narrow lane ahead made her look up and she caught her breath and stifled a cry as she saw the shimmering canopy of web and tangled mass of threads that hung across the entrance of the Shambles. Somehow she had found her way back to the place that she dreaded most. She rose to her feet and stumbled backwards on the uneven cobbles. The canopy of webs quivered and trembled and countless eyes were suddenly watching her in the darkness and holding her with their cold, pitiless gaze. Her muscles felt as though they were tied in knots; her feet were leaden on the cobbles. She was trapped and too terrified to escape. Then soft music sounded from a dark alleyway just ahead of her and the spiders blinked and turned toward the sound, releasing her from their spell.

Syrenea stared at the dark entrance. There was something familiar about the whispering sound. Suddenly two silver bells drifted across the alleyway on the icy night wind and landed on the canopy of webs that guarded the entrance to the Shambles. "Mumblers!" she gasped as the sound of the windbells rolled down the tangle of threads and echoed through the darkness, but her face clouded with a frown as she glimpsed Naul, the master mumbler, slip across the narrow alleyway and duck beneath the tangle of webs without a sideways glance. Half-forgotten words of intrigue and whispers that had passed between Pinvey and Mertzork while she was their prisoner rushed into her head and she recalled Naul's birth ties to Erek the healing woman.

"Traitor!" she hissed. "Dabbler in treachery!" she spat after the vanishing hems of his saffron robes.

Somewhere quite close to the entrance of the Shambles a footstep scraped on the cobbles. Syrenea looked wildly around her and ran for the dark entrance where the master mumbler had hidden. She stumbled on the steep stone steps and grazed her knees before she recovered and began to climb. Looking up, she saw the sheer, frost-glittering walls of the hall against the starlight. She knew that now she could find the way and bring word of the mumbler's treachery to Marrimian's ears.

* * *

Vetchim lay in the beasting pit where the healing woman had savagely kicked him. Slowly the darkness cleared from his mind. He gasped for breath and clawed at the mass of fine silken threads that she had woven around his tongue in an endless knot, striking him dumb. His head ached, the blood pounded in his ears, and as he rose to his feet he saw that his hands and knees were grazed and bloody from his headlong fall into the pit. He moved slowly and painfully toward the entrance of the cage, waiting, listening for the clatter of the crones' boots on the cobbles above the pits and the angry marshmen shouting against Mertzork's treacheries, but there was no sound. Nothing save the distant roar of mudbeasts foraging in the quickmarsh broke the eerie silence. Vetchim pushed against the bars of the iron door and it swung open. He began to work his way up toward the Hurlers' Gate. He would have worried more about the silence and the absence of the marshmen who had pledged themselves to Marrimian, but the knot that had been wound around his tongue had begun to choke him, forcing him to stop and suck in gasps of air. He tried to swallow but the more he moved his tongue the more the knot tightened and arched it against the roof of his mouth, blocking his throat.

"The scullion," he thought desperately. "The scullion will know how to break the spell."

Vetchim remembered how Ansel had thwarted

the healing woman's magic when she had brought
Marrimian into the Shambles to seek refuge from
the frozen ice wind. He could not remember quite
what the scullion had done but he knew that she
would help him: she had pledged herself to him in
the shadows of the Hurlers' Gate. He forced his
fingers away from his mouth and, fighting against
the rising panic; slowly crossed the broad space
above the beasting pits, searching for sight of the
Hurlers on their high chairs watching and record-
ing everyone who tried to enter the city. But their
chairs lay empty and broken. The door to the guard
hovel was smashed, hanging off its hinges. The
gates were deserted. The healing woman must have
used her magic to spirit the Hurlers away, he
thought, moving cautiously between the broken
chairs. He slipped into the city, where he looked up
above the mass of narrow streets to the sheer, towering wall of Glitterspike Hall. He steadied himself
and drew in shallow breaths as he clutched the
corner of a rough, mud-slapped wall. There was
something cold and sticky beneath his hand. He
snatched it away and stared at the strands of sticky
black thread that now clung to his fingers. Slowly
the realization came to him that they must be
threads from the crones' riddle of flying rags and he
moved along the wall; searching for, and finding, a
sparse trail of threads. These led him through a
maze of lanes and alleyways to the foot of a steep
spiral stone stairway.

Vetchim stumbled, his head roaring and dizzy,

his face purple from lack of breath. He began to climb the twisting stairs. Ahead of him he caught the sound of light footsteps, a woman's footsteps, but they vanished and the sun had set before he reached the top of the stairs, gasping for breath. He felt along the walls of each of the gloomy alleyways that opened out before him, looking for the trail of sticky thread that would tell him the crones' path. And the thread led him toward the entrance to the Shambles. He recognized the hags' canopy of threads and abruptly stopped and crouched, pressing himself into the shadows. He knew that he dare not enter but while he waited, puzzling which alleyway would take him up toward the hall, he noticed that there was someone hiding almost opposite him, also watching the entrance, and beyond, further down a steep lane, a woman pressing herself against the damp stone wall. After a few moments the man opposite stood up and Vetchim realized by the color of his robes it must be the mumbler, Naul. He watched him trick the spiders into following the sweet music of his windbells and slip unseen by them beneath their guarding webs. Then he heard a hiss of hatred and saw the woman run into the dark entrance where the mumbler had crouched. He frowned, realizing that it must have been her footsteps that he had heard when he began the climb through the city. He watched her slip out of sight and then he rose to his feet and followed her as she ran up the steep stone steps. From the cut and rich embroidery of her gown he guessed that she had come from Glitterspike Hall and he hoped that she would lead him to the doors of the hall itself, but he was forced to fall back: the webs were choking him and he could keep up with her no longer.

7

A Feast of Triumph

*M*ARRIMIAN hesitated for a moment on the threshold stone of the great hall. It lay wrapped so silently in evening shadows that she could hear the crackle of the hoar frost that the night wind painted on the broken shards of the crystal windows. On the Glitterspike feather patterns sparkled and shimmered in the darkness. She felt someone pause beside her and caught the faint shuffle and scrape of the feet of the hall folk and the sobs and cries of the frightened children in the passageway behind her.

"We must light the hall as best we can and clear away the dead marshmen before we sit down to the feast that Ansel's scullions have prepared," Krann whispered, breaking the eerie silence, making her start.

"But there is so much ruin and destruction," Marrimian frowned as Krann took a spark from her and lit it, sending huge shadows leaping across the hall, made by the mounds of rubbish and the litter of corpses.

"Take no heed, mistress," Ansel muttered

grimly, clapping her hands to summon the hall folk and give them their orders. "Those not helping with the feast can build the funeral pyres for the dead beyond the great doors of this hall. Those who plagued us with all this ruin can burn while we eat."

"But . . ." Marrimian broke off and spread her hands helplessly as Ankana brought the children to the threshold stone and they screamed in terror at the echoing vastness of the hall and clung to the birthwoman's blood-red apron tails.

Ansel frowned at the children, not quite sure how to act with them. She set a huddle of scuttles and washwomen fussing around them, then turned, took Marrimian's arm and gently led her toward the dais of the throne where a large group of scuttles and servers were working to set up the long eating boards for the feast. Mallets fashioned from marshoak wood drove home the black ebony dowels that held the eating board to the trestled legs and the long benches were dragged into place with noisy laughter and shouts.

"Mistress," Ansel murmured, sniffing loudly and wrinkling her nose. "Can you smell the feast? Now doesn't that smell better than those raw roots and bitter leaves that we had to eat in the marshes?"

Marrimian wrinkled her nose and caught the longforgotten, sweet smells wafting beneath the kitchen archway. "Ansel, you are a wonder," she smiled and then she caught the look in Treasel's eyes and remembered how the marshgirl had kept them all alive on the raw roots and leaves and berries that she had gathered while they were crossing the marshes.

Turning, she took Treasel's hands. "You must forgive Ansel, she has a raw edge to her tongue. She knows as well as I do that without the food that you found for us in the marshes we would have died."

Ansel frowned and bit her lip as she stared down at her feet. Treasel laughed and linked her arm with the scullion's. "Already the smells from her kitchen are making my mouth dribble . . ."

A tall ragmen coughed politely, to interrupt the marshgirl, and then bowed to Marrimian. "The pyres are ready for burning, my Queen."

"My father, Lord Miresnare?" she asked, her voice trembling as she cast an anxious glance toward where he had lain amongst the loops of heavy iron chains.

The ragman hesitated and glided backwards a pace as if he feared her. "We laid your father on a single pyre before all the marshmen and we have laid your sisters from the daughtery on another pyre beside his."

Marrimian glared angrily at the ragman. "You have disobeyed me. I said that my sisters were to burn with the marshmen for casting little Treyster out of the daughtery to scavenge for food for them while they cowered in safety."

"But, my lady," the ragman pleaded. "It did not seem right to toss their frail, gowned bodies so carelessly amongst the marshmen. They were the daughters of this hall and they deserve a little respect, for all their faults. It would only have dishonored them further." He fell silent and bowed his head, waiting for Marrimian's anger to fall on him.

"How dare you thwart my judgments . . ." she hissed, her lips trembling and pinching into a tight, bloodless line.

"But they are women, my Queen. Your sisters are women, despite what they did," the ragman cried. "You commanded us to treat all women with respect. You . . ."

Marrimian lifted her hand and silenced the ragman. Gradually she turned over his words in her mind and her face softened. Perhaps the ragman and the dusters and all the other men of the hall had heeded her words. Perhaps this was the first step. "You have shown much compassion toward my sisters. I shall not forget it. Now seek out a lampwick that he may fire the pyres."

"Mistress, it is time for the feast," Ansel cried, clapping her hands.

Marrimian dismissed the ragman and took her place at the center of the long eating boards. Ankana and the children filled the benches on her left hand while Krann, Treyster and Treasel sat on her right. The clatter and bustle of the kitchen swept through the hall. The succulent smells of the feast wafted through the crowds who were clearing the mounds of refuse and setting everything to rights. It made their mouths water with anticipation. One by one they put their brushes and brooms aside and began to hurry toward the long eating boards.

"There will be places for everyone. There's no need to push and shove," grumbled Ansel, making sure that everyone was seated before she gave the signal to the scullions to bring in the feast.

Ragmen craned their long, thin necks. Scuttles and hoemasters turned and glanced anxiously over their shoulders, their murmurings falling away into silence. A child cried out, only to be hushed by Ankana as Ansel called, "Now, bring in the feast."

With a sudden rush and a clatter of footsteps a long procession of bake cooks, fish cooks, roasting cooks, basters and underscullions filed into the hall, their arms full of pots and pans of every shape and size. Steaming kettles of pink-shelled crawlers, fresh-baked trenchards, rounds of cheese all decorated with the finest copper cutting wires were brought in. Bubbling cauldrons of blue cabbage and trays of apselgathers were carefully carried by the underscullions. Scuttles darted forward setting crystal cups brimming with an amber wine and every eating tool that they had been able to find upon the tables.

Ansel, her fat, dimpled cheeks flushed with pride, motioned all the cooks and servers to their places. "It is a feast to celebrate your triumph, mistress. It is to show our joy that you touched the Glitterspike and drove the marshmen from Glitterspike Hall forever."

Ansel's voice sounded clear in the silent hall, yet she wrung the corners of her apron tails nervously between her fingers as she surveyed the feast. It looked so meager now that it had been served out, shared between so many.

"It is the best we could prepare," she stuttered.

"The marshmen had sacked the kitchens and the scullions have had to scour every nook and cranny and sift through every scrap of the shattered wreckage of the crystal houses. They have dredged the fish moats and searched all the salting larders and herb rooms to prepare what lies before you. And yet the feast is still not half worthy of you, my mistress, the first Queen of Gnarlsmyre."

Marrimian rose to her feet as Ansel sat down heavily on the long bench, her face bright scarlet.

"The feast is a wonder beyond my wildest dreams, Ansel. You are truly the greatest overscullion . . ." Marrimian paused. There was someone beneath the high entrance archway. A figure was stumbling forward across the threshold stone.

"Syrenea!" Marrimian cried, seeing her sister stagger and then fall to her knees as she tried to cross the hall. Krann and two hoemasters ran to her and helped her to the long table.

"Pinvey and that murderous marshman, Mertzork, are plotting against you with that evil hag the healing woman," Syrenea wept as Marrimian gathered her up in her arms. "Alea is their prisoner and I only just managed to escape as those foul, black-ragged crones led us down toward the Hurlers' Gate."

A low gasp of fear spread through the hall folk but Marrimian hushed them into silence as Syrenea spoke again.

"Can . . . can . . . can you ever forgive me for following Pinvey's wild whisperings?"

Marrimian looked down at Syrenea's torn and

bloodied gown and at the black bruises Mertzork had made when he had cruelly taken her for his pleasure. "It is you, sister, who has suffered the most. But I will help put right the wrongs that Pinvey has done to you. There is nothing for me to forgive because I love you. Here, sit close to me and eat and share this feast of triumph that Ansel and the scullions have prepared."

Krann frowned and leaned across urgently to touch Syrenea's arm, making her jump. "You must tell us everything you have heard while you eat," he murmured, drawing back a little as he saw the fear that his closeness had brought to her face.

Syrenea shuddered and pushed away a trenchard brimming with steaming pottage. "The healing woman dropped spiders on us. It is as though I can still feel their cold claws beneath my gown every time I think about the Shambles."

"Naul? Did you see Naul the master mumbler?" Marrimian asked in a hushed whisper.

Syrenea brought her hand up to her mouth. "Yes! Yes I did," she gasped. "I saw him slip into the Shambles as I was finding a way back up to the hall. First he threw two of his windbells on to the canopy that guards the entrance and then he ducked beneath the hanging threads and vanished in a blink of an eye."

"There! I knew it!" Marrimian hissed, making every head turn toward her. Her knuckles were whitening with anger. "The master mumbler has gone to plot and scheme with his mother, Erek, the healing woman, in the Shambles. I shall have his blood if he ever dares to show his face in this hall again. Mark my words, scullions, ragmen, dusters: if you ever catch the slightest whisper of his wind-bells, capture him, bind him in the chains that once shackled Yaloor and bring him before me."

Krann shook his head sadly but he kept his own counsel. Now was not the time to cast doubts amongst the feasters at the long eating boards or set dark shadows of fear of what Mertzork and Pinvey might be plotting somewhere in the marshes beyond the Hurlers' Gate. Quietly he beckoned two of the hoemasters and bid them slam shut the great doors of the hall and bolt them against any who tried to enter without Marrimian's leave.

The noise and clatter of the grand feast was dying down. Ansel pushed her empty plate away and glanced around slowly at those who sat at her mistress's table.

"This is some realm—and to think we struggled through the quickmarshes to win this," she muttered under her breath as her eyes flicked over the large crowd of ragmen, dusters and hoemasters who had stayed in the hall and pledged themselves to Marrimian. For all their pledges they appeared awkward and ill at ease amongst the cooks and scullions and they sat with their arms held tightly against their sides, taking the food from their platters with quick, bird-like movements. "I'll teach them to be easy with us and to eat even quicker," she whispered to Treasel with a wicked gleam in her eye.

Suddenly Ansel stood up and clapped her large

hands to signal the feast's end, and the scuttles, who by the lore of the kitchen could glean the scraps from the table, leapt up with shouts of delight and swarmed between the ragmen and the hoemasters and devoured every last crumb that had been left on their plates.

"Easy, be easy," cried Marrimian, a look of anger crossing her face, but she laughed as Ansel clapped her hands again and the scuttles vanished beneath the long eating boards to search for crumbs beneath the ragmen's feet. Cries of terror and startled looks spread through the ragmen and some of them half rose in confusion, but Ansel called out to the scuttles and sent them back into the kitchens loaded down beneath piles of empty bowls and platters.

"Things may be different now," Marrimian laughed as she held Ansel's gaze, "but if the scuttles are to join us at the table they must learn some manners."

Ansel blushed and muttered excuses for them as she quickly left her place and hurried to Marrimian's side to whisper, "If there's to be any more sitting at table, mistress, we'll have to find something to put on it. There's nothing left in the kitchens; the larders and herb rooms are empty; nothing now swims in the fish moats and the only thing there is plenty of in the crystal houses is broken glass!"

Marrimian frowned at the scullion's words and looked past her voluminous apron tails to the crowd of ragmen, dusters and hoemasters, fidgeting awkwardly in their places. She was at a loss to know what she should do.

Krann touched her arm lightly and made her turn quickly toward him. "Your hoemasters are gardeners—send them out to forage, command them to sift again through the wreckage of the crystal houses and every one of those courtyards the scullion led us through to reach this hall. Tell them to gather everything left that we can eat, but more importantly, make them search for seedlings, no matter how small. They must bring back seedlings and shoots that can be replanted. Tell them to leave no hanging basket unsearched," he whispered.

Marrimian looked along the table at the silent huddle of grim faces. "You tell them. You have such a way with words, they would do it for you quicker than if I commanded them." She reached for Krann's hand and implored him with her smile but he drew away from her and shook his head as he whispered softly, "You are their Queen; it is what you have striven for. You must tell them; they must respect your judgments and decisions from the very beginning."

"But surely we will rule together. We will share the throne," she hissed, the smile fading from her lips as she saw a faraway look clouding Krann's eyes. His mind was longing for something she could not even understand. "We shared everything. There were no secrets. I helped you to lay the beast that haunted your beginnings; that is what has made our love so strong," she whispered angrily, feeling that now she had triumphed he was drawing away from her, shrinking from her touch.

"No," began Krann, trying to smile and to reassure her and yet knowing of the world of difference that lay between them. His yearning to return to Elundium was so strong and yet to tell her of it would seem a betrayal of her love for him that had flowered in the marshes.

"Marrimian . . ." he whispered, leaning forward, but a cry of terror and a rush of footsteps beneath the kitchen archway made him rise from his chair and spin around, his dagger already in his hand.

The two hoemasters he had sent to bolt the doors were running into the hall with some scuttles, their eyes wild with fear. Pots, dishes and plates were sent flying into the air as they scattered in every direction. Ragmen, dusters and hoemasters and all the cooks and scullions alike rose from the long eating boards and sent the benches clattering backwards on to the floorstones behind them. Ansel and Treasel crowded on either side of Marrimian while Krann, with giant racing strides, ran toward the kitchen archway.

"Beware! There is a marshman in the hall. He lunged at us as we returned from locking the doors. He must have hidden in one of the corridors, waiting to attack us!" cried one of the hoemasters in terror. Krann paused, then dodged to one side of the archway and crouched with drawn dagger, ready to strike. He motioned silently to all the ragmen to snatch up knives from the eating boards and to spread out across the hall, then he held his breath, steadied his racing heart and listened. He could hear shuffling footsteps in the gloomy darkness and short gasping breaths. A figure emerged, half crawling, half staggering, beneath the archway. Another faltering step and it would be in the hall. Krann gasped in horror as the figure reached out to him.

"Traitor! Traitor!" Ansel screamed, the fury in her voice making Krann jump as she rushed toward the marshman, dagger ready.

Vetchim gasped for breath, his mouth choked and drooling loops and trails of sticky gossamer thread. He fell to his knees and held out his empty hands toward the charging scullion. But she was blind to his gesture as she bore down on him.

Krann looked quickly at the kneeling, exhausted marshman and saw tiny spiders crawling over the mess of threads blocking his mouth. "This is Erek's work," he hissed, turning toward the enraged scullion. He sensed that she knew nothing of the crones spinning through the Hurlers' Gate and the foul magic they must have cast on Vetchim. Krann glimpsed, with his second sight, all the hurt and betrayal that Ansel thought Vetchim had caused her and her mistress. Springing forward, he flung himself at her, knocking the breath from her and sending her tumbling sideways, the dagger flying harmlessly from her hand as she rolled over and over amongst the litter of the joust.

"Hold her . . . hold her down," cried Krann as he staggered back on to his feet. "Stop her from reaching the marshman."

Ansel struggled, her face purple with rage, as Treasel and two strong scullions pinned her down. Marrimian ran across the hall and scooped up the dagger. She turned angrily on Krann, who was kneeling in front of Vetchim, holding a steadying hand on each of his shoulders and carefully examining the mess of threads that hung down from his mouth.

"Those marshmen deserted you, mistress," Ansel cried, catching her breath. "Every one of them who pledged themselves to you before the Hurlers' Gate has vanished into the marshes. And this one is the worst of them all, mistress, because . . ." She stumbled over her words as tears of despair overwhelmed her. She thought of all she had lost with Vetchim's betrayal of his pledge to her. "This one is the worst because if he was true to us he would not have deserted the Hurlers' Gate. He wouldn't have broken the pledges he made to both of us," she wept, her huge shoulders trembling, her dimpled chin pressing down on her chest.

"You are too quick to judge him, scullion," Krann answered, rising firmly to his feet. Turning sharply to her, he showed her a dozen trailing loops of gossamer which hung down from his fingertips. "Look at the price that Vetchim must have paid for standing alone against the healing woman and her gathering of crones."

Krann thrust the loops under Ansel's nose and his anger rose as she recoiled in horror at the tiny white spiders, no larger than the pins the thread-needle women used, that ran backwards and forwards, weaving more tangles of thread between his fingers.

"Now tell us what you know of the marshmen beyond the gates," he insisted as he tore the threads from his fingers and crushed them under his boot.

"Too much has been hidden," interrupted Marrimian, her eyes blazing with anger. "Both of you must tell me what you know of the marshmen."

"They have gone, mistress," muttered Ansel, struggling back on to her feet. "That's all I know. They betrayed their pledges and left, but of those spiders' webs hanging from Vetchim's mouth I know nothing, I swear."

"Indeed you know nothing—none of us really knows what happened beyond the gates—but you would allow your judgment of this wretched marshman to be colored by some pledge he once made to you?" Krann snapped at Ansel and the kitchen folk and the hall folk shuffled forward, tightening their circle around Vetchim as they stared in horror at the mess of dangling threads that choked him.

Krann smiled and pointed down at Vetchim. "I would venture that if he could speak, the first words he would utter would warn his Queen of Mertzork and Pinvey's treachery."

Krann sought out Ansel again and held her gaze. "Perhaps he was searching for you, scullion, searching for the one person in all Gnarlsmyre whom he believed could break the strangling, choking spell the healing woman must have wound around his tongue."

The scuttles and scullions whispered and nudged each other. Ansel, her mind full of confusion, blushed scarlet and wrung her hands in her apron tails as she glared the whisperers silent. She slowly advanced toward Vetchim, towering over him as he knelt on the hard floorstones of the hall, and as the watching circle edged forward she took his hands into hers and searched his eyes. Large tear drops formed in the corner of her own as she saw the strength of the love that had carried him to search through the city for her. She reached out and touched the loops of sticky threads which writhed and twisted, making Vetchim choke and gasp as the tiny spiders drew their tangle of threads away from her fingers and took them deeper into his throat. He clamped his fingers around his neck and sank back, dizzy for air.

"The spiders! They cannot abide my touch and they are choking him. What can I do?" Ansel cried, turning desperately toward Marrimian. "Please help me, mistress," she begged.

Marrimian turned helplessly toward the scullion. "I know of nothing, nothing, that would untangle these threads," she said as she stared at the wretched marshman.

Treasel elbowed her way to Ansel's side and whispered, "In the marshes we would use a forked branch from the mangle tree to catch the poisonous toads that live amongst their roots. Once we had trapped them between the prongs of the stick they could not harm us with their venom, no matter how much they hissed and spat. Perhaps there is something here amongst the mounds of refuse from the joust, or in the kitchens, something that has the same knobbly smoothness as the mangle branch that you could use to pluck those fine threads from Vetchim's mouth without touching them."

"You'll use nothing from those heaps of reeking rubbish!" thundered Ansel, but her black looks softened and she began to fumble and search beneath her voluminous folded apron, seeing that, for all her wildness, there was a gleaning of wisdom in the marshgirl's words. "I will find something to untangle that healing woman's magic," she whispered, her eyes smiling into Vetchim's as she looked down into his wretched purple face. She wanted to reach out and tear the threads from his lips, to gather him up in her arms, but she knew that she dare not touch him, that his next strangled breath, his life, depended upon her.

"There are knives upon the eating boards," Marrimian called out softly, "and my dagger has a razor's edge."

"I have a pair of silver-edged crimping shears: they would cut through the tangle of threads," ventured a timid needlewoman, pushing her way through the circle.

"Fire tongs—they would tear them out," cried a scuttle, eager to be the first to help the overscullion. "There are at least a dozen fire irons hanging by the roasting pits. I could run and get . . ."

"No, no," interrupted a leathery-skinned hoemaster as he forced his way to the front of the crowd. "You would do best to gouge that vile mess of threads out of his mouth with one scrape of a sharpened onion hoe. I'll hone the blade for you myself."

"But no—that could tear half of his mouth away with it," cried Ansel in horror, spinning around as one of the fish cooks touched her arm.

"Use a handful of straithooks; they'll catch hold of anything that wriggles with their barbed heads."

Ansel's face drained of color as she thought of those hooks tearing through Vetchim's tongue.

"Thrust a beating iron into his mouth and crush those horrible white spiders. Spin the iron between your hands and then drag the tangle of threads out," rumbled a huge laundry scrubber as she folded her arms across her chest, holding the long, rusty iron in her fist.

"Get back to your wash tubs, you foolish woman," cried one of a group of pastry cooks. "The only thing a beating iron is any use for is knocking the season's filth out of smelly clothes." She hurried over to Ansel. "The only thing that could hold those threads still while you pluck them out of his mouth is a pair of sweetmeat nippers. They are just right for catching hold of awkward things.

Ansel frowned and reached out a hesitant hand but a chorus of voices rose all around her offering every tool and utensil that could be found in the hall. The crowd suddenly broke up as footsteps echoed through the mounds of rubbish and figures ran backward and forward through the flickering lamplight. The kitchen folk and the hall folk were dodging and ducking around each other in the race to be the first to find just the right implement to untangle the threads.

"Prickers—curved prickers," shouted one of the needlewomen, feeling herself carried forward as the crowd surged back again and closed in around Ansel and the kneeling marshman. "Their tiny hooked blades will hold on to the finest thread," she cried breathlessly.

"Give us room—give this helpless marshman room enough to snatch what breath he can," Ansel thundered as she raised her fists at the eager crowds, but a smile tugged at her dimpled cheeks and she reached out to touch each of the hooks, blades and tongs of all the various tools that were thrust toward her.

The crowd fell back a pace, giving a murmur of approval as she chose a serrated gutting knife, a pair of sweetmeat nippers and a handful of straithooks and prickers.

"There, I told you she should choose my hooks," murmured the fish cook, her face breaking into a smile.

Ansel glared the fish cook into silence and forced her fat fingers through the handles of the nippers. The dusters and the hoemasters stood on tiptoe and clung to the tall ragmen's shoulders to get a better view while the kitchen women shuffled and edged nearer, their apron tails crushed anxiously in their clenched hands as Ansel bent over the marshman. Somewhere at the back of the crowd a child cried out in the waiting silence.

Ansel sucked in a shallow breath and pursed her

lips tightly. She could hear the sound of her own heartbeat pounding in her ears as she opened her fingers and widened the curved jaws of the nippers. Slowly she pushed them toward the sticky mess of threads that hung out of Vetchim's mouth. Her hand trembled and she hesitated as she tried to still the jaws of the nippers on either side of the threads. Beads of sweat sprang up on her forehead and began to trickle down into her eyes, stinging them and blurring her sight. She blinked and once again tried to summon her courage, knowing that she held the life of this man in her fat, fumbling fingertips. Fear froze her and visions of his face blackened and gasping for breath should her hand slip filled her mind. Her lips began to quiver and the muscles across her broad shoulders knotted as she fought to control the panic that had seized her.

"Take deep breaths. You have the skill and the courage to thwart the healing woman's magic. Nothing is beyond you, Ansel." Krann's voice suddenly filled her head; he was there beside her, his strong hands upon her shoulders as he bent and peered into the sticky mass of threads.

"But . . . but I am so afraid," Ansel stuttered through a chatter of teeth. "I do not know where to start. How can I ever clear a way through these choking threads? The spiders will spin forever faster."

"Yes, you will do it. You must unravel every one of them and kill every spider. Start now, start with that one there," whispered Krann, pointing to a single sticky thread that trailed out behind one of the swarm of tiny white spiders that was about to squeeze back into Vetchim's mouth.

"Now, be quick," hissed Krann and Ansel, without another moment's hesitation, snapped the nippers shut and crushed the spider. At the same time she thrust the straithooks into the tangle of threads and held on tightly as the webs of magic seethed and wriggled, the spiders trying to break them free of the hooks and choke Vetchim to death.

Ansel gave a shout of surprise and staggered forward as the straithooks twisted and dragged against her fingers. Krann snatched up two of the hooks as they slipped through her fingers and thrust them into Treasel's hands. "Run—run as fast as you can, between the columns. Wind the thread around the Glitterspike, keep uuraveling it as fast as you can."

Ansel released the nippers and snapped them shut, crushing another swarm of tiny spiders that poured through Vetchim's mouth, scuttling over the unraveling threads as they tried to draw them back into his mouth.

"Hold on to that marshman. Don't let the uuraveling threads pull him over, keep him steady!" Krann shouted, urging the strongest of the dusters and the heaviest of the hoemasters to crowd in behind Vetchim and hold him down hard upon the floorstone as Ansel snatched every straithook and curved pricker and thrust them into the seething mess of threads that was spilling out of Vetchim's mouth.

Willing hands grasped the handles of the hooks and every scuttle, ragman, needlewoman and laundry scrubber raced across the hall with trails of sticky thread snaking out behind them. Vetchim choked and gasped, his own hands clamped tightly about his throat as he tried to fight off his urge to panic, to gulp and swallow for another breath. His face blackened, his eyes bulged out of his head. He was dizzy and his mouth burned and stung from the spider's bites. He began to sink into nightmare dreams as he swayed limply backward and forward between the tug of uuraveling threads and the strong grips of those who held him.

Faraway he could hear the snap of the nippers in Ansel's hands. They sounded just like a shoal of marshfish biting at the evening dragonflies that hovered over the stagnant pools in the marshes. A voice was calling to him, shouting his name. He blinked and looked up. The scullion's huge face was swimming toward him, laughing at him, crying. Tears were coursing down her cheeks and splashing on to his face.

"Breathe—breathe," she was shouting, waving the bloodied nippers at him, their curved blades a mess of crushed spiders' carcasses.

Vetchim gasped and felt the air rush into his throat. He tried to swallow but there was still a tight tangle of threads around the base of his tongue.

"Breathe slowly," Ansel whispered, working a handful of new hooks into the last tangle of threads and unraveling them one by one. Casting aside the last hook, she took his hand and gently helped him to his feet. "All the spiders are dead," she smiled.

Vetchim moved his tongue and puffed out his cheeks as he swallowed huge gulps of air.

"Will he ever be able to speak again?" whispered one of the scuttles standing close to them.

Vetchim smiled at Ansel and clasped her hands. Then he kneeled before Marrimian and tried to warn her that Erek had woven black spells over the marshmen. The words came out in slow, choking gasps as he began to tell her of Mertzork's and Pinvey's treacheries before the Hurlers' Gate, then his voice rasped and fell to less than a whisper.

Ansel smiled, her face blushing bright scarlet with joy. She held Vetchim's hand. "The words will come easier, mistress, if I take him to the kitchens and soothe his throat with sweet honeys."

Marrimian smiled and nodded. There was laughter in her eyes as the scullion hurried Vetchim out of the hall. Ansel turned back toward the archway and caught sight of the endless strands of gossamer threads woven between the columns and around the Glitterspike, shimmering in the rays of the flickering lamplight, and she saw the measure of help that the people of the hall had given her. She opened her mouth to thank them, searching for the right words, but Marrimian laughed softly and ushered her on.

"Go, take him to the safety of your kitchens, for you are pledged to be together."

Krann smiled at Ansel's blushes but he followed the marshman and the scullion thoughtfully with his eyes. There were a dozen important questions that he wished to ask Vetchim about Mertzork's and Pinvey's treacheries before the Hurlers' Gate and he wanted to know the healing woman's part in it all. They were questions that only the marshman could answer but he knew that they would have to wait until the scullion had soothed his throat. Turning, he ran his fingers across the shimmering strands of gossamer that hung between the columns and they broke and melted away at his touch.

"So much for your magic, healing woman," he murmured yawning.

The reed lamps that Krann had lit before the feast were beginning to gutter in their iron baskets and die down, and long night shadows were spreading rapidly across the hall. The feasters were dispersing, grouped in tight huddles and whispering about the healing woman's evil powers, and slipping noiselessly away to their sleeping chambers beneath the low archways.

Marrimian sought out Krann amongst the thinning crowds. Her face looked pinched and tired and she glanced nervously over her shoulder at the lengthening shadows. "I cannot sleep alone. I fear Pinvey's hatred and the healing woman's evil. I fear that they may have slipped back into the hall. There is a sleeping chamber that I use high above it. Will you come with me?" she asked shyly.

Krann laughed softly as he looked into her eyes. "Lead on, my Queen. I will follow you to the ends of Gnarlsmyre."

Marrimian took his hand and led him across the hall and up a winding stone stairway to the chamber. She bolted the door and sank wearily down amongst the jumble of sleeping rugs. "Come, hold me, lie with me just as you did in the marshes," Marrimian breathed in a tired whisper as she looked up at Krann silhouetted against the shimmering ice stars in the sky beyond the window frame.

Krann half turned and smiled down in the darkness. "I will be but a moment. I just want to look out across the sleeping city," he answered softly.

"You will stay here with me now that I have touched the Glitterspike? You will, won't you?" Marrimian asked, her words slurring and running into one another as, despite her fear of Mertzork and Pinvey, sleep overtook her. "You will, won't you?" she murmured, stretching out her hand and lacing her fingers with his.

Krann felt her fingers tighten and tug heavily against him as if she sensed his yearning to return to Elundium, as if she feared that he would melt away into the darkness. "Yes. Yes, I will stay with you," he murmured as she fell asleep and her hand slackened. Gently he untangled her fingers and slipped her hand beneath the warm sleeping rugs.

Krann sighed softly and smiled as he gazed down at her. She looked so frail, so small and alone among the jumble of rugs. "Without your love I would know nothing of my beginnings. It was only through our touching and love-making that I learned why those nightmare voices haunted me and drove me through the Shadowlands and the swirling fogbanks into the dreary wastes and marshes of this land of Gnarlsmyre," he whispered, leaning forward to brush at a stray wisp of hair that had fallen across her forehead.

His fingertips touched her smooth skin and they burned and tingled just as when he and Marrimian first touched in the marshes. A vision of Elundium rose to fill his mind. Cool shadows and shafts of bright sunlight patterned the forest floor; distant hoofbeats echoed on the Greenway's edge, mingled with the sweet scent of crushed pine needles. There was a figure with firegold hair, and soft laughter filled the silent forest. The sound rose up to him.

"Fairlight. Is that you, Fairlight?" he sighed. The figure had looked like the childhood friend who had first led him to the Rising to watch the Shadow-treading and begin the journey to face his night-mares.

He reached out to touch the vision but it melted and folded into the shadows, leaving a hollow, empty yearning inside him.

"Tomorrow. I'll begin the journey tomorrow. There is still so much I must find out about my beginnings in Elundium." But he paused as he caught sight of Marrimian amongst the sleeping rugs and his promise not to leave her while Mertzork and Pinvey were still loose in the marshes echoed in his head. He slowly turned from her and shivered as he gazed at the frozen ice stars sown across the night sky and felt torn in two. Torn between his love for her and his yearning to return to Elundium.

He clenched his fist and stared bleakly out toward the dark rim of Gnarlsmyre and thought of his home far away, beyond where the ice wind rose and began to blow across the wastes of mire and quickmarsh. It gathered the crystals of frost and rime ice in its bitter fingers as it wove between the tall bulrush stems and brittle branches of the marshoaks. He could hear it in the night silence, moaning and whispering as it probed every thundercrack and gap in the Hurlers' Gate, rattling the locks and tapping on the window shutters as it found its way into the city. Faster now it moaned and whined through the narrow, empty lanes and steep, twisting alleyways, trembling the heavy canopy of spiders' webs that hid Erek's lair, deep within the Shambles. Up, up it rose with the sharp scent of far away in its howling breath as it chased between the spires and towers of Glitterspike Hall to paint the window of their sleeping chamber with the crackling feathers of hoar frost.

"I'll return one daylight. I know I must, when Pinvey's treacheries have shriveled to nothing and Marrimian's throne is safe," he breathed to himself as he slipped silently beneath the sleeping rugs and closed his eyes.

8

Queen of the Marsheries

*P*INVEY gripped Andzey's neck firmly between her thighs to keep her balance and dug her fingernails into his scalp as she drove him relentlessly forward with her heels, making him stumble and stagger to match Mertzork's pace where he strode ahead of them. The flat, dreary horizon was now broken by the shapes of crudely woven shelters: rough, mud-slapped, windowless hovels with steep, conical roofs, crowding together, leaning against one another, on spindle-thin, rickety stilts above the marshes.

"Queen of the Marshes," Pinvey muttered in disgust, choking on the rank marsh gasses bubbling out of the oozing mire that stretched away on either side of the narrow path they were following.

Pinvey cursed Marrimian for stealing the throne from beneath their noses and forcing them to flee from the city. Her hatred of her sister boiled up afresh as she twisted on her shoulder-perch, looking back over the heads of the marshmen who were strung out on the narrow path behind her, and saw the great ridge of Gnarlsmyre and the steep, crowded roofs of the city clustering below the sheer stone walls and towers of Glitterspike Hall. She watched them shimmer and vanish in the heat haze burning from the marshes. She slapped angrily at the swarms of stinging insects that rose in dense clouds from the bubbling pools of slime, and muttered Erek's name beneath her breath as she realized that it was too late: she had been over-hasty to be the queen of this miserable wilderness.

Kicking her heels savagely into Andzey's sides, Pinvey turned her back on the city and swore that she would exact every grain of revenge on Marrimian, and on the healing woman, and on . . . She caught sight of her younger sister, Alea, struggling to keep her balance in the ankle-deep mud that washed across the path and smoothed out the marshmen's footprints as soon as they appeared. For a moment she stared down at Alea, hating her helplessness almost as much as she hated everything else in this dreary waste of endless quick-marsh. Her lips parted in a cruel sneer as she watched the marshmen closest to Alea prod her along with their iron spikes; they were afraid to go too close to her in case the venomous spider that Erek had slipped beneath the folds of her gown scuttled on to them.

"Beg them to carry you, sister, offer them your pleasures for a ride," Pinvey taunted, but Alea, stumbling along in the slippery mud, had no time to look up. She barely heard the goading words as she sprawled on her hands and knees in the hot, stinking slime that oozed up between her fingers.

"You are a hopeless fool, sister," Pinvey mocked as Alea struggled back on to her feet, "if you thought for one moment that I would ever share any of my triumphs with you."

Alea wiped at the stray knots of hair that had fallen across her forehead, smearing her face with streaks of cold, wet mireslime as the marshmen behind her prodded her forward. Her eyes narrowed as the iron spikes pricked her between the shoulders. She opened her mouth to curse at Pinvey but felt the venomous spider wriggle and move down beneath her breast and dropped her gaze and swallowed her anger. She wept bitter tears of regret that would have brought Pinvey to shrieks of laughter had she not already turned away to shout at Mertzork.

"How much further do we have to travel through this miserable wasteland of mud to reach your marshery?"

"It's over there—just beyond these reed beds," Mertzork shouted, throwing the words carelessly over his shoulder without a backward glance as he turned and vanished amongst the reeds.

"Quickly, keep up with Mertzork," Pinvey hissed, kicking her mount with her heels and making him gasp and choke on the webs bound across his mouth as he struggled to match Mertzork's pace.

Andzey reached the narrow entrance between the tall reed stems but in his haste he stumbled in turning and his foot sank into the soft mud beside the path. Desperate to keep his balance as the stink-

ing slime oozed up, he clutched at the reed stems and pulled them roughly against Pinvey.

Pinvey screamed and hurled a string of curses down on his head as the razor-sharp reeds scraped against her arms and legs. "I'll cut off your ears with one of these stems and make you eat them!" she snarled. Andzey found his footing and hurried along the twisting path.

It was dark amongst the reeds and the tall, shriveled flowerheads arched high above her head, swaying and touching, rattling softly against each other like so many black forgotten flags in the hot stifling air. The path twisted and turned as it followed some hidden spine of rock below the mud and gradually the reeds began to thin out and the sky to brighten overhead. Sunlight penetrated the forest of reeds and cast moving shadows across the path. Mertzork was just ahead of them. He called over his shoulder, commanding them to skirt the channel carefully, and then he vanished, following the path to the left toward an island of marshoaks that towered over the edge of the reed beds. Andzey slowed as he reached the edge and kept well away from the channel that opened out before them. Pinvey cast her eyes across the waste of stinking green mud and saw what looked like a forest of rotten tree stumps and sunbleached branches lying half submerged in the mire. But she shuddered as she realized that the branches were a forest of bones, mudbeast bones, some with rag ends of flesh and strings of gristle still hanging from them.

Something moved on the far side of the channel,

perhaps disturbed by their passage through the reeds. Cruel, pitiless eyes blinked and stared at Pinvey and she gave a cry of terror as a pindafall bird that had been feasting on the bones shrieked, spread its leathery wings and rose lazily into the air.

"Run! Make for the cover of the reeds," shouted Mertzork, cursing Andzey's slowness as the bird soared across the channel, its leathery wings clattering in the stifling marsh silence.

Andzey took one fearful glance at the bird swooping down on them and stumbled as fast as he could toward a dense clump of reeds where the channel of bones turned to the left. The carrion bird was getting closer, its shadow rippling over the edge of the reed bed. Pinvey cried out and cowered over Andzey's shoulders, clawing at his face and almost blinding him with her fingernails.

Alea, who had only just reached the edge of the reed bed, saw the carrion bird swoop toward Pinvey. She wanted to shout out and urge it to tear off her sister's head but her fear of the spider that clung somewhere beneath her gown forced her to swallow her desire for revenge. The marshmen who had goaded and driven her across the quickmarsh pushed her to the side of the path, making her flounder amongst the razor-sharp reedstems while they hurled their spears at the swooping bird. Two spears spinning high into the air struck the pindafall glancing blows on its wing tips, making it turn and shriek and snap its jaws in rage as it circled out over the channel. Flapping its wings, it soared high above the marshery and turned toward the city, vanishing into the shimmering heat haze, the humming clatter of its feathers gradually fading into the heavy marsh silence.

Pinvey laughed and shouted after the bird, cursing it, telling it to be quick and tear Marrimian's head from her shoulders. Spitting at the bubbling mud to rid her mouth of the taste of fear, she sat upright upon Andzey's shoulders and looked about her.

She swept her gaze beyond the bone-choked channel to where she could see steep, conical roofs of woven reeds showing above the shriveled flowerheads. "That must be the marshery," she muttered to herself as she kicked Andzey hard, bruising his ribs with her heels, and they passed through the last of the reeds. But she hesitated as they reached the edge of the channel and Andzey began to stride out on to the worn path of stepping stones that crossed the heaving mud. She dug her fingernails into his scalp, hissed at him to go slowly and stared across the channel to the muddle of rough, mud-daubed, woven shelters perched on tall, rickety stilts above a low strand of earth and rocks.

"Queen of the marshery!" she muttered in disgust, her hatred of the healing woman tightening in her stomach. She had been tricked into leaving the city for this dreary huddle of hovels.

Pinvey half turned and would have forced Andzey to retrace his footsteps but the reed beds behind her were filled with marshmen who had taken her as their Queen and followed her across the marshes. As she faced them they saluted, lifting their arms up to their foreheads and twisting their hands into horn shapes on either side of their heads.

"Queen of the marsheries!" she hissed scornfully under her breath and she turned slowly back to look at the mounds of reeking rubbish and discarded bone litter that choked every scrap of dry land and overflowed into the bubbling mud. She shuddered and reluctantly dug her heels into Andzey's sides to force him to carry her across the channel. As they drew close to the marshery a foul reek drifted out to meet them. She wrinkled her nose and the stench made her eyes smart and water. She leaned forward, frowning and swatting at the cloud of insects that droned around her head as she watched dark shapes on the edges of the marshery. Some were solitary, wading slowly in the mud, others were formed into a circle on the edge of the channel. Andzey brought her closer and the stench became worse. She saw that the shapes were of women, miserable, filthy creatures dressed in rags. The solitary ones were toothless old hags bent over, sifting their hands through the black slime, as if searching for something that lurked beneath the bubbling surface. The groups of younger women were holding strips of raw beastskin which still had flaps of flesh hanging from them. They chewed on the beastskin repeatedly, tearing at the loose gristle and flesh with their teeth, spitting into the mud before plunging the skin deep into the mire. They would then scrape it clean with their fingers before slowly beginning to chew on the hide again.

Pinvey swallowed the bile that had risen in her

throat. She looked away from the women toward the crowded forest of stilts that supported the marsh peoples' dwellings and she saw that every post and pole was hung with strips of stinking beastskin, stretched and draped to cure in the sun. The soft marsh wind stirred the drying skins and before she could raise her hand to cover her nose she choked on the terrible stench of corruption that wafted over her. Waves of dizziness washed over her and the unfamiliar noises of the marshery and the dull slap of the beastskins being plunged beneath the surface of the mud began to fade as her head began to pound. Her grip on Andzey weakened. Faintly, far away, mixed with the buzz of the insects that swarmed around them, she heard a voice. It was calling, shouting at her. Pinvey blinked and shook her head. The tall stilts, the dirty hovels and the decay came swimming back into view and there, less than a dozen paces away, standing on a mound of rubbish, was Mertzork. He was calling her name, welcoming her, calling her the Queen of the Marsheries, as he swept his hands up across the huddle of huts and pointed at something.

"Queen? Who would want to be a queen of all . . ." Pinvey's words died in her mouth and she swallowed them in one gulp as she followed Mertzork's hands and looked up to see the people of the marshery staring down at her.

She gripped Andzey's ears and leaned back, craning her neck. There were hundreds, perhaps thousands, of faces. Some were frowning, some were leering, but most of them showed startled surprise.

She narrowed her eyes against the sunlight and shaded them with her hand. She brushed her hair away from her forehead and looked from hut to hut. Every doorhole, every ledge and foothold was crowded with these ragged marsh people. The women at the edge of the marshery had stopped chewing on the rawhides and closed in behind her. The white-haired elder marshmen were muttering together in a cluster of larger huts in the center of the marshery, leaning across the narrow gaps between their hovels and touching hands, shaking their heads. They had heard whispers of the wild rumors from far-off marsheries, rumors of a woman who had ridden a mudbeast. They had heard that some of these marsheries had proclaimed her Queen and now they looked down with troubled eyes at Mertzork, who was strutting about the marshery as if he were a marshlord.

"Queen?" sneered a young marshman who stood below the lowest of the elders' huts. "There are no queens here in the marsheries, nor anywhere else in Gnarlsmyre, save in men's minds as they talk beside the fires."

Immediately, the startled silence was broken; voices laughed and sneered from all directions. Mertzork snarled and shouted to the marshmen emerging from the reed beds, telling them to hurry and defend their Queen. The woven huts suddenly began to sway, the tall stilts to tremble and quiver, as the marsh people started to swarm down to the ground below.

"Give her to us, Mertzork," shouted a handful of

leering marshmen. "We'll show you what to do with a woman stolen from the city of Glor!"

The hide-chewers moved closer and spat at Pinvey and the boldest of them strode forward and reached out mud-engrained fingers to snatch her from her shoulder perch. Mertzork lunged forward with his iron spike but Pinvey was quicker, lashing out with her heel and striking the woman under her chin, sending her reeling backwards into the heaving mud.

"I *am* Queen!" she screamed, clamping her knees tightly around Andzey's neck and spinning him toward the huts. Her face was blanched with rage that these miserable, ragged marshscum should dare to sneer at and mock her.

The younger, braver marshmen, anxious to be among the first to reach this city woman, ignored the cries of their elders and slithered down the stilts of their huts, landing with practiced skill amongst the piles of rubbish. The first two rushed forward. Mertzork struck out with his iron spike, spearing the leader through the throat. Pinvey loosed the dagger she kept well hidden beneath her skirts and slashed at the second attacker, opening up his face and blinding him with one brutal stroke. Mertzork was upon him before the swarms of insects that plagued the marshery could settle on the raw, bleeding gash or the helpless youth could utter one cry. He laughed as he dropped his sharpwire over the boy's head and pulled it tight. He forced the lad down on to the ground before Pinvey and buried his face in the filthy piles of litter between Andzey's feet.

"Kneel! Kneel at the feet of my beast of burden," cried Pinvey. "Kneel before your Queen, the Queen of this miserable marshery and of all Gnarls- myre!" she hissed, her voice edged with a murder- ous rage that this youth, this ragged urchin, had dared to rush at her, and as she watched Mertzork tread his face down into the filthy mud she threw her head back in a pitiless shriek of delight.

The crowds of marsh youths who had followed the lad, tearing the drying beastskins from the hooks and pegs as they tumbled to the ground and hurried to reach Pinvey, now hesitated and drew back into the shadows of their huts, retreating amongst the forest of rickety stilts. They slipped over the heaps of slimy skins in their efforts to escape the wild woman's dagger.

The young men gathered and crouched in a wide, fidgeting circle, whispering together. They feared this woman. Her voice was different from any woman's they had ever known; her gown shim- mered like molten gold, tracing every curve and sensuous secret of her womanhood. Yet woven through all this wild beauty they could sense cruel savagery. Their whispers rose into startled cries as they saw the edges of the reed beds fill with hordes of unfamiliar marshmen and word quickly spread through the crouching circle that this wild woman must be the one who had tamed the mudbeasts and these marshmen now swarming into the marshery behind her must be all the marshlords, hunters and

waders who had gathered in the great city of Glor
to joust for the firstborn's hand.

"She must be the eldest daughter of Glitterspike
Hall," whispered one of the voices from the circle.
"These marshmen must have taken her from their
Queen." The circle widened and broke as the grim-
faced marshmen from the reed beds surged forward
to stand behind Pinvey.

Pinvey had heard the marsh youths' whispers
and threw her head back and shrieked with laughter as she saw their fear of her spread through the
circle. She had cared nothing for queens, and less
about who ruled Glitterspike Hall or Gnarlsmyre,
before her cursed sister, Marrimian, had stolen the
throne for herself. In the days of the joust Pinvey
had stolen what others toiled for, she had sought
out their secrets and their weaknesses and had used
them without the slightest qualm and had taken
whatever she wanted. But now everything was different. Now she was hungry, no, ravenous. She
wanted power to take her revenge on Marrimian, to
crush her beneath her heel and grind her into the
floorstones of Glitterspike Hall. She could see the
beginnings of that power in the eyes of these people
who scratched out their miserable existences in
these marsheries. The healing woman had not been
wrong in sending her out here to raise an army. She
could easily twist these ragged creatures into be-
lieving that she was the one who had tamed the
mudbeasts. She would use every rumor that Marrimian had started when she had ridden one of
those filthy beasts.

"Kneel! Kneel before your Queen the Beast-Rider!" she cried, driving Andzey forward a pace as she licked lazily at the drying blood on the blade of her dagger.

Some of the marsh youths half rose and some crept forward out of the circle, only to crouch or sink back fearfully into their places when the tall, spindle-thin ladders that reached up into the shadowy, rough-cut doorholes of the larger hovels bent and creaked as the elders of the marshery descended. The crowds that huddled beneath the hovels shrank back, their whispers dying to nothing.

Pinvey watched the elders shuffle toward her, picking their way through the mounds of reeking rubbish, only to stop a handspan beyond the sweep of her dagger. Her eyes narrowed and her lips tightened into a sneer of contempt at their ragged, dirty robes and the shredded remnants of once fine, and heavy beastskin cloaks that hung from their shoulders.

"Who are these wizened creatures?" she mocked, slashing her dagger toward them. "Kneel, kneel at my feet," she hissed impatiently, but her voice faltered and trailed into silence as she stared at their faces.

"They are the elders. The elders of our marshery; they make all the judgements, they are the law," Mertzork whispered, and for the first time in all the days that she had known him and savored his murderous ways she felt him quail and shrink beneath another's gaze.

Pinvey tried to laugh and sneer and to drive Andzey forward so that she could slash at their faces and break their gaze, but Andzey would not move no matter how hard she cut into him with her heels, and the elders just stood as still as gnarled marsh-oaks, staring at her with their watery, unblinking eyes, and their motionless gaze made her shudder. The stillness showed in each wrinkled fold of leathery skin that neither twitched nor flinched though the marsh insects crawled across their faces.

Voices began to whisper amongst the forest of stilts and dark figures half rose to peer down at the elders. Children cried and the oozing mud in the channel popped and bubbled, sending sluggish ripples against the shore of the marshery. The marshmen who crowded behind Pinvey and who had already pledged themselves to her in front of the Hurlers' Gate pressed forward, demanding that the marsh people kneel before their Queen. But they hesitated and shrank back as the elders raised their hands, palms outwards, and pushed against the stagnant air. Without appearing to move they swayed and shuffled closer together until their grizzled heads of white hair touched and then as one they pointed their gnarled fingers toward Mertzork and Pinvey and began to chant, their voices sounding no louder than the wind that blew across the summer reedbeds. As they sought the truth of who it was who stood before them their eyes took in every thread of finery with which Mertzork had adorned his body since he had left the marshery to follow in his father's footsteps at the beginning of the season of the joust. It was finery that he had no right to wear while his father lived, and if his father was dead then Andzey, his elder brother, who had left many days ago following the disquieting rumors of his father's murder and the talk of the woman who could tame beasts, was the rightful heir. Frowning with disquiet they had watched Andzey, the rightful heir to Fenmire Marsh, stagger as a beast of burden beneath the weight of this wild woman dressed in a gown of molten gold as he bore her across the channel and up on to the dry land of the marshery. Now they whispered about the strands of gossamer thread bound across his mouth as a gag and the swarming spiders that clung to the shimmering webs hanging across the front of his jerkin, between the woman's feet, and they cried out for the truth of the wild rumors that had reached them and asked if this was the woman who had tamed the mudbeasts and ridden one beyond Rainbows' End. They wanted to know if this was the woman who was so powerful that she had entered the city of Glor to claim Lord Miresnare's throne and all the marsheries across the length and breadth of Gnarlsmyre as her own to rule. And lastly they asked for Mertzork's part in all of it and why he strutted so boldly before them. Suddenly the chanting stopped. The elders held their breath and waited for the answers to their questions.

"She is Pinvey, a daughter of the Glitterspike," stuttered Mertzork, overcoming his terror of the elders, who held the power of life and death in their judgments. "She is the beast-rider, the one who tamed the mudbeasts." He smiled secretly and grew bolder. The elders had blinked and dropped their piercing stares. There was a flicker of belief in their eyes. They were digesting the lies and using them to turn the wild rumors they had heard into truth.

"I touched the Glitterspike. The throne and all Gnarlsmyre is mine!" Mertzork shouted, "and Pinvey is my Queen. Ask the marshmen who have pledged themselves to us," he cried. And drawing out the heavy, squirming web of venomous spiders that Erek had thrust into his hands before the Hurlers' Gate, he turned toward the crowds of marshmen and swept the web across their faces, making them stagger backwards as the spiders scuttled over his fingers.

"Ask them! Ask them who rules," he cried triumphantly.

Pinvey twisted on Andzey's shoulders and stared at Mertzork, her eyes glittering with hatred as she realized that he was stealing every thread of power over these wretched marsh people that he could.

"Tell the elders, tell them!" he hissed, catching sight of her hatred and sneering at her as he advanced menacingly on the marshmen.

Grimly, with fear in their eyes, the marshmen kneeled and called out Mertzork's name, then raised their hands to their foreheads and chanted that Pinvey was their Queen. As their chants died down the marshmen suddenly parted and Alea, driven on by her captors, stumbled into the clear space at Andzey's feet.

"She is mine. She serves only me," cried Pinvey, seizing Alea's sleeve roughly before Mertzork could turn back toward them, but he only laughed and shrugged his shoulders, casting aside any thoughts of the pleasures he had taken from Alea, for they were nothing but the shadows of a mere moment compared to what now lay at his fingertips. Turning away from the women, he met the gaze of the elders.

"Now you must kneel and pledge everything to me. Every footstep of dry land, every thicket, every reed bed, island of marshoaks and grove of mangletrees. Everything will be mine, the new Lord of Gnarlsmyre." Mertzork laughed as his words filled the silence but he caught the look of hatred and rage in Pinvey's eyes and added, "And you must bow to Pinvey and take her as your Queen and submit to her every whim and fancy."

Slowly the elders began to bend their knees, then hesitated, their minds troubled. They sensed that Mertzork had twisted the truth in some way and that he and the wild woman on Andzey's shoulders held some strange, unknown power over the marsh people who crowded behind them.

"There are rumors that your father is dead. Tell us if he lives and why he did not take the throne; and surely Andzey is not a mudbeast—why does your Queen ride him?" one of the elders queried, taking a step forward.

Mertzork snarled and was upon him before the words finished pouring from his mouth. He was afraid that doubt in even one of the elders would unravel his threads of lies. The webs trembled in Mertzork's hands and a black spider scuttled across the elder's throat and he fell—his scream of terror cut short—clawing at the spider as it bit him.

The echo of Mertzork's voice sounded across the marshery. "My father is dead. Andzey is my Queen's beast of burden because she has freed the mudbeasts to roam toward Rainbows' End, as they always do when the wet seasons are about to begin. Now who else doubts my right to rule? Who else will taste my spiders' bites?" he snarled at the elders.

"I ride whatever beast I choose," laughed Pinvey cruelly as she saw the Elders step quickly away from Mertzork. She leapt to the ground, thrusting the silken reins into Alea's hands, and strode toward the elders, eager that they should submit.

"Kneel, or I will set the spiders on to you. Be quick or I will blind your watery eyes with one slash of my dagger blade!"

The elders fell to their knees in terror of this savage woman. Mertzork kicked Andzey behind his knees, making him stumble and fall, then let a handful of the spiders run across Andzey's jerkin as he tore a ragged hole in the webs that gagged his brother and goaded him to tell the elders how their new lord and master had murdered their father, but Andzey was in fear of the spiders and he merely looked away and hung his head. Mertzork ordered Alea to lead Andzey down to graze in the bubbling mud of the channel, where all dumb beasts were caged before they were driven into the city for the joust.

Pinvey watched Alea stumble through the

marshmen, leading Andzey after her, and laughed and shouted to her, telling her to keep her beast well tethered and to be careful that the spiders didn't bite them.

"I'll teach you, sister," Pinvey muttered spitefully and she turned and passed through the kneeling elders, treading uncaringly on their outstretched fingers as she looked up through the forest of stilts at their miserable hovels that gently swayed in the marsh breezes.

"That one shall be mine to weather out the wet seasons before I return triumphant to Glitterspike Hall," she called over her shoulder to Mertzork as she pointed up at the largest of the elders' dwellings. "And my beast and Alea shall share a cage woven from branches of marshoaks which shall be hung in the shadows below my doorway and none shall touch them or speak to them on pain of death."

"Come, my Queen," laughed Mertzork, delighted that the elders had swallowed his lies. He caught Pinvey up in his strong arms and lifted her off her feet. "Let me carry you up into your royal chambers!"

Mertzork paused on the tenth rung of the ladder and slowly cast his gaze across the crowds of startled, upturned faces and he laughed, his cruel mouth splitting into a sneer as he saw so much fear in the marsh peoples' eyes. But he knew there was still hatred for him amongst the elders and that he must destroy their power before they spoke out against him.

"Elders!" he called, snapping the fingers of his

free hand. "Your power to judge my people is broken; you are banished to grub for roots on the outer edges of the marshery and you shall weather out the wet seasons amongst the branches of the marshoaks on that island beyond the reed beds."

The crowd stirred below him and whispers spread as the elders retreated toward the stepping stones that led across the channel, but Mertzork merely laughed, lightheaded and dizzy with the power that his lies had given him.

"There will be a feast!" he cried. "A feast to mark my triumphant return. Dark meats from the pindafall carcasses will be roasted over open fires, live wriggling crawlers will be swallowed, bowls of toads' eyes and juicy slugs and leeches will be boiled with tender marshroots." He paused, smacking his lips in anticipation as he watched the marsh people on the ground below begin to hurry about their tasks, but they paused and looked up as he spoke again. "And I shall choose any woman I want, to chew and soften my beastskins while I eat. Send only the youngest and those with the strongest teeth to squat in the shadows beneath this hut. And there will be wrestling jousts and sharpwire matches to choose the best among you as my captains to accompany us to the city of Glor when the wet seasons end." The shouts for Pinvey and Mertzork, led by the marshmen from the Hurlers' Gate, took many minutes to fade into silence before the people of the marshery began their tasks.

Alea stumbled along the edges of the channel, the gossamer reins held tightly in her hands as she tried to shut out the noises behind her. Andzey opened his mouth to whisper to her but the spiders on his jerkin swarmed up on to his shoulders and he sank into a terrified silence. Everyone they passed shunned them. Now they were passing close to a group of women who stood knee-deep in the mud as they softened leathery strips of mudbeasts' hide between their teeth.

"Queens and their likes, why don't you stop tormenting Andzey?" shouted one of them. They all spat at Alea and vented their hate as they drove her away.

"It's not her fault," shouted Andzey through the ragged hole in the webs. "She's as much a prisoner as I am. If she tries to help me the spiders will kill her."

A figure moved in the mud beyond the hide-chewers, its voice cackling with laughter. Alea looked up and blinked away the tears of despair that burned her eyes and caught her breath as she saw a filthy bundle of rags and bones move quickly toward them.

"Don't you know anything of a woman's secrets?" the creature whispered, glancing anxiously back at the group of hide-chewers who had turned away from them and were now plunging the rancid beastskins beneath the mud.

"I dare not even speak. The spiders will bite," Alea gasped, shrinking away, but the woman merely laughed, showing a mouth of withered gums.

Deftly the old woman reached out, plucked one

of the spiders from Andzey's jerkin and stroked its swollen abdomen. "Watch," she whispered. Gently, using a finger and thumb, she teased out the venom and let it drip harmlessly into the heaving mud. "It will not hurt you now that I have milked it and drawn its teeth."

Andzey watched the spider scuttle across the woman's bony arm and his eyebrows drew into a frown. "I know you," he whispered. "I brought you toads and spiders' webs and you soothed my cuts and bruises. You lived in the branches of a dead marshoak on the edges of the manglegroves beyond Fenmire Marsh. It was a wonderful tree, hung with a thousand secrets."

The filthy wretch laughed again, only now there was anger and hatred in the sound. "You didn't mock me for gleaning secrets from the mud, but your half-brother, Mertzork, did. He burned down my marshoak and threw all the secret potions that I had spent my life gathering into Fenmire Marsh. I am shunned by the marshery and banished to forage for scraps where I can, but I would help you, Andzey."

Alea stared at the filthy old woman and saw a glimmer of hope in her cacklings. "Show me again. Teach me how to draw the spiders' venom and we will take your revenge on Mertzork and my sister Pinvey," Alea urged softly.

The poor wretch threw back her head and peals of silent laughter shook her meager frame. "It's justice I want, not revenge. Revenge is its own poison which eats a body up and blackens its heart," and she plucked another of the spiders from Andzey and dropped it into Alea's hand. "Be gentle. Squeeze it softly, draw the poison sack between your finger and thumb."

Alea shuddered but did exactly as she was told and the spider's venom dripped slowly from between her fingertips on to the ground at her feet. She looked up to thank the woman and ask her name but the old creature had vanished: only her shadow showed where she waded away from them through the mud. Marshmen were closing in all around, shouting and cursing at them to return to the center of the marshery, to clamber up into the cage that awaited them beneath Pinvey's chamber. Alea dropped the harmless spider back on to Andzey's sleeve and her eyes softened into a secret smile of hope before she turned toward their cage.

9

The Great Dyke

K*RANN* stared out through the broken crystal windows across the high walls of the city to the gathering storm clouds that blackened the horizon. He shivered as a cold gust of wind tugged at his cloak. A rumble of thunder sounded in the distance and jagged forks of lightning cut stark shadows across the endless leagues of mud and mire beyond the city. Below him, the hall echoed to the shouts of the children they had rescued from the birth chambers as they ran and dodged between the groups of ragmen and dusters who were clearing away the last of the refuse of the joust. Krann heard the bustle and noise but didn't turn or look down, even though the children shouted his name. He felt a burden of problems weighing heavily on his shoulders and he had to riddle them out.

"Where and what can we harvest next?" he muttered, shifting further along the stone windowsill so that he could look down at the gang of hoemasters whom over the last ten daylights since the joust he had set to work weeding between the cobblestones, instructing them to take care to include every nook and cranny of the rough, mud-plastered walls of the houses that made up the maze of narrow lanes just below the hall. They were moving slowly through the ruin that the marshmen had left, painstaking, with their small, curved hoes and their thrifty hooks as they worked through every crack or fissure in the jumble of stonework and cleaned out every living stalk or leaf.

Krann smiled and nodded as he watched two of the hoemasters prising up the thin velvet-soft strips of moss that grew on the dampest walls, carefully loosening and pulling free their tangle of roots before laying them in the dampened wicker baskets. He was not sure what they would do with these gleanings from the upper thoroughfares of the city but Treasel had said that they were just like the mosses that grew on the marshoaks and safe to eat once they had been boiled. He could see that they would never be able to harvest enough to feed the hall folk but what worried him even more was that the people of the city had grown wise to what these small gleaning gangs were doing and as their own food ran out and they became hungry they resented their foraging through the streets. Only yesterday an angry crowd had stoned a group of hoemasters and driven them back into the hall before they tore down two whole alleyways of hovels in their search for food. Krann had seen the helms of Lord Miresnare's guards in the crowd and, since they had deserted Marrimian, he feared that they might try and storm the hall. He sent out every man that he could spare, arming them with staves and daggers to defend the hoemasters while they worked and watch over the great doors while they remained open, but he believed that it would only be a matter of time before the guards urged the mass of city folk to rise up and overrun the hall and take what little had been harvested.

Krann shifted further along the windowsill and craned his neck to look down to the ruins of the crystal houses where every scullion and scuttle that Ansel could spare from the kitchens was working shoulder to shoulder with the rakes and hoemasters, sifting through the broken crystal. Marrimian had ordered them to stack the largest sheets of crystal carefully against the walls of the hall while they searched for every seed head that they could find in the wreckage. Krann started to smile again as he saw the hoemasters' leather-pouched apron pockets swell with the gathered seed, then jumped and frowned as a flash of lightning lit up the hall. He stole a glance at the black thunder clouds that lay heavily on the horizon as a distant peel of thunder split the dense air. He had heard the hoemasters muttering against the wet seasons when, for days beyond counting, the rain fell so heavily that it turned every roof into a waterfall and every lane and alleyway into a raging torrent that washed the bones of the great ridge of rock on which the city stood bare of every grain of earth or speck of dust that had fallen and clung to it during the dry seasons. Slowly he had come to realize the importance of the crystal houses in this dreary land of marshes and mires that lay below the great ridge of rocks. He sighed and wished that just a few, perhaps a handful of craftsmen, glaziers, masons or black-smiths, from the city had pledged themselves to Marrimian. Then they could have made a real be-ginning; they could have started rebuilding.

Footsteps sounded on the broken gallery and he turned, narrowing his eyes against the shadows of the hall, to see Marrimian picking her way across the splintered rafter beams toward him. His smile turned to a frown of concern as she reached the windowsill and he moved quickly to one side to give her room beside him to gaze out across the city. Her face looked pinched and drawn as she plucked anxiously at the collar of her gown.

"Do you fear the city folk will rise up against the hall, or that Pinvey has slipped back into the city?" he asked her quietly.

Marrimian bit her lip and shook her head. "I . . . I . . . I fear that everything I have striven to achieve is falling apart. Everything," she muttered miserably.

"But look, the hoemasters are gleaning every-thing they can in the upper lanes and alleyways, and the scullions labor tirelessly in the ruins of the crystal houses. The Hurlers watch the marshes for any sign of Mertzork and Pinvey and we guard the doors of the hall against the city folk. Surely we are winning," he said, quickly pointing down through the broken window to avoid her touch.

"Krann—look at me, Krann," she whispered softly, making him swallow and turn toward her.

"Although you share my bed during the frozen hours of darkness you have drawn away from me ever since I touched the Glitterspike. During the hours of daylight I have looked for you and called out but you are never near, you are always somewhere else, marshaling the hoemasters or organizing the ragmen. I would share this throne with you. I would share everything with you, but you have become distant from me."

"There is so much to do, a whole city to feed," he answered, looking away, but he felt wretched that his yearning for Elundium had driven a wedge between them.

"Whatever troubles you it goes much deeper than a worry over gleaning for food. We share that burden. Tell me what really troubles you," she insisted, reaching for his hand, but he hesitated at her touch and she let her own hand drop to her side and blinked back the tears that filled her eyes.

"It was different in the marshes," she whispered bitterly. "Then you lay with me and used me to discover your beginnings. Then you needed me and clung to me and called it love. I was surely a fool to turn deaf to Ansel's warnings: she saw you more clearly than I did."

"No! No! I did love you—no, I *do* love you," Krann cried, wringing his hands together. He sought for the words to tell her of his yearnings to return to Elundium without them sounding like a shallow betrayal of his promise to stay with her until her throne was secure. Slowly he lifted his eyes until he held her gaze. "You showed me my beginnings, yet what we glimpsed barely cast a ripple on the surface of all those unanswered questions in Elundium. One daylight I must go back. I yearn to know more. I must ask Elionbel, my half-sister, and Fairlight, my only friend . . ." Krann hesitated and swallowed and then carried on quickly, almost stumbling over the words. "But I promise I will not leave you here struggling alone, clinging to what you have won. I will stay beside you until your throne is secure, that much I promise, no matter how many seasons it may take; but that does not stop my yearning for home."

"Yearning for Fairlight! That is why you have drawn away from me. Your love for me has shriveled, has it not?" cried Marrimian through trembling lips. "Through our touchings you know that there was some good in your beginnings and that you can return to her, and now you cannot bear to touch me."

Krann shook his head bleakly and looked out across the marshes. "No, Fairlight was my friend, my only friend, as close to me as any sister, but I do not love her as I love you. But I do yearn to see her and Elionbel and ask them both a thousand questions." Krann paused and gripped Marrimian's hands tightly in his. "When we touch you tear aside a dark curtain and I can see and smell the Elundium that I yearn to return to, yet my love for you denies me that journey. That is why I shrink away from you, to avoid the hurt."

Marrimian frowned and bit her lip as she thought back over all that they had been through together, wondering how she had not realized the depth of his yearning. She had thought that the love flowing between them would bind him to her, that he would want nothing from his life in Elundium and that he would share the throne and all her triumphs forever. She looked up at him, her eyes glittering with tears, her voice trembling as she spoke. "Then may I never touch or lie with you again? Is that my reward for loving you and showing you the beast that haunted your beginnings?"

"Touch me! Hurt me! Prod at the wound I cannot heal," he cried hopelessly, throwing his hands up in the air and sucking in a shallow breath as he tried to tell her that it was his yearning for Elundium that had split them apart, not a lack of feeling in him.

A loud clamor of children's voices from the hall below interrupted them. Krann turned and pointed down to where Ankana was gathering the girls from their games around the Glitterspike, bringing them close to the scarlet tails of her blood apron. "Your triumph is almost complete. We have journeyed to the very cradle of *your* beginnings. Ever since we brought Ankana into the hall you have plagued her with an endless thread of questions about every day, every hour, of your lost childhood. Would you now deny me my chance of seeking those same answers beyond Rainbows' End, in Elundium?"

Marrimian turned away from him, her shoulders trembling. She gripped the stone windowsill and shook her head. "No. No, I would not hold you for one moment against your will. If I had the wings of a pindafall bird I would gather you up and soar above those storms that shroud Rainbows' End and deliver you back to Elundium where your heart yearns to be . . ."

Marrimian fell silent and tears burned her eyes and trickled hotly down her face. She felt so alone, so empty. "Would . . . would you take me with you? Take me to your land of Elundium?" she asked quietly as she stared out of the window and brushed at the streaks of salty tears that wetted her cheeks.

Krann stared down at her in surprise and hesitated, stuttering as he tried to answer without hurting. Here in Gnarlsmyre she was the Queen, and yet she was in many ways so raw and untutored, so different from the people in his land of Elundium, and he feared that the people that he had grown up amongst would mock her and shun her as they had shunned him and make her feel awkward and out of place. "Yes! Yes, of course. But my people might turn against you, they . . ." His voice trailed away.

Marrimian caught a glimpse of the hesitation. "It is Fairlight! It is Fairlight you do not want me to meet!" she cried, her jealousy boiling up in anger. "This talk of your people turning against me is nothing but a cloak of lies! You have lied about your love and you have used me. All this talk of touching is nothing more than words to ease your conscience and smooth your path back to Fairlight! Well, you can go for all I care. I would not hold you for one moment against your will. But you will not get far, Krann, no matter how much you may long to leave," she cried, stabbing her finger through the broken window at the darkening horizon. "You can dream of her all you want but you are trapped here, here in Glitterspike Hall, until the wet seasons have passed."

Krann looked past her shoulder and saw the last bright archway of rainbows flicker and vanish beneath the advancing storm clouds.

"The wet seasons have begun at Rainbows' End," Marrimian whispered bitterly, "and the mires and marshes will have vanished beneath the floods long before you could ever get there."

Krann stared at her for a moment, his lips thinning with anger, thinking that she had judged him too harshly through her jealousy, and yet he saw her hurt and loneliness and knew that he had selfishly driven her to it. His eyes softened and he smiled and reached out and clasped her hands tighter in his. "Fairlight was as a sister, my only friend. You must believe it. I have never loved anyone or anything as much as I have loved you. It was here with you as we crossed the marshes that I first discovered love. My yearning to know myself completely has nothing to do with the differences between our peoples."

Marrimian frowned and would have pulled away from him, her mind jumbled with confusion, but his grip tightened.

Krann laughed and threw his head back. "Jealousy of Fairlight has clouded your vision. It makes you imagine shadows and see false meanings in every word I utter. I would hesitate to take you amongst my people until I have banished the fears that they heed over my beginnings, but once they have accepted me for what I am then I would gladly have you at my side amongst them," he said.

"But one instant you cannot bear my touch because it reminds you of what you cannot have and the next your grip is hurting me. What am I to think?" Marrimian cried wretchedly. "Where is the truth in all these words?"

"Look! Look at me," Krann urged. "If there had been nothing between us, if I had merely used you to discover my beginnings, surely, armed with that knowledge, I would have left your land of Gnarlsmyre the moment you touched the Glitterspike. Surely I would have vanished quietly before the shouts of your triumph had faded away. The fact that I am here beside you should be proof enough of the love that flowered in the marshes."

"But my touch hurts you," she whispered sadly. "I do not understand how to love you without causing you pain."

Krann smiled gently and drew her to him. "It hurts me because it shows me brief glimpses of myself, the one I left behind shrouded in other people's lies and half-truths, and I yearn to set them right. But my hurt is nothing to the pain it has caused you and I am truly sorry."

Marrimian looked away and thought for a moment and began to see the truth. Perhaps she *was* jealous of Fairlight, jealous of anything that would take him away from her. She frowned and looked up at his silhouette as he stared out of the broken window at the steep rock ridge behind the hall.

"What lies over there?" Krann asked. "Do those ledges and overhangs of rock flood in the wet seasons? How can we reach them?"

Marrimian smiled to herself as she watched him and she reached out a hand to brush against his sleeve, knowing that she had no right to stop whatever path their love took, that it was clouded and veiled in mists of the future. Krann was here with her now and she must use whatever time they had together to strengthen their love against the moment when the rainbows once more flickered on the horizon's rim and she must let him go. "That is where the hill sheep are kept for the Allbeast Feast graze, but it is dangerous ground of loose rocks and narrow cracks and chasms," she replied, shaking her head to scatter the thoughts of what might or might not happen between them in the future. "Why do you ask?" she frowned, moving closer to him and standing on tiptoe to follow his gaze out toward the crumbling ridges of gray rock.

"If there are sheep grazing those rocks there must be earth and grass. There must be enough earth to plant out the seed and shoots that the hoemasters have gleaned from the wreckage of the crystal houses, but if that fails the sheep could be our only hope of food once the rains begin." Turning, Krann pointed to the blackened horizon. "How many daylights will pass before the rains reach the city? How much time do we have to do the planting?" he asked.

"The wet seasons move slowly across the marshes from Rainbows' End. There may be ten daylights, twenty, perhaps even thirty: it varies from season to season. The mumblers always foretold that the rains would begin when the rainbows vanished. But how will you plant? Surely the rain will wash the seeds into the marshes. The steep lanes and alleyways of the city become raging torrents and the courtyards always flood. That is why everything was always grown in the crystal houses."

Krann tried to remember the hill farms and terraces of Elundium. "There were narrow strips of earth cut into the steep hillsides in my land," he answered, frowning as he tried to recall what they had looked like. "Yes, they were bordered by rough stone walls and after the heavy storms the water used to cascade in sparkling fountains and waterfalls through gutter spouts in the base of each wall. People would travel leagues to watch the curtains of water boiling out of those thick stone walls."

"But these are crumbling ridges of rock, not hills. Only the hill sheep and ravine goats can wander safely there," cried Marrimian.

Krann laughed and shook his head at her. "We will use the lower slopes. We must or we will starve. If everyone helps we can build thick walls and build the earth in steep ridges that will let the water drain out through the walls. Yes, that is our only chance to feed the people of the hall and the city. Quickly, call the hoemasters, gather everyone into the hall. Tell them to bring everything they can to hoe and dig and rake and build."

"You must tell them, it is your idea," cried Marrimian as Krann sprang away across the splintered rafter beams.

But he laughed again and waved his hand as he leapt down into the hall, calling over his shoulder, "You are Queen, the idea must seem to come from you. Give the hoemasters their heads and let them discuss the terraces and they will offer you countless seasons of their knowledge, some they have almost forgotten because they have never had the need to use it."

"But where are you going? Surely you will talk to the hoemasters?" questioned Marrimian, hurrying from the window.

Krann shook his head and lengthened his stride toward the high-arched entrance. "I will take extra hoemasters and ragmen down to the gates in case the rains drive Mertzork and Pinvey back to find shelter in the city and then I will follow the city wall toward those high ridges of rock and search for the best places to build the terraces."

"Wait," cried Marrimian, making him stop. "Don't go out beyond the wall alone. There may be marshmen or pindafall birds. Take as many of the men folk as can be spared from gleaning roots: they will find you the quickest road down to the Hurlers' Gate. And take Treasel: she will know if any of the plants or roots you find beyond the walls are edible."

Krann turned toward the kitchens, lifting his

hand to wave his thanks to Marrimian, and she watched him vanish beneath the kitchen archway, wondering if she would have the courage to let him go when the time came and they stood together beneath the bright archways of Rainbows' End. Sighing, she called for the scullions to assemble everyone who had pledged themselves to her and climbed wearily down to the dais in the center of the hall.

"Terraces will flood, mistress," called an ancient hoemaster from the back of the crowded hall. "The earth will turn to mud and pour out between the stones at the base of your walls."

"No, they won't, not if you ridge the earth to follow the slope of your terrace; that would allow the water to drain away," called out another gardener thoughtfully.

"We could use the lower slopes where the blue cabbage and borage flowers and husk corn were grown, but they flood so easily when the level of the marsh rises," grumbled one of the hoemasters toward the front of the crowd.

"Perhaps we could build a dyke, a huge bank of rocks and earth, that would keep the marsh water out," called a young apprentice gardener.

A sudden hush fell across the hall as heads turned and craned to look at the young lad.

"You'll be wanting to drain the marshes next," shouted a voice and the silent, uneasy gathering erupted into shrieks of laughter, using the youth's inspiration as an excuse to mock the whole idea of terraces, dykes and banks beyond the city.

The apprentice blushed scarlet and hung his head in shame as he saw that by speaking out of turn he had led them into ridiculing his Queen. "I know I could do it! I know I could!" he cried, angrily clenching his fists at the crowd.

Marrimian frowned at the mocking laughter and fiercely clapped her hands. The hall fell silent again. She smiled at the young apprentice and beckoned him forward. "What is your name?" she asked kindly.

"Tregond," he answered, his voice dry with embarrassment.

"You shall be my dyke builder," she said firmly as he bowed before her. "Search out Krann, who is exploring those ridges of rock beyond the city wall for the best places to build the terraces. He told me that there are many such wonders in his land of Elundium and he will help and advise you."

"It will flood, mistress," grumbled a voice amongst the ancient, leathery hoemasters. "Everything beyond the Hurlers' Gate and the high wall vanishes completely beneath the huge torrent of mud and water that pours down every steep lane and alleyway of the city."

Tregond blushed uncomfortably and began to retreat into the crowd, humiliated and ashamed. Marrimian hesitated and looked this way and that as the arguments became louder and louder for and against building a dyke. Suddenly she clapped her hands again for silence. "Choose your helpers," she commanded Tregond. "Since the learned hoemasters are at a loss you must start at once. Find Krann and tell him that I have sent you to build a dyke around the city. Go—quickly," she commanded, silencing all those who were against the idea.

The crowd muttered and murmured for long moments after Tregond and forty strong young helpers had left the hall. He had chosen his assistants from amongst the youths who tumbled the wheelbarrows and served the hoemasters, and the scuttles who helped the scullions and those they had served felt aggrieved at their loss. Marrimian waited and turned over in her mind what she could say to these hall folk. The sound of the footsteps of Tregond and his helpers had faded and the whispered mutterings of the crowd had subsided, and now every face had turned back toward her. She caught sight of the old birthwoman with her gaggle of children hanging on to the tails of her apron and she remembered Ankana's words counseling her to be herself and change nothing. Yes—she must be honest; that had always been her way. She swallowed, took a deep breath and began.

"You will starve, just like my sisters starved locked in the daughtery, if you do not use every moment to build the terraces and the banks and dykes that will keep the marshes away from around this city," she said quietly, looking from face to face.

"But you promised to feed us if we pledged ourselves," grumbled a knot of disgruntled ragmen.

"Yes, and boiled moss and gutter sweepings are

all that has wet my bowl so far," cried another voice from the crowd.

"Now you tell us that we must leave the safety of the hall and venture beyond the Hurlers' Gate and risk our lives on the edges of the marshes," cried a bencher, his eyes wide with terror.

"There is no other choice," Marrimian shouted, clapping her hands to quieten the crowd. "The crystal houses lie in ruins. The smoke houses and the fish moats are empty. Our only chance of surviving the wet seasons lies in the seeds and shoots that you have gleaned from the wreckage of the crystal houses. We must build the terraces beyond the city walls and plant them or we will starve to death!"

The crowd stared at her in shocked silence. Ankana looked over her shoulder at their blank faces and laughed softly as she hobbled forward, the children still clinging tightly to her apron tails. "Few of them have ventured beyond the great doors of Glitterspike Hall, mistress, let alone put their noses outside the Hurlers' Gate. They have always lived in terror of the outside, the marshes and the wild marshmen who roam there. Only some of the scuttles and scullions, the harvesters and the gatherers have ever been out of the hall," she whispered to Marrimian.

"But the young barrowers and scuttles were eager to follow Tregond to begin work on the dyke," frowned Marrimian. "Why did they not hesitate?"

"Because they are young, my lady, and their

minds are full of adventure and they have not yet become set in the ways of their elders," whispered the birthwoman.

Marrimian looked quickly around the hall. "They must venture out to build the terraces and the city folk must follow them or we will all starve to death."

Ankana thought for a moment, resting heavily on her sticks. Sighing, she gripped both sticks in her left hand and slowly turned and snatched a long-handled hoe from a gardener who stood just behind her. "You'll have little use for this hoe if you're going to spend your last days sulking in this hall. I can find a better use for it loosening the clods of earth in the terraces that my Queen is going to build beyond the Hurlers' Gate. I'm not afraid of going outside!" she said in a voice loud enough for everyone in the hall to hear. Turning back, she hobbled over to Marrimian as a wave of whispering swept through the hall. "Well, that's given them something to think about," she grinned. "Now you lead us out, my lady; the children and I will be just behind you."

Marrimian smiled down at the frail birthwoman and gripped her arms. "But you can barely walk and there are at least a thousand rough-cut steps in those narrow, twisting lanes and alleyways, and they are still choked with broken masonry and piles of rubble. No, Ankana, you have suffered enough for the daughters of this hall without being buffeted and blown off your feet by the marsh winds beyond the Hurlers' Gate. Stay here with the children in the safety of the hall."

Ankana shook her head fiercely and said, "It will shame many who are younger, quicker and stronger and they will follow you beyond the Hurlers' Gate if I walk beside you."

Marrimian laughed, then linked her arm through Ankana's and slowly led her toward the high-arched entrance. The children kept pace with them, dancing around asking questions all the while of what lay beyond the Hurlers' Gate, and the women of the hall began to follow one by one. Behind them the crowds of ragmen, benchers, dusters and hoe-masters fell silent until one voice called out, "You are abandoning us and breaking your promise. You are leaving us here to starve."

Marrimian paused beneath the archway and then turned and shook her head. "There is a place for everyone who is brave enough to follow me, and there will be food for all those who help me build the terraces."

"You say that Krann knows how to build terraces and dykes—will he be with us? And will you lead us out and labor too?" cried a hoemaster. As Marrimian nodded he hurried through the crowds with his heavy pouches of seed thrown across his shoulder. "Then I will follow you," he said eagerly, joining the scullions and the scuttles and following them beneath the archway.

"But what if the marshmen attack us, or a mud-beast climbs up out of the marshes?" asked one of a tight knot of ragmen, reluctant to move from the furthest edge of the hall.

"Krann has taken extra guards down to the Hurlers' Gate. We will set them to watch the terraces while we work," answered Marrimian.

"The mudbeasts have vanished as they always do when the wet seasons begin," coughed Vetchim as he and Ansel fell in behind Marrimian.

Heads nodded, voices rose amongst the ragmen and slowly, step by step, the crowd moved forward. Marrimian smiled to herself as she overheard a group of hoemasters behind her debating the best way to lay terraces and deciding to ridge up the earth between the drainage channels that would empty through the retaining walls. Just in front of the hoemasters the fish cooks were eagerly discussing how they would be able to catch the marshfish that were rumored to swim in the waters on the edges of the marshes.

Marrimian cast one final glance back into the emptying hall to the tall finger of crystal that shimmered and glittered beneath its featherings of hoarfrost and she beckoned her sister, Treyster, and took her hand. "You know, father missed the real wealth and riches of this hall. It's not there, trapped in the Glitterspike; it is in the people, in the skills and knowledge that they carry. He never discovered it because he never looked for it."

"This is where you must start to build the dyke. There is a broad ledge of rock beneath the reed bed," Krann called over his shoulder to Tregond and his gang of helpers. He had waded out into the marsh and used his gift of foresight to follow a narrow spine of rock that lay just below the surface of the bubbling mire.

"He has strong magic. He can walk on the marshes and barely dampen his boots. I can't see how we will ever be able to cross with the heavy baskets of rocks and earth," muttered one of the dyke builders, nervously wishing he hadn't been so eager to follow Tregond.

"He has the power of fire at his fingertips. I have seen him light the reedlamps in the great hall by just touching them," whispered another as they watched Krann hammer thin iron stakes deep into the reed bed to mark where they should lay the foundations of the dyke.

Krann looked up and called to Tregond to bring two of the barrowers with trenching spades out on to the reed bed and then vanished amongst the reeds. Moments later he reappeared and laughed as he watched the dyke builders hovering on the edges of the mire take a tentative step and then retreat as their feet vanished beneath the bubbling mud.

"Wait! I will show you the path," he cried, striding back along the zigzag route. "Keep close to me and place your feet in my footsteps," he ordered, wiping at the trickles of sweat that were pouring down his forehead and stinging his eyes. The dark thunder clouds on the horizon's edge had made the stifling marsh air still hotter. The mire was bubbling and letting off a foul stink that made him dizzy and light-headed.

"Follow carefully," he called back as he moved slowly along the narrow spine of rock.

Twice Tregond slipped and would have floundered had he not caught hold of Krann's sleeve and steadied himself, and all three of the dyke builders were trembling and breathless with terror by the time they had climbed on to the reed bank.

"I'm sinking! There's nothing but mud beneath these reeds," cried Tregond, clutching at a handful of reeds and pulling them free of the soft mud.

"We'll never be able to build a dyke here!" shouted one of the barrowers, floundering forward in the reeds as his feet sank beneath the liquid ooze.

"Keep still and pass me that trenching spade. You'll sink no deeper if you stop blundering about," muttered Krann. The stifling heat and the clouds of stinging insects that were buzzing around his head had shortened his patience and frayed his temper. He took the spade and forced his way through the reeds until he reached the farther side of the bank. Working backwards, he dug a narrow trench across the reed bed and piled the soft clods of fibrous sludge well to one side.

Resting on the spade, he pointed to the narrow channel that was already filling with a sluggish, black, watery mud, swirling and eddying around their feet. "Watch the mire that you crossed to reach this reed bed," he smiled rubbing his dirty hand across his face.

"It's magic! Look the whole surface of the mire

is moving toward the channel," cried one of the barrowers.

"Krann is draining the marshes!" shouted Tregond, waving his arms at the dyke builders on the higher ground.

"There is no magic," muttered Krann crossly, "and I'm not draining the marshes, simply this small puddle that we crossed. Now follow me and use your eyes and tell me how much magic you can see."

Following the narrow channel, he led them through the reeds to the farther edge of the reed bank. "Well, tell me what you see."

Tregond blushed at Krann's anger and pushed the last of the reeds aside and caught his breath. "The marshes are lower beyond these reeds. There are tall reed banks and bands of marshoaks everywhere. I had always thought the quickmarshes were a great flat expanse—it *looks* flat from the upper levels of the city or through the windows of Glitterspike Hall."

Krann smiled, a little ashamed at being so cross at the youth's ignorance of the world he lived in. Tregond had only seen the marshes at a distance, through the heat haze as the marsh gasses burned. Krann held up his hand and cupped the palm. "Your land of Gnarlsmyre is like a hollow dish riddled and honeycombed with ledges and spines of rock, all of different heights and thicknesses. They are the secret paths that lie just beneath the marsh that the marshmen use and they stop the rainwater of your wet seasons from draining away over the waterfalls of Rainbows' End. It is the honeycomb of rocks that forms all the mires, swamps and quick-marshes that spread out in every direction as far as we can see."

"But the reed banks and the islands of marsh-oaks—how are they formed?" asked the young apprentice, scratching at the tangle of unruly hair that hung down across his forehead.

Krann laughed and pointed down to the soft, dark, greenish mud that had oozed up over their boots. "The broader ledges have silted up and the roots of the reeds have held the mud together, forming it into banks and islands. All I have done is to cut a channel through the silt and the reed roots to allow the mire that we crossed to reach this bank and drain into the lower stretch of marsh."

Tregond waded through the sticky, soft mud over the top of the bank and clutched clumsily at the thick reed stems, breaking them and scattering them into the channel, before reaching the far side of the bank. He stared out across the lower marsh of bubbling, stagnant pools, tufted with clumps of rank reed grass, toward the scattered islands of ancient marshoaks and the tall reed banks that shimmered in the heat haze. He frowned and leaned forward as far as he dared and watched the thick sludge of the mire ooze and slop out of the channel Krann had dug across the bank. It fell in stinking, sluggish ripples that slowly spread out and sank in a hiss of bubbles below the surface of the lower marsh.

"What would happen if you dug channels in that

reed bank over there?" he asked, glancing over his shoulder to where Krann was resting his hands on the smooth handle of the trenching spade and staring down into the narrow channel he had just dug. "Would this lower marsh drain away?"

Krann blinked and swatted at the clouds of insects that darkened the stifling marsh air above his head before looking up. "What?"

"The marshes—could you drain them all if you cut channels through every reed bank?"

Krann laughed and shook his head. "We could drain most, but not all. Some of the levels are higher than this one. If we cut through those reed banks the marshes beyond would simply flow back and flood us, but . . ." Krann hesitated and glanced down into the channel and then crouched and trailed his fingers through the mud, holding them against the sluggish flow.

"What is it?" Tregond asked, struggling to free his feet from the mud and hurry back across the reed bank.

Krann looked up and pointed to the broken reeds that had fallen into the channel. "We are draining everything—not just stagnant water. Look how the mud has built up against those reeds that you snapped off and let fall into the channel. We must somehow stop the mud from escaping or there will be nothing to plant the seeds in behind the dyke." He paused and bent lower over the channel. "Look, something is swimming through the channel. I think it is a . . ."

Tregond crouched down and without a moment's thought plunged his hand into the swirling mud. He felt a sudden stabbing pain in his hand as something pricked his finger and sharp spines cut into his palm. "It is a marshfish, you have caught a marshfish!" Krann shouted as the thrashing fish slipped and wriggled through Tregond's fingers and fell back amongst the fibrous roots of reeds. It flapped up a shower of sticky mud as it struggled to reach the mire.

Tregond had snatched it up again, hugging it desperately to his chest, when a loud voice from the firm ground above the marsh thundered out through the stagnant air. "Put it in your pocket, fool! Don't allow it to escape again!"

"Ansel!" Krann cried, looking up at the huge scullion where she stood with Vetchim at her side. She lifted her voluminous apron tails and began to splash her way determinedly across the mire, following the zigzag path Krann and Tregond had taken to reach the reed bank.

"Did you teach her how to walk on the marshes on your journey from Rainbows' End? Look, she can find the secret path just as easily as you did!" Tregond cried, trying to cram the wriggling fish into his largest pocket and crushing its sharp fins on the tynes of a thrifty hook and an onion hoe that he kept there.

Krann smiled and shook his head. "The marsh is draining: that spine of rock that we followed is showing just above it now," he laughed and, reaching out with both hands, he helped Ansel climb awkwardly up on to the soft reed bank.

"Clumsy oaf!" she grumbled a little breathlessly, glaring at Tregond with a face as black as thunder as she snatched the wriggling fish from his hands. She smoothed its broken scales and thrust it carefully into her apron pocket. "There'll be nothing but a mouthful of sharp scales and bones to savor if you handle it anymore," she muttered, wiping the smears of mud from her fingers with a muslin cloth that hung from her apron ties.

Vetchim climbed up beside the scullion and stared down at the drainage channel. "The marshes," he whispered hoarsely. "The marshes are vanishing."

Krann laughed softly. "It is only a beginning, it's . . ."

Vetchim looked up and gripped Krann's arm. "Look! Look over there in that reed bed. I'm sure something is moving."

Krann narrowed his eyes and followed the marshman's pointing finger. A mudbeast suddenly bellowed and reared up, its long horns glistening with marsh slime. Vetchim breathed a sigh of relief as the beast turned away from them and disappeared into the tall reeds.

Ansel suddenly slapped her forehead. "I nearly forgot," she cried. "Seeing that boy mauling that precious marshfish between his clumsy fingers and hearing that mudbeast bellowing drove it out of my mind."

"What is it? What have you come to tell me?" Krann asked.

"Mistress Marrimian says that she has found

fields, hundreds of them, beyond a shallow river just around that bend in the city wall. They are all overgrown with vines and creeping weeds. The hoemasters say that they were abandoned before the last joust and that they always used to flood when the rains came, and our Queen says you are to come as quickly as possible to settle the hoemasters' arguments and tell them about dykes and banks and all those things that you have in Elundium to keep the water out."

Krann was about to laugh and tell the scullion that there was no water to keep out, that there were no swamps or marshes or endless drenching rains, when suddenly the surface of the mire began to ripple. Bubbles burst upon its surface and fins, the fins of a huge marshfish, cut through the swirling crust.

"Marshfish! Marshfish!" Ansel cried with delight, forgetting all about the hoemasters and dykes, her face beaming. "Don't let any of them escape, catch them as they swim into the channel!" and she tugged at the large muslin cloth and, pulling it from her apron, kneeled in the stinking mud to hold it across the end of the channel. "Bring your sacks, fish kettles and every pot and pan you can carry. Bring more from the hall," she shouted to the procession of passing scuttles, scullions and hall folk who were carrying heavy baskets of rocks along the edge of the mire to build the first terrace. "Hurry, hurry and there'll be a fish supper for everyone," she shouted as Tregond and the two barrowers that

Krann had led on to the reed bank began to gather up armfuls of the flapping fish.

"Quickly, stuff the fish into my apron pocket and help me block the channel," she cried. "Use the thick reed stems, weave them into the edges of the muslin. I'll never be able to hold it on my own and we can catch the rest of the fish once we have kettles and sacks to put them in."

"Ansel, you are a wonder," Krann laughed as he helped the two barrowers weave a rough nest of the strongest reed stems round the bulging muslin cloth and force the ends of the stems securely in amongst the reeds that grew in the farther end of the channel. Straightening his back, he watched the trickle of murky water seep through the cloth and spill down into the marsh below the bank. "Not only have you stopped our supper from escaping, you have also stopped most of the mud from draining away!"

"We could cut dozens of channels and block them all with these woven reed cloths," ventured one of the barrowers as he wiped the mud from his hands.

"And we will grow as fat as the kitchen girls on an endless feast of marshfish," laughed one of the other barrowers but swallowing his words as he caught sight of Vetchim glaring at him from where he squatted beside the huge overscullion. Vetchim slowly began rising to his feet, a marshfish clenched in his hands.

"I . . . I . . . I meant no harm," the boy stuttered, blushing scarlet and looking awkwardly away.

"Bear no mind to him. He's just a foolish youth,"

Ansel laughed, her frown vanishing into a wide, dimpled smile as she turned away and began to scoop up the marshfish that were flapping at the edges of the reed bank. Vetchim watched the young barrower for a moment, muttering curses under his breath.

"Leave him, leave him," Ansel chided, tugging at Vetchim's sleeve. "We have too much to do catching our supper to worry over harmless kitchen talk."

It had not been that long ago that the people of the hall had said whatever they pleased, no matter how much it stung her feelings, and she rather enjoyed having Vetchim beside her watching over her.

Krann left them catching marshfish on the reed bank and hurried away.

The cluster of small fields that Marrimian had discovered lay close to a shallow river beyond a line of black ebonies and pink-barked trees. Krann found the hoemasters sitting nearby in heated debate about what seeds to plant where and how quickly the fields would flood once the wet seasons began.

"We will start to build the dyke over there where these fields meet the sheer rock face of the great ridge," Krann insisted, breaking into the argument and pointing from the high cliffs along the bank of the river and out into the marshes to where he could see Ansel. "It will stretch out into the reed bank, where we have just dug a channel, and sweep a great curve to the Hurlers' Gate. Yes, it will begin in the shadow of that waterfall where it cascades down the rock face of that last steep ridge."

"But all these fields will become a lake trapped by your dyke," grumbled a dozen voices in the crowd. "Any breaches in the dyke to allow the water to drain away will also allow the swollen marshes to flood back through."

"No, not if we raise the level of the fields and lay drainage channels over the top of the dyke," Krann answered slowly, catching sight of Treyster on the river bank and lifting his hand to wave. He smiled as he saw that she was carrying the bow of black ebony wood and quiver of arrows that he had fashioned for Marrimian on their journey across the marshes. He began to turn back toward the hoemasters when a flock of hill sheep clambering along a narrow ledge near the top of the closest ridge of rocks caught his eye and he beckoned secretly to Marrimian and whispered to her as she drew close to him.

"Take your bow back from Treyster and arrowstrike as many of the sheep on the ledge as you can before they scatter and vanish from sight. The scullions can draw and roast them over open fires here on the river bank. It will silence all those who grumble against you for not providing food and it will give your hall folk new heart to have full bellies and make them work all the harder." Krann paused and glanced over his shoulder at the wide expanse of marshes behind him.

"What is it?" Marrimian hissed drawing close, her hand tightening on the bow she had been given.

"The marshes seem too quiet," Krann warned. "I feel that we are being watched, it is as if a thousand eyes are staring silently at us."

Marrimian shivered and swept her gaze across the tall reed beds and toward the silent island of marshoaks that shimmered in the heat haze. "There could be an army of marshmen out there," she worried. "Pinvey could be crouched on any of those marshoak islands waiting to attack. We had better set more guards where you are building the dyke."

Krann nodded silently and then pointed up to the sheep. "And you had better be quick and arrow-gather those sheep."

"But I cannot kill them. I have never once loosed a single arrow against a living thing. You only schooled me to aim at dagger scratches on the marshoaks' bark."

"If Pinvey is out there waiting to attack us then you'll soon be killing more than sheep. You are our Queen, show them your strength," hissed Krann forcefully. "You must appear strong and afraid of nothing."

"I am always the one who has to do the grisliest tasks to prove my strength. I doubt if your ladies in Elundium would ever have to stoop to such slaughter. I doubt if your sister Elionbel or Fairlight would ever dirty their . . ." Marrimian hesitated, swallowing the last words of her sudden anger, as she saw the hurt she had caused him reflected in his eyes.

"My sister, the Queen of Elundium, fought at Thane's side and she has arrowstruck more enemies than I care to remember. Our warrior women are some of the best archers in the land and they would flinch at nothing when nocking a spine on to the string. And you forget, when you misjudge them, that they are not clamoring to be Queen."

Marrimian frowned and bit her lip, silently cursing the jealousy that had flared up inside her. "Forgive me," she whispered as Krann turned to face the large crowd of hoemasters and hall folk who had gathered to hear his wisdom on dykes and banks.

She reached and gently touched his sleeve, making him pause and look back over his shoulder. "I did not mean those hurtful words against Elionbel or Fairlight or any of your women of Elundium, but sometimes this struggle to prove my right to rule overawes me and the fear of Pinvey lurking in the shadows hones a brittle edge to my tongue."

Krann shook his head and laughed softly as their eyes met. "We cannot help but chafe and tear a little at each other's pride as we try to prepare against these wet seasons. Nothing worth doing is ever easy. Remember, as you draw back each arrow that you nock on to the bow string, to take a deep breath and think of Mertzork peering through the reed stems. Think of that treacherous healing woman watching you from a secret window in the Shambles as you sight the arrow shaft upon the sheep. Now, move closer to the ridge and do it quickly before anyone watching us sees you hesitate or the sheep move out of sight."

As he turned he heard her footsteps fade away

behind him and he looked at the sea of waiting faces. "What do I know of dykes and banks and keeping back the swollen marsh waters?" he muttered to himself as he racked his mind for every half-forgotten picture of the hill farms and terraces of Elundium that he must have ridden through a thousand times. He wished now that he had not dismissed it all with a casual glance. Dimly he remembered processions of people winding slowly up through the terraces carrying baskets of rocks and earth to fill the breaches the winter storms had caused to the wide stone walls.

"You must work in teams," he ordered, nodding gravely to give his counsel more weight. "And the strongest of you must carry baskets of rock and earth out on to that reed bank while the others lay the foundations and pound the earth in between the stones. It must be raised to the height of two men, stretching from the Hurlers' Gate in a great arc to that sheer wall of rock behind us. And while we build the dyke the scuttles and all the women of the hall can carry baskets of earth down from the higher ground to raise the levels of these fields behind the dyke. The hoemasters will ridge each finished strip of land and sow the seeds they gleaned from the wreckage of the crystal houses . . ." Krann paused for breath and anxiously glanced across the marsh toward the heavy thunder clouds that blackened the horizon. "We must hurry to raise the dyke before the weather breaks."

"But the path across the mire is only wide enough for one. It will take forever to carry the baskets of rock out on to the reed bank," cried a voice in the crowd.

Krann frowned as other voices rose, grumbling and muttering against building the dyke, saying how hopeless it was to start something that could not be finished. For a moment Krann's face darkened with anger beneath his fringe of frost-white hair. Why were these people from the hall so weak? Why did they shrink from the simplest tasks that they believed were beyond the endless routine of their narrow lives within the hall? But his face softened as he looked at their frightened, bewildered eyes and he saw that if they had been stronger or more adventurous Lord Miresnare would never have been able to rule them with such tyranny and then Marrimian would never have been able to claim the throne and the right to rule over them without an army to strengthen her claim. He looked out over the marshes to the marshoak islands as he tried to think up an answer to their grumbling.

"We could carry all the heaviest baskets of rock and earth across the mire during the frozen hours," called out a harvester. "The whole mire will be safe to cross once it has frozen."

Krann blinked and looked at the harvester. "Yes! Yes, of course, we could move a mountain of earth during the frozen hours."

"But we will freeze to death!" wailed a dozen ragmen's voices.

"We will lose our way and stumble over the reed bank in the darkness," cried a bencher.

Krann laughed and shook his head. "I will set torches here on the high ground and on the farther edge of the reed bank to light your way in the darkness and there will be extra guards to make sure you don't fall over it."

"Grumble, grumble, those ragmen and dusters are always complaining," called out a large thread-needle woman as she lifted a tall woven basket on to her shoulder and motioned to those who had been sitting with her to begin moving the earth from the higher levels. "Leave them here to grumble," she sneered, "And by the time they stop to draw breath we will have filled in the mire and made it safe for everyone to walk upon, frozen or not."

"It's not just the carrying and the cold we mind but what about all these guards? Whatever are you so afraid of? What is it out there that makes you keep staring at the reed beds?" asked one of the ragmen.

Krann tried to laugh. "Oh, they are keeping watch for mudbeasts."

"Marshmen more like. You are afraid of that murderous Mertzork attacking us, aren't you?" insisted the harvester.

Krann tried to smile at the cluster of women as they hesitated and crowded together and he opened his mouth to urge them forward when a ragged, untidy figure sprang up from the shadows of one of the low walls. "There are no marshmen out there in the reeds. I should know, I was out there before the sun came up. I am not afraid to go out there now and cut an armful of reeds to lie with each basketful of earth. If we lay them together it will stop the soil from washing away when the wet seasons begin."

"Well, if the reedcutter says there are no marshmen out there I believe him," cried one of the women.

"But he cannot work with us, he's not one of the hall folk. He has no right to be here," grumbled a hoemaster.

"There are rumors in the city that Marrimian, the firstborn, has claimed the throne and that she is a just Queen who feeds all those who pledge themselves to her," stuttered the reedcutter, stepping back a pace as angry faces turned toward him and figures half rose to chant and curse him.

"All are welcome," Krann began, when an arrow shrieked through the air behind him. The bleating cry of a ravine sheep and the musical rattle of its bell were cut short as, arrowstruck just behind the shoulder, it reared up and plunged from the ledge on to the rough ground below.

"Look! See how our Queen handles that long bow of black ebony wood better than most of her father's archers," murmured a chorus of voices, anger against the reedcutter forgotten as the folk watched another two of the ravine sheep plunge to their deaths with arrows through their hearts.

"She is a great lady," cried one of the ragmen in anticipation of roast supper.

Krann smiled and quietly beckoned the reedcutter forward. "You could serve your Queen well by keeping a sharp eye open for marshlords while you are cutting the reeds," he whispered, "and it would earn you a place at her table if you would bring her word of everything you see." The crowd had moved away from the reedcutter, their minds and eyes fixed on Marrimian as she reached back into the quiver for another arrow. The young man nodded, bowed hurriedly and ran down the path that led to the reed bank.

Marrimian, deaf to the rising murmur of approval from the crowds behind her, gritted her teeth and tried to shut out the bleating screams of the ravine sheep as they reared and scrambled to escape, running backwards and forwards along the ledge. Krann slipped through the crowd of hall folk and hurried to her side.

"You have arrow-gathered enough sheep to feed everyone laboring here on the edges of the marsh," he said quietly, putting his hand on her arm. "Now you must organize the scullions to dig fire pits and send the scuttles to gather fuel." Krann hesitated as his eyes followed the remnants of the flock of sheep scrambling along the ledge toward the higher ridges, their bells clattering shrilly in the narrow gullies and deep ravines that lay hidden by the towering spires of wind-cracked rocks. "Perhaps we should catch those sheep before they vanish," he murmured.

"Why?" frowned Marrimian, reaching back for another arrow as she raised her bow. "They would be better smoked or salted for us to eat during the wet seasons."

"But if we caught them I think we could milk

them and make cheese," Krann began. He wasn't at all sure how you milked a sheep or made cheese but he caught sight of Ansel and Vetchim climbing up out of the marsh on to firmer ground and breathed a sigh of relief. "Ask Ansel, I'm sure she knows, she will tell you."

"Cheese? Rounds of hard cheese are only served at the lower tables," Marrimian sneered, but she hesitated as she realized that the days of high and low tables were a thing of the past and that they must harvest everything if they were to survive the wet seasons. "I will send the nimblest scuttles up on to those ledges to catch the sheep," she answered, turning back toward the marsh to call for the youngest barrowers and scuttles but she gave a cry of surprise and almost dropped the bow from her hand as she saw the heavy baskets and bulging sacks of flapping, wriggling marshfish that Ansel and a dozen scullions were carrying between them.

"Where are you going with all those fish? Where did you catch them all?" she laughed as a large, black-scaled marshfish jumped out of Ansel's apron pocket and flapped its spiked tail in the air.

"Ankana, quickly, come here," Marrimian cried. "Bring the children, tell them to leave those baskets of earth that they are filling and come over here to see the marshfish that Ansel has caught. Soon we shall have such a feast."

"The marshes are full of fish if you know where to catch them," muttered Vetchim, wiping the black marsh slime off his hands.

"But only half of these fish are for eating, mistress," interrupted Ansel, puffing out her cheeks. "We must save the rest and use them to breed more fish."

She muttered, glaring at the noisy children who had crowded around her and were bending down and picking up the flapping fish and tossing them into the air with shouts of delight. "Every scrap of food is precious—these fish are not playthings, they must not be wasted," she grumbled, snatching one up and pushing the children away from her apron tails as she stowed it in her pocket.

Marrimian frowned at Ansel. "You must be gentler with the children," she chided.

"There are plenty of fish for them to tickle in the marsh. But we must hurry if we are to make a fish moat over there in those hollow rocks," Ansel explained, hoping to excuse her impatience with the children as she cleaned the slimy mud and fish scales from her fingers. She pointed past the long, winding procession of ragmen and dusters who had begun to carry their heavy baskets of rock and earth down to the narrow path that led out on to the reed banks. "That would be the best place for a fish moat, in that outcrop of rocks," she said.

"But why don't you carry the fish back up into the city and use the fish moats there? They are already dug and lined with stones," Marrimian said, trying to suppress her laughter at the ooze of slime and mud leaking out of the scullion's voluminous pocket and through the bottoms of the sacks and baskets. "Surely all the fish will be dead by the time you have filled those rock hollows with mud and water?"

Ansel glanced darkly at the steep, gabled roofs of the city in the distance and shook her head. "There'll be nothing to eat in the city soon and I'll not stock the city folks' larders for them. The fish that die we will eat; the rest will breed in the rock pools for us to catch in the wet seasons."

Marrimian turned and followed the scullion's eyes toward the city and a fear that had nagged at the edges of her mind since they had passed through the Hurlers' Gate rose to the surface. She remembered all the grim-faced, silent folk who had stared out of every door arch and window crack as she led the people of the hall down through the city.

Five times Marrimian had brought the procession to a halt and proclaimed that she now ruled in her father's place but no one had come forward. Each time she had called for the city folk to follow her and plant the seeds of the future along the edges of the quickmarsh, but the ironmasters, chandlers and wheelwrights had all sneered at her. Her voice had been drowned out by the slamming of their doors and the rattling of their closing window latches; but worse than the heavy silence that followed, muffling the city, had been the faintest echo of laughter, of wild crones' cackling, though no one else in the procession had seemed to hear it. The laughter had been in the air at every dark twist and turn in the lower lanes and steep winding alleyways, laughter that threaded Pinvey and Mertzork's names within its mocking whispers and sent

cold shivers of helplessness down Marrimian's
spine. She blinked and shook her head to dispel the
hollow feeling of dread that gnawed at her bones
and she caught Ansel's arm.

"You had better hurry. Go quickly before all that
stinking mireslime drains out of your apron
pocket," she cried, urging all the scullions loaded
down with sacks and baskets of wriggling marshfish to hurry toward the outcrop of hollow rocks.
"Some of the children can help you to fill the hollow with mud and water," she shouted as Ansel
vanished amongst the heavily burdened lines of hall
folk carrying their baskets of rocks and earth down
to the quickmarsh.

Marrimian divided up the children and sent the
eldest ones to follow Ansel while the youngest went
back to help Ankana scoop the rich, dark earth into
baskets.

"The sheep, we must catch the sheep," Marrimian frowned, picking out a dozen of the nimblest barrowers and scuttles from the passing lines
of workers and sending them armed with crudely
woven rope halters to scramble on the narrow
ledges of the great spines of rock that towered behind Glitterspike Hall and catch as many of the
ravine sheep and hill goats as they could find.

The reedcutter suddenly appeared through the
bustling crowds and bowed hurriedly before Marrimian. "There were marshmen on the furthest
reed bank a way beyond the dyke, but they vanished when they saw me watching them."

Marrimian frowned and lifted her bow. "Was my

sister Pinvey or Mertzork amongst them?" she asked quickly.

The reedcutter shook his head. "They were too far away to see, my lady. I can't say how many were there."

"Were they armed?" Krann asked, looking anxiously across the marshes.

"I saw only four or five of them clearly, ragged-looking hunters with iron spikes."

Treasel called out and waved, making them look up. She was leading a long line of kitchen girls up from the marshes, their arms laden with dripping marsh roots and flowering vines that they must have just gathered from the far side of the reed bank.

"These will sweeten our tongues and fill our bellies . . ." She gasped as she caught sight of the rows of sheep carcasses that lay beside the freshly dug fire pits, but before she could ask about them Marrimian took her aside.

"Did you see any marshmen hiding in the reeds?" she hissed.

Treasel nodded. "Yes, out there beyond those marshoak islands. But they vanished when they thought we had noticed them."

Marrimian turned and gazed out over the marshes. A hoemaster caught her attention by coughing politely and asked about building reed shelters for those who were resting or eating so that they would be protected against the frozen hours of darkness. Marrimian tried to turn back toward the crowds, only to face more questions on every side.

"Watch the marshes closely. Guard the dyke builders, but do not use your bow unless they are attacked," she called, thrusting the bow into Krann's
hands.

"You will need cauldrons to boil those roots. Collect as many as you can carry from the hall kitchens,
ask Ansel," she muttered to some scullions, turning
as her eyes swept over the higher ground in search
of the best place to build shelters against the cold.

"Build the shelters up there amongst those rocks,
between the rows of gnarled marshoaks, near the
drainage channels," she ordered the waiting hoemasters before she listened to the bewildered dusters who had sought her advice about moving a large
rock. She quickly sent them to where Krann stood
amongst huge piles of stone with the bow of black
ebony in his hand, telling them that he would know
best.

But no matter how hard she worked or how
many questions were asked of her on every side she
could not forget the smoldering anger in the eyes of
the city people as they closed their doors against her
and she worried about what they would do when
hunger had tightened their belts and the wet seasons began.

Sudden angry voices from the fire pits made Marrimian frown. She could hear Ansel's voice above
the others shouting them down and quickly sent
away all those who had crowded around her with
their questions and slipped through the slow-
moving lines of ragmen and dusters, bent beneath
their heavy baskets, and climbed up to the higher

ground. Ansel was standing beside a fire pit, her fat legs splayed apart, her hands on her hips, towering over a frightened scuttle.

"I won't have it, mistress, not in the kitchens of the hall, or here on the edges of the quickmarsh," Ansel thundered, her face blotched with anger as she glanced over her shoulder toward Marrimian. "The moment my back is turned to organize the fish moats these scuttles ruin the meat. Look! Look at those carcasses over there with their dirty fleece and skin still hanging in ragged strips. These girls were ready to roast them with half the entrails still dangling between their hind legs. They would not be fit to serve to the lowest marshscum, let alone to the Queen of Gnarlsmyre and the people of her hall."

"But the marshmen stole the sharp gutting knives from the kitchens and there are no gutting slabs out here," wailed the frightened scuttle. "Every time we tried to skin the carcasses they slipped and dragged in the dirt and . . . and . . ." The scuttle burst into tears and crawled toward Marrimian as she begged protection from Ansel's rage.

"There's no excuse," grumbled Ansel, advancing on the scuttle. "You should have spread reeds beneath the carcasses." And she reached down and took the scuttle's gutting knife out of her hand and pressed her own plump-fingered one against the cutting edge.

Marrimian looked down at the scuttle. Part of her wanted to smile and soothe her and send her into a shadowy corner of the kitchen to wipe at her tears, but this rough strip of ground was their kitchen and the rocks and bare earth where they stood were their tables and chairs. They could not return to the hall until the dyke and terraces were finished and the seeds and shoots planted. The thunderstorms were coming closer with every hour and every mouthful of food was precious. "Ansel is the overscullion. I will not cast my shadow over her judgments; it is to her you must plead, but . . ." Marrimian paused, her face drawn and serious, "if she finds that it was your laziness in the honing that caused your gutting knife to be blunt and spoil the meat then I will judge you before the people of the hall who labor here on the edges of the marsh and with their hunger they shall set your punishment."

"None of us has ever gutted or skinned a beast on our own before," cried the scuttle. "No one has ever shown us how to hone a gutting knife, but we did try to sharpen them with those stones over there beside the fire pits. Look, you can see the marks our blades have made upon them."

Ansel's face softened. "Scuttles!" she grumbled. "Why did none of you speak up?"

Another of the frightened scuttles crept forward. "You were in such a rush, throwing orders over your shoulders, none of us dared to ask you or answer you back, but we did the best we could."

"How would you judge them, Ansel, overscullion?" Marrimian asked, catching her eye.

Ansel frowned and puffed out her cheeks as she bent down and searched amongst the jumble of stones and rocks that littered the rough ground around the fire pits. "First," she muttered, selecting exactly the right sharpstone and picking it up, fitting it snugly into the palm of her hand. "Firstly I will teach them how to hone a sharp edge to their knives and then I will overwatch the skinning and the gutting of these carcasses, but I will ask you, mistress, as our Queen, to judge if they have cooked them to your satisfaction. You must judge if the meat is fit to eat."

Marrimian laughed, pleased that Ansel had taken the scuttles under her wing rather than chiding and making them cower with harsh words, and it made her smile secretly to see the respect the scuttles held for her as they followed her every movement and hung on her every word of kitchen wisdom. She remembered how, before her father Lord Miresnare had driven her and Ansel out of the hall to perish in the frozen darkness, the scuttles had mocked and cruelly teased the overscullion in the kitchens of the hall.

"Will you light the fire pits, mistress?" Ansel called, looking up, and she caught the smile in Marrimian's eyes. She blushed with pleasure and fussed around the scuttles as she heard the spark light and the sharp crackles of the flames spreading through the kindling wood.

Marrimian yawned as she wondered how many days had passed since they had begun to build the dyke and raise the cluster of small fields into steep narrow terraces that stretched from the sheer spire of rocks down to the lip of the dyke where it looped out into the marsh. Night and day had seemed to blend together in a never-ending stream of heavy baskets of rock and earth and she had hardly noticed the frozen hours of darkness as she labored in the guttering torchlight between the steeply ridged rows of young shoots and seeds that the hoemasters had planted in the terraces. She had taken her turn along with all the other hall folk pounding the stones that formed the drainage channels firmly down between the rows, and it was only now as she sat on the highest terrace snatching a moment's rest, huddled inside her cloak against the frozen hours and picking clean the bones of a boiled marshfish that Ansel had brought her, that she felt the bitter marsh winds ruffle her dirty hair and shivered. She threw the bones of the fish away and spat out the sharp grains of sand and dirt that ground between her teeth.

"It's impossible, mistress. It matters not how many times the scuttles wash the meat and fish that they prepare, sometimes more than a dozen times, and they use whole bundles of reeds to lay it on before they cook it, but the dirt still creeps into everything," apologized Ansel, brushing at the streaks of dirt on Marrimian's gown.

Marrimian pushed her hand away. "The night wind has changed direction. Can you feel it?" she muttered, half rising as she watched the billowing swirl of smoke from the fire pits that had been drifting between the flickering torches set on the high rim of the dyke. The smoke was eddying and swirling back across the terraces and drifting toward the city, carrying with it the mouth-watering smells of their roasting meats and fish.

"I can feel a dampness in the wind," answered Krann through a mouthful of boiled marsh roots from where he sat, two rows below her in the terraces.

"There is a smell of wet mangle roots in the air," whispered Treasel, "that always means that the wet seasons have begun to flood the marsheries beyond the Fenmire reed beds."

"How soon will it begin to rain?" Krann asked, quickly swallowing the last of the slippery roots and rubbing his gritty fingers together to clean off the worst of the dirt.

Vetchim leaned forward and scented the icy night wind from where he crouched beside Ansel. "Two days—perhaps three . . ." he began, when suddenly screams and shouts near the fire pits brought everyone leaping to their feet.

"Look down there, the city folk are raiding our kitchens. They are stealing the spit-roasting carcasses," shouted Ansel, hurling aside the spiked tail fin of the marshfish she had been sharing with Vetchim and catching at his sleeve. The two of them leapt to their feet and ran toward the wide wall that bordered the terrace, tripping and stumbling over the steep ridges and furrows of earth.

"The bow of black ebony—quickly, use it. Climb up on to that wall, it overlooks the fires," Krann shouted to Marrimian, thrusting the bow into her hands as he leapt to his feet and snatched up the closest guttering torch. "Follow Ansel and Vetchim down to the fire pits," he cried to the others who had been chewing on strips of roasted meat and boiled marshfish with them on the high terrace. "Help the scullion drive the city folk away from the fire pits and out into the center of the terrace. Then we can surround them."

Marrimian clambered on to the high wall that bordered the terrace, snagging the hems of her skirts on the rough-laid stone. As she stood upright her fingers trembled and she reached back into the heavy quiver slung from her shoulder, feeling for an arrow. She looked down across the rows of terraces toward the shadowy figures who were running and scattering back toward the Hurlers' Gate in the flickering torchlight. She nocked an arrow on to the bow string and sucked in a shallow breath. She felt her anger tighten and steady her fingers. She felt anger that these same people of the city whom she had offered a place here beside her planting for the future should try to steal what they would not work for. Narrowing her eyes, she tensed her arm and drew the arrow back until the flight feathers lightly touched her cheek.

"Where are you, thieves?" she muttered, searching the milling crowds fanning out through the steeply ridged furrows. Hesitating, she eased the arrow and began to lower the bow. It was impossible to tell amongst the leaping shadows who were the thieves and who were the hall folk.

Suddenly Marrimian caught sight of two swarthy figures, ironmasters by the look of their clothes. They were running toward the dyke on the edge of the torchlight, carrying a ravine sheep carcass still slung on its roasting spit between them. "Thieves!" she hissed through tight lips as she lifted her bow and loosed two arrows that shrieked through the darkness toward the dyke. One of the ironmasters screamed and stumbled forward. The heavy carcass slipped from his shoulder and fell into a drainage furrow between two freshly planted ridges of earth.

The other ironmaster cursed and pulled the wounded man toward the steep side of the dyke. He glanced fearfully over his shoulder as Marrimian loosed another arrow that buried itself in the steep bank a handspan from his feet.

Krann and Vetchim, leading the strongest hoe-masters and dusters and a grim-faced line of kitchen folk along the walls of the lower terraces, quickly surrounded the city folk and hemmed them in within a ring of flickering torches.

"Kill them! Drive them into the marshes!" shouted angry voices in their closing circle.

Marrimian heard the anger and hatred that boiled up in the voices of both the hall folk and the city folk and she quickly lowered the bow and jumped lightly down to the next terrace. She began to run toward them following a wide drainage channel down into the flickering circle of torchlight.

"There will be no killing!" she shouted breathlessly, bursting through the line of scullions as the uninjured ironmaster on the top of the dyke sneered and goaded the hall folk, and urged the city folk to attack.

"Call yourself a queen, a leader," he spat. "You are no more than a weak prettier and you are wrong if you think that this rag-bag of hall folk can stop us taking what we want!" He spat again and began to climb back down toward the sheep carcass where it lay half hidden between the furrows.

"Be still!" Marrimian whispered to Krann as he made to leap at the ironmaster. "I am the Queen and I must show these city people that I have the strength."

Marrimian reached back into her quiver and drew out an arrow and nocked it on to the bow string. For the merest moment, no more than a flicker of an eyelash in the torchlight, she hesitated. The bleating cries of the ravine sheep that she had slaughtered to feed her people still haunted her and she had felt sick and dizzy after loosing the two arrows at the ironmasters. She knew that it was anger that had steadied her hand but the anger had gone now and in its place was a cold dread knotting her stomach and paralyzing her muscles as she tried to draw the bowstring tight.

The ironmaster saw her hesitate and laughed, sensing her weakness, and he reached out with blackened hands to snatch at the iron handles of the roasting spit skewered through the body of the sheep. "You are a weak woman who doesn't have the stomach for killing or the strength to stop us from taking what we want. Know your place, prettier—scrabbling for scraps beneath my table!"

The ironmaster's sneering words cut Marrimian to the quick and she heard in them the echo of so many of the cruel taunts that her father had hurled at her for being a daughter—a mere woman—and her fingers burned and tightened around the bowstring as the muscles tensed in her arms.

"No! You will take nothing that you have not worked for," she answered quietly as she sighted her arrow, and her voice was now edged sharper than the cutting knife in Ansel's hand.

"Queens cannot rule in Glitterspike Hall," the ironmaster scoffed, deaf to the firmness in her voice and the groaning creak of the bow as she pulled it taut.

"You'll next be telling us that there's truth in the rumors that you rode upon a mudbeast and walked unharmed through the circle of beasts to touch . . ." The arrow shrieked across the terrace, cutting short his words as it struck the ironmaster in the center of his chest, driving him backwards and pinning him against the steep wall of the dyke. He gasped and clutched with desperate fingers at the arrow shaft, his eyes bulging in disbelief. His mouth opened and closed as blood bubbled up into his throat and dribbled out of his open mouth, down his chin. He kicked out once and slumped forward, tearing the blade of the arrow free from the bank of earth and rock as he fell.

"Who else will dare doubt me?" Marrimian asked as she reached for another arrow, her voice cutting through the startled silence that filled the circle of flickering torchlight. "Who else will step forward and touch that sheep's carcass or try to take what we have labored to build here on the edge of the quickmarsh?"

A frightened whisper spread through the people of the city. They edged closer together, trampling the rows of neatly ridged and freshly planted crops as they looked for a way to break out of the circle.

The wounded ironmaster on the top of the bank struggled to his feet. "Run! Flee!" he shouted. "She can't kill us all at once. Run back toward the Hurlers' Gate. These hall people and that queen don't know the ways of the city folk; they will never be able to find us in the maze of lanes and alleyways. Lord Miresnare's archers will help us hunt her and her hall folk down as they try to return to Glitterspike Hall."

The whispers within the circle hushed to nothing. The city folk drew tightly together, their eyes glittering in the torchlight as they sought the weakest spot in the circle. Suddenly, with a great shout, they surged forward toward the line of scullions. There they met gutting knives, fire irons and blackened roasting spits in the shadowy darkness. The city folk with their daggers and spears fought desperately to break through the scullions' line. Marrimian saw bloody blades rising and falling in the torchlight and all around her she heard screams of agony.

"Enough! Enough!" she shouted, making all those who fought within the circle hesitate. "There will be no more killing. I will not have these terraces run with the blood of any more of my people," she cried.

Reluctantly the hall folk drew back, muttering and cursing, but they left wide gaps in their circle of torches for the city folk to pass through.

"There will be a place and food for everyone who accepts me as their Queen and who works with me for the future," she called out as the city folk began to slip through the gaps in tight, defensive groups.

"Food," sneered a voice among the city folk. "Everything that you have planted will flood and wash over that silly dyke into the marsh or vanish beneath a lake of flood water."

"There are drainage channels . . ." Marrimian began angrily but another voice laughed.

"You'll never be able to harvest anything, not until the wet seasons have passed and the raging torrents that pour down every lane and alleyway and boil through the Hurlers' Gate have dried up. And even if you can find a way down through the city we will be waiting for you and we will pick you off one by one, and if you stay locked up within the hall you will have starved to death long before the end of the rains!"

Before Marrimian had a chance to answer someone sneered, "Anyway we shall have the food the healing woman has promised us."

"I will barter with you during the wet seasons," Marrimian shouted. "There is no food in the city; the crystal houses are destroyed. When the healing woman fails to keep her pledge to you and your belts tighten with hunger, if you bring the products of your skills to the doors of the hall I will exchange them for the food grown in these terraces at the marshes' edge. Now let us see who will keep and who will break their promises."

But the escaping crowds merely laughed at her and ran heedlessly through the terraces, crushing the newly planted shoots and seedlings carelessly beneath their boots, causing as much ruin and destruction as they possibly could before they reached the steep dyke where it was banked up against the sheer wall of the city twenty paces from the Hurlers' Gate. For a moment they were silhouetted on the rim of the dyke against the torchlight that spilled through the high arches of the gateway. Cursing, they shook their fists and tore up the loosest rocks and stones from the top of the dyke and hurled them at the terraces. They sneered and laughed at Marrimian for sparing their lives and mocked at her for showing them that she was a weak and worthless prettier.

"If the city folk start attacking us when we pass through the Hurlers' Gate then we'll never reach the hall again and we will drown out here without proper shelters when the rains begin," cried a ragman.

"You should have let us slit their throats, mistress: that would have silenced them. Then they wouldn't be able to hide in the dark alleyways and wait to waylay and murder us," grumbled Ansel, wading between the steep rows of earth to look at the dirt-encrusted carcass of the sheep where the ironmasters had dropped it.

"No, Ansel," Marrimian answered firmly. "I showed my strength merely to a handful of iron-masters and wheelwrights, but if we had killed them all we would have had the whole city turn against us."

"We must find another way to travel up and down from the hall," muttered Krann almost to himself as he scratched at the burning itches that had suddenly broken out on the backs of his hands and all over his face.

"I think there is a narrow path that twists and snakes up over that spine of rocks behind the hall," called out one of the scuttles, blushing and stumbling forward into the torchlight as two of her friends gave her a forceful shove. "We followed it when we were gathering up the ravine sheep and it took us less than ten strides away from the top of the city wall. You can almost reach out and touch the tall, reed-woven window screens set high in the wall of the herb larders just beyond Ansel's kitchens."

"We must search out this path at once," urged Krann slapping at his cheeks and raking his fingers through his hair.

"What's the matter with Krann and the children? What's making them scratch?" frowned Marrimian. The air around them was very still and her voice seemed to echo all about her, and then her skin too began to itch and burn.

"It's the thunder mites," Treasel laughed, lifting up her forearm into the torchlight to show how it was covered with a wriggling mass of tiny black insects no larger than the point of an embroiderer's needle.

"Krann is not used to our thunder mites and they burn his skin, just like they are burning the children's." The little girls were screaming and crying as they fled to hide beneath Ankana's apron. "Quickly, we must cover them with a layer of mireslime: that will soothe their skin and kill the mites."

"Listen! The rumbles of thunder are getting closer," Treyster warned, touching Marrimian's arm. "Somehow we must set guards to stop the city folk from destroying these dykes and terraces."

Krann shuddered as the icy cold mireslime the scuttles poured over his head trickled down the back of his neck, but he was relieved that it stopped the terrible burning sensation.

"We will need straight-grained wood from the black ebony trees that grow beside the river to make bows and spear shafts. We must arm ourselves in case the city folk try and attack again. Choose the strongest of the hoemasters and ask them to drag every seasoned, windblown bough they can find up to the top of the highest terrace. Everyone can help to carry them up from there and into the hall. Take Syrenea with you to help search out the straightest boughs. Be quick," he called to Treyster.

"Crones! Filthy crones," shouted Ansel, making everyone on the terrace turn abruptly toward her and then follow her pointing finger toward the Hurlers' Gate where the black-ragged hags had suddenly appeared, spinning and dancing on the rim of the dyke in the shadow of the Hurlers' Gate.

"I wish we had caught those foul hags when we had the chance, before we entered the hall and you touched the Glitterspike, mistress. I would have wrung their miserable, treacherous necks. I'll lay my cleanest apron on it that the crones and that healing woman, Erek, are the ones who goaded the city people into attacking us and trying to steal what little food we have."

Marrimian watched the crones disappear one by one as their cackling shrieks of laughter faded away into the heavy thunderous air. "No," she answered wearily, shaking her head. "Killing them would have been my father's way. He ruled this city and all the dry lands of Gnarlsmyre with bloody hands and I will not tread willingly in his footprints. Have you forgotten already, Ansel, that Erek told us how he sacked the Shambles in search of magic to sire an heir and how he drove all the healing women out into the quickmarshes to perish because they could not conjure up what he desired? Well, I'll wager all the precious heartstones in the Glitterspike against your apron that those wretched crones you would strangle without a moment's thought are all that remain of those helpless healing women that my father banished."

"But they threw venomous spiders at us! And they dealt in treachery by helping your sister, Pinvey, and Mertzork—and I have heard you curse Naul, the master mumbler, when you realized that he was one of them. Why have you suddenly allowed your mind to change and find pity for them, mistress?" Ansel muttered, frowning, at a loss to understand her Queen as she snapped her fingers at the closest of the scuttles and hurried them as they dragged the sheep's carcass up out of the dirt and took it away to wash it thoroughly.

Krann smiled at Marrimian's judgments of the city folk and the crones, and cracked the layer of marshslime that had dried across his face. Marrimian was showing a real glimpse of compassion and he knew that it would give her great strength. In time it would be the one quality above all others that her people would love her for. He had seen it when fate first crossed their paths in the water meadows, but then it had been the merest whisper beneath her sometimes brittle surface.

Marrimian laughed softly. "I do not like them more, Ansel, only I seem to see them more clearly now. I see them for what they are, the helpless victims of my father's madness." Frowning, she turned on the scullion. "What would *you* have done, Ansel? What would you have done if the healing woman had ruled over your kitchens and endlessly plagued and terrorized you to serve up dishes that were beyond their season. What would you have done if she had beaten the scuttles and driven the cooks and scullions out beyond the Hurlers' Gate to perish in the marshes? Surely anger would have gnawed at your heart and revenge would have blackened and twisted you, and perhaps with the passing of the seasons that revenge would have goaded you into poisoning a sweetmeat or souring the wine into vinegar."

"Well, they make my skin crawl with their cackling laughter and those riddles of sticky black rags that they wear that always seem to cloak them in so many shadows," muttered Ansel.

"I'm sure that the riddle of rags is a disguise—a protection," Marrimian began, when Treasel suddenly called out, and as she lifted up her hands to shout the first glistening drops of water fell.

"The rains! Quickly, mistress, quickly, we must seek shelter. The rains have begun!"

10

A Bundle of Bright Lilies

*P*INVEY began to descend the rickety ladder as she followed Mertzork down from the cluster of hovels that she had chosen as her royal chambers in the marshery, but she paused as she drew level with the cage of woven branches where she kept Andzey and Alea as prisoners. She watched the swarm of spiders that clung to the webs they had woven on their clothing and between the bars of the cage and she sneered at their wretchedness as she carelessly threw a strip of maggoty, half-eaten, raw flesh into their cage.

"Eat it, sister, or I will whisper and those spiders will nip you," she gloated, bubbling with delight at the blanching look of horror that crossed Alea's mire-smeared face as she hesitated and then slowly reached with trembling fingers for the meat.

Andzey laughed and spat at Alea, then snatched up the strip of crawling flesh before she could touch it and crammed it into his mouth. "Make the spiders bite her," he growled through a mouth full of meat, a triumphant smile creasing the corners of his mouth and spreading across his bloated cheeks, yet his eyes were hard as he held Pinvey's gaze.

Pinvey snarled and hissed at him in anger for spoiling her moment of pleasure as she taunted her sister, for she had known better than anyone in Glitterspike Hall how squeamish Alea was about her food and nothing had delighted Pinvey more than to slip wriggling insects into her pottage or to spit on her meat and then whisper about what she had done moments after Alea had swallowed it.

"Steal the feasts that I throw to her! Starve her if you like, but I will find something much more tasty and I will have your hands bound behind your back before I force her to eat it," she sneered, turning her head and glancing down as she heard Mertzork calling to her, urging her to hurry. He wanted to start the wrestling jousts and sharpwire contests to choose the strongest and most cunning captains for their assault on Glitterspike Hall. The sneer on her face hardened into a glare of hatred as she watched Mertzork jump to the ground and thrust aside the throng of kneeling marsh people, treading on feet and fingers as he strode toward the thrones that stood on the highest footstep of the dry land of the marshery.

"Thrones!" she muttered with contempt as she glanced at the two roughly carved chairs he had forced the elders to whittle from the thickest boughs of the marshoaks that grew on a small island beyond the reed beds and the channel of mud. They could have been a mockery of the crudest scuttles' chairs crowding the darkest corners of the kitchens of Glitterspike Hall but to these miserable marsh people they were a symbol of power and she knew that, no matter how fast she clambered down the ladder and ran across the backs of the kneeling throng that crowded the foot of her hovel, Mertzork would reach the thrones before her, and to thwart and spite her he would choose the one that was set slightly higher, with the softer, reed-woven seat.

"Move closer together and kneel very still or I will reach down and slit your throats," Pinvey hissed at the huddled marsh people below her as she reached the foot of the ladder and began to walk out across their backs, moving as quickly as she could without appearing to hurry. She had no intention of dirtying her feet in the filthy refuse of the marshery or allowing the bubbling, stinking mud of the channel that surrounded it to touch her skin and her first task as the Queen of these wretched people had been to make sure that they kneeled or lay for her to walk across whenever she descended from her chamber. She had made them clear a path through the mounds of rubbish so that Andzey would not trip or stumble and throw her if she rode him out into the reed beds.

The moment that Pinvey descended and her eyes vanished below the level of their tiny cage Andzey spat out the mouthful of rotten, maggot-crawling meat, his face gaunt and twisted with disgust. "That will teach her to try to torment you," he muttered, smiling softly at Alea, and he reached out to try to wipe her arm where he had spat at her.

Alea shrank away from him and turned her head away. "Don't touch me," she hissed.

His face darkened in confusion and he snatched back his hand. "I was only trying to help you, to save you from having to eat that rotten strip of meat," and he sat back on his haunches as he probed and prodded inside his mouth, scraping out a handful of the fat white maggots that must have wriggled out of the meat and crawled into every soft fleshy corner of his mouth. Spitting and choking, he hurled the maggots through the bars and snatched up the strip of crawling flesh and threw it after them into the bubbling mud of the channel. He cursed bitterly at Mertzork and Pinvey for what they had done to them.

Alea shuddered and drew further away from him, pressing herself against the bars. "She hates being thwarted. She'll do something much worse next time if she guesses that you are trying to help me," she whispered miserably, "and if you push her anger too far she'll make the spiders bite us. What then? What when she finds that we have milked their venom and drawn their teeth? She'll probably have some of those marshmen kill us, the ones who follow her everywhere. That is if she doesn't dagger us to death herself."

Andzey shook his head and brushed aside the scuttling spiders, tearing through the webs that they had spun across Alea's sleeves and bodice, and he tried to touch her and draw her toward him.

"No, don't," she cried angrily. "It's wretched enough being here as a prisoner without you trying to maul me all the time. I'm sick of being touched."

Andzey threw up his hands in despair. "We are both prisoners. Perhaps together as friends we could find a way to thwart them before the wet seasons end and they march on Glitterspike Hall, because I am sure that they will kill us before they leave the marshery."

"Friends? Make friends with a marshman? Do you think I'm mad?" Alea snapped, turning on him angrily. "Do you think I would spend one moment with you if . . ." She fell silent and looked away, ashamed of her anger, ashamed that she had attacked him yet again when he had tried to help her, but it unnerved her being so close to this wild marshman. She had expected him to maul her once they had milked the spiders' venom, to take her for his pleasure whenever he wanted to, but he had not, he had been gentle and kind and she felt confused and angry.

Andzey sighed and thoughtfully dangled a spider by its thread from his fingertip, spinning it slowly around and around. "No matter how much you hate me we must work together or they will kill us. Remember, if she does make the spiders bite us we must yell and scream and thrash our arms and legs. I'm sure she'll be too impatient to watch us for long."

"She'll never fall for that. I should know, I know how cunning, how hateful, how . . ." Alea fell silent and large tears of helplessness blurred her eyes and trickled down her dirty cheeks.

"No! No, that's where you are wrong. Impatience is one of Pinvey's greatest weaknesses," hissed Andzey fiercely. "I have watched her just as closely as I watch my brother flex his greed and practice his lies and treachery and I am beginning to know every tender spot, every weakness, in both of them, even those weaknesses that they have not realized in themselves."

"Yet Mertzork captured you so easily before the Hurlers' Gate," Alea answered harshly, turning on him with a sharp edge to her voice. "If you had known him that well we would not be their prisoners now, would we?"

"He had changed," Andzey muttered. "He had become more murderous and more clever with his lies. I never thought for one moment that the healing woman and those crones would cast their spells over the marshmen, and suddenly I was alone against him."

"There you see—it's hopeless! Even working together won't make any difference, we'll never find a weakness in either of them," whispered Alea in despair.

Andzey laughed softly. "That's where you are wrong. Look at them both, so wrapped up in their jealousies and hatreds."

Alea pressed her cheek against the bars of their cage and looked down toward the two thrones.

"There is a bitter rivalry between them," he whispered, his face splitting into a grin. "It is born out of their selfish thirst for power. Watch them closely and look at the way Mertzork leers and laughs at your sister as he sprawls in the higher of the two thrones, dirtying the seat of her chair with his marsh-smeared feet. And look how her eyes have narrowed with anger and her lips have thinned and become pinched as she strives to hide her hatred of him and to control it before the people of the marshery. It is one thing to force the people to kneel while she treads them down and quite another for her to swallow Mertzork's taunts before them. Their rivalry is their weakness, I am sure of it!"

Alea looked down between the forest of rickety stilts that supported the huts and she shivered as she watched her sister reach her throne. All trace of rivalry seemed to vanish as Mertzork and Pinvey touched and momentarily clung together before Mertzork broke free of her and lifted his hand to signal for the wrestling jousts to begin. But there was a ruthless coldness in their shrieks of pitiless laughter as the champion of the joust suffocated his helpless victims in the shallow mud on the edge of the marshery and the brutality of it all made the hairs on the nape of Alea's neck prickle with horror. She shook her head.

"It is hopeless to think that we can ever overwhelm them. Look! Look how the people of the marshery laugh and clap with them and the young hunters and waders crowd around Pinvey's throne seeking to touch her. Together they have so much power over your people."

Andzey looked down and swept his gaze across the kneeling throng who had crowded in behind the thrones and he smiled as he saw how they watched Pinvey and Mertzork and all the favorites they had chosen, following their every movement with a look of veiled hatred in their eyes. "A handful follow them, yes, but the majority of my father's people do not love them. They are like the hunted beasts of the marshes and are falling back before the hunters, bowing and kneeling and seeming to serve them, but like the mudbeasts they are drawing them into dangerous mires and swamps and are awaiting their time to strike back. Watch how the young girls of the marshery crowd around my brother's throne, needling and pricking at Pinvey's jealousy as they touch him and offer him every pleasure. And see how your sister competes with him by devouring the champions of the wrestling with her eyes and thrusting out her breasts in that transparent gown of molten gold as she wets her lips with the tip of her tongue and tastes the secret pleasures she would gladly share with them. These are not the ways of our people, despite what you have heard of us. Her wild lust and her rivalry for power will, I'm sure, eventually destroy them both."

Alea laughed but with no trace of humor. "Pinvey doesn't care who he takes his pleasure from, she'll merely laugh and urge him on to take who or whatever he wants, just . . ." She hesitated, shuddering, her face drawn and white beneath the filth of the marshery, as she remembered her ordeal at Mertzork's hands. "Just as she did when he wished to take Syrenea and me while we were searching for a way through the mumblers' mazes into Glitterspike Hall. I think she enjoyed it more than he did, goading him and helping him to tear loose our skirts and petticoats, ripping them off and holding us down on the cold stone floors of those dingy corridors while he brutally took us, sneering and laughing..." Alea fell silent, swallowing the shame and disgust, her cheeks burning as she turned away from Andzey. She had not wanted to tell him, to pick loose the raw scab that she had grown across those nightmare moments, and she dug her fingernails into the palm of her hands, clenching her fist so tightly that the blood trickled and oozed out between her knuckles. Her hatred of Pinvey boiled through her veins and made her shoulders tremble. "One day I'll kill her for what she made him do to me," she hissed, pressing her face harder against the bars.

"She hates him now for touching the girls of the marshery. Look, her eyes blaze with jealousy," whispered Andzey, trying to comfort her and adding gently, "Not all marshmen are like my brother. She must have goaded him to rape you, to hurt you, because she hated you so much."

Alea blinked away her tears and looked back at Andzey. "Does it matter in your eyes what Mertzork did to me? After all I'm just a woman, to be taken for pleasure, to be soiled and left wretched and dirty and . . ."

"No, no, please don't think of yourself like that," he whispered quickly, the urgent pleading in his voice making her catch her breath. "You were the victim of your sister's hatred and my brother's brutality. You were powerless to stop them and . . ." He hesitated, his face pale beneath the layers of dirt and grime. As he shook his head fiercely the rag ends of the gossamer spiders' webs that hung down in forgotten loops and tails from his ears swayed from side to side. "I understand why you hate me now and I promise that one day I will avenge what my brother did to you." He paused and drew in breath as he searched for the words to tell her that not all of the marsh people were like Mertzork, that some of them even held women in high esteem, but a sudden strangling shout from the edge of the marshery made them both turn and press their faces against the bars of the cage.

Andzey gripped the bars, his knuckles whitening with anger as he looked out to where the sharpwire matches had begun. "My father had put a stop to this butchery," he muttered grimly as he turned his head and hid his face in shame when the first luckless marsh youth slipped and lost his footing and his opponent ducked behind him and, looping the sharpwire down over his head, wrenched it tight. The youth staggered and fell heavily to his knees in the bubbling mud. He struggled to rise, his eyes bulging and staring wildly at the shouting crowds, but as he gasped for air his tongue turned black and swelled to choke him and he thrashed and kicked and clawed at the strangling wire tightening around his throat and tried to free himself with frantic, muddy fingers.

Mertzork leaned forward, licking his lips and watching the youth's bloated face turn a darker

shade of indigo. He laughed and raised both of his
hands with his thumbs pointing inwards, then
drew them sharply away from his throat. The
marshman holding the wire gave a shout of triumph and jerked both of his hands wide apart. The
wire tightened savagely and the youth's head lolled
forward, his shoulders trembled once and he
slumped down, making a sluggish ripple in the mud
as the victor of the match loosened the wire, gave
him a final shove between the shoulder blades and
pushed him out of sight beneath the bubbling
slime.

"Blood! It's better if we see blood!" panted Pinvey, slapping lazily at the swarms of insects that
droned above her head. "Have those who would
jostle and thrust to be our champions sharpen a
cutting edge to their sharpwires so that they slice
through skin and flesh—so that the heads . . ."

"Quiet! Quiet you fool!" hissed Mertzork, glancing frantically over his shoulder toward the noisy
crowd that surrounded them. Drawing closer to
Pinvey, he whispered, "It is forbidden in every
marshery across the length and breadth of Gnarlsmyre to sharpen the wires; it is against all the laws
to take heads."

Pinvey laughed softly and mocked him with her
eyes. "I thought you were the King of these
wretched people. I thought that you made and
broke the laws as you pleased."

Mertzork glared hatefully at her. "It's not that
easy. There are some traditions and laws that even
I dare not break or try to change."

Pinvey held his gaze as she sensed a weakness in him and she curled her lip in a silent sneer and prodded ruthlessly at him. "The sharpwires that you brought into Glitterspike Hall were honed to a razor edge, but now you are afraid . . ." she whispered, "afraid that this rabble of marshscum will see through the lies that you have told them if you change so much as one silly law!"

"No!" Mertzork hissed, his face darkening with anger. "In the city of Glor and Glitterspike Hall it was different; the laws of the marshery do not stretch beyond the beasting pits. There I could do as I pleased."

"Then you are afraid," Pinvey laughed. "You *must* be afraid, because I care nothing for anyone's laws, not here in these miserable swamps and stinking wastes of mud nor in Glitterspike Hall itself. I am the Queen and I do as I please!"

"Then you are a fool," Mertzork snarled, catching his breath and trying to swallow his rage as he sought to explain to her in low whispers how dangerously she trod amongst his people. "The punishment for carrying a sharpwire with a cutting edge is death. The fear of that punishment is enough to disarm every man here in the marsheries but if you have your way and encourage your champions to carry sharpened wires neither of us will be safe, because anyone who schemes to seize what we have taken can creep up behind us and silently take our heads."

"But I am the Queen!" she hissed, her eyes narrowing into murderous slits. "No one would dare!"

Mertzork opencd his mouth to answer but she had turned away and was calling loudly to the marshgirls she had appointed as her ladies-in-waiting to attend to her needs.

"Your games tire me," she snapped, turning sharply back to Mertzork. "I shall ride out through the reed beds on Andzey's shoulders and force Alea to collect a basket of the brightest marsh flowers to bring a little color into this miserable marshery."

"There are dangerous swamps beyond Fenmire Marsh," Mertzork muttered as two of the young marshmen who had won their wrestling jousts went to fetch Andzey and Alea from their cage beneath Pinvey's chambers. "Be careful, they are treacherous places to wander alone."

Pinvey held Mertzork's gaze and snapped, "I shall take a handful of our champions. They will take care of me!" Her eyes told of secret passions and she wet her lips and caressed her thighs in anticipation as she let her gaze wander away from his over the crowds of young marshmen that thronged around the throne.

"Choose who you like. Take them all," Mertzork replied carelessly as he turned back toward the two youths who were crouching in the bubbling mud on the edge of the marshery, waiting for his signal to continue with the sharpwire matches. But he was quick to catch the eye of every one of the young champions that she beckoned to come forward and his murderous gaze made them hesitate.

* * *

"Do you see them quarrel?" Andzey asked quietly. "Do you see how Pinvey goads Mertzork?"

"They are both consumed with jealousy," Alea nodded, but she shivered with fear, realizing they were summoned, and wished for a moment she could move closer to Andzey. The ladder led to their cage shook and the lower rungs began to creak as the two marshmen climbed up toward them. "But how can we use that jealousy to thwart them? Mertzork has surrounded himself with a gaggle of marshgirls and my sister is picking as many champions for her pleasure," Alea muttered hopelessly.

"My brother was always cunning and ruthless but he has changed so much since he followed our father out into Fenmire Marsh to hunt for a mudbeast to take to the joust at Glitterspike Hall. Would you tell me everything, no matter how trivial, that you learnt of him while you were lost in the corridors of the hall? Anything that might show me a weakness?"

The spiders began to scuttle across their clothes, warning them that the two marshmen had reached the top of the ladder and drew back, keeping their fingers well away from the bottom of the cage. Alea looked up at Andzey for a moment and hesitated. He smiled at her and held her gaze.

"Together we can thwart them, I know it!"

Alea felt her cheeks flush. There was something about this marshman. Perhaps in better times she might even have liked him. She sighed and shrugged her shoulders. "Mertzork was obsessed with the magic of the healing woman," she whispered, turning her head away from the marshmen, a little ashamed of herself for offering up her secrets so easily. "He was always putting the dried-up husk of a hedgehog she had once given him upon the ground and cursing it for not showing them the way."

"Hedgehog?" Andzey hissed, his eyes widening with interest.

Alea nodded seriously. "He put it down every time the corridor forked and he would stare at it for hours and then kick it savagely or hurl it up against the roof and then follow whichever of the passageways it rolled into."

"Follow us down and keep your distance," growled one of the marshmen, trying to mask his terror of the spiders as he reached up and swung open the door of their cage.

"When did he first use the hedgehog? Was it alive then or did the healing woman cast a magic spell over its carcass?" Andzey asked quietly, moving as close as he dared to her, his lips almost brushing against her ear as he followed her toward the open door of the cage.

Alea wanted to draw away from him but she resisted and whispered back, "I heard him boast once to Pinvey that there was not a nook or a cranny in all Gnarlsmyre that the hedgehog couldn't find a way through. It was alive when the healing woman gave it to him; she had wound a gossamer thread around it and all he had to do was to hold the end of the thread and the hedgehog would show him the way. Once it even saved him when the frozen marsh crust shattered beneath his feet and . . .''

"Stop your muttering and hurry down. Your Queen is waiting,'' shouted one of the marshmen, rattling the ladder fiercely.

Andzey's mind was racing. Alea had not shrunk away from him and he had learned more of his brother in those few moments than in all the seasons they had spent together in the marshery. "I will take Pinvey through the reed beds to an island thick with marshoaks where wild hedgehogs sometimes gather, crossing the marsh crust to weather out the wet seasons. If you see one, hide it beneath your skirts and bring it back,'' he whispered as he crawled through the doorway and slowly descended the ladder.

Mertzork heard the crowds of marshmen behind the throne fall silent and he snapped his fingers angrily to stop the sharpwire match before turning to see the two marshmen leading Andzey up to the throne. "Take your ladies-in-waiting,'' he sneered at Pinvey as he rose from his seat and drove the frightened marshgirls into a huddle beside the Queen from where they were hovering just behind the throne.

Pinvey mounted Andzey and turned him back toward Mertzork's chair. As she did so Mertzork caught sight of Alea and his cruel mouth split into a leering smile. In two strides he was beside her, touching and fondling her, more to annoy Pinvey than to take his pleasure. He remembered all too well her wailing cries and the way she had frozen and shrunk back from his touch. But Pinvey seemed hardly to notice as she wriggled more comfortably on Andzey's shoulders, pressing her thighs tightly around his neck.

Mertzork grew tired of touching Alea and pushed her to the ground but as he dropped his hand he caught a look of pure hatred in his brother's eyes. "You are jealous of me, brother," he sneered, reaching out and pulling Alea roughly back to him. "The spiders' bites are harmless to me. I can take her whenever I please . . ."

"No you cannot!" snarled Pinvey, catching the thread of Mertzork's words and gripping Andzey in a stranglehold with her thighs as she twisted around to face Mertzork. "She is my sister and serves no one, not even the King, unless I offer her to you. Use one of those marsh harlots that you are so fond of," she hissed, kicking Andzey so hard in the ribs that he stumbled and would have fallen had not Alea broken free of Mertzork's clutches and rushed forward to steady him, as the crowd, terrified of the spiders, gasped and drew back. For a moment their eyes met and Andzey smiled. Pinvey stared down and Alea blushed and stepped back, white-faced, and a frightened silence spread between them. Pinvey's lips tightened and began to curl back across her teeth, while her eyes hardened into narrow slits of hatred. Alea bowed her head and tensed as she felt her sister's gaze cutting into her. Her fingernails dug into the palms of her hands as she waited for a string of curses or vicious blows to rain down upon her head.

Pinvey suddenly laughed, making Alea catch her breath and look up. "That's more like the little sister who used to trail along on the hems of my skirts in Glitterspike Hall, looking after all my wants, fetching and carrying for my every whim and fancy. You have been so quick to save me from falling into this filthy mud and slime that, as your reward, I shall let you take your pleasure with Mertzork after the evening feast."

Alea shuddered at the look of triumph in Mertzork's eyes and saw the muscles in Andzey's jaw tense as he clenched his teeth in helpless rage.

Pinvey was turning him toward the stepping stones, goading him with her heels to the edge of the marshery. "Take me to the island of marshoaks beyond the reed beds where the brightest flowers grow," she cried and the throng of champions prodded at Alea, driving her before them with the gaggle of waiting women, and they began to file out across the channel of bubbling mud.

"I want those flowers. Pick those orange ones over there," Pinvey ordered, stabbing with her fingers toward a mass of brilliant petals and leathery lily pads that lay in the center of the bubbling mire between the marshoak islands. Alea cried out as the marshmen prodded at her with their iron spikes, laughing, and drove her out from the bank to flounder in the oozing mud.

"Gather a heavy bundle of flowers or I will send you back again," laughed Pinvey ordering Andzey to set her down. She lay back amongst the young champions who had come with her and, settling

down on the soft black earth of the island, abandoned herself to the pleasure of their touching.

Andzey watched helplessly as Alea sank and
floundered in the shallow, swampy mud on the
edge of the island. She had taken less than a footstep
from the bank and already the swamp was swallowing her up. He wanted to cry out, to warn her to
follow the lines of bubbles or to clutch at the lily
stems whose roots grew along the edges of the secret paths that crossed the swamps, lying hidden
just below the surface; but he knew that to call her
would show Pinvey clearly that he cared and he
feared that she would use such knowledge to destroy them both. Yet if he remained silent Alea
would drown in the swamp. Shrieks of laughter
erupted from behind him and he glanced quickly
over his shoulder to see Pinvey writhing, clutching
at two of the marshmen while she urged the others
to take their pleasure amongst her ladies-in-
waiting. Screams and shouts echoed across the island as the youths leapt up and began to chase the
women between the crowded marshoaks. Andzey
had but a moment to warn Alea and show her
where to tread. He slipped quickly and quietly between the trees and hurried to where she had been
floundering in the swamp.

"Alea . . . Alea, where are you," he hissed as
loudly as he dared, searching desperately amongst
the tall clumps of reeds that grew along the bank.

A movement in the lily beds made him look up
and catch his breath. "Alea! How did you cross the
swamp?" he called, cupping his hands to his mouth,

directing the sound of his voice away from the island and toward her.

Alea looked up at the sound of his voice and
swayed awkwardly, scattering a handful of bright
lilies and other flowers that she had gathered, and
they were swallowed by the bubbling mud. Andzey
thought that he saw a shadowy figure reach out and
steady her and quick hands help to gather up some
of the scattered flowers.

"Alea, who is with you?" he hissed, frowning.

"Beast! Where is my riding beast?" Pinvey
shouted impatiently, tiring of the marsh youths and
rising from where she lay among the marshoaks.

Andzey half turned, hesitating. "Follow the lines
of bubbles," he called out to Alea anxiously, knowing that he must hurry. He watched her glide between two lily beds in the shadows of the low,
overhanging branches, on a distant island, laden
with brilliantly colored orchids. She waved once
and then vanished beneath the trees.

Pinvey glared down at the dripping wet, heavy
bundles of orchids and water lilies that Alea laid
carefully at her feet. "Your skirts are barely
muddy," she muttered. "I should send you back for
more."

Alea fell to her knees and began to arrange the
flowers into neat piles, asking anxiously which ones
she should collect and offering to run back across
the swamp immediately. Pinvey yawned at her eagerness and waved her aside. The fun of sending

her sister out into the swamp had evaporated, especially since she seemed to enjoy doing it. She had tired of these willing marshmen. The pleasure of lying with them was not so great when she could do so openly. Lying with the ragmen and dusters of the hall had been so much fun. The excitement of the secrecy, the hot whispers, the planning and the risk of being caught had all fueled her lust.

She wrinkled her nose at the overpowering stench of the swamps and slapped at the insects that hummed and droned constantly around her head. She hated these wretched marshes and she yearned for the dry, echoing corridors of Glitterspike Hall.

The anger swelled up in her. "Enough of this foolery," she cried fiercely, turning on the marshmen and her ladies-in-waiting, who had crowded noisily around her. She silenced them with a piercing stare. "You would roll in the dirt and filth of these marshes forever while Marrimian struts as Queen through the corridors of Glitterspike Hall. Get back into the marshery and hone a cutting edge to your sharpwires. Learn to fight, to kill, and ready yourselves to sack the city of Glor and overrun Glitterspike Hall, because I want Marrimian's head. I want . . ."

Pinvey stopped and swallowed her words, realizing that she had already said too much. There could be no Queen in Glitterspike Hall—*she* was the Queen. Quivering with rage at her own stupidity, her face blotched and blackened and a froth of white spittle appeared on her lips. "Back! Go back to the marsheries," she hissed to the startled youths who had shrunk away from her as she ranted and raged to herself and they wondered what they had done to fuel her anger and whom she was cursing in Glitterspike Hall.

"Back! Back!" she shouted, brushing aside their hesitant questions and stamping her feet on the wild orchids in fury, scattering the bundles of marsh flowers that Alea had gathered.

"I will bring the flowers," Alea offered and reached down with quick fingers, but Pinvey pushed her roughly aside.

"I want no more flowers. I want my sisters' heads spiked on the archway high above the Hurlers' Gate. I want an end to these stinking marshes!"

"Keep well away from her!" Andzey whispered to Alea as she stumbled and scrambled up from her knees in front of him. "Your sister is filled with a murderous rage."

"Beast! Beast! Carry me back," Pinvey shouted impatiently. Alea retreated from her and followed the line of silent, hurrying marsh youths and the huddle of frightened women back through the swamps.

Andzey breathed a sigh of relief as the door of their cage slammed shut behind them. "I thought that you had drowned in that swamp while you were gathering the flowers. I searched and searched and never for a moment gave up hope and suddenly you were amongst the brightest lily pads. But it is beyond me how you got there. I would swear that

I saw a shadowy figure beside you, but in a blink it was gone."

Alea smiled at his concern. "I would have drowned and been sucked beneath the mud. I was floundering and sinking deeper with every step when suddenly that old woman, the one who used to live in a tree hung with secrets and who moves as stealthily as a shadow along the edge of the marshery—the one who showed us how to milk the venom from the spiders—she was beside me. She whispered and muttered underneath her breath, cursing Mertzork all the while and his savage Queen, and she dragged me back into the shallow mud. She made me tie curled strips of bark on the soles of my feet and then she helped me glide across the swamp and gather up the bundles of marsh flowers for Pinvey."

Andzey laughed softly. "That old woman must have taken a liking to you to teach you to use bark sledges. They are a woman's way of crossing the swamps to harvest roots and berries. One day, in better times, I'll find her the biggest marshoak tree in all Gnarlsmyre and tie precious treasures to every branch for keeping you safe."

"One day," sighed Alea, her voice bleak with despair. "If we ever live to see it."

Andzey wanted to reach out and comfort her but he hesitated, afraid that she would shrink away from him again. "Did you see any hedgehogs?" he asked in a whisper.

Alea shook her head. "No. But I asked that old woman where I could find them and she told me that she hadn't seen a hedgehog for the last two seasons anywhere near the marshery."

"Oh well, it doesn't matter," sighed Andzey, shrugging his shoulders. "It was a silly idea anyway. Did the old woman say anything else?"

Alea opened her mouth to speak and then shut it again and shook her head. She felt her cheeks flush as she turned away from him. She was certainly not going to tell him that the old woman must have been spying on them because she had chided Alea for the way she treated him, or that she had told her quite sharply not to judge Andzey with the rest of the marshmen.

"No, she said nothing," she murmured.

The mood of the marshery changed abruptly the moment that Pinvey returned. The shouts and screams of pleasure echoing through the crowds who were watching the renewed sharpwire matches fell to sullen, frightened whispers as she cursed them and ranted at them for brawling in the mud.

"Call yourselves lords! Call yourselves hunters!" she sneered, sweeping her mocking gaze over the crowds who filled every footstep of the low hump of dry land that rose above the marsh. "Warriors indeed," she muttered beneath her breath with contempt. "Warriors who let a miserable herd of mud-beasts drive them out of Glitterspike Hall and chase them down through the streets of the city to hide in these wretched marshes. If you were men you would have returned and attacked! You would have sacked the city!"

Mertzork frowned and hunched forward in his throne, listening closely to her continual mumblings and rantings, and he would have sneered and laughed at her and chided her impatience but he caught the scent of a growing fear in the marshery. They were afraid of the savage change in her; it was making them doubt her and the boldest marshmen were beginning to shuffle toward the stepping stones that crossed the channel. They were beginning to gather up their iron spikes and spears and whisper that there was still time to scatter to one of the other marsheries before the rains began.

"You are a fool to push our warriors too impatiently," he muttered, drawing her aside. "Can't you see that your rages are turning everyone against you? Where is the laughter? Where is the woman who chose champions and who claimed to be the Queen of the Marshery?"

"Queen? Queen of this miserable huddle of hovels? Queen of this stinking crowd of marshmen? Have you forgotten how Marrimian drove us out of the city?"

Mertzork glanced sideways at her and hushed her into silence. "You must be patient. Remember that we withdrew from the city to weather out the wet seasons here in the safety of my marshery, or have those rages driven reason from your mind so that you have forgotten why we fled? Have you forgotten that the mudbeasts wrecked the crystal houses and that the people of the city will starve to death during the rains? Have patience, encourage the marshmen to be ready to journey back to the city when the rains stop. Offer iron spikes to your faithful servants. Every marshman will follow us when the floods recede."

Pinvey thought on his words slowly and nodded her head. She laughed with relief for the first time in many days and called for her ladies-in-waiting. Murmurs of approval broke out near the throne and rapidly spread through the crowd. People laughed and eagerly followed her talk of easy pickings when they returned to the city.

But although Pinvey had changed outwardly before the people of the marshery, inside her impatience and jealousy of Marrimian boiled over and she secretly clenched her fists and ground her teeth. Her eyes narrowed and glittered brightly with anger and in the privacy of the royal chamber she would rage at Mertzork and demand to attack Glitterspike Hall immediately. Attack before Marrimian could rally the people of the city to fight or close the city gates against the marshmen.

Mertzork would yawn and shrug his shoulders and turn to her and whisper, "What can Marrimian do? The city lies in ruins, and there is no food to feed the people. Have patience. Go to sleep."

"But she has already tricked us out of our triumph and stolen the throne from beneath our noses," Pinvey whispered. "What if she parades herself on the high archway above the Hurlers' Gate when we attack the city? Many of these marshmen will recognize her as the real beast-rider, the real Queen. We should attack now before she can do anything to prevent us."

Mertzork was sickened by her continual moaning and finally he sat up and gripped her wrists and stared at her in the darkness. "There is no time to attack before the rains begin. Listen to the thunder," he whispered fiercely. "But it might stifle your impatience to know that I have sent word to every marshery from here to Rainbows' End commanding all the marshlords and their hunters and waders to gather here the moment the floods recede. I have ordered them to accompany us into the city for a triumphant crowning. No one from the outlying marsheries will have seen Marrimian and they will not doubt your right to be Queen. They will be hungry to fight with you and seize every dry footstep of land from the starving people of the city. Now let us have some peace and quiet."

Pinvey shrugged her shoulders and forced a bitter smile across her lips but her eyes still burned with impatience to be free of everything to do with these wretched, stinking marshes. She shifted her gaze and stared up through the gaps in the rough thatch of their chamber. "The stars have vanished," she muttered.

Mertzork laughed at her in the darkness. "The wet seasons are about to begin and when the stars shine again Marrimian's head will be spiked above the Hurlers' Gate."

Pinvey laughed harshly. "Then I shall count the raining days impatiently!"

* * *

Andzey waited until Mertzork and Pinvey's voices died down in the hut above their cage. "Did you hear what they said?" he whispered to Alea.

Alea crouched down close to him and nodded silently. There were tears in her eyes as she whispered, "It's so hopeless. Even if Marrimian does survive the wet seasons the city will be overrun. Everything will be destroyed."

"No," Andzey muttered grimly. "We must never give up hope, never, never." He smiled at her gently, wishing he could brush at the drying tear streaks on her cheeks.

Later that night when the cooking fires of the marshery had burned down to less than a few glowing embers and the ice wind blew across the quickmarshes, rattling the brittle reed stems and freezing the marsh crust in the channel, Andzey blinked awake. The rumbles of thunder drew closer and stark flashes of lightning burst out across the darkness. A hunting dog barked somewhere below their cage, its echo mingling with the growing storm that was sweeping across the frozen marsh toward them. But these weren't the noises that had made Andzey start awake. The hairs on the nape of his neck prickled as he reached out a hand to touch Alea and warn her, but he froze as the cage swayed and he heard the rungs of the ladder that led to their tiny prison creak. He looked about the bare floor desperately for something to defend Alea with, fearing that his brother had sent one of his murderous captains to kill them while they slept; but there was nothing to hand. A spider scuttled across the back of his hand and he snatched it up, holding it in his palm and pinching its soft abdomen between his finger and thumb as he held it ready to hurl through the bars into the face of their assassin the moment he appeared above the floor of the cage. He hoped that terror of spiders would make the intruder lose his balance and topple backwards.

The ladder creaked again and Alea stirred in her sleep and cried out. Andzey tensed his arm and drew it back. The ladder shifted slightly; a filthy hand gripped the bars of their cage and a cackling voice hissed at them to be quiet or they would wake the whole marshery. Andzey hesitated and stared at the hand as it felt between the bars, searching for the widest gap. There was something familiar in the voice. He dropped the spider and shook Alea's arm, clamping his hand over her mouth to stifle her cries as she woke. She struggled against him, her eyes wide with terror, the movement making the whole cage rock and sway.

"Be still!" he hissed. "The old woman is here, who saved you from drowning in the swamp. She must have crept through the guards who watch the channel."

At that moment he heard tiny claws scrabble at the bars of the cage behind him and the spiders that clung to his jerkin scuttled and vanished into the hidden folds of his sleeves. Andzey spun around and stared down at a small bundle of prickly spines that was moving toward them across the floor of their prison.

"It's a hedgehog," Alea whispered, peering around his shoulder.

The old woman's head suddenly appeared above the floor hissing at them to be quiet. She stared up into the black shadows of the huts above that shut out the starlight. "You are making enough noise to wake a roost of pindafalls," she muttered, glaring at them and licking nervously at her withered gums as Andzey caught the hedgehog and held it up in the palm of his hand.

"It was the only one I could find," the old woman whispered. "I searched all the marshoak islands well beyond Fenmire Marsh for one with more than a finger's thickness of flesh on its bones but . . ."

"It's not for eating, woman," Andzey whispered. "It's for . . ." A hunting dog barked on the edge of the marshery and voices cursed it from somewhere below, in the forest of rickety stilts.

"Take care, the guards are close to us," Alea whispered, reaching out to touch the old woman's hand, but she had already vanished into the darkness without the slightest creak of the ladder.

Andzey stared down into the marshery and thought that he caught a glimpse of a shadow as lightning flashed in the sky across the frozen channel, but before he could blink it vanished into the reeds. "I owe you much, old woman," he whispered as he offered the hedgehog to Alea, asking her to hold it for a moment while he unraveled a gossamer thread from the webs that the spiders had woven

across his shoulders. He began slowly to wind it around the hedgehog's prickly spines. "Now I shall destroy you, brother, with the very threads of magic that you have used to destroy everything you touch."

"Listen, I can hear raindrops," whispered Alea, resting the hedgehog for a moment and pointing up to the steep conicled roofs of the marshery above them.

Andzey listened and then slowly nodded as he unwound another loop of thread. "The wet seasons have begun. We must hurry to make this hedgehog into a spindle of thread and keep it well hidden until the rains stop and the floods recede."

11

The Bitter Taste of Revenge

*T*HE air had grown darker and the bleak, flat landscape of quickmarshes, swamps and mires that stretched endlessly away toward Rainbows' End was slowly vanishing beneath the advancing storms. Low thunder clouds, black and menacing, boiled toward the city; the lightning flashed and crackled, sending stark shadows leaping and plunging down the narrow, winding streets and airless alleyways. Rain squalls lashed the low marshoak islands and beat down on the reed beds that lay just beyond the great dyke of earth and stones the hall folk had built out into the marshes. The deluge bent the tall, slender reed stems and snapped off the brittle, withered flower heads as it swept toward the Hurlers' Gate.

Yet as the wet seasons closed in about the city there had seemed to be a moment's silence before the first raindrop fell and the rumbling thunder-claps broke between the sheer towers of Glitter-spike Hall. A moment of calm, filled with anxious shouts and running footsteps, filled with the sound of slamming doors and window latches echoing in the empty streets before the roar of the rainstorms drumming on the steeply gabled roofs and the endless rumbling of the thunder drowned out all the other city sounds.

Naul sensed that moment in the blind darkness of the narrow rock tomb beneath Erek's hovel where she and her gathering of crones had locked him away until he renounced the house of Miresnare and swore to help her destroy Marrimian.

"The rains will flood the chamber!" he cried out in panic as the rough rock wall that pressed in around him suddenly began to sweat and worms and beetles wriggled out of every crack and crevasse and began to swarm up the walls, crawling toward the crack of light that edged the ill-fitting trap door above his head. Panic overtook him and he cried out, begging Erek to let him breathe on the searching mirror once more and show her that he had renounced the house of Miresnare and turned his back on all his mumbling days. He wanted to show her that he would help them destroy Marrimian, but even as he tried to shout the words to gain his freedom from the stifling chamber where he had been buried alive his tongue stuttered and he sank down in the darkness and wept tears of hopelessness. He could not betray Marrimian even though his life now depended upon it. He could not become a part of his mother's black, venomous revenge against her. He was the master mumbler; truth and honesty were ingrained in him and part of his very essence. Even Erek's magic could not overwhelm that.

Faintly above the trap door he could hear the measured tramp of the crones' boots. They were dancing in a tight circle, chanting his name and weaving it into every spell and shout of sorcery to destroy the power of his own mumblers' magic, to blacken his conscience and sour his soul against the house of Miresnare and make him a part of what they had become. He laughed harshly and struck his fist violently against the wet rock wall of his tomb and tried to shut out their chanting, remembering that moment when Erek had caught him spying on her. At first she had thought that he had come to her, her child, her son, returned to swell the power of her revenge against the Miresnares, and she had laughed and drooled over him, touching and pawing him with her crooked fingers and showing him a thousand secrets all at once. But the crones had found the windbells that he had tossed into the canopy to distract the watching spiders and they had grown suspicious and had whispered against him and she, to quell their doubts, had thrust the searching mirror toward him.

"Breathe, breathe all the truth. Show this gaggle of hags just how much you hate Marrimian and the way she stole the throne," she had murmured, stroking the silken softness of his saffron gown.

But her cooings and murmurings had quickly turned to shrieks of rage and the mirror had trembled in her fingers as it showed the truth within him. His breath had dulled the glass, ghosting it with shadows, but slowly, as the beads of moisture formed, they etched a glistening picture of Lord

Miresnare proclaiming the joust and Marrimian snatching the jousting cup from Mertzork's hands. It showed how she had drunk from the cup and claimed her right to joust for the throne and then dashed the cup into a thousand pieces at her feet. The crones had crowded closer, hissing and muttering against Naul. The glass had shown strange pictures if he was truly against Marrimian. Then the tiny beads of moisture melted together and the picture changed. Now the hall was in riot; beasts bellowed and roared; marshmen fought and cursed one another, and Marrimian, casting aside her cloak of beastskin, walked between the shackled beasts that guarded the Glitterspike and touched the veins of molten silver that lay beneath its feathered skirts of hoarfrost. It was the very moment that she had claimed the throne and all Gnarlsmyre as her own.

"Lies! Nothing but lies. This is not the truth!" Erek had shrieked, rubbing at the drying glass with a cloth of the finest gossamer; but she could not wipe away Naul's truth. The glass had lain spoiled in the palm of her hand, still holding the clear picture of Mertzork and Pinvey fleeing from the hall.

The shadows of the crones had leapt forward in the crackling firelight and filled the hovel, closing in upon Naul where he crouched at Erek's feet. They had cursed him and called for his death; he knew too much of their secrets and they foresaw that he would carry them to Marrimian and she would use them to destroy the Shambles and drive them out, just as her father had done before her.

Erek had stilled the crones with a stab of her

fingers and then driven them back into the darkest corners of her hovel before clutching at Naul and pulling him closer to her. "You are of my blood," she had hissed, rubbing her hand over his head. "Lord Miresnare stole you from my birth webs and held you in his power, but now you are free of him and his cursed daughter. The crones have destroyed all the mumblers and smashed their pine-oil lamps. You are free to join me in my hatred of the Miresnares and strengthen my power for revenge."

Erek had paused and wiped at a loop of saliva that dangled from her chin; she had stroked the top of Naul's head as she continued. "And it shall all be yours once we have destroyed Marrimian. You shall rule the house of Miresnare."

Naul had looked quickly around the hovel. His gaze had taken in the swarms of spiders that clung to every beam and the tangled loops of hanging threads that festooned the ceiling and he had shivered as he had seen the murderous gleam in the crone's eyes and he had shrunk as he realized how much the desire for revenge had blackened and twisted her thoughts. "But what of Mertzork and Pinvey? Surely you have promised them. . . ?"

Erek had clapped her hands to silence him as she threw back her head and cackled with laughter. The crones had mimicked her, their mouths split into shrieks and cackles as they danced around the room. "They are nothing and they shall have nothing," Erek had sneered, as she drew her dirty nails across her throat in a strangling gesture.

Erek had reached into a dark alcove behind

where she sat and brought out of it a dirty iron goblet, its rim stained and spoiled with streaks of bright red rust. "Drink from the cup of my revenge. Show us that you have renounced your former master," she had whispered, thrusting the full goblet toward him.

Naul had shivered as the crones had crowded in around him and he knew that they would have killed him if he had not drunk. "Die! Death to Marrimian!" He had tried to sneer the words and make them convincing but the sounds choked in his throat as he had reached for the cup. He had brought it to his lips, determined to taste the bitter revenge that Erek had fomented against Lord Miresnare and Marrimian, but the bubbling liquid had made his head spin. It had burnt his lips and turned to ashes on his tongue. He had cried out and staggered, falling to his knees, and Erek had snatched the cup before he could spill it and the crones had borne down on him in a black mass of swirling rags with jagged daggers in their hands.

"No! He is of my blood! He is the very root of our hatred against the house of Miresnare; we must keep him a prisoner until we have thwarted the power of the mumblers' magic that still flows through him. We will lock him up until we have purged him of the poison that Lord Miresnare has forced into him. He will remain in the darkness below this house until his breath wipes clean the foul lies that he has engraved upon my mirror." Erek had dragged the crones from him and driven him down to this tomb.

"I will never never be free," Naul whispered to himself as he rested his hand against the cold, wet rock. But now, above him, the bolts of the trap door were being drawn back. Light spilled down into the narrow tomb and he looked up, blinking as a shaft of light reflected from the spoiled face of the searching mirror that Erek dangled over him.

"Breathe on my mirror," she shouted.

"Breathe on the mirror," chanted the crones as it dangled, twisting and turning over him, and they hung over the trap door, their hoods and bonnets and riddles of black rags blocking out the flickering firelight from the room above and covering him in an airless, stifling darkness.

They whispered and muttered impatiently against him and spat venomously down into the narrow hole. The mirror swung slowly backwards and forwards as Erek dangled it just above his head. "Breathe on it. Breathe on the glass," she hissed.

Naul hunched his shoulders. "How? How can I hide the truth? How can I ever escape to warn Marrimian of the hideous human carcasses that Erek is going to feed to the people of the city when the rains begin?" he whispered to himself as the cold lens of the mirror brushed against his cheek.

The crones fell silent as the mirror touched his lips and in that moment while they craned forward, watching the glass and waiting for his pent-up breath to ghost his truths upon it, he heard the sound of the rain drumming on the steep, gabled roofs of the Shambles. He smiled in the stifling darkness and let the sound of teeming rain fill his head. He pictured the swollen gutters of boiling water, the curtains of raindrops pouring off the glistening eaves, the steep, narrow alleyways awash and the winding stone steps now raging waterfalls. He laughed as his breath wet the glass, for he had found in the deluge lashing the steep streets of the city a power far greater than all his mumbler's magic and all the pent-up, blackened hatred of Erek and her crones. A power that could, without one magic spell or whispered curse, change the face of all Gnarlsmyre as it swept across the marshes and help him escape from Erek's clutches. He thought of nothing but the pounding rain as his breath misted the mirror.

The glass was roughly jerked up and away from him. Voices hissed and muttered and he heard the whisper of a gossamer cloth wipe the mirror clean. "It shows nothing now. Nothing but the rains lashing the city," cursed a disbelieving voice.

"Make him breathe on it again: that will show if he has tricked us with his mumbling magic," shrieked one of the crones.

Erek gently lowered the mirror back toward his lips, longing to believe that they had destroyed the mumbler's magic within him. "Breathe, breathe upon it, my child," she murmured, licking at the dribbles that escaped over her sunken gums as she smiled triumphantly down into the darkness.

"The rain, the rain that washes everything clean, that purges the gutters and polishes the drains," Naul mumbled over and over to himself as he breathed on the mirror and allowed the thunderous downpour to fill every corner of his mind.

"Look. Look at the picture: the roofs and the flooding alleyways. Look, there is nothing of the cursed Miresnare or his daughter; he thinks of nothing but the deluge," cried Erek, passing the glistening mirror from hand to hand, and one by one the crones reluctantly nodded their heads.

"Let him drink from the cup of revenge," urged one of the crones. "If we have truly destroyed his love of the Miresnares our broth will taste sweet and wholesome to him and it will surely nourish him after his ordeal in the dark."

Erek hooded her eyes and looked down into the narrow tomb. "Yes! Yes," she whispered, quickly reaching down with her thin, crooked, leathery fingers to help the crones lift Naul up into the firelight.

He fell to his knees, dizzy and weak with hunger, his eyes screwed tightly shut against the brightness of the flickering flames on the firestone.

"Drink, drink," Erek soothed, pushing the cup against his lips.

Naul blinked and tried to pull back as the sulphurous fumes of the bubbling liquid burned his nose and he caught a glimpse of the crones' suspicious eyes watching his every movement as they crowded around him.

"My lips are cracked and parched," he whispered, gripping the cup with both hands. "Let me wet them gently on the rim and savor the sweetness of your broth before I swallow it," he begged as he brought the cup slowly to his lips and let the sound of the pounding rainwater that was flooding the gutters soak into him and he filled his mind with the thought of swallowing mouthfuls of pure, icy rain. He tilted his head back and tried to gulp at the vile liquid but it foamed against his lips and boiled between his teeth as it washed hotly across his tongue. He staggered backwards, choking for breath, retching and dizzy from the stench of revenge that filled the cup, but with all his willpower he clenched at it and held it against his lips, knowing that his life depended on his next move. His teeth chattered against the iron rim but he could not force himself to swallow no matter how hard he tried. The crones were muttering impatiently and prodding at him with their sharp fingernails. He stared desperately up into the cobweb-shrouded rafter beams and tried to snatch his last glimpse of daylight. There amongst the forgotten tangles of webs and dusty gossamer threads he saw glistening with the reflections of the flickering firelight— raindrops.

They must have leaked between the steep, weather-beaten slates of the roof and trickled silently down the hanging loops of thread, making them sag beneath their weight, swelling ready to drop on to the dusty floor of the hovel. Unbeknown to the grumbling crones, the whole roof of Erek's lair was now sown with sparkling raindrops. Naul saw the ones directly above his head tremble and begin to fall; he moved the cup and they splashed, one by one, into the bubbling liquid and their purity weakened the foul brew.

"Drink! Drink or be buried alive," chanted the crones, swaying backwards and forwards as they gathered tightly around him in anticipation.

Naul lifted the cup high above his head and swayed in rhythm with the crones as he chanted. "I am with you. I renounce the house of Miresnare," he gasped, forcing the words through trembling lips and he held the cup up as long as he dared, to catch the precious raindrops.

"Drink! Drink now," Erek shrieked, impatient to see if he was truly one of them.

Naul lowered the cup to his lips and drank three long swallows. The crones stared at him, brushing irritably at the scattering of raindrops that dripped on to their heads, hissing and bubbling as they soaked into the rags they wore.

Naul thrust the cup back into Erek's hands. "Do you doubt me now, Mother?" he rasped, forcing a smile to his shriveled lips to hide the agony where the liquid from the cup of revenge had burnt them raw.

For a moment a shadow clouded Erek's face. She stared down at him and scratched at the dry, wrinkled skin beneath her chin, murmuring and muttering under her breath as if she herself doubted that the power of her revenge could have purged him of all his mumbler's magic. "Come. Come here, child, and let me listen to your secrets," she whispered, pulling him to her and scratching at his eardrum with her fingernail before she pressed her ear against his.

Erek listened and suddenly threw her head back and cackled as she let him go. "There is nothing of the Miresnares! Nothing but the sound of the pounding rainstorms that lash the city!"

She beckoned the crones to gather around them and she made Naul sit down beside her on the floor in the very center of their circle while she schemed and plotted how best to butcher the carcasses of the poor wretches that she had snared in the webs of the Shambles for seasons beyond counting and were now hanging and ripening in her curing houses.

"They must not know whom they eat," muttered one of the crones.

"They must think it is the flesh of the mud-beasts," cackled another as she cracked her swollen knuckles one by one.

"Carve the flesh cleverly," whispered Erek. "Chant spells over each ripened fillet and wet it from our cup of revenge and it will poison the minds of the people and blacken their hearts completely against Marrimian and they will be ready for the doubts and false rumors that we will feed them."

Naul shuddered, his narrow shoulders trembling as he listened to the depths of depravity in the huddled circle of hags. He lifted his eyes above the shadows cast by their riddle of rags, desperate to escape, knowing that he must somehow warn Marrimian, but how?

The crones' mutterings had fallen silent all around him. Naul blinked and saw that they were watching him, following his eyes as he sought a way to escape. He laughed nervously, dropped his gaze and shrugged his shoulders, but Erek, catching a whisper of the thoughts in his mind, thrust the searching mirror against his lips.

"What were your thoughts, child?" she hissed at him, her eyes narrowing with doubt, and Naul realized as the cold lens of the mirror touched his lips that he must never think of Marrimian or of the people of the hall, or consider what was right or wrong, while he was trapped here in the Shambles. He rolled his eyes up toward the glistening raindrops that hung from the rafter beams and let the sound of the beating rain fill his head and he thought of nothing but the bones inside the rotting carcasses that hung in his mother's larder.

Erek shrieked with laughter as the mirror filled with a hazy, muddled picture of piles of moldering bones and she stroked and pawed at his scalp, sorry that she had ever doubted him. She whispered and dribbled over the collar of his mumbling gown and praised him for being a clever child and showing them how they must dissect out every bone from their sweetmeat.

"We could make broth from the bones," cried one of the crones, "and mince the gristle into a wholesome pottage. Nothing need go to waste."

They all laughed and Naul let a breath of relief whisper out between his teeth as one by one the crones began to turn away from him.

"I could help you carry the food to the people of the city," he offered, sitting forward on his haunches. "I know every twist and turn in the lanes and alleyways beyond the entrance to the Shambles."

Erek paused and the crones turned back toward him as she spoke. "You have returned, my child. This was beyond my wildest hopes and I would be a fool if I ever let you out of my sight again. Our sweetmeats and every one of the wholesome treats that fill my larder shall be piled high in the entrance of the Shambles for the city people to take, but you may willingly help us to pick the skeletons clean and wet each offering with our revenge."

Naul nodded silently as he sank down amongst the crones, forcing his lips into a smile and touching the gnarled and crooked fingers that reached out to join him with their evil plotting, but his heart was filled with bleak helplessness. There was no way for him to escape. They were going to keep him within their circle forever.

12

The Wet Seasons

EVERYTHING glistened and smelled of damp.
The great hall was fogged with a fine, wet,
drifting drizzle and every reed lamp that
Krann had lit hissed and guttered damply in the
gray light of the wet seasons, throwing only weak
shadows across the slippery floorstones. Hoemasters, scuttles, benchers and dusters hurried backwards and forwards across the hall, shaking the
raindrops from their oiled weather-cloaks and
wide-brimmed, rush-woven hoods and stamping
the mud from their bark shoes before they carried
the heavy baskets of roots and edible shoots that
they had harvested from the terraces into the kitchens. Ansel's voice could be heard beneath the low
kitchen archways; she was shouting and cursing the
gatherers for bringing more mud and filth in the
bottoms of their leaking baskets into her kitchen
than food for her to cook.

Ragmen and dusters, grumbling against the gray
days, were busily clearing the last mounds of the
marshmen's refuse out of the maze of corridors and
passageways that sprawled around the hall. They

were piling the rubbish into maggoty, rotting heaps just beyond the doors of Glitterspike Hall where the floods of the wet seasons would wash it down through the lanes and alleyways of the city and out through the Hurlers' Gate into the marshes beyond. The noise of masons' chisels and carpenters' hammers echoed dully in the gloom. A handful of masons and carpenters had come to the doors of the hall, thin and hungry, just after the wet seasons had begun and bartered their skills for food. They were now busy repairing the slender, fluted columns and broad walkways of the high galleries.

Marrimian dismissed the crowds of hall folk who had sought her daily counsel. The needlewomen, rakers, servers and dressers had been ordered to go about their allotted tasks and she called after them, "If you find a glazier who can repair these leaking windows lurking in the corridors of the hall send him to me," and she laughed softly and wrung out the hems of her skirt as she slowly rose from the throne.

"Mistress, mistress," Ansel called breathlessly, her cheeks flushed and blotched from hurrying. She opened her mouth to speak and then remembered the new custom that the hall folk insisted upon to gain an audience with Marrimian. She turned back to the Glitterspike and awkwardly touched the feathered patterns of hoarfrost that clung in sparkling skirts to the sheer finger of crystal, muttering crossly and snatching her hand away as the coldness of the frost burned her fingertips. "It's not natural," she grumbled blackly, rubbing at her sore fingers.

Marrimian stifled a breath of laughter at Ansel's clumsiness as she asked gently what all the fuss was about.

"It's those harvesters, mistress," the fat scullion answered crossly. "I don't know what's got into them but they are fetching more mud and marsh-slime into my kitchens than roots or vegetables for me to cook. Look! Look at the trail of mud and slime that they have left across the hall and that's not half as bad as the mess in my kitchens!"

Marrimian frowned and glanced quickly across the hall. Puddles of mud and a trail of scuffed and dirty footprints led from the narrow bridge that they had built between a disused window arch of the herb larders across to the ridge of rocks that led down to the terraces behind the hall.

"What do they say to your complaints?" Marrimian asked, turning back to the scullion.

Ansel shrugged her broad shoulders and fidgeted with her apron tails. "They are always complaining that the terraces are a sea of mud, mistress. They don't have the time to wash the roots and vegetables for everything is flooding. The marsh beyond the dyke is beginning to wash back down into the drainage channels. But I told them bluntly that there's no way that the dyke can be at fault. I told them as plain as I'm standing here that Krann knows more about building dykes than they know . . . than they know . . ." Ansel stuttered to a halt, her face purple with anger. "I . . . I . . . I told them that the land of Elundium where he comes from is full of terraces and dykes as large as . . ." Ansel fell silent, her huge hands held high above her head.

Marrimian smiled at the scullion. "I will speak to the builder of the dykes when I can find him. I will tell him how you sing his praises and I will order that all the harvesters must clean the mud from the roots and vegetables before they bring them into your kitchen. But . . ." Marrimian frowned with an edge of worry in her voice, "but what of the ones who guard the dyke? What do they say of the terraces or the swollen marshes beyond the dyke? What do they say about the flooding when they wait at the kitchen archway for your scullions to serve out their pottage?"

Ansel thought for a moment as she wrung her broad hands together. "They used to grumble much about the city folk throwing stones or loosing stray arrows at them from the safety of the Hurlers' Gate but that was before the lower alleyways and lanes of the city became a raging torrent. Now it's not so easy for the people to reach the gates and since the ragmen and the dusters cleared the mounds of refuse out of the passageways of the hall the ironmasters and their like have taken to plundering the heaps of rubbish under cover of darkness as well as trying to steal from the terraces. But our guards barely talk of the dyke at all, save to complain about the endless rainstorms that seep through the layers of grease on their weathercloaks, numbing and chilling them."

Marrimian stopped two ragmen who were shuffling across the hall carrying between them a heavy iron cauldron piled high with the refuse of the joust. "Build the mounds of rubbish well away from the doors of the hall, where the deluge is fiercest," she ordered. "Then the rainstorms can wash it away more quickly. That should put a stop to the city folk's plundering."

"Mistress," Ansel called, making Marrimian turn back toward her as she pointed a fat finger up toward the tall shattered crystal windows on the far side of the hall. "Krann is here now, mistress." Krann was standing where he often did during the daylight hours, looking out toward Rainbows' End.

Thanking Ansel, Marrimian quickly gathered up the damp hems of her skirt and hurried across the hall to climb the new stairway that the carpenters had built up to the gallery. But when she reached the head of the stairs she hesitated and looked sadly down at Krann where he leaned against the cold, damp stonework of the window, silhouetted forlornly against the curtain of rain. She frowned and bit her lip as she wondered what she could do to stop him yearning for his home in Elundium, far beyond Rainbows' End. She had offered him everything—her love, her life—but still she saw the pain deep within him, in his unguarded moments, although he strove so hard to hide it from her. She knew that it was not the nightmare monsters which had haunted his birth that filled his head now and gave him such pain and longings; these she had silenced with their touching and banished to mere shadows. But she still feared that a love for Fairlight burned somewhere inside him and she knew that it was beyond the power of her love to extinguish it or to put right the thousands of wrongs and whispered half-truths that he had grown up amongst.

Marrimian shivered, fearing the day when the rainbows would once more shower brightly upon the horizon, knowing that somehow she would have to find the courage to let him go back, no matter how much it hurt her, that to try to hold on to him would destroy whatever love he had for her. She swallowed her fears and, brushing a stray lock of hair out of her eyes, moved silently to the windowsill to stand beside him. Krann felt her presence and turned his head, blinking his wet eyelashes. He smiled and pointed out at the heavy curtain of rain beating down on the steep, glistening roofs of the city.

"When will it ever stop?" he shouted above the roar of the water pouring out of the swollen gutters and the steady, thunderous hiss of the countless waterfalls that cascaded and boiled down every winding flight of stone steps and every twisting alleyway to gush out through the Hurlers' Gate and into the flooding marshes.

"It will rain for an age of days yet," she shouted back, but he barely nodded as he stared out at the drifting rain squalls and the shrouds of mist and low clouds that enveloped the city, blotting out everything beyond it.

"There is trouble in the terraces," she called against the noise of the rain, touching his sleeve and drawing him away from the window. "The hoe-masters are saying that the floodwater beyond the dyke is seeping back into the drainage channels and flooding the terraces."

Krann frowned and listened anxiously to every-thing that the scullion had related to Marrimian, angry with himself that he had done nothing but gaze through the broken window toward Rain-bows' End, selfishly thinking that he had done enough to help Marrimian by building the dyke and the steep terraces behind it. He had allowed himself to wallow in his impatience and self-pity since the deluge began. He turned quickly, climb-ing up on to the stone windowsill, and leaned out between the jagged sheets of crystal, staring down toward the top of the dyke and the swollen flood-waters that lapped against its outer lips. The veils of mist thinned for a moment and drew apart and in the moment before they closed and shrouded everything again in their gray wetness he glimpsed the wide lake of water that stretched out from the lips of the dyke over the marshes and across to a dark reed bank that lay in the distance.

Scrambling back down to the floor of the gallery, he shook the icy raindrops from his cloak and wiped the water out of his eyes with a muslin rag that the scullion had given him soon after the wet seasons had begun.

"There is a bank of reeds that edge the marsh beyond the dyke. It must be damming the water draining out of the terraces," he muttered almost to himself as he paced to the balustrade of the gallery where he gazed down into the hall below, lost in thought.

"Will everything that we planted be flooded?" Marrimian asked anxiously hurrying to his side.

"Yes . . ." Krann began but his voice faded into silence, his eyebrows creasing into a frown, as he leaned on the rail and watched two of the children who were squatting down beside one of the muddy puddles that the harvesters had left on their way to the kitchens. "Boats!" he whispered as he watched one of the children push a blunt splinter of wood across the muddy water and send sluggish ripples toward the other child, who had stretched out her hand, waiting to push it back. Turning around, Krann laughed and grasped Marrimian's hands.

"I had never imagined it would rain as much as it has. I had thought that the marsh beyond the dyke would easily swallow all the rainwater that would pour out of the drainage channels."

"But boats . . . what are boats?" interrupted Marrimian, staring down at the children. "How can they help us to save the terraces from flooding?"

Krann laughed softly as he realized that on the journey across this land of swamps and quickmarsh he had not seen one raft or boat. He had seen the bark sledges that the harvesters used as shoes to cross the soft mud and swampy water but nothing that resembled a boat. Without another word he took Marrimian back to the broken window and carefully drew her a picture of a boat in the beads of moisture that clouded the crystal.

"We could ride in the boat across the floodwater

beyond the dyke and out to that reed bank and
perhaps, if the level of the floods beyond is lower,
we could cut channels through the earth to drain
the waters threatening to flood the terraces," he
explained patiently, but as he spoke the seeds of an
idea began to flower. "We could begin the task of
draining all the swamps and mires of Gnarlsmyre—all the way to the great waterfalls of Rainbows' End!" he added, his eyes shining with
excitement.

"But . . ." Marrimian tried to catch his flying
cloak tails and remind him of the endless leagues of
swamps and quickmarsh that lay beyond the city,
but he leapt down the broad staircase, taking the
treads three at a time, deaf to her as he shouted for
the carpenters to gather around him.

Krann soon had the men carve a crude skeleton
of a large flat-bottomed boat from the rough boards
of timber that they had cut to finish the galleries.
The boat slowly grew into the shape Krann had
marked out on the floor of the hall in the shadow
of the Glitterspike. Night had darkened and smothered everything in its black wet mist, but Krann
would not let them rest and brought fresh reed
lamps.

The ring of hammers pegging the planks of
marsh-oaks together and the scraping thump of
rough sacking soaked in grease being forced with
flat masons' chisels into every crack between the
planks echoed through the gloomy hall all night. By
the first gray flicker of morning light the boat was
finished and the hall folk crowded around whisper-

ing and pointing while Krann stood back, his hands on his hips and a broad smile of satisfaction on his face.

Marrimian stood beside him, realizing that as their Queen she must ride in the boat without showing the slightest trace of fear. She held the bowl of pottage that Ansel had brought her from the kitchens and savored the scent of tunsole leaves as she watched, and listened to the hall folk's whisperings about the boat. There were rumors rippling through the hall, fresh from the guards who had returned from the dyke. They said the city folk were clambering on top of the city wall and calling out that the terraces would flood before two days had passed and that all they had labored to achieve would be washed away. The whispering hall folk looked anxiously at Marrimian and Krann as they stood together beside the boat.

"Will you not break your fast before riding across the water in that . . . that boat?" Ansel asked of Krann. She gave it a wide berth and a suspicious glare as she offered him a bowl of the pottage and a crust of black husk bread to soak it up.

"Do you fear the boat?" Krann asked with an edge of laughter in his voice.

"Fear it? I'm not afraid of such a thing, but it's just not natural floating on water," Ansel grumbled. "Water's for fish and birds, not for the likes of things that look like giants' shoes." She glared down at the boat with her broad hands planted on her hips. "I'll lay a scuttle's life on it that if you build another, one of the giants who live beyond

Rainbows' End will come looking for his new set of shoes."

The hall folk did not know whether to laugh or shiver with terror at the scullion's words. She had traveled beyond Rainbows' End and knew much more of the world past the Hurlers' Gate than they did. Krann saw their indecision and the fear that her words had sown in them. He beckoned Ansel to come close to him and whispered, "There *are* no giants beyond Rainbows' End. I would swear my life on that. But in Elundium the ferrymen use boats just like this one to ferry people across wide rivers and lakes, and even the horses that you loved from my stories traveled in them," and he urged her to dispel the fears that she had started because some of the folk from the hall would have to ride with him in the boat and help to dig channels through the reed bank.

Ansel's cheeks flushed, showing blotchy purple, as she realized what her careless words had done. She thought for a moment and then muttered, "Giants! What a fool I am: they hate the rain and you'd never find them traipsing through the swamps and mires of Gnarlsmyre to look for a set of new shoes!"

All around her sighs of relief rippled through the crowd but she had hardly given them time to catch their breaths before she called Vetchim to come out of his warm corner by her baking ovens. She beckoned him forward and boldly patted the stern post of the boat as she pointed to the narrow seats. Then she told the hall folk, "In Elundium horses sit on those seats while the ferryman takes them across lakes and rivers."

The crowd surged around the boat, craning their necks and giving nods of approval as they hung on every one of Ansel's words. "If these boats are good enough for our Queen and the horses of Elundium to travel in then Vetchim and I will ride across the floodwater in one of them and dig channels in the reed banks," declared the scullion, folding her arms so firmly across her bosom that she defied any argument.

Vetchim looked down at the boat, touched the stern and laughed. "Why, it's just like a huge bark sledge, except this has places to sit."

Krann hid a smile at the thought of horses sitting on the seats and Vetchim's idea that it looked like a sledge. Stepping back, he began to choose the strongest-looking hoemasters to accompany them in the boat. Carpenters carried it above their heads out of the hall and down through the terraces to the edge of the dyke.

Marrimian shivered and drew her slippery, grease-smeared hood tighter against the pouring rain. She looked out across the swollen lake at the dark smudge of reed bank that showed faintly through the drifting mist.

Suddenly a shower of stones skipped across the rainbroken water beyond the dyke and voices jeered and cursed her. A badly aimed arrow struck the top of the dyke forty paces from where Krann had ordered the boat to be lowered into the water.

"The boat! Quickly, get down into the boat!" cried Krann.

In her anger Marrimian forgot her own counsel. She snatched a bow and a quiver of arrows from Treyster and, turning toward the sheer walls of the city, aimed at the crowd of dark shapes silhouetted on the top of the wall.

Krann spun round and put his hand upon her arm. "Do not kill any of the city folk. Aim high above their heads if you *must* loose an arrow," he cried.

"But why?" hissed Marrimian, breaking loose from his grip and drawing the feathered flight of the arrow taut against her cheek. "Why should I show any longer a moment's mercy to these city scum when they have tried to steal the crops we grow upon the terraces? You know that they would kill us now if our guards were not here, or have you forgotten the attacks on the harvesters they make at every opportunity and how they curse and stone the hall folk if they dare to venture down into the city? Listen to what they are shouting: they are mocking you, the dyke builder, they are laughing at you for building a terrace of lakes to drown everything that we have planted."

"They are only words," he whispered fiercely. "They are the shouts of desperate people. Listen to the hopelessness in their voices: it is the humiliation of defeat. They know the seeds and shoots that we have planted have flourished in these terraces, that you have harvested enough to feed the people of the hall, while they, through their stubbornness, have gone hungry. Offer them the barter that the others gave you, their crafts and skills in exchange for food at the doors of Glitterspike Hall. Their voices echo how close they are to accepting it and when they see these floodwaters drain away, making the terraces safe, it will weaken them still further. There is no need to kill them."

Marrimian hesitated, easing the arrow from the bow string. "Are you sure your boat will reach the reed banks and that you can drain the floodwaters seeping back into the terraces?" she asked, casting a quick, doubtful glance down into the boat.

Krann laughed and beckoned the scullion forward. "If it takes Ansel's weight, then you have my promise on it."

"I'd rather have our Queen murder every ironmaster and every lampwick than be the first to step down into that boat!" muttered Ansel, but she reluctantly tottered to the lip of the dyke and looked down grimly at the craft.

Krann laughed at her fears and jumped lightly into the boat. Whispering to her to remember the horses of Elundium, he reached up with both hands toward her. Huffing and grumbling, she slithered awkwardly down the steep side of the dyke. Vetchim and two hoemasters held her, their hands thrust beneath her armpits, while she felt for the bottom of the boat with her toes. Marrimian stifled a cry of concern as the scullion wavered, then lost her balance and sprawled into the bottom of the boat in a tangled mess of muddy, wet apron tails. The boat rocked wildly from side to side and waves broke over the edge. It settled lower in the water, but did not sink.

The crowd silhouetted on top of the city wall suddenly jeered louder and as they saw the scullion sit up in the boat hurled a shower of stones toward her.

"You see it floats, even with our weight," called out Krann, urging Marrimian to be quick before the crowd were lucky aiming their stones.

Marrimian turned, threw back her hood and shouted through the pouring rain toward the dark figures standing on the wall. She offered once more to barter food for their skills if they would accept her as their Queen.

"Queen of fools, who would try to float out across the floods," jeered a host of voices.

"How can we barter with a dead Queen?" called out a gaunt ironmaster and those close to him muttered and nodded. But although they cursed and jeered, Marrimian heard the doubt in their voices. There was a whisper of fear, perhaps even a glimmer of jealousy and a grudging respect for all that she had done to try to feed the hall folk.

She bent the bow and aimed the arrow high above their heads to vanish in the curtain of rain and laughed as the crowds ducked down behind the wall. "Killing you would be easy. The people of the hall are well fed and strong and Krann has taught us the ways of Elundium with spears and long bows while you are all weak and hungry. But that would have been my father's way, to stifle you with force. I will have none of the fear and terror that he spread amongst you. Remember, the doors of Glitterspike Hall are open from dawn to sunset to every one of you for peaceful barter," she shouted before she turned toward the boat and, grasping Krann's hands, clambered lightly down the steep side of the dyke.

"Set extra guards along the dyke until we return," she ordered a waiting hoemaster who helped her down into the boat.

Ansel and Treasel moved to make room for her while keeping a firm hold on the hard wooden boards they were sitting on, digging their fingernails into the grain of the wood as Marrimian settled in between them. Her movements made the boat rock from side to side.

"Mistress! Mistress!" Ansel cried out as her stomach turned over and over and her bright red oven-scarred cheeks drained of color.

"Why don't you crouch with Vetchim and the hoemasters if you are so frightened?" laughed Marrimian, pointing down to where they were already huddled with the trenching spades in the stern of the boat.

"I can't mistress, not if I'm to look after you."

Marrimian smiled at the scullion's face, white and taut with terror, and opened her mouth to thank her, but Krann called out, "Sit still! Sit very still or you will upset the boat," and he dug the long pole he had fashioned for steering into the steep wall of the dyke and pushed them clear of the bank.

Ansel wailed and clutched at her stomach, screwing her eyes tightly shut. Treasel buried her head in her hands as the boat began to move across the flooded marsh. Marrimian glanced over her shoulder toward the widening gap of waves and ripples that broke the surface of the water behind them and felt a small thrill of terror run through her.

"Watch out for our return," she shouted to her sisters Syrenea and Treyster and the scattering of guards standing along the lip of the dyke and she turned to look ahead at the dark smudge of reed bank drawing closer to them through the sheets of rain. She caught a glimpse of the sheer walls of the city crowded with silent, watching figures as Krann moved carefully along the boat, pushing the long pole deep into the water on either side, directing their craft toward the reed bank. Small waves slapped and broke against the bow, sending widening ripples back against the dyke. Ansel groaned and leaned over the side as her stomach churned over and over.

"Queen? Queen of fools!" cackled Erek, rubbing her wet hands together as she watched the boat vanish into the drifting rain and mist from one of the secret holes in the great wall that the crones had been using to spy on the terraces. "Now is the moment. Stir up the city folk to overrun the hall. Make them steal all that has been harvested from these miserable terraces," she whispered to the two crones who crouched beside her. "Spread new rumors amongst them. Tell them I will barter the roots and vegetables that the hall folk have harvested and stored in the hall for the cured flesh of mudbeasts I have saved so carefully and which now awaits them in the entrance of the Shambles."

"But our sweetmeats are not ready," muttered one of the crones.

"No matter," shrieked Erek. "Whip up a frenzy amongst the city people and shadow them when they burst into the hall. Carry fire secretly beneath your riddled rags and take everything that has been harvested. Burn and trample everything underfoot so that if that Queen of fools ever returns she will find nothing but ruin."

Shrieking and springing through the rain-washed lanes and alleyways, the crones began to weave their treachery at every window latch and door crack throughout the city.

Ansel began to feel better and opened her eyes. She shrieked and flung herself against Marrimian. "Mistress, mistress," she stuttered as she rocked the boat violently. "There are trees beneath us! I saw marshoaks and wildflower bushes and clumps of reeds and . . ."

"Sit still!" shouted Krann angrily as the violent motion of the boat almost toppled him into the water. He staggered, clutching the long pole, and drove the boat in hard amongst the reeds that grew along the bank.

Broken reed stems scoured and scratched against the flat underside of the boat and waves of mud sprayed up over the bow as they hit the bank. "Grab hold of the reeds," shouted Krann as the boat stopped with a shudder and began to drift backwards away from the bank, sending him sprawling on his knees in the bottom of the boat.

Marrimian reached out and held on to the reeds that dripped forlornly over the edge while Krann climbed back on his feet and gently nudged the craft in close to the bank. He scrambled up across the sticky, rainsoaked mud as he searched for something to tie the boat to. Marrimian bunched up her skirts and with Treasel beside her climbed up after Krann, at times both sinking to their knees in the soft, squelching mud before they reached the top of the bank and forced a passage through the dense reeds that grew there.

"Your Gnarlsmyre has become a sea of lakes," Krann called out above the sound of pouring rain as he pointed into the gloomy, drifting mists and rain squalls beyond the reeds.

Marrimian could see the dark shapes of reed banks and swollen, flat stretches of water and everywhere the tops of drowned bushes and trees. She rubbed the rain from her eyes and peered ahead. "What will happen when all the floodwater we have crossed drains into the lake beyond this reed bank? Surely it will overflow back through the bank and eventually drown the terraces?"

Krann frowned and slowly nodded, then after a moment's thought he shook his head. "No, not if we cut channels in all the reed banks that we can reach with this boat. If we drain enough of the water dammed by these banks of reeds there will be no flood."

* * *

Marrimian stood up cautiously in the boat, stretched her aching arms and blew on her numb, raw fingers. She had lost count of how long she and the other two women had been on their hands and knees bailing out the rainwater from the bottom of their boat. They were all cold, soaking wet and filthy dirty from floundering in the sticky mud as they helped to drag the boat across each new reed bank, and they had to empty it of rainwater each time before they could begin to drag it out of the water.

"How long will this nightmare go on, mistress?" Ansel cursed from where she kneeled in the bottom of the boat gathering up the floating muslin cloths she had spread in the cold rainwater and wringing them out over the side.

"I really don't know. Perhaps until it stops raining," Marrimian muttered wearily, shivering as a rain squall lashed her face.

Krann suddenly appeared on the top of the bank above the boat. "Vetchim says that there is something familiar about this place. We caught a glimpse of something strange beyond this reed bank, half hidden in the mist. We are going to try and cross to take a closer look. Bring the boat along that side of the bank. He thinks there is an island of half-submerged marshoaks. You can just see the tops of the trees further along to your right whenever the mist clears. If he is right, you can tie the boat to one of the trees and wait for us." His voice carried to them against the noise of the rain drumming on the reed stalks.

Marrimian shouted back that none of them was very good at steering the boat, but he had already vanished back into the reeds. Clumsily she tried to use the long pole and twice nearly capsized the boat as it veered away from her and ploughed into the reeds that grew close to the bank. The bow was riding up over broken stems that lay just beneath the surface of the floodwater. "Let us pull it along, mistress," pleaded Ansel. "Let's reach out and catch hold of the reedstems that grow beside the bank and gently pull it along."

The wild rocking motion of the boat as it lifted up out of the water had terrified Marrimian and she quickly nodded. Laying the long pole in the boat she crouched with Ansel and Treasel to reach out and clutch at the brittle reed stems and ease the boat toward the dark mass of marshoak branches emerging above the reeds in the drifting shrouds of mist and rain.

"Surely those trees should have lost their dark clusters of leaves when the wet seasons began?" Marrimian called out to Treasel.

The marshgirl frowned as she peered through the mist toward the dark canopies of leaves. There was something familiar, something menacing, in their shapes and she opened her mouth to call out and warn Marrimian when the boat suddenly ground and grated over the first of the hidden marsh-oak branches that lay just beneath the surface.

"This is far enough," cried Ansel in terror of the boat capsizing as it juddered against another thick branch and she leaned over the side of the boat to grasp at a handful of hanging twigs to stop them drifting further in amongst the trees. She noticed something bobbing up and down in the water. It brushed against the bow of the boat and then slowly floated past her, making her lean further out and try to look down at it. Ansel caught her breath as she stared down and saw a small naked body, a child's body, in the water. The skin was bleached gray and wrinkled and its fingers and toes were hideously bloated. "Mistress! Mistress!" she cried in horror, letting go of the handful of twigs and sinking down dizzy in the bottom of the boat. "There was a child! I saw a . . ."

"I know this place," Treasel hissed, cutting across the scullion's gasp of horror and making Marrimian turn to the wild-eyed marshgirl. "This is the marshoak island on the edge of Fenmire marsh and over there, beyond the trees and that reed bank, lies the marshery of Mertz, the marshery the elders banished me from, the one where Mertzork . . ."

"Mistress, look!" cried Ansel, gripping Marrimian's arm and shaking it forcefully. Both women looked up into the dark tangle of branches above their heads. "There are people up in the branches. I can see their eyes in the shadows above us, they are staring down at us, hundreds and hundreds of them," she hissed, loosing the dagger from beneath her apron.

"It wasn't leaves that you saw, mistress," whispered Treasel fearfully as she tried to push the boat away from the trees. "It was strips of beastskin and all the rag ends of old beastskin cloaks of the people of the marshery who could not find a place in the huts to weather out the wet seasons."

Marrimian put her hand on Treasel's arm and whispered to her to be still. She looked up, her eyes widening in the gloom, and saw the silent, wretched, bone-thin figures that clung to every branch and bough beneath the leaking canopy of rotting beastskins. She moved closer to Treasel and was asking her why so many of them had been driven out of the marshery when a child screamed and weakly struggled in the weary hands of one of the marsh women in the lower branches. It fell with flailing arms and legs and landed with a loud splash in the murky waters beside the boat. The woman made no attempt to rescue the tiny child, she merely stared helplessly down through the tangle of branches as it thrashed its arms weakly and vanished beneath the bows of the boat.

"Quickly, catch hold of it before it sinks!" cried Marrimian, throwing herself across the boat and making it rock violently as she grasped the child's arm and hauled it roughly out of the water to safety. The wet child, no more than a trembling, shivering bundle of bones, stared at her with large, iridescent eyes.

"Have you no feelings?" Marrimian shouted up toward the silent, staring faces above her. "Don't you care if the child drowns?"

Ansel took the child from her and wrapped it up warmly in her apron, and the voices suddenly started whispering above their heads, blending in with the driving rain which was beating down on the canopy of beastskins. Here and there the marsh people crowded in the branches brought their hands to their foreheads and twisted their fingers into horn shapes.

"Who are these people?" Marrimian asked Treasel in a hushed whisper.

Treasel looked up and swept her gaze through the shadows beneath the dripping canopy. "Normally it is only the weak and the old, or those who have displeased the elders, those who cannot fight for a place in the marshery, who seek refuge in the branches of the marshoaks until the floodwaters recede. They survive by chewing the bark of the trees or catching the crawlers and leeches that feed on the rotting corpses of those who grow weak and fall helplessly into the water, just as that child fell from its mother's arms."

"But I could not let it drown," interrupted Marrimian in a frightened whisper, her lips trembling at the brutality of these marsh people's lives.

"But you have stolen the food from their mouths by saving that child," whispered Treasel, looking nervously up at the sea of bleak, hunger-ravaged faces that stared down at them. "Remember, mistress, out here in the marshes the strong feed off the weak. It is the way of my people . . ."

Treasel's voice faltered and her eyebrows creased into a frown. She had been looking up for the

slightest sign of movement, expecting at any moment that the tree dwellers would drop into the boat and strangle them with rusty sharpwires, when she caught sight of the wrinkled faces of elders perched in the highest boughs.

"There are hundreds more crowded into these marshoaks than would normally shelter here. There are elders, I think, and many of the marshmen who pledged themselves to you at the Hurlers' Gate," she murmured, reaching out with her left hand to grip at a twisted branch the boat had drifted against and flexing her arm to push them out of the way of the trees.

"Do you mean they are the marshmen who worshiped me as the Beast-Rider? The ones with Vetchim whom I commanded to guard the city? The ones the healing woman turned against me?" Marrimian asked quickly, her mind racing, as she stopped the marshgirl from pushing the boat further.

"They will kill us, mistress, if we stay another moment," Ansel muttered urgently shielding the crying child with her weather-cloak. She glared up into the crowded branches and made sure that she still had hold of her dagger.

"No," hissed Marrimian firmly. "They once pledged themselves to serve me. They are as much my people as are the people of Glitterspike Hall and the city of Glor and I must care for them. I will not abandon them here in this wretched place."

Without another word she stood up in the boat, cast back her high weather hood and looked up toward the crowds who huddled beneath the leaking canopy of stinking beastskins.

"It is the real Beast Lady," whispered voices amongst the marshmen in the branches. "It is the one we pledged ourselves to in the shadows of the Hurlers' Gate."

"Who amongst you," Marrimian cried, "would renew that pledge to the firstborn daughter of Glitterspike Hall, to the one who tamed the mudbeast and rode upon its back and walked between the savage beasts shackled around the Glitterspike to touch that finger of crystal and claim the throne and all Gnarlsmyre? Who amongst you would call me their Queen and follow me back through the doors of the hall where food and safety await?" She paused and cast her gaze slowly across their startled faces.

"Mertzork told us that *he* had touched the Glitterspike," muttered one of the elders in a doubting voice, "and Pinvey, his Queen, claimed to have been the beast-rider." He shook his thin, wrinkled face from side to side in confusion.

"Why should we believe you when Pinvey rode amongst us upon Andzey's shoulders?" asked another of the elders.

"Andzey is not a beast and they are ruling us with a tissue of lies!" cried a marshman, lowering his voice quickly as he looked anxiously over his shoulder to where the marshery lay hidden by the mist and then he added, "Ask any of us for the real truth, that is, any one of us who is brave enough to tell how the healing woman and her gathering of hags held us in such terror with her magic spells and her swarms of poisonous spiders. She made us bow to Mertzork and take Pinvey as his Queen. She forced us into breaking our pledges. But I for one am ashamed of what I did."

Uneasy whispers broke out beneath the canopy. The elders shifted in the branches and sent a shower of rancid, bitter-tasting raindrops from their rough shelter of hides into the boat. Their whispers became chants and Marrimian heard her name pass from branch to branch. The huge trees began to sway as if tugged by a sudden wind as the marshmen stirred. The huddles of wretched hide-chewers and old women with their children tied to them and every one of the marsh people who clung to the lower branches leaned out as far as they dared to stare down at the woman who had really tamed the mudbeast.

"It was Marrimian who touched the Glitter-spike," called out a hesitant voice close to where the elders perched. "I know she tells the truth because I was there in the great hall. I saw her walk between the shackled mudbeasts."

The whispers and chants fell silent. Heads turned and necks craned to catch a glimpse of the marshman who had spoken.

"If this is the truth then all of you deserve to die," called out one of the elders gravely. "Every marsh-man, marshwader and marshhunter who, having pledged himself and then broken his pledge and turned blind eyes to Marrimian's triumph, should be punished. And we, the elders of this marshery, deserve no better for swallowing Mertzork's lies and allowing him to seize the marshery."

"His story of touching the Glitterspike made me uneasy," muttered another of the elders.

"Ulloreto questioned their triumph and look what they did to him," called another.

Marrimian clapped her hands impatiently. The day was drawing to an end and gloomy, gray shadows were gathering beneath the canopy of dripping skins. There was no time for argument. "It would seem to me that you have suffered enough for following Mertzork and my sister since clearly they cared nothing for you if you die of cold and starvation." She paused and thought for a moment. "There is room enough for all of you in Glitterspike Hall, and food and warm clothes, but only for those who renew their pledges and are prepared to serve me and make amends for their treachery."

"What do we do? What will become of us?" cried a voice in the lower branches from amongst the huddle of women and children.

Marrimian turned awkwardly in the boat and smiled up at the wretched, filthy creatures and asked them, "Who would you choose to follow—my sister Pinvey or me?"

The women whispered and mulled together and one of them called out, "Pinvey has treated us cruelly. We could do no worse chewing the hides you throw to us and gleaning the rinds and scraps that fall from your table."

"They are wild and dangerous—don't bring them into the hall, mistress!" hissed Ansel, staring up at the mass of filthy faces in the branches overhead.

Marrimian looked down at the scullion, her eyes blazing with anger. "They are starved and wretched and close to death, just as Treasel was when we rescued her from the marshes. Would you rather we had passed her by?"

"Oh no!" Ansel answered, catching the look of hurt in the marshgirl's eyes.

Treasel suddenly stood up beside Marrimian and shouted toward the crowd of ragged figures beneath the canopy.

"There is no fighting for scraps of food in Glitterspike Hall: you'll have to mind your manners and earn your place at table by bartering with your skills . . ."

"Your Queen will never take us into her hall to mingle with the likes of you city women," sneered one of the old women. "She'll treat us no better than Mertzork or that woman who calls herself his Queen; she has no use for a haggle of hide-chewers and bent old harvesters who can't even comb through the mire for roots and grubs to feed themselves."

"She'll simply choose the strongest marshmen and use them to fight the army that Mertzork is going to lead against the city when the wet seasons end and the floods recede," cried out another of the women, shaking her fist at Treasel. "She'll leave us here to rot in these marshoaks."

"No!" cried Treasel, throwing back her weather hood so that they could recognize that she had come from the marshes. "My mistress would never turn anyone away from the doors of Glitterspike Hall: she cares for all her people, even the weak and the old."

"You would treat us equally with the marshmen and take us all into your great hall?" asked a host of startled voices as all the women clinging to the lower branches peered down at Treasel. The whisper went amongst them that they remembered the elders banishing her to die in the marshes for spoiling the hides that she had been given to soften with her teeth.

"All those amongst you who pledge to serve me shall have a place in Glitterspike Hall," Marrimian called again, silencing the last of the murmured doubts in the branches.

A voice suddenly called out from the tall reed stems on the bank stretching away toward the flooded channel and made the tree dwellers shrink back into the shadows. "Marrimian, where are you? Shout so that I can follow your voice!"

Marrimian turned to Treasel, her eyes bright and shining. "It is Krann! I had almost forgotten about him. Here! We're over here!" she shouted cupping her hands to her mouth against the noise of the rain.

Krann with Vetchim beside him and the two hoemasters following wearily in their footsteps, broke through the reeds close to the spreading marshoak branches. "The reed bank is too wide to dig a channel through, we must find our way back to the city before darkness falls and . . ." Krann's voice fell away to nothing as he saw the canopy of rotting beastskins and the crowds of wretched, filthy figures sheltering beneath it.

"Wait there," Marrimian called to him. "We will push the boat across and collect you. You must meet the marsh people Mertzork and my sister Pinvey banished to starve in these marshoak trees. We are going to ferry them all back to Glitterspike Hall."

Krann was about to shake his head and tell her to leave these wild marsh people where they were. He felt it would be madness to allow them to overrun the hall. But as he looked up into the tangle of branches he caught a look of hope in their bone-thin, desperate faces. He saw the way they followed Marrimian with their eyes as she moved the boat out from beneath the trees. They looked as if they feared she might vanish for ever in the curtain of driving rain.

"You are a greater queen than I ever imagined," he muttered, almost to himself, as the boat bumped in amongst the reeds, and Vetchim, catching Krann's words, vigorously nodded his head.

"Yes. She is the Beast-Rider. She is our Queen," he agreed as he reached out and caught hold of the bow of the boat.

Krann looked up at the crowds of silent, staring faces as the boat glided in amongst the branches and ground shuddering to a halt. "We'll never ferry all these marsh people back to the edge of the dyke before night falls," he whispered with concern.

"I have promised. If we go back without them they will think I have broken that promise." Marrimian frowned, looking out at the drifting rain squalls and the darkening mist closing in around the marshoak trees. She reached out and clutched a dead and withered handful of thin branches overhead to keep her balance but they broke off in her hand. "The canopy of beastskins has kept these twig fingers fairly dry," she whispered quickly as an idea began to form in her mind. "We could make torches out of the dry twigs and weather out the night here amongst the marshoak branches and we will listen to everything that Mertzork and my sister, Pinvey, have done during their reign of terror in Fenmire Marshery."

Krann didn't attempt one word of argument. He saw what power Marrimian held over the marsh people and he smiled at her in the deepening gloom beneath the leaking canopy. He cut a thin strip of fabric from the hem of his weather-cloak, wrung it out and bound it tightly around the bundle of twigs, making sure that a stout branch lay in the center of the bundle as a handle.

"Warm the spark in the palm of your hand before you try to crackle it alight," he whispered, reaching up to break off another handful of twigs for the second torch and giving orders to the hoemasters and the scullion to make as many torches as they could.

Marrimian crouched in the bottom of the boat and held her breath as she crackled the spark. The marsh people were at a loss to know what was happening and gasped and clung tightly to the thick branches overhead as the spark blazed alight between her fingers and sent small flames dancing amongst the tops of the bundles of dead twigs. Marrimian lifted the blazing torch above her head, using it to light the next one Krann and Treasel had finished binding together. And then, one by one, as the hoemasters and Ansel bound more, she touched and lit them and passed them up carefully to the marsh people.

"I cannot offer you food until we reach the doors of Glitterspike Hall," she called toward the flickering torchlight, "but I can give you warmth and light to thaw out the coldness of your bones through the long night of darkness that stretches ahead of us. And when the first light of dawn breaks through the mist and rain we will begin the journey back across the floodwater . . ." She paused and frowned. The marsh people were clawing at the leathery bark of the branches all around them, tearing it off in narrow strips and holding it out in the dancing torchlight toward her.

"They are offering you their food," Treasel whispered. "They are offering to share everything they have. I have never known this happen before. Please do not refuse to take it, mistress," she begged.

Marrimian smiled at the marshgirl and reached up and took a handful of the tough curls of bark. Keeping one for herself, she passed the others to those in the boat. "Tonight," she cried, lifting the bark strip to her mouth, "tonight we shall feast on the delicacies from the marshes," and to a rising chorus of murmurs of delight above her head she bit into the tough and bitter-tasting strip of bark. She heard Ansel groan and glanced down to see a shudder of disgust cross her face. "Eat it all," she hissed to her. "Do not show these people a blink of disrespect or I will make you eat the bark of every tree that you can see from the windows of Glitter-spike Hall."

Grinding the fibrous bark between her teeth, Marrimian swallowed the first sour mouthful and looked up into the flickering torchlight that reflected from the rough underside of the canopy of dripping beastskins. The marsh people had shifted on their branches and drawn into tight knots around each of the guttering torches as they chewed on the bark. They were whispering together and holding out their hands toward the dancing flames, sighing and murmuring as their leaping shadows raced between the branches.

Krann stood up beside Marrimian with a bundle of new torches in his arms. "You must ask them if your other sister, Alea, is still alive and Pinvey's prisoner," he whispered, making her start and forcing the color to drain from her cheeks.

"I had forgotten all about Alea," she cried, her voice stilling the marsh people in the canopy above her. The sudden silence was only broken by the rattle of the pouring rain in the reed beds beyond the circle of their torchlight.

"Alea? Is that the name of the poor wretch guarded by Pinvey's spiders?"

Marrimian spun round toward the speaker, almost capsizing the boat. "Have you seen her?" she asked, searching the faces of the women for the one who had spoken. "She has locks of night-dark hair and stands this high beside me and she wears . . ."

The voice cackled again, cutting across Marrimian's words. "Yes, the one you ask about is Pinvey's prisoner. She crouches in rags and tatters, caged beneath the chambers Pinvey uses in the marshery. Pinvey treats her more cruelly than anyone else," she added, spitting out a mouthful of bark.

"We must rescue her before dawn breaks," cried Marrimian but the women huddling down around the guttering torches and even the elders and the marshmen in their high branches shook their heads.

"We dare not go near her," called out one of the marshmen. "Pinvey used to offer her to us for our pleasure when she ordered her to lead Andzey down from the cage where they are kept together but there are venomous spiders hidden in the pleats and folds of her ragged gown."

"Would you have touched my sister?" Marrimian asked, her lips tightening and her eyes blazing with anger. "Would you have taken her against her will and added to her misery?" An uneasy silence spread through the branches and wherever she looked the marshmen dropped their gaze.

"Yes, we might have used her, before we saw the way that Andzey respected her. That is the way it is here in the marshery with prisoners, especially with women that are stolen during the jousts from the city of Glor," called out a hesitant voice above Marrimian's head.

"Andzey is the rightful lord of this marshery and we would follow his ways if he were free. Your sister, Alea, was haughty at first and shunned Andzey's help but now she sits closer to him," called out one of the old women.

"We hated her at first for her high-handed ways," said another, "and we cursed and spat upon her when she led Andzey by the gossamer reins that the healing woman had bound across his face down to where we chew the beastskin hides in the mud on the edge of the marshery."

"At first we thought that Alea was a part of Pinvey's cruelty, that she enjoyed watching Andzey crawl on his hands and knees through the mud," added another woman, "but she has changed; she helps Andzey when he stumbles."

And everywhere beneath the leaking canopy voices muttered and whispered Alea's and Andzey's names and talked of the spark of love that seemed to have been kindled between them inside their cage of spiders' webs.

"I could guide you in that floating platform close to the marshery, just close enough for you to see where their cage hangs above the floodwater, but if we drift too close and the spiders scent us there will be danger for both of them," hissed one of the bolder marshmen. "Though all you will see is a tangle of gossamer webs woven between the bars, thicker than the cloak that hangs from your shoulders."

"Then I dare not try to rescue them, I dare not risk killing them both," Marrimian muttered wretchedly sitting down in the boat and drawing her weather-cloak tightly against the cold.

"No," whispered Krann, sitting down close beside her. "You must trust their lives to fate; there is no other choice."

Close to them, sitting astride one of the lowest branches, her swollen feet dangled in the murky water, a shadowy thin old hag wrapped in rags saw the despair in Marrimian's face. She wanted to reach out to touch her shoulder and comfort her, but she hesitated, fearing to reveal that she had taught Alea to milk the spiders' venom. There were too many listening ears beneath this leaking canopy, too many telling tongues belonging to the waders and the hunters and even to some of the hide-chewers that she did not wholly trust. They might not believe this Queen of the Glitterspike with her talk of food and dry clothes and might trade her secrets for a dry corner in one of Mertzork's huts above the floodwater. Her secret had reached the tip of her tongue but she shook her head, snapped her mouth shut and slipped back unseen into the shadows.

Dawn shivered through the branches, its cold, wet fingers probing every secret pleat and hidden fold of Marrimian's weather-cloak. She blinked her numb eyelids, stamped her frozen feet on the bottom of the boat and looked up into the dreary, gray-black shadows beneath the beastskins in the branches. The torches had long ago burned down to spluttering sparks that hissed as they vanished in the ink-black water. The marsh people were sitting statue-still amongst the boughs of the trees, watching her, waiting silently to see if she would keep her promise.

"It will take days, endless days, to move all these people," grumbled Ansel as she rocked the fretful child they had saved from drowning.

Krann looked out into the drifting curtain of mist and rain toward the last of the reed banks they had cut through with drainage channels. "It would be quicker," he whispered to Marrimian, "if we ferried the strongest of the marshmen on to the reed banks and got them to widen the drainage channels so that we could steer the boat through into each of the flooded marshes."

"Yes! That would indeed be the quickest way," she cried and called the strongest marshmen down into the boat.

"No, leave the strips of beastskins where they are," she called up through the branches to the descending marshmen. "There will be new clothes, warm and dry, for you in Glitterspike Hall."

"There, I told you that she would choose the strongest men and leave the rest of us here to die," muttered one of the women, but a few moments later she had to swallow her words. Marrimian and Treasel, leaving Ansel with the child in the boat to go and get everything ready in the hall for their return, climbed awkwardly up into the slippery branches and settled down amongst the marsh people, calling to the elders to choose who should make the first journey when the boat returned.

Marrimian glanced back over her shoulder through the drifting mist and rain to the vanishing cluster of huge marshoaks and the crowds of waiting marshfolk still clinging amongst the branches. She frowned and fidgeted, impatiently pulling at the knots and ties of her weather-cloak. She had wanted to send at least a dozen boat-loads of the marsh people back before she made the journey herself to reassure them that she would keep her word. But Ansel's message had changed all that. Impatiently she looked up at the marshman standing in the stern of the boat, poling it through the muddy waters toward the wide drainage channel that she could see in the dark bank of broken reeds through the mist ahead of them.

"What did Ansel mean? What exactly did she say when she gave you that message? What did you had happened in the hall?" she shouted against the rattle of the rain beating on her hood, asking the marshman for the twentieth time what disaster had befallen the hall while they had waited for the dawn to break beneath the marshoaks.

The marshman shrugged his shoulders as he fought to hold the boat in the center of the swirling channel the floodwaters had cut through the soft mud of the marshes. "She said that you were to hurry back, my Queen. She said that trouble had brewed in your absence and that . . ." He glanced

down as he shouted his answer against the roar of
the rain and his pole snagged on some unseen tangle of roots beneath the water. The boat suddenly
slewed across the swiftly moving muddy water and
shuddered from end to end as it rode up on the
branches of a stunted tree lying just beneath the
surface.

"Keep the boat straight!" cursed the marshman
in the bows, throwing the words across his shoulder as he fought against the rocking movement.
Thrusting his pole in amongst the tangle of hidden
roots and branches, he forced the boat back into the
swirling channel.

Slowly the boat forged toward the gap in the reed
banks. The banks looked higher now the floodwaters were draining away, a steep mass of glistening
mud and broken, dripping reed stems, their blackened, shriveled flowerheads trailing forlornly in
the water. The floodwaters were racing through the
narrow channel, tearing and sucking at the sheer
walls of soft black mud that Krann and the hoemasters had widened for the boat to pass through. The
marshmen sweated and fought against the swirling
tide, thrusting their poles deep into the mud, the
silt and dirty water breaking across the bow. Suddenly the boat surged forward through the gap and
Marrimian saw on either side of them that the
floodwater had almost completely drained away.
There was just a narrow river that flowed between
wide pools of mud and stark marshoaks standing
forlornly above the clumps of reeds and marsh
grasses that had been hidden when they had first set

out this way. Black pindafall birds sat hunched upon the bare branches, their leathery wings wet and glistening in the gray morning light as they waited for the rain to stop so that they could fly again.

"Look! Look at the city!" gasped a dozen voices in the boat. "It's so big . . . it's so . . ."

"Those towers—look, they vanish into the clouds," cried one of the marsh women.

Marrimian leaned forward, sweeping her gaze across the guards who crouched on the high wall of the dyke and looked for Krann or Ansel as the dark walls of the city and its steep, rain-bright roofs, the stone walls and towers of Glitterspike Hall emerged through the heavy curtain of rain and mist. As they touched the bank of the dyke Ansel ran forward to meet them.

"Mistress, mistress—there's been murder and treachery!" she cried, her face blacker than thunder clouds, her quivering jaw thrust out angrily as she grasped Marrimian's hands and helped her up on to the bank. "Those city scum, those ironmasters whose lives you spared, they invaded the hall the moment our backs were turned!"

"Invaded the hall?" Marrimian cried, turning and straining her eyes as she looked up at the sheer towers and high window arches. "Tell me, what has happened? Where is Krann?" she asked, gripping Ansel's arm. "Where are my sisters, and Ankana and the children? We must gather everyone with a bow or a spear—we must fight and drive them out of the hall."

"There's no one left for us to fight, mistress," Ansel muttered bitterly, clenching her fists. "Those city scum fled from the hall the moment our guards appeared, but not before they had almost killed Ankana and done as much damage as possible. And stolen everything that they could lay their thieving hands upon!"

"Ankana? They have hurt Ankana? Quickly, take me to her," Marrimian cried angrily, turning away from the huddle of marsh people who had clung together on the top of the dyke beside her.

She began to climb as quickly as she could up through the terraces toward the hall. The marsh people heard the anger in her voice and began to whisper and glance anxiously up at the narrow terraces that rose in steep steps to the sheer walls of the hall.

"What shall we do with these ragged marsh folk?" asked the hoemaster who was guarding the dyke.

Ansel threw her hands up helplessly and looked along the rim of the dyke to where the other guards crouched facing the Hurlers' Gate and the high walls of the city. "How should I know? You had better escort them to the hall." She frowned and nodded her head. "Yes you had better take them to the hall while you send the boat back across the marshes."

Ansel looked pale and drawn as she began to climb up through the terraces. "I had better hurry," she muttered. "Ankana is close to death and my mistress will need me."

"Ankana, why!" Marrimian cried as she clambered through the highest terraces. "Who would hurt the birthwoman? She is so kind, so gentle."

Krann suddenly appeared above her and stretched out his hands to pull her up to the top of the last remaining wall. He looked gaunt and white-faced and there were tears in his eyes. He hurried her forward. "Come quickly. Ankana is close to death."

Marrimian ran beneath the high archway into the great hall. The acrid stench of smoldering wood and burnt cloth made her wrinkle her nose but the sound of children crying made her turn quickly toward the Glitterspike. "Ankana," she cried seeing the frail birthwoman. She was surrounded by the children and several court healers, their figures gray in the dull light of the hall. She was half-sitting, half-lying against the Glitterspike. Krann had wrapped his weather-cloak around her shoulders but Marrimian could see that she was swathed in burnt rags, her hands and face smeared and encrusted with drying blood.

"Ankana, what has happened?" Marrimian called, forcing a path through the burned and broken chairs and tables that littered the hall, barely noticing the blackened remains of the new gallery and the fire scars on the fluted columns or the smashed and buckled iron fire baskets—the destruction that the city people had caused when they attacked the hall.

Throwing off her weather-cloak, Marrimian fell

down on her knees beside the frail birthwoman and gently gathered her up into her arms.

"There is nothing more we can do for her," whispered one of the healers.

"Surely there must be something? Why did the city folk do this? Why did they want to hurt such a gentle soul?"

Ankana coughed, a dribble of blood wetting the corner of her thin lips, as the sound of Marrimian's voice made her blink and slowly open her eyes. She frowned, trying to focus, and turned her face toward Marrimian's voice. "Is that you, Marrimian? I tried to stop them but there were so many. They came to destroy everything, to ruin all that you had struggled to achieve."

"Why did the guards let this happen? Where are the men I set to watch the doors?"

Marrimian turned angrily toward the crowd of hoemasters and hall folk who hovered in the shadows. Her eyes blazed with anger, making them afraid to come forward. She dabbed at the blood at the corners of Ankana's mouth with a white linen cloth that Ansel had breathlessly pressed into her hands.

Ankana struggled in Marrimian's arms. She lifted her burnt arm and tried to point toward the throne with bloody fingers that had been broken and hacked to the bone. The marsh people from Marrimian's boat had followed Ansel up through the terraces and into the hall and were crowding now beneath the high-arched entrance and gazing fearfully at the Glitterspike. Silently they watched the heartstone as the veins of molten silver shimmered and flickered beneath its featherings of hoarfrost and they remembered the rumors that had told them of the beast, Yaloor, who had been shackled to that towering finger of crystal, and in that moment, as they stood spellbound by its beauty, they caught sight of the crumpled figure of the injured birthwoman. As she lifted her arm to point to the throne they scattered back away from the entrance, fearing that she would strike them down with magic curses dripping from the ends of her bloody fingers.

"The guards fought valiantly, Marrimian," Ankana whispered, "but the city people overran them and trampled them into the floorstones of the hall. It was the crones who drove them into such a frenzy, who led them into the hall under cover of darkness."

Ankana sighed and let her arm sink down on the burnt and crumpled folds of her blood apron. Marrimian looked through the gap that had opened between the frightened children crowding around her.

The throne lay in splintered ruins. She stared speechlessly at the high headrest that had been hewn into three pieces and at the once beautifully ornate armrests now axe-riven beyond repair. "Why? This ruin and destruction has the stink of Naul about it—to destroy my father's throne . . ." she whispered as she caught sight of the deep beast-skin seat with its inlays of gold and silver scrolls, ripped open and set alight. She watched for a moment as a wispy thin spiral of blue smoke drifted up to vanish amongst the rafters of the gloomy hall. "But I cannot understand why he would want to hurt *you*. His mumbling magic protected you from my father's hatred of the daughters that you birthed and reared in the birthchambers."

Ankana heard Marrimian's words and looked up, searching for her face as death misted her eyes. She shook her head feebly as she found Marrimian's hand. "No, it was the crones," she said, gripping tightly with her bloody fingers. "The mumbler was nowhere to be seen in the hall. It was the crones."

Ankana sank a little in Marrimian's arms and a smile of reassurance flickered across her lips. "But I knew you would return, child, despite the crones' taunts. They said you had drowned in the marshes."

She knew that her long vigil at the base of the Glitterspike was drawing to an end and she sighed softly, just as so many of the children that she had birthed had sighed as they sought comfort from her at the day's end when the frozen darkness gathered in the corners of the birthchambers.

"I would know your voice anywhere . . ." Ankana murmured, feeling Marrimian's arms gently embrace her, "anywhere in this echoing hall of whispers."

"Rest, rest, do not weary yourself," Marrimian soothed as she blinked back her tears and dabbed at the gaping axe wounds on Ankana's neck and arms with an oiled cotton rag that the helpless healers had given to her. But the frail birthwoman struggled weakly and shook her head, bright bubbles of blood wetting her lips as she fought to speak.

"They came because they were jealous, because you were succeeding, because . . ." Ankana gasped for breath. Her body trembled in Marrimian's arms but she opened her eyes and stared blindly up at the shimmering finger of crystal as if seeing it for the first time. "They struck just after nightfall. I heard the screams of our guards as the city folk speared them to death and the cackling chants of the crones in the darkness as they burst into the hall. I saw their leaping shadows stretching long across the floorstones as they burned the galleries and raised their axes to destroy the throne. The crones were blind to my presence beneath Threadneedle archway as they led the city folk in their orgy of destruction. They went shrieking and shouting toward the Glitterspike, crying out that you had perished trying to float across the flooded marshes and that they would tear down the one bright symbol of your power, the power that the house of Miresnare had always held over the people of Gnarlsmyre."

Ankana's voice faltered and Marrimian bent over her to wipe at the trickles of blood drying on her chin. But the birthwoman would have none of it; she sensed that the shadow of death had closed its fingers on her shoulder and she fought to continue. "I could not save your throne, child, but I ran out and called to them to watch the flooded marshes for your return and I drove them back from the Glitterspike with my bare hands. They merely hesitated in their rush, a blink, just enough time for one of them to spin away and look out at the dawn breaking across the marshes, and then they rushed at me."

Ankana's eyelids drooped and she fell silent, her head nestled against Marrimian's breast. Marrimian fought back her tears and looked up at the Glitterspike. There she saw Ankana's dark bloodstains and tiny splinters of bone embedded in the shimmering skirts of hoarfrost that clung to the finger of crystal. She shuddered, realizing that the frail birthwoman must have raised her arms to ward off the frenzied crones as they struck at the Glitterspike with their axes, and she shook with rage as she thought of what they had done. But when she looked closer at the skirts of frost, searching for the rivening axe strokes, she found none, not even the slightest fracture in the lace-fine, crystal patterns to mar the beauty of the glistening stones or the veins of molten silver that lay just beneath the frozen surface.

"The crones have failed to spoil the Glitterspike with even one axe mark," Marrimian whispered, dabbing gently at Ankana's lips. "And as for the throne, I shall have the carpenters fashion a new one. Your name, Ankana, your title as mother of all the daughters of this hall, shall be carved across the headrest."

Ankana shivered as she heard Marrimian's voice, it drifted to her as a distant echo. "Marrimian," she whispered, frowning and struggling against the touch of death and the clamor of the voices of long-dead friends growing louder in her ears. She knew that there was something, some message, some dreadful warning, that she must tell Marrimian. "The crones, the crones," she gurgled, bright bubbles of blood swelling and bursting on her lips as she fought to remember. Her eyelids flickered open and she stared up at the towering finger of crystal that rose above her and it all came rushing back— the wild chants and the screaming shouts as they swung the axes. "They boasted that they have stored enough sweetmeats and smoked mudbeast flesh in the Shambles to feed the city people for two wet seasons. But Erek would only barter them for the roots and vegetables that we had harvested in the terraces. That was why the city folk overran the hall—to steal what we had grown. They will take what they have stolen to the entrance of the Shambles. Be warned, Marrimian: don't let the hall folk touch those sweetmeats; they are poisoned, spoiled by the healing woman's hatreds. Don't let them have any."

Ankana sighed, her voice melted away into nothing as death gathered her up. Her head sank forward and her last breath ghosted faintly across Marrimian's hands.

"Ankana, Ankana," Marrimian wept helplessly, knowing that she could not call her back. She rose to her feet with the limp, frail body of the birth-woman held tightly in her arms and hot tears of anger trickled down her cheeks. She blinked and shook the tears from her eyes, forcing herself to look at the ruin and devastation that the crones had brought into the hall.

Dimly in the gray light she saw Krann leading a tall figure toward her through the wreckage. The ragman bowed before Marrimian and opened his mouth to say something, but Krann spoke first.

"This is the ragman who found Ankana defending the Glitterspike."

The ragman spread his hands. "We were resting, sleeping after laboring in the terraces, warming ourselves in the kitchens, when we heard a terrible commotion here in the hall and smelled burning. We snatched up our spears and bows and came as fast as we could, but the hall was in riot. A mob of ironmasters and lampwicks were rampaging all over, burning and looting, and there were crones everywhere, chanting and trampling on the newly harvested food laid out to dry on the long eating boards. And some of them hewed at the helpless birthwoman as she tried to defend the Glitterspike."

"But you slept through the screams of the guards who were being speared to death in the entrance of the hall? You did nothing? You let the mob of city folk kill Ankana?" Marrimian shouted, advancing on the frightened ragman and thrusting the burned, blood-smeared body of the birthwoman toward him.

"The . . . the . . . the crones must have cast spells over us that bound us in sleep. When we did wake the mob was wild and crazed with their magic," he cried, stumbling backwards. "They had set light to everything they could lay hands on and when we tried to drive them out they turned on us, shrieking and shouting. They would have overrun us if the crone who had perched herself up there above the burning gallery by the crystal window had not cried out that you, great Queen, were returning with the breaking dawn. She shrieked and cried that you were riding in a craft across the floodwaters and you had savage marshmen with you. The mob hesitated, then turned and fled in panic and the crones, seeing that the crowd were in retreat, spat on the trampled food and sneered at us as they spun away and followed the fleeing ironmasters and city scum through every door and dark crack in the hall. Their fading voices mocked us for following you, the firstborn daughter of the hall, and they laughed. They shouted that when we had tired of nibbling roots and berries here in the hall, there were real dark-flavored meats and wholesome sweetmeats for us to eat a pace inside the entrance of the Shambles. They said that they would be piled there, ready for the taking."

When she had dismissed the ragman Marrimian frowned, then turned anxiously toward the trampled mess of vegetables and fruits that the people of the hall had struggled so hard to harvest from the terraces.

"Don't worry about that, mistress, those cursed black hags spoiled less than they thought," muttered Ansel. "Everything that was harvested before Krann built the boat and had already dried is still safely locked away in the storage larders beyond the furthest kitchen archway. There will be plenty to eat."

Marrimian turned to the scullion and the ghost of a smile hovered at the corners of her mouth as she thought of Ansel's thoroughness, but her lips quickly drew into a thin, bloodless line of worry. She motioned Ansel to come close. "I know there is food enough to feed us all," she whispered gently as she laid Ankana's body down on the dry weather-cloak that the scullion had spread on the floorstones between them. "That is not what fills me with dread." She hesitated as she searched for the words to express the fear that nagged at her.

"What is it? What worries you, mistress?" hissed Ansel, drawing her eyebrows into a black frown.

Marrimian looked down at Ankana's blind, staring eyes. The scullion reached forward and drew the eyelids shut and carefully folded the edges of the weather-cloak across the dead face.

"She warned me, Ansel, she warned me about the meats within the Shambles and that the healing woman is offering them to the city folk; and that will mean they do not have to barter with us for food. But worse than that, she warned that Erek has poisoned the meat and it will turn the hall folk against me if they eat it."

Ansel thought for a moment and then laughed. "Where could that poisonous hag have found enough meat to feed her brood of crones, let alone the people of the city? Anyway, even if she has managed to hoard some rotten carcasses and spoil the meat no one from the hall will touch it, mistress. There's nothing to fear; our food is wholesome and good to eat."

"You are wrong," whispered Marrimian. "Watch that ragman, the one who told me what the crones had whispered. His eyes are constantly straying toward the archway that leads to the entrance of the hall, the archway closest to the path down to the Shambles. He is dribbling and licking his lips for the taste of meat. Remember, without the carcasses of the mudbeasts there are no meats here in the hall. We have survived the wet seasons on the flesh of plentiful marshfish, and roots and berries that we have harvested from the terraces, but I fear that he hungers for the cured meat from the smokehouses and his hunger will draw him and everyone else in the hall down into the Shambles."

"I'll kill him before he reaches the door arch, before he can whisper what he heard," hissed Ansel reaching for her dagger, beginning to rise to her feet and turn toward where the ragman was standing.

"No! No, that won't do any good," whispered Marrimian firmly, shaking her head as she put her hand on Ansel's arm to stop her. "The rumor of the sweetmeats that lie just inside the Shambles will have already spread throughout the hall."

"But we could block every entrance, mistress, we could set guards . . ." Ansel began, but Marrimian cut across her words with bitter laughter and she swept her hand across the rows of gloomy empty archways that lined the hall.

"Where could we find enough hall folk whom we could trust? Who wouldn't hanker for the rich, dark taste of the smokehouses as these dreary wet sea-

sons chill and numb them to the bone, and what of
these marsh people we have just brought into the
hall? What would you make them—our prisoners?
Do we watch every morsel of food they eat?"

Ansel glared at the silent crowds of wet and filthy
marsh people who still clung huddled together beneath the high entrance of the hall and she
shrugged her shoulders, wishing that Marrimian
had left them clinging to the branches of their
marsh-oak trees. She turned her head and looked up
to the ragman where he hovered a dozen paces
away and she cursed him and every other ragman,
hoemaster and duster that they had left guarding
the hall, keeping her words under her breath. She
cursed them for letting the crones overrun the hall
with their whispers of foul meats.

"Then what can we do to stop the people of the
hall crowding into the Shambles to gorge themselves, mistress?" Ansel asked, at a loss to know
what to do as she looked up to Marrimian and
shrugged her shoulders.

Marrimian commanded the hallwardens to
gather the hall folk in the great hall and to offer
food and warm clothes to the people from the
marshes. Then all must pay homage to Ankana for
defending the Glitterspike before she was laid upon
her funeral pyre. Marrimian turned and for a moment stared at the ruined throne. She listened to the
hall folk as they entered, whispering and crying
with despair as they saw the birthwoman's body,
and she tried to answer Ansel's question. She
spread her hands helplessly. "There is nothing that

we can do but watch and wait. We cannot stop anyone going to the Shambles."

Darkness had pulled its black wet shroud over the city and the last bright ribbon of dancing sparks hissed and spluttered into glistening ashes on Ankana's funeral pyre. It had been set upon the cobbles before the doors of Glitterspike Hall so that Erek and all her crones and every one of the murderous city folk who had rampaged through the hall could see the homage and honor that Marrimian bestowed upon her. Marrimian had whispered her last farewells to the birthwoman as the center of the pyre collapsed in a blaze of white sparks, then she had slipped into the shadows between the flickering reedlamps and hurried to her sleeping chamber high above the hall.

Now, alone, she wept at the hopelessness of it all, resting her forehead against the cold, damp stonework of the window frame as she stared blindly out into the darkness and listened to the numbing roar of the pouring rain beating on the roofs below and the gushing rush of the rainwater as it filled and flooded through the gutters. Behind her she heard the liftlatch of her door click open and she half turned, her tear-wet eyes now blazing with anger, her fists clenched and her lips trembling.

"It is all so hopeless. The healing woman and her crones are destroying everything," she began as Krann quietly shut the door, crossed the darkened room and gathered her in his arms. He had seen the look of haunted despair in her eyes and knew that he must go to her. Now he saw her silhouetted against the window frame and that spark of love that had once burned so brightly in him crackled and blazed with new fire and it sent the shadows of his yearning for Elundium back into the hidden corners of his mind.

"We have shared everything—our triumphs and our despair," he whispered, gently brushing at the tear stains that scarred her cheeks and holding her tightly against him as huge sobs shook her shoulders.

"But Ankana was so weak, so helpless," she wept. "And in a way her struggle to survive stood for everything that we have tried to do. And the crones just cut her down. It is an omen, a warning that everything else will fall apart and crumble to nothing around us."

"But we have drained the marshes that were threatening to flood the terraces and we have gathered all those wretched marsh people into the hall. With careful measuring there is still enough to feed everyone despite what the crones destroyed in their attack. Everything is not lost."

"Ankana's death is the beginning of our ruin, or were you deaf to what the crones were chanting, and did you not hear the marshmen's whispers while we sheltered with them beneath their rotting canopy?" she cried, pulling fiercely away from him and turning back toward the curtain of rain beating on the window. "Did you not hear how they whispered in terror of Mertzork and my sister Pinvey

and the awesome power those two are gathering to
attack the city when the wet seasons end? And Pinvey has claimed to be the one who tamed the mudbeast and calls herself the Queen of all Gnarlsmyre
and she forces the marsh people to follow her. Tell
me, Krann, who will I have to stand with me to
defend the Hurlers' Gate when she marches into
the city? Who will there be left once all the hall folk
I have struggled to feed have deserted me for the
sweetmeats the healing woman and all her filthy
crones have piled up inside the entrance of the
Shambles?"

Marrimian fell silent, clenching her hands in
hopelessness, and she let her forehead sink down
against the cold, wet stone of the window frame.

"But you are seeing dark shadows in these rumors. You are seeing only the lies and the half-
truths," Krann offered, stepping close to her.
"Pinvey and Mertzork fled from the hall when you
touched the Glitterspike in your triumph and although they are seeking shelter with the people of
the marshes in that miserable huddle of huts above
the floods I doubt if any one of the marshmen will
follow them willingly when the wet seasons end.
And as for those sweetmeats, surely none of the hall
folk would touch meat those black hags have prepared? Surely they would rather feast on Ansel's
broths and pottages?"

Marrimian laughed bitterly and pointed down
through the swirling black mist, the wind and rain
that beat against her window, to faint points of
light moving through the narrow alleyways below.

"How can you talk to me of jumping at shadows when the rumors and lies of your beginnings drove you to flee from Elundium through the Shadowlands in search of the truth? Look—look down there. Are those mere shadows or hollow rumors or are they storm lanterns that flit from alleyway to alleyway as the people of the hall, the people I have struggled to feed, find the quickest way down into the Shambles?"

Krann frowned as he leaned forward and looked over Marrimian's shoulder toward the watery lights moving in and out between the steep, crowded roofs. "But why are they deserting you? I don't understand. They cannot be hungry."

Marrimian sighed wearily and turned away from the window to face him in the darkness. "Because they crave the taste of meat. It is that which lures them into the Shambles. I am sure that the healing woman and that treacherous master mumbler, Naul, are using their sweetmeats somehow to poison the people against me. Ankana warned me with her dying breath that Erek had tainted the meat, but I can do nothing to stop the people going."

"But *we* have fed them meat! We have killed and roasted many of the hill sheep and . . ."

Marrimian laughed harshly and threw her hands up into the air to silence him. "Our worlds are so different. Krann, here in Gnarlsmyre everything that is not freshly harvested goes moldy during the wet seasons. Food is scarce and everything that is to be kept must be cured in the smokehouses over smoldering fires of black ebony wood and dried vines and herbs gathered from the crystal houses. The curing smoke darkens the meats and gives them a rich, aromatic flavor that stays with you forever once you have tasted it. It becomes a craving. My father used his knowledge of the craving for the meat of the mudbeasts to control the people of the city; it gave him untold power over them."

Krann turned his head away for a moment and watched the tiny flickering lamplights vanish between the roofs below. "No!" he whispered, shaking his head. "The crones were lying. Remember, when Ansel was leading us up through the city she brought us through Chimney Lane. There was no more than a wisp of smoke then in the tall chimney stacks of the smokehouses because none of the mudbeasts the marshmen had driven into the hall to joust against Yaloor was slaughtered. Remember, you broke the beasts' shackles and set them free. There cannot be anything to eat in the Shambles, no matter what lies and rumors the crones spun when they overran the hall. Erek cannot thwart you like this."

Marrimian suddenly remembered that awful night when Ansel had led her down into the Shambles to seek help and shelter from the healing woman when Lord Miresnare, her father, had banished them both from the hall to perish in the frozen darkness because she had demanded the right to joust against the marshmen for the throne.

"She has all manner of terrible things dangling above her firestone!" she gasped, shuddering as she remembered those tightly wound cocoons smeared with soot and dribbles of tar that spun and turned in the smoke of her fire. "It doesn't matter what flesh they are being fed, the craving will make the people greedy to devour it and one taste of the poisonous spells that the meat must be riddled with will turn them all against me."

Krann took her into his arms. "You must have courage," he whispered firmly. "Not everyone will follow the crones' whispers. Ansel and Vetchim are with you; so is Treasel, and I doubt if any of the marsh people you have brought into the hall have ever tasted the meats from the smokehouses. They will not desert you easily."

"But I feel so alone, betrayed, so weary of the struggle. I don't even know if I want to cling on to the throne." Marrimian wept as he gathered her up, carried her across the darkened chamber and laid her on the deep pile of sleeping rugs heaped on her bed.

"We are together," he whispered, "and through the love we share we have a power that soars above all the poisonous treacheries and hatred that are spun in the Shambles."

And he brushed his lips against hers and felt their softness and his kiss became stronger and they held each other tightly, just as they had done in the darkness of the water meadows. She felt the love that had once flowed between them well up and rekindle. It made her dizzy, her heart beat wildly and her fingers burned and tingled.

"Krann," she whispered breathlessly, pulling back slightly from him and, looking up, she traced every lock and curl of his hair as it was silhouetted against the window of her chamber. "Won't this hurt you and bring back those memories? Won't it make you yearn for Elundium if we touch too intimately?"

She felt him smile in the darkness and the warmth of his breath ghosted against her cheek as he whispered, "My love for you has overpowered my longing to return to Elundium. It has melted away that shadow that stood between us."

"Krann . . ." Marrimian began but her voice faded to a murmur as he kissed her again, and as their fingers sought and found each other, loosening belts and buckles, unlacing every secret knot and tie, the despair and the hopelessness that had overwhelmed her faded into a distant echo.

Hungrily they touched, their legs and arms entwined. Krann pushed her down amongst the sleeping rugs and she arched against him, crying out as he quickened, "Krann, I love you, I love you." She gasped and clung to him as she felt him tense and the heat of their passion flooded through her. Sighing, she wrapped herself more tightly about him and felt as if they were floating, drifting through the darkness on quilts of feather softness, and the sound of rain beating on the crystal window and the warmth of Krann against her lulled her to sleep.

Krann woke and shivered in the darkness. He had been dreaming of moving through the grasslands of Elundium. Battle Owls were stooping silently through the shafts of evening sunlight that broke up the forest gloom and far away upon the edges of the dream he had caught the sound of muffled hoofbeats of the wild war horses, soft laughter and the whispered echo of blackbirds on the Greenway's edge. He reached out to touch the dream, to hold it tightly between his fingertips, but it faded from him into the darkness. Sadly he sighed and drew one of the sleeping blankets up over them both and for a long moment before sleep once more overtook him he looked through the tiny rivulets of rain that trickled down the window and he knew that now there was no going back.

13

A Moment of Indecision

NAUL held his breath as the outer door to Erek's hovel slammed shut and the heavy iron liftlatch clicked into place. He listened carefully, counting the voices of the crones as they shrieked and chanted of the armloads of sweetmeats they were carrying from Erek's larder into the entrance of the Shambles for the people of the city. The rough scrape and clatter of their boots gradually faded into the night, but it was as he feared: he had counted one voice short amongst the crones. He had overheard their whispers against him even after he had sipped the cup of their revenge and he knew that they did not wholly share his mother's belief that he was by now one of them and guessed that they would watch his every movement. Silently he let his breath escape between his teeth, hunched his narrow shoulders and began to steal secret glances between the rows of hideous human carcasses that hung in their soot-smeared cocoons of gossamer thread from every hook and rafter beam. They twisted and turned in the yellow trails of smoke that rose from Erek's curing fires.

"I'll thwart every one of them somehow—every single treacherous one!" He fell silent beneath the weight of his hopeless task, catching his useless muttering threats in his mouth and forcing a thin, bloodless smile across his lips to hide his despair as he caught sight of the wrinkled hag who had been left to watch him. She was huddled beside the door-stone of Erek's smokehouse, wrapped tightly in her riddle of black rags, hissing and muttering to herself, oblivious to the dribble of poisonous spit that hung from her chin. Naul began to turn away but she caught his eye and held his gaze. He could feel her probing, searching inside him, and he snatched his eyes away and threw his head back to stare up into the darkened rafters.

Turning his head from side to side, Naul listened for the sound of the rain beating on the steep gables of the roof. Leaking raindrops splattered on to his dirty face and he let the sound of the deluge lashing the city fill him to overflowing before he turned back and stared at the crone. His eyes were now full of watery innocence. The crone, unsettled by that second's glimpse of the thoughts that he strove to hide, spat at him and cursed him beneath her breath.

She snapped her crooked fingers. "Start butchering a new row of sweetmeats. Start in that row where you stand," she hissed, pointing through the haze of yellow curing smoke with her bloody gutting knife, "and leave no clue, no splinter of bone or careless cut, that will give the city folk the slightest hint of what they really eat."

Naul tried to laugh to hide his revulsion and show his eagerness to do her bidding and he curled his lips back across his teeth and spat on the curved butcher's blade he held in his right hand. He ran his thumb along the cutting edge.

"Here, come here, you fool; take the cup of revenge and wet each fillet of meat as you carve it," cried the crone, impatient to continue her chanting, as she held the rusty iron cup brimming with the foul liquid and pushed it toward him across the soot-streaked floor of the smokehouse.

Naul bowed his head to her and hurried between the rotting carcasses, bumping and barging them aside in his haste to reach the crone. "But I thought that you would want to fillet each carcass and spice each tender morsel of meat yourself. I did not think you would trust me with such important tasks," he soothed. "I thought I was just to fetch and carry."

But the crone waved him away, fixing him with a glassy, penetrating stare. "You have watched us begin the butchering; now I shall be able to watch you better if you do it," she cursed.

Naul began to lift the cup of bubbling foulness carefully with both hands. The liquid frothed up over the rim and Naul staggered forward to steady it. The windbells hidden in the folds of his sleeves touched their tiny clappers and whispered sweet music.

"Silence those filthy bells; there is an echo of your mumbler's magic in their harsh music," hissed the crone.

"Yes! Yes, of course, at once," Naul answered,

quickly pressing his arms to his sides to stifle the sound in his sleeves. He retreated amongst the carcasses but once he was out of sight of the crone and his back was turned he smiled and nervously licked his lips. He had never dreamed that they would allow him actually to butcher the carcasses. The crone's cursing and ranting against the music of his windbells and her giving him the cup of revenge had made him see the beginnings of two ways that he could stop the people of the city from eating these poisonous offerings. He slipped quickly between the hanging bodies, pretending he was choosing the ripest to butcher first. He searched the gloomy rafter beams, listening through the drumming sound of the rain for the whispered drip and splatter of the raindrops that leaked through the roof. He found what he sought quickly and stole a glance over his shoulder at the crone before he dared to grin at the long crack in the weatherworn tiles above his head. It glistened with raindrops in the flickering firelight.

Stepping beneath the crack, Naul felt the ice-cold splash of pure water strike his chin. He could have laughed and shouted for joy as it trickled over his chin and down his neck but he knew that to utter one sound would turn the crone's eyes toward him. Stepping back, he kneeled down on the wet floor and carefully set the iron cup of revenge beneath the steady stream of sparkling raindrops. "I will thwart you all!" he murmured to himself as he watched the pure droplets of water splash into the dark and bitter brew. The surface of the liquid frothed and boiled up over the rim of the cup, darkening the bright rust stains before it spread in a widening, bubbling stain of hatred across the dirty floor of the hovel.

"Carve the meat, you idle fool!" shrieked the crone, making Naul jump and snatch up the butchering blade. He heard the scrape of her stool as she rose from beside the doorstone.

"I'm choosing the ripest," he called, swallowing his horror and revulsion at what he now had to do.

Reaching up with his free hand, Naul caught hold of the dangling corpse that twisted and spun in the smoke closest to him. The crone advanced a dozen paces toward him and watched him with burning, penetrating eyes as he pressed the tip of the butchering blade into the side of the carcass.

"Cut it cleanly and be quick. There must be crowds flocking into the entrance of the Shambles now that the rumors of our sweetmeats have spread throughout the city." And she turned away from him, chanting a watching spell.

Naul shuddered as he felt the soft carcass beneath his fingertips. It was almost spongy under the layers of sticky, soot-smeared threads of the cocoon. He knew as he cut into the threads that he must not falter or show a moment's hesitation. But nothing could have prepared him for the sight of the layers of gray, rotting flesh and the ripe stench of decay that billowed up all around him as he sheared through the last binding threads and they sprang apart. He staggered backwards, pushing the carcass away from him, choking on the stench of corrup-

tion as the knots of sinews and bundles of muscle fell away from the crumbling bones and spilled out of the cocoon. His stomach tightened and the bile rose in his throat. The carcass, with all its glistening, gray flesh and slippery entrails trailed through the smoldering curing fire as it swung back toward him. He flung out his arms to ward it off and sent the carcass next to it spinning through the smoke. The windbells hidden in his sleeves touched and whispered out their music once again and the crone was disturbed by their whispering. She rose from her stool again and rushed toward him, her riddle of black rags fanning the smoke of the curing fires and making a dense yellow fog.

"You have spoiled the meat, you useless mumbler!" she shrieked, pushing him roughly aside. Going down on her hands and knees, she began to gather up the loops and bundles of rotten flesh in her arms before the flames of the fire greedily devoured it.

Erek heard the commotion from the smokehouse and flung open the door. She hissed the crone into silence.

"I was trying to cut the cocoon open but the flesh inside was so soft and slippery that I dropped it," Naul explained, spreading his thin empty hands imploringly toward his mother.

Erek stared at him for a moment, searching his blank face for the slightest hint of deceit, but found nothing except his eagerness to please. She turned her hooded eyes on the crone and snapped her fingers at her. "*You* were supposed to prepare the sweetmeats. You push my child too hard: he knows nothing of our delicacies or how we prepare them here. Let him merely dip each slice into the cup of revenge and he can carry them one by one and lay them in the entrance of the Shambles."

"The cup! Where is the cup of our revenge?" snarled the crone, fixing Naul with murderous eyes, as Erek turned on her heel and left the smokehouse.

"I will fetch it, I will fetch it," cried Naul, ducking beneath the rows of dangling corpses and leaping over the curing fires, desperate to reach the cup before the crone discovered that he had left it beneath the leaking drips of rainwater.

"Here it is," he soothed, wiping the rim dry with the tail of his dirty saffron gown before he handed it to her, trying to hide the slightest trace that any of their evil liquid had been spilled.

The crone muttered. She looked at the froth of bubbles that covered the surface and cursed him under her breath as she began to fillet the rotten strips of flesh. Naul dipped each one into the bubbling cup and then piled as many as he could carry in his outstretched arms, left the curing house and hurried toward the entrance of the Shambles.

"Be quick or I shall send the spiders to find you," the crone cackled evilly, slamming the door shut on him and returning to dissect the next carcass.

Naul heaved a sigh of relief. The rain lashed his face and he breathed fresh air again as he hurried away from the lair bowed beneath the weight of rotting fillets. It took all his strength of will not to cast the putrid strips aside, to make his escape from the Shambles, and run as fast as he could for the safety of Glitterspike Hall. He knew the power of the craving for the dark rich meats of the smoke-houses that would be gnawing at all the people of the city. He had overheard the crones talking and plotting, boasting of how they had murdered An-kana, the birthwoman, and how through their lies and rumors spread throughout the hall and through every street in the city they were luring the people away from Marrimian, controlling them through their craving for meat. He knew that if he should try to escape, the shadow of his mother's revenge would swallow up the city and follow him to the ends of Gnarlsmyre; it would snatch him back and bury him alive in the tomb beneath her hovel for trying to turn against her. He knew that he must stay in the very center of her webs and destroy her power from within.

Naul slowed his pace and looked up at the sag-ging, wet canopy of webs that now hung in rags and tatters across the narrow alleyways. In all his seasons as master mumbler he had never known such a ferocious storm lash the city and he smiled to see how the canopy had been torn and broken by the force of the deluge. Twisting and turning, he craned his neck, searching for watching eyes, but there were none. The storms had driven the spiders out of the canopy to seek shelter in the dry cracks and corners. He stopped and kneeled on the cold, wet cobbles, piling the reeking strips of corruption against the wall of the alleyway. He looked quickly from side to side and listened for the crones, but there was nothing save the angry shouts of the crowds in the entrance of the Shambles and the sound of the rain on the steep roofs all around him. He reached into the secret folds of his sleeves and drew out one of his precious windbells for a moment and looked at it. He cupped it in the palm of his hand, then rattled it gently and, lifting his head to one side, listened to its sweet music.

"You were once the symbol of my mumbler's magic. People fled in terror as they heard your shrill whisper; you warned them of my coming and they hid lest I set eyes on them and ill-fated them in our dance of foresight. They thought I might foretell their death before the sun set. Perhaps an echo of that fear still lives in the people. Perhaps if I were to place a windbell into each fillet. Perhaps . . ."

Naul fell silent, then shook his head, sprinkling raindrops gathered in the wrinkles of his brow across the rotting meat. Out here, beyond the airless stench of his mother's smokehouse, what had seemed a strength against her now seemed a hopeless gesture. He could almost picture that screaming crowd in the Shambles' gateway fighting and brawling, daggers drawn, grabbing every morsel of meat before he had put it down, tearing out his precious windbells and flinging them aside, trampling his magic underfoot as they gorged themselves. He had begun to slip his windbells back into his sleeve, defeated and overwhelmed by the power of his mother's hatred, when he noticed that the surface of the meat had become scarred and pitted by the rain. He bent closer to the stinking pile and then threw his head back and let out a shout of laughter. The raindrops were burning into the meat and dissolving its outer layer and he realized that the bright, glistening surface of the meat that he had shuddered to touch must have been etched clean by the raindrops in the cup of revenge. He reached back into his sleeve, withdrew some bells and put one into every strip of flesh.

"They may do no good at all but they are all that I have to offer."

Gathering up the pile of flesh, he hurried on toward the entrance of the Shambles. "You must run faster," hissed the crones, suddenly swarming all around him, snatching the meat out of his arms. "The city folk are crazy with hunger. Go back and bring us more sweetmeats."

They drove him back into the Shambles but as he retreated beneath the torn and sagging webs he saw figures crowding forward out of every dark entrance and gloomy alleyway. They were shouting and fighting with one another and in amongst their leaping figures he saw ragmen and dusters carrying large pieces of meat carefully hidden beneath their weather-cloaks.

"Hurry! Hurry!" shouted the crones, flapping their riddle of wet rags at him. Naul turned and ran through the alleyways of the Shambles and felt the weight of despair again bow his shoulders. There would never be enough windbells hidden in the folds of his sleeves to stop all the people of the city from touching his mother's sweetmeats.

Andzey had watched the floodwaters surge through the muddy channel, covering all the secret paths and every dry footstep of the marshery as they crept slowly, day by day, up the rickety stilts that supported the huts. Now the waters were lapping dangerously close to the bottom of their cage and he, Alea and the swarms of spiders huddled in the shadows beneath Pinvey's hut. He had rattled the bars and shouted until his jaws grew numb as he pleaded with Pinvey and Mertzork to let them climb up into the safety of the huts above, but both Pinvey and his brother had sneered and spat down on them, shouting above the roar of the storms that lashed the marshery that they could drown for all they cared. Then Pinvey had hesitated and carelessly thrown a gnawed bone to Andzey.

"For my beast. To keep him strong enough to carry me triumphantly into Glitterspike Hall," she had mocked before vanishing from the entrance of her hut.

Mertzork had laughed and gloated as he took one last look at their wretchedness. "Now you can see that I have taken everything that might have been yours, brother. Everything!"

And then he had turned his back on them and crawled into the hut, pulling the rough door of woven reeds tightly shut behind him to keep out the weather.

"The floodwaters! They will swamp this cage, won't they?" Alea asked, reaching up with a shivering hand to brush at the strand of wet hair that clung to her forehead.

As she moved she felt the swarms of spiders that were supposed to guard them move beneath her soaking cloak. They had scuttled under her clothes to seek a dry corner from the pouring rain but the water had found its way even into the tightest folds of the cloth.

Andzey began to shake his head as he stared out at the swollen waters. "Normally the floods only reach the tenth rung of the ladders and even in the worst of the wet seasons that I have ever known the floods only covered another two rungs of the ladders. But . . ." he hesitated. "This time the waters move faster, swirling and tugging at the rickety stilts. This season I fear that they will rise at least another six rungs on the ladders."

Alea looked through the bars to the spindly thin ladder that would have led them to safety had her sister known the slightest trace of compassion. It stood beneath their cage and she silently counted the dripping rungs that showed above the floodwaters. "Then we shall drown," she muttered, her face drawn into a wet mask of misery.

Andzey frowned and looked up at the dark shape of the huts above. He made sure that no one was watching before he felt beneath his beastskin cloak and brought out the hedgehog that the wild old marshwoman had brought them on the night that the rains had started.

"Watch how the raindrops run off the surface of the threads that I have wound around it," he whispered, holding out the animal that now looked more like a thick spindle of thread than the wriggling bundle of spines that had been thrust through the bars to them. The drifting curtain of rain that soaked their tiny prison scattered on his binding of gossamer threads.

"How can that silly hedgehog help? How can anything help us? It would be better to eat the wretched thing now and at least die with a full belly. I have forgotten what eating is after trying to survive on the foul-tasting bodies of these dragonflies that fly through the bars of the cage. And those disgusting leeches and crawlers that live in the swirling waters between the stilts of this marshery that you catch by dangling the rotting strips that you tear from your cloak." Alea fell silent and turned away from him with tears of hopeless despair brimming in her eyes.

Andzey looked at her trembling, wet shoulders. He wanted to reach out, to touch and hold her, to gather her up in his arms and carry her to the driest hut in the marshery, to put an end to this nightmare existence. But he was as much a helpless prisoner as she was as he knelt there on the filthy, wet floor of the cage, and he felt the burden of their helplessness press down on him. He clenched his free hand in rage and struck out at the bars, of their cage, hissing at her, "You must not give up now!"

Alea's shoulders stopped trembling, but she did not turn to him as she muttered miserably, "Why?

What does it matter now? What does anything matter if the floodwaters are going to drown us?"

"We have to survive—we have to," he snarled, grinding the words so forcefully between his teeth that she turned back toward him and stared into his tortured eyes. "We have to survive because . . ."—he was whispering, his lips quivering as he fought to mask the anger that boiled inside—"my murderous brother Mertzork and your black-hearted sister Pinvey have cheated and lied and tortured everyone their lives have touched and if we don't survive their crimes will go unchecked and unpunished!"

"You only want revenge and it has blinded you to our helplessness. It is the wish for revenge that feeds your anger and makes you reach for the impossible."

"Oh no," Andzey answered fiercely, thrusting the hedgehog toward her. "I want justice, not revenge. It is the wish for justice that has driven me to clutch at every thread of hope no matter how slender and which has given me the strength to survive despite our wretchedness."

"But we can never bring them to justice even if we survive the rising floodwaters," Alea muttered helplessly.

"I think you are wrong. And we can survive." Andzey laughed softly as he shook off the last of the raindrops that had gathered on the threads wound around the hedgehog. "The rain does not penetrate the threads if they are bound tightly together. I noticed that whilst I was winding the threads around this creature, look he is bone dry beneath them!" Andzey smiled and gave the hedgehog a final shake before hiding it beneath his cloak again.

"But I do not understand. How can these flimsy spiders' threads stop the floodwaters from drowning us?" Alea frowned. She had never grasped why Andzey had questioned her so thoroughly about the hedgehog that the healing woman had given to Mertzork to show him the way through the city, or why Andzey had so laboriously made this poor little creature into a mirror image of it.

"We will use the spiders as shuttles and pass them backwards and forwards through the bars. We will build a covering of their silks that is tighter than the weave of your gown," he whispered.

"If it keeps the floodwaters out it would also keep out the rain, wouldn't it?" Alea asked quietly, catching at the edges of his idea and seeing in it a moment's shelter from the driving deluge.

She reached beneath her cloak for a handful of the damp, bedraggled spiders and set them on the floor of the cage, close to the bars, stroking and tickling their soft underbellies to make them scuttle in and out. Andzey laughed and pointed down to the swarm. "Look, they must have been listening; they are leaving their sticky trails of thread woven tightly between the bars!"

"They weave the cocoon so fast. Look, it is already a finger span high. And the driving rain is running down the outside!" Alea cried in excitement, forgetting to keep her voice to a whisper.

Pinvey must have heard them for suddenly her voice shouted out from the shelter of the hut above.

They both scrambled into separate corners of their cage and smothered the scuttling spiders with their cupped hands, trying to keep them from her ruthless gaze. They heard her rush door scrape back.

"Quiet! Be quiet!" she snarled. "You are disturbing my sleep. One more sound from either of you and I'll cut your cage loose and let it sink beneath the floodwaters. That will silence you forever!"

The reed door scraped again above their heads and Andzey risked an upward glance and then let out a sigh of relief. The hurrying spiders slipped between his fingers and contrived to scuttle backwards and forwards once again through the bars.

Alea stared at the growing cocoon and gingerly reached out to touch its sticky, drying threads and feel the strength of it with her fingertips. She frowned and looked up at the hovering dragonflies that had just flown in through the bars of their cage, their wings shimmering with raindrops in the gray, misty light. "How will we eat?" she asked suddenly as Andzey's hand shot out toward one, snapping shut around it. "When the spiders have finished weaving their cocoon and it completely covers the bars you won't be able to dangle strips of beastskin in the floodwater to catch leeches and crawlers and the dragonflies won't be able to fly in."

"I will make small windows above the level of the rising water." Andzey laughed softly. "I will make windows both to catch our food and to watch for the end of these wretched wet seasons." He paused thoughtfully and plucked the wings from the dragonfly, passing the soft, wriggling body to her as he watched the rising waters touch and swirl around the bottom of their cage.

"There is something very different about this wet season. Look at the color of the water flooding through the channel; look how it is staining the spiders' threads," he whispered.

Alea bent forward and stared toward the muddy waters and then shrugged her shoulders. "It looks just like the rivers of bright mud that run down the rocks behind Glitterspike Hall, spreading out in swirling patterns across the marshes."

"Well, I have never known such bright ribbons of colored mud to reach the marshery. Normally the floodwaters in the channel are black or a blackish green."

"Well, what can it mean?" asked Alea anxiously as she moved closer to him, but all Andzey could do was to shrug his shoulders and watch for an end to the drifting curtain of rain.

An ironmaster cursed and spat out the foul-tasting strip of flesh that a wheelwright had brought to barter for a new iron tire. "Even the pindafall birds wouldn't touch that!" he snarled, stamping on the meat and squelching it under the heel of his boot. He turned his back on the wheelwright in disgust and began walking toward the shelter of the over-hanging gallery that edged his courtyard.

"That's never the flesh of a mudbeast. The healing woman and her crones have lied to us," muttered the ironmasters. The quenchers and everyone in the courtyard nodded in agreement.

"It's time we burned down those Shambles and drove those cursed crones out into the flooded marshes for filling our heads with lies. For turning us against bartering with this new Queen," shouted a striker, raising his long-handled forging hammer above his head.

A lampwick laughed. "Don't be a fool, everything in the city is far too wet to burn."

"Perhaps this Queen Marrimian would still barter with you if you had the sense to try," interrupted the ironmaster's woman from the dark entrance of her kitchen.

The ironmaster thought for a moment and then shrugged his shoulders. "She'd be a fool to offer us anything but death after the way we rampaged, killing and burning, through the hall."

"She's taken carpenters and harvesters, and some glaziers into the hall since then," muttered one of the quenchers. "I have seen them making their way up there and none of them has returned. Perhaps if we . . ." The quencher hesitated and spread his empty hands.

The ironmaster stared up at the sheer, wet walls of the hall through the driving mist and rain. "Perhaps . . ." he murmured softly, beckoning the lampwick to where he stood at the edge of his cold, damp forge.

* * *

Marrimian stretched up on tiptoe and pressed her nose against the new pane of crystal the glaziers had just finished setting into the stone window arch at the far end of the high gallery. Krann stood with her. Behind them the carpenters were busily replacing the last of the charred rafter beams and floorboards that the crones had tried to destroy, but Marrimian was deaf to the rattle of their hammers and to the bustle of the hall below as she looked down at the glistening, rain-wet roofs of the city. She began to turn away to call after the retreating glaziers to go to the kitchen archway for their rewards when she hesitated and looked through the window again, her forehead drawn into a troubled frown.

"I don't understand it," she muttered, reaching out for Krann's hand and entwining her fingers with his as she drew him close to her. "Look! Look down there," she whispered. "See those drifting smudges of dirty smoke that hang in the air above the courtyards where the ironmasters have their forges. There are people hurrying through the narrow alleyways between the chandlers' houses."

Krann gazed over the streets below and shook his head. "But the people have been making their way toward the entrance of the Shambles ever since the crones spead the rumor of their foul offerings of meat that lay waiting there."

Marrimian watched the shuffling crowds for a moment. "No. It looks different now. It's almost as if the city is coming back to life. The smoke of the ironmasters' forges is belching up and people are hurrying about their daily tasks."

"And more and more of them have been gathering at the doors of the hall to barter their crafts and skills for food, despite those rumors of meat for them at the entrance of the Shambles . . ." Krann added thoughtfully as he swept his gaze across the bustling streets below. "It's gone!" he cried suddenly, making Marrimian start. "The Shambles! I can't find the shroud of gossamer threads that covers the roofs of the Shambles!"

Marrimian leaned forward. "It's down there, beyond the empty chimneys of the smokehouses and that steep narrow, winding, stone stairway." She laughed softly as she pointed to the huddle of weather-bleached roofs that protruded as starkly as a skeleton of hide-bound bones through the torn rag ends and loops of webs that now hung in damp tatters from every eave and broken gutter of Erek's lair.

"The storms must have filled those canopies of spiders' webs and the weight of the rainwater has torn them down. Look! Look! I can see the crones scuttling in and out of Erek's doorway."

Krann smiled and nodded as he picked out a handful of shadowy figures moving furtively about in the entrance to the Shambles. The fury of the storms had torn away the shrouds that had once hidden all Erek's secrets. "I can even see the piles of meat that lie just inside the entrance."

Krann suddenly felt Marrimian's hand tighten on his. "Naul!" she hissed, pointing down into one of the alleyways close to Erek's lair. "Look there, it's that cursed mumbler carrying bundles of that foul meat in his arms toward the entrance. I knew he was steeped in his mother's treacheries. I knew he was working against me!"

"Mistress, mistress! Krann! Come quickly!" Ansel called breathlessly as she climbed the stairway up to the gallery. Marrimian and Krann turned sharply away from the crystal window just as the scullion reached the stairhead and forced a passage between the carpenters, cursing and muttering to them to get out of her way.

"Mistress, there is something you must see," she cried, wringing her apron tails anxiously between her fingers and casting thunderous glances at the carpenters kneeling just behind her. "You must come quickly," she insisted, turning and rushing back to the stairhead.

Vetchim had been waiting at the foot of the stairs and he fell into step hurrying beside Ansel as she led Marrimian and Krann across the hall and through the main corridor toward the hoemasters' courtyard. Ahead of them, beyond the scullion's bulk, Marrimian could see a small crowd of ragmen, scuttles and laundry scrubs blocking the narrow corridor, bending down to stare at something on the ground.

"Make way for your Queen! Stand back! Stand back!" Ansel shouted angrily and the crowd shrank back, their frightened whispering fading into silence.

"What is it?" Marrimian asked as she drew closer,

wrinkling her nose and choking at the foul stench that had now filled the vaulted passageway.

"That," Ansel muttered darkly, pointing down to the gray rotting strip of flesh that lay in the center of the passageway, "that is one of the crones' sweetmeats!"

"Well, there's nothing sweet about it. Nothing would even tempt me to touch it!" gasped Krann, stepping hastily backwards for a breath of fresh air.

Marrimian swallowed and tried to hold her breath as she stepped closer to examine the reeking sweetmeat. She straightened her back, her eyes blazing with anger. "Which one of you dared to go against my warnings?" she hissed, glaring at the frightened crowd that huddled beyond the strip of rotting meat.

"It doesn't matter who dropped it, mistress," Ansel muttered loudly, her voice heavy with disgust. "None of them has the courage to own up because every one of them is probably guilty of disobeying you and slipping out of the hall at one time or another to follow the rumors of what lies in the Shambles and to satisfy their craving for the flesh of the mudbeasts. That is not what I brought you here to see."

"Well, what did you bring us here for?" Krann asked impatiently as he interrupted the scullion in his haste to get far away from this reek of corruption that was making him stagger with dizziness.

"Listen," the scullion whispered as she stepped purposefully forward and pushed the meat with her foot.

It swelled up against the toe of her boot and rolled over and the crumbling web of sinews that held it together fell apart. The crowd gasped as the clear sound of a windbell broke the silence in the corridor and they stumbled backwards away from the tiny pealing bell as it rolled toward them across the damp floorstones.

"A curse on Naul and all his mumbling magic," cried Marrimian, angrily clenching her fists. "It wasn't enough that he plotted against my father and used his mother's venomous spiders to keep the lesser followers of his magic in their mumbling cells. Now he invades my hall with the sound of his windbells, once sewn into his gown as a measure of his magic!"

"Oh no, mistress," Ansel whispered, turning quickly to Marrimian to quell her anger. "The sound of the windbells used to strike terror into anyone who heard them. Surely you remember that to hear the windbells meant that the mumblers would foretell your fate. These hall folk still fear the mumblers' magic and none of them will now touch this meat."

Marrimian stared down at the tiny windbell where it lay on the worn floorstones in the center of the passageway. She laughed softly and muttered under her breath, "You have tried to be far too clever for your own good, Erek. If you think you can use my father's mumbling magic to serve your own ends you must think again!"

And she strode forward, stooped down and gathered the windbell up in the palm of her hand. She felt its fragile coldness as she shook it at the frightened huddle of hall folk, making them cry out and cover their ears against its shrill music.

"There are more of these foul sweetmeats, mistress," Ansel muttered grimly as she pointed with a blunt finger into the warren of dark and narrow corridors and gloomy, rain-washed courtyards that opened off the main passageway. "They are lying everywhere, spoiling the air with the stench of corruption."

"We haven't tasted the crones' sweetmeats, great lady," cried a distraught voice in the crowd. "It's true that we went against your warning but we crave the dark-tasting flesh of the mudbeasts. We were driven to it. Please forgive us."

The voice fell silent, its fading echo mingling with the sound of the pounding rain and the gurgling rush of water pouring out of the gutter spouts.

"Forgiveness!" Marrimian hissed angrily, breaking the frightened silence. "You ask me to forgive you for going against my warnings?"

"The whispering of the crone, echoed through the hall luring us into the entrance of the Shambles while you were rescuing the marsh people, my lady," cried another voice from the crowd.

"Everyone hungered for the taste of the meat; there was such a crush in the entrance of the Shambles as the crones thrust the meat into our hands. Even if you didn't want to take the sweetmeats the crowd swept you along," called out a voice. "They smelled so foul that I would have left without touching them but the crones would not let us leave without taking the meat."

"They cackled spells and vile chants at us when we tried to drop it and said that they would set their spiders on us if we wasted so much as one delicious mouthful. But . . . but . . ." The voices hesitated and fell silent.

"But what? Why did you not eat the meat? Once you had disobeyed me thus far why did you stop?" questioned Marrimian, looking slowly from face to face, searching in the crowd until a tall, stooping ragman shuffled forward.

"Forgive us, great lady," he begged. "But we could not overcome our cravings. It drew me step by step down into the entrance of the Shambles, but the crones' offerings are vile, tainted strips of rotting flesh that stink of corruption and I for one could not bear to bring a single mouthful of them to my lips."

"The crones have lied to everyone in the city," muttered a hoemaster, stepping awkwardly to stand beside the ragman, glad to unburden himself of his guilt. "That is why more of the city folk are waiting at the doors of the hall every morning. Everyone is beginning to realize. These sweetmeats that the crones tricked and forced us into taking with their spells and curses were never the flesh of any mudbeast that has ever roamed in the mires and marshes of Gnarlsmyre, of that I am sure."

"I heard the sound of the windbell inside that rotting piece of meat, that is why I dropped it," interrupted a scuttle. She had snatched her chance to tell the truth and beg her Queen's forgiveness, and she carried on with barely a pause to draw more breath. "I knew that I dare not throw it away, not even in the darkest lane or alleyway of the city. The crones are everywhere, spying and chanting curses against the city folk for shunning their sweetmeats. That is why I had to bring it into the hall, to find some dark corner to bury it or throw it away, but as I entered the corridor I stumbled on the uneven floorstones and heard the shrill mumbler's music inside the meat. I threw it up into the air and as it hit the floor and broke apart I saw the windbell, shining as pure and bright as the ice stars sown across the night sky. But as it lay there its music did not stop, it echoed around me, cursing me for disobeying your warnings, shouting to me for breaking my pledges to you and creeping like a thief into the entrance of the Shambles to taste the crones' sweetmeats."

"Would any of you take this strip and taste the flesh if your Queen freely offered it to you now that you have seen the mumbler's windbell inside it and have heard its haunting music?" Krann asked the crowd slowly.

Low murmurs ran through the people and every one of them began to shake their heads.

"The mumbler's magic will ill-fate anyone who hears its music," called out one of the dusters.

"Even if the meat were not so foul I for one would not dare to touch it now for fear of the master mumbler's magic. He would weave me into his dance of fate," cried a threadneedle woman, keeping her hands over her ears in case Marrimian shook the bell again.

Marrimian stared at the crowd thoughtfully and paused for a moment. Clearly the master mumbler still held a terrible power over the people of the hall, a power that she must destroy before Erek sought some other way to use him against her if she was to hold on to the throne. She must capture him the moment he took his first step outside the entrance of the Shambles.

"You shall become my watchers," she said firmly, sweeping the hand that held the windbell across the crowd. They scrambled away from her as its shrill music filled the vaulted passageway. "That shall be your punishment for disobeying me and creeping into the entrance of the Shambles. You shall spend your days and nights watching the lanes and the alleyways just beyond the door of the hall, listening for the rattle of bells, so that I shall know when Naul leaves the safety of the Shambles."

Marrimian beckoned to the scuttle who had brought the strip of rotting flesh into the hall and sent her to fetch the bow of black ebony and the quiver of arrows that hung beside the throne. She told her to warn Treyster and Syrenea and the door wardens to be on their guard and bring her word if the master mumbler so much as dared to show his nose in the hall.

Krann watched the scuttle vanish in the gloomy corridor and slowly turned to Marrimian. "Do not judge the master mumbler so hastily," he warned quietly. "There is something about him that I am not sure of. Something in his eyes and the way he defended your right to touch the Glitterspike. There is something . . ."

"Judge him hastily?" Marrimian cried, cutting off Krann's words. "He is guilty of black treachery and I will kill him if he ever dares to set a foot inside this hall."

Krann shook his head. "No! Those are an echo of the words that your father would have used. Those are not your words, nor is it the judgment *you* would use. Remember, whatever Naul's intentions were when he vanished from the hall, the fear of his magic is what is stopping the people of the hall from touching Erek's sweetmeats. Perhaps that, and the foulness of her offerings, is what is driving all the city folk away from the Shambles."

"That may be true, but what of Erek and her gathering of crones? They will not come begging forgiveness at the doors of the hall, I'm sure of that. Naul is with them, remember. We saw him creeping through the alleyways of the Shambles close to Erek's lair and his arms were loaded down with foul, stinking sweetmeats. I fear that she will find another way to frighten the people of the city with the power they see in his magic. I must kill him. That is the only way to be sure of . . ."

A sudden rush of footsteps made Marrimian fall silent and spin round. "Mistress, mistress!" Ansel's voice carried over the heads of the marsh people as she hurried toward them, her apron tails billowing out to brush and rub against the damp stone walls of the passageway on either side. "There are more ironmasters, lampwicks, wheelwrights, chandlers and others this morning than on any other day since the wet seasons began. They are all flocking to the doors of the hall. They are crying out that the crones have tried to trick them with lies and poisonous meats and now they are all clamoring to barter their crafts and skills for food. They are calling your name as their Queen, Queen of all Gnarlsmyre. What shall we do?"

Marrimian stared at the scullion and brought her hand up to her open mouth. "We must let them into the hall, of course," she cried. "Throw open the doors—fill the long eating boards!"

"But the lampwicks are empty-handed, mistress; they haven't got a reedstem between them; and some of the ironmasters are only carrying bags of rusty iron filings. Shall I turn those who have little or nothing away again?" Ansel asked, thrusting her jaw out in a scowl.

"If they have come freely and are not armed, if it is not one of Erek's treacherous schemes, then I would let them all into the hall," urged Krann.

Marrimian thought for a moment. "The lampwicks cannot harvest until the floods have receded. Let them all have a place and tell those who are empty-handed that they can barter a promise and a pledge to serve me for some food from the table."

"But we will never have enough to feed everyone!" Ansel cried indignantly. "Not if anyone who lives in the city comes begging with empty promises at our door."

"Then spread what we have thinly, be sparing

and waste nothing," answered Marrimian before turning her back toward the hall.

"Come quickly, word is that she is letting everyone into the hall," shouted the wheelwright as he hammered on the ironmaster's bolted door.

Above his head a window latch rattled open and the ironmaster's head appeared.

"Come on," cried the wheelwright. "The great doors of the hall have been jammed solid since daybreak with the press of harvesters and chandlers all fighting for a place at the Queen's table. Come now or there will be nothing left."

"What of the crones?" asked the ironmaster anxiously, lowering his voice to avoid being overheard.

"They have been shrieking and spinning through the streets of the city, cursing us for shunning the sweetmeats."

The wheelwright laughed and shook the heavy, wet leather bag of stones that hung from his belt. "They'll spin away from us all the faster under a hail of stones."

Krann leaned on the balustrade of the high gallery and looked down across the crowds that now thronged the hall. They had been gathering in greater numbers every morning, spilling through the outer doors to do their bartering as the first streak of gray, wet morning light cast a weak shadow from the Glitterspike. At first he had laughed at the shouts of barter that had echoed backwards and forwards between the colonades of fluted columns but now he shook his head in dismay at the piles of useless objects they left to litter the outer edges of the hall before they joined the slow-moving queues to be fed at the long eating boards.

On some mornings there were boiled pink crawlers or flesh from a roasted marshfish with strips of watery blue cabbage and the gritty leaves of sandleeks cooked in their own juices. But on other days the people had to make do with some rusk baked from husk corn or the bitter black bread made from the marshoak acorns that the harvesters had gathered using Krann's boat to cross the marshes.

"What will become of those piles of wheels, the hooks and the hoes, the jugs and pots and pans that we have no use for here in the hall? What are you going to do with this whole jumble of useless rubbish?" he asked Marrimian, sweeping his hand across the bustling crowd below as she came to his side.

Marrimian looked down at the milling people and smiled as she picked out an ironmaster haggling with one of the ore carriers over the last rusty rock in the bottom of his basket, offering him a large piece of his crust of black bread and a bowl of sandleeks for the contents of his basket. "Everything has its place; nothing shall go to waste," she murmured. "Watch carefully, follow that ironmaster down there and you will see that he does more than merely barter for his food, he uses that barter to trade for ore and for wood for his forge. Look over there in the shadows of the stone columns; there are groups of strikers and quenchers who will barter their skills and strengths with the ironmaster for a part of the food that he has exchanged for his bag of nails or set of iron hoes or whatever he has brought into the hall."

Krann followed the ironmasters for a moment with his eyes and then frowned and shook his head. "No, you make this chaos seem too neat, too simple and orderly. You have not explained away those ragged figures that come into the hall empty-handed, take what they please from the long eating boards and then spend their mornings sifting through the piles of rusty rods and iron tools. They pick up a twist of yarn here and a newly woven basket there without so much as a thank you to anyone. Look, there is one of them clambering over that pile of iron hooks, there—just beside the kitchen archway!"

Marrimian followed his pointing finger and then softly laughed. "He's a lampwick—he'll be searching for a new hook to trim the reed stems that the reed cutters will bring when the floods recede. Normally he would barter the light in the reed lamps using his store of reeds gathered before the wet seasons but when the marshmen overran the city they probably stole most of his stock and burned the rest. We must be patient with the harvesters and all those who cannot go about their daily tasks: they will repay their barter in full when the wet seasons end."

Krann sighed and shook his head. "I think the crones will curse the rain so that it never stops. I swear we will never see the sunlight again."

Marrimian turned and laughed at him and drew him away from the bustle and the shouts of barter that were filling the hall. "Their power is weakening. The city folk chase them and stone them if they dare to show their faces in the street."

She took him to stand beside the tall crystal window at the far end of the high balcony. "Listen!" she whispered. "Listen to the sound of the rain."

Krann tilted his head to one side and listened, his forehead wrinkling into a frown, then he quickly turned and pressed his nose against the pane of crystal, looking out at the dreary, drifting curtain of rain. "It's getting lighter! The sound of the rain is fainter!" he cried, grasping Marrimian's hands and spinning her around.

"The sky is getting paler!" Marrimian laughed with him and nodded. "The season has been gradually changing for many days and before too many tomorrows have passed the sun will break through the clouds!"

"How many tomorrows?" Krann cried, clapping his hands with delight.

"Very soon now and then when it stops raining the marshes will begin to drain away in no time at all and . . ." A sudden commotion in the entrance of the hall made them both turn and rush back to the balustrade.

Below them they could see one of the watchers Marrimian had sent to watch the entrance of the

Shambles running across the hall toward the foot of the stairway that led up to the high gallery. "The crones! Erek and the crones are loose in the city. They are rushing up toward the hall in one shrieking riddle!" he gasped catching sight of Krann and Marrimian at the head of the stairway.

"What of Naul the mumbler?" Marrimian hissed, her fingers tightening on the ornate bannister rail.

"He runs before them, great lady," the watcher added breathlessly. "The crones are screaming and cursing him and howling for his blood." He fell silent and glanced nervously over his shoulder toward the high-arched entrance as if he expected Naul with the crones at his heels to burst into the hall at any moment. Marrimian reached for the bow that hung from her shoulder. At that very moment the voices of the crones shrieked and cursed and the rush of their footsteps echoed in the winding corridor that led from the great doors into the hall.

"Naul!" Marrimian snarled as she reached into the quiver that hung at her waist and nocked an arrow on to the bow.

The crowds that thronged the high-arched entrance split apart and scattered in terror at the screams of hatred that poured out of Erek's mouth and the shrieks and curses from her gathering of black-ragged hags who ran close on the mumbler's heels as he burst into the hall.

"Come no further, you treacherous mumbler, or I will arrowstrike your black heart and end your life forever," Marrimian cried, drawing the feathered flight of the arrow back against her cheek, feeling the bow string cut into her fingers as she leveled the blade of the arrow at Naul's heart.

"Marrimian . . . I sought only to serve you, to make amends for my mother's treacheries," the mumbler cried, stumbling over the torn hems of his saffron gown and falling to his knees close to the Glitterspike.

Erek let out another shriek of hatred as she raced across the hall toward where Naul kneeled. She spun the crones round to stand between him and the crowd. "He is mine, mine, and I alone have the right to kill him!" she hissed, her eyes narrowing into murderous slits.

Her venomous hatred bubbled on her lips as she swept a long, curved dagger out of the sleeve of her ragged cloak and held it high above her head. "He is mine, I tell you, and he will die for washing away the cup of revenge that we so lovingly brewed against this house of Miresnare."

"And for poisoning our sweetmeats with his nasty little bells," cursed one of the crones, spitting at Naul.

"Your revenge was wrong, I had to destroy it," Naul cried, twisting around toward his mother. "Lord Miresnare was seized with madness when he sacked the Shambles and snatched me from your birth webs, but to harbor such hatred, and plot such terrible revenge, was as wrong. My mumbler's magic gave me the power to know the truth and through it I can see how wrong both he and you have been."

The crones suddenly closed in on Naul, leaping and scratching at his face to silence him. Krann stared at the mumbler as he tried to ward off the black hags.

"He was trying to help you, Marrimian," he cried, leaping forward to rescue Naul.

He strode in amongst the hideous hags, plunging his dagger at their sticky riddle of flying rags, cutting and tearing through them as he fought to drive the crones back.

Erek spat at Krann as she brought her dagger up high above Naul's head to make the killing stroke. For a moment she held Marrimian's gaze with her murderous eyes. "You have not the stomach, firstborn: you cannot loose that arrow. You are nothing but a weak prettier and you shall have nothing—not the throne nor one single dry footstep of Gnarlsmyre. Mertzork and Pinvey shall snatch it all from you and I shall take my child's heart which your father stole from me so many seasons ago. You shall have nothing . . . nothing!"

Double-handed, she brought the dagger sweeping toward Naul's neck. Marrimian steadied the bow and loosed the arrow, sending it shrieking across the hall. Erek cried out once as the arrow blade struck her chest and sent the dagger flying from her hand. The force of the blow drove her backwards through the crones and across the hall, tumbling her over and over the floorstones. Spiders swarmed in the dark, secret folds of her clothes and as she came to rest in a bloody crumpled tangle they scuttled out of every pleat and fold of her cloak and spread in a black, shifting tide all around her.

Naul saw Marrimian release the arrow and felt the draft as it shrieked through the air above his head. He heard his mother's scream behind him as it struck her. He rose, spun round and ran to her, treading heedlessly through the swarming spiders, then gathered her up in his arms and wept as he rocked her gently backwards and forwards.

The crones, wounded and bleeding from the fury of Krann's attack, heard the arrow scream across the hall and turned as one, screaming and clutching at their black rags as the arrow struck Erek. When it shattered her breastbone and pierced her heart each one of them felt the arrow through the webs of deceit and treachery that they had wound between themselves.

"Erek! Erek!" they wailed as the very essence of their magic drained from them and their riddle of rags began to melt and shred from their shoulders. They turned and tried to run toward the high archway that led out to the brightening sky but their footsteps slowed and dragged on the floorstones. Their backbones creaked and bent beneath the weight of all the evils that they had ever plotted and schemed in Erek's lair.

Ansel, hearing the commotion in the hall, rushed to Marrimian's side as the crones were trying to escape. "I will cut their throats," she thundered, snatching up her gutting blade as she strode after them, her eyebrows drawn down into a grim furrow of hatred.

"No, there will be no more killing in this hall," Marrimian called out as she dropped the bow and ran down the stairway and across the hall to where Naul kneeled.

Ansel stopped as she heard Marrimian's voice; she was but a stride from the closest crone. "Evil old hags!" she hissed, giving the hobbling crones a look of disgust before she turned reluctantly back. "Mistress, they will escape and vanish into the Shambles to plot and scheme against us. Remember, they plotted to kill you and they overran this hall the moment our backs were turned, they tried to burn it down and . . ."

"I said no more killing," repeated Marrimian firmly. "Look at their crippled bodies, Ansel, and try to remember that they were once healing women before my father drove them out into the marshes to die. I will not have their blood spilt in this hall; they are a part of the tragedy of my father's madness. Look how weak and helpless they are now that Erek is dead. They can barely shuffle over the threshold, let alone run away and vanish. Remember, the Shambles cannot hide them now: the force of the storms has torn down the canopy of webs that covered their evil plots and the spiders that once wove them will surely perish now that Erek is dead. Take Vetchim and Treasel and a dozen of our guards and escort the crippled crones down into the Shambles. But while you are there throw open every door and window and let a fresh wind blow away the last shadows of Erek's treachery."

Ansel turned her head toward the shuffling crones and her glare of anger and hatred changed to one of pity and compassion for she saw them trying to cover their wizened nakedness as their riddle of rags fell from their shoulders. "Cover them with your cloaks," she ordered, turning sharply on a group of ironmasters and lampwicks who were staring at the wretched women. As they fumbled at the clasps of their cloaks she hurried forward, unfastening her apron ties, and cast her apron around the closest crone.

Marrimian reached the edge of the black tide of spiders that had swarmed out of Erek's clothes but she hesitated to go any further for fear of the spiders running beneath the hems of her skirts and crawling up her legs. She looked down and shuddered at the mass of twitching legs and convulsing underbellies that she could see all heaped together and she realized that the spiders must be dying.

"They were a part of the terror that my mother wove in her lair within the Shambles, they cannot survive without her," Naul whispered not looking up, brushing at the tear stains on his face.

Marrimian swallowed her revulsion, trod her way across the spiders and kneeled down beside him. She gathered her courage and looked down at Erek's face, half expecting her to leap up and hiss and snarl, her lips bubbling with bright venom, the hatred and hunger for revenge etched into every crease and wrinkle, but there was nothing but a sunken and pitifully aged face that stared blankly back at her through blind, dead eyes.

"Your arrow blade has purged her evil and now, through her death, I have found the mother who bore me and wrapped me in her snuggling clothes," Naul whispered softly, gathering up Erek's body, and rising, he turned toward the weak rays of watery sunlight that showed beyond the high-arched entrance to the hall.

14

A Thread of Magic

*H*OT mists drifted between the rickety stilts of the marshhuts and vaporous clouds of steam, heated by the morning sun, rose from the draining reed beds. Everywhere water dripped from the opening flowerheads and the budding branches of the black ebonies and clusters of marshoaks that stood above the emptying marshes. Herons and waders, rising in vivid clouds of color, moved from channel to channel, fighting and squabbling, as they fished the water lily beds. Sinister pindafalls, lean and hungry from sheltering through the wet seasons in their roosts and caves above the beasting pits, were hunting across the marshes, their leathery wings smoothing black shadows over the pools of bubbling mud as they soared in widening circles around the marshery. Far off, beyond Fenmire Marsh, a mudbeast bellowed, awakening Andzey.

Quickly he shook Alea awake. "Look!" he whispered peering through the tiny window in the cocoon that had covered their cage. "Look and you will see the sourwings flying low across the reed

beds toward the great ridge of Gnarlsmyre. Their
wings brush through the tops of the bulrush heads
as they try to escape the pindafalls."

Alea shivered in the cold morning air, pulled her
damp cloak more tightly around her and gazed at
the tiny fingerspan shaft of sunlight spilling
through the window in the cocoon. Hesitantly, as
she heard the rattle of the bulrush heads, she
reached out and warmed her fingertips in the sunlight. Andzey thrust his fingers through the bars
and tore another long hole in the cocoon and
dropped the tangled bundle of threads into the
swirling waters of the channel below their cage.

"Mertzork must have heard that mudbeast, it heralds the end of the wet seasons and will waken him
from his deepest sleep," Andzey whispered urgently. "Be quick, help me strip away this cocoon
before he opens the door of their hut. They mustn't
know how we have used the spiders."

Above them they heard a movement. Pinvey's
voice rose, cursing Mertzork and demanding that
he open the door. Alea worked desperately beside
Andzey, tearing through the webs, gathering the
mass of broken threads and forcing them through
the bars to float away on the receding floodwaters
racing through the channel. Suddenly she stopped,
the reed-woven door above them was scraping
open, she sank back into the furthest corner of the
cage away from Andzey, bundling the remaining
tangle of webs behind her. She glanced up, expecting a hail of curses, and saw Mertzork's cruel face
silhouetted against the clear blue sky. He was

frowning and shading his eyes against the low morning sunlight and staring out across the marshes. Alea turned her head and followed his gaze.

"Look," she hissed to Andzey, pointing toward a forest of spear tips she could see moving above the reeds. "There are many marshmen traveling through the reed beds toward us," she muttered darkly. Pinvey crowded the door beside Mertzork and blinked her eyes against the bright sunlight as she peered out of the hut.

"Look! Look, they must be my army—the warriors that you sent for before it began to rain," she cried excitedly.

Looking down, she glanced into the cage, her face hardening with the hate she felt for her sister. "Prepare my beast. Ready him for me to ride in triumph into Glitterspike Hall," she hissed, snapping her fingers at Alea.

Mertzork turned his head toward the island of marshoaks that loomed in the thinning mist just beyond the furthest end of the reed bed and for a moment he watched the mass of black rotting beast-skins draped over their upper branches as shelter for the poor wretches who had been forced there to weather out the raging storms of the wet seasons. He cupped his hands to his mouth and shouted, causing a commotion in all the huts that crowded on either side.

"Come down out of the trees, you idle hide-chewers and mud-sifters. Come down! Come down! Prepare to march on the city of Glor!"

Rush-woven doors scraped open on either side of their hut and dirty, shaven heads appeared, crowding every doorway. Eyes blinked in the sunlight and fingers scratched at the swarms of tiny mites and insects that crawled across unwashed skin.

Mertzork glanced at the wakening marshmen on either side and cursed them for their idleness, shouting furiously. "Cast your nets in the waters of the channels and light roasting fires. We must eat before we march on the city of Glor."

Suddenly the long, spindle-thin ladders that led to the drying ground below were bending and creaking as the marshmen swarmed down. They were fighting and cursing at one other as each one tried to be the first to cast the bundles of finely woven nets slung across their shoulders into the muddy, swirling waters of the channel.

"They are hungry after their long fast," Andzey whispered. "Much more hungry than we are; they have not eaten dragonflies, leeches and mud crawlers."

Alea shuddered as he continued. "But the channel will be full of marshfish and huge pink shell crawlers that are carried with the floodwater far out into the marshes."

An angry shout from the edge of the channel made him fall silent and he leaned forward, pressing his face against the bars. He frowned as he watched the line of marshmen pulling their empty nets out of the water. Mertzork began to descend the ladder cursing the fishermen and ordering them to cast their nets further out. He paused as he drew level with Andzey and Alea in their cage.

"Brother!" he sneered, curling his lips back across his yellowing teeth. "My Queen will have no further use for her beast when we reach the city and I shall, therefore, kill you between the Hurlers' Gate!" Laughing cruelly, Mertzork descended and was out of sight before Andzey could open his mouth to reply.

"It's hopeless," Alea whispered in despair. "We'll never be able to lift a finger . . ."

Andzey hushed her into silence. "They are merely threats and taunts against what he sees as our helplessness, but listen to the angry shouts below; come here and look down at the channel: there is something wrong." Andzey laughed softly to himself. "Not everything is how my brother would like it: there are no fish, there is not even a crawler in the nets, and the floodwater is flowing through the channel differently than usual. It has washed away all those piles of bones and changed the shape of the marshery." They watched Mertzork searching for the path of stepping stones that used to lead to the reed beds. He kept glancing toward the marshoak islands where he had driven the lesser hunters, the elders and all the women, young and old, whom his favored followers had not chosen to take up with them into the safety of their huts. The marshoaks were too silent; surely those wretches should have scrambled out of their branches and crossed back on to the dry land of the marshery the moment that it appeared above the receding floodwaters?

"Are they all dead?" Alea asked, looking across the reed beds to the towering marshoaks that stood so silent beneath their shrouds of rotting beast-skins.

"I really don't know," Andzey whispered. "Many will have starved and slipped from the branches to drown and others will have died of the cold, but . . ."

"Prepare my beast of burden!" Pinvey hissed at Alea, rattling the bars of their cage with the blade of her dagger and making both of them jump and spin around. They had been so engrossed in looking for signs of life in the marshoak branches that neither of them had heard Pinvey descend the ladder. For a moment her eyes narrowed suspiciously and she reached through the bars and pinched at the lean, wasted flesh of Alea's arm.

"You have survived the wet season too easily, sister," she muttered, hate-ridden.

"I . . . I . . . I caught dragonflies . . ." Alea began, the disgust at what they had had to eat showing clearly on her face.

Pinvey sneered and then burst out laughing. "Then they shall be your delicacies, sister. I shall send out the best hunters to catch a basket of the fattest dragonflies for your daily feast."

Gloating with delight as the horror of this etched across Alea's face, Pinvey unlocked the cage and turned her head to glare impatiently down at the lines of marshmen who had waded dangerously far out into the swirling channel in desperation to fill their nets. "Get back here, you fools," she cursed, "and throw away those useless nets: there is food enough for every one of us crammed in the larders of Glitterspike Hall."

"Don't march today, please don't . . ." Alea begged but Pinvey sneered at her helplessness through the bars and continued to descend the ladder.

"Please don't march . . ." Alea began again but Pinvey's cruel laughter cut her short and her pitiless voice floated up to them.

"Prepare my beast, sister, for my triumphant return into Glitterspike Hall. We shall begin the march immediately!"

Alea sank back on to her haunches in the tiny cage and large tears of despair trickled down her cheeks. "It is all so hopeless. Mertzork will kill you the moment we reach the Hurlers' Gate and Pinvey will . . ."

"No," whispered Andzey, and there was a hint of laughter in his voice that made Alea fall silent. She looked up to see a smile crinkling the skin around his eyes. "You care, then? You care a little that my brother will kill me?" he asked, hesitantly reaching out his hand toward her.

Alea blushed and lowered her eyes. "Yes, I care," she whispered, touching the tips of his fingers gently with hers and catching her breath as he gripped her hand and made her look up at him.

"We must travel now," he whispered forcefully, "now, while the marshes are still swollen and dangerous to cross, while the secret paths are still difficult to find. I'm glad your pleading with your sister has made her all the more determined to start today."

"But why? How can that possibly help us?" frowned Alea, moving closer to him. He lifted the hem of his cloak and patted the hedgehog hidden beneath his jerkin.

"Now that I know you care I will risk everything to defeat my brother and Pinvey so that we can spend the rest of our lives together. All we need is one moment's hesitation from Mertzork, just a flicker of indecision as he searches for the path!"

Mertzork's voice suddenly floated up to them. He was speaking in hushed and anxious whispers to Pinvey just below their cage as he pointed toward the silent marshoak island. He was telling her how he had found the dripping branches beneath the skin canopy totally deserted. "Some magic must have spirited them away," he hissed fearfully.

Pinvey gave the island a casual glance and shrugged her shoulders. "What does it matter what happened to them? They were nothing to us; we are better rid of them. Let us march now on the city of Glor and leave this wretched huddle of huts and swamps behind."

"No, the marshes are still too swollen to travel and what if your sister, Marrimian, has armed the city people against us?" muttered Mertzork uncertainly. "I think we should prepare the marshmen for battle before we leave."

Pinvey threw her head back and laughed at his

indecision. "There is nothing to eat here unless you wish to feed your marshmen on bowls of mud, and while we are waiting and licking this mud from our lips perhaps the magic that spirited away those creatures from the marshoak island will snatch our warriors too!"

Mertzork turned angrily on her, aware that the marsh people had stopped casting their nets and were crowding forward to listen. "You forget, I know these marshes better than any marshman and I say it is too dangerous to travel," he snarled.

"And you have forgotten," hissed Pinvey, her eyes blazing with anger, "that Erek and her crones promised to destroy my cursed sister, Marrimian, and to be ready to welcome us into the city the moment the wet seasons ended."

Mertzork hesitated and glanced over his shoulder at the silent crowds that had shuffled closer between the stilts of the marshery. A ladder creaked and the crowds hurriedly moved apart, looking up to see Alea and Andzey descending from their cage. Alea had readied Andzey for the journey across the marshes by putting a bridle of gossamer threads down across his face but it did not cover his eyes or mask their looks of triumph at Mertzork's indecision.

"We march now, this very moment!" Mertzork snarled, turning his back on Andzey.

Mertzork hesitated for what seemed to be the thousandth time as he floundered in the warm, bubbling mud and felt for the path that he knew must lie somewhere just ahead of him. He cursed his decision to march on the city before the marshes had properly drained. He had thought that the journey would be difficult but he had not expected the land to have changed so much after the flooding.

"What are you waiting for? The city lies just ahead of us, I can see the setting sun reflecting from the towers of Glitterspike Hall," shouted Pinvey, her impatient voice rolling across the dark, mud-covered reed beds, the upturned marshoaks and scrub bushes whose broken, roots were etched black against the evening sky.

"Wait where you are while I find the path across this mire. I will climb up on that reed bank. I should be able to see the Hurlers' Gate from there," Mertzork shouted back to her, glancing, with hatred in his eyes to where he had left her sitting astride Andzey's shoulders on a low, muddy bank of broken reeds. It was so easy for her, always demanding everything so impatiently. *She* didn't have to find the path. For a moment he thought of turning back and telling her to lead them and then allowing himself to gloat while she foundered and vanished as the clinging mud pulled her down. He half turned but then shrugged his shoulders and thought better of it. He still needed her for now, though once inside Glitterspike Hall, once he had the throne, then things would be different.

Mertzork's foot found the narrow path and he slowly moved forward, sinking at times up to his waist as he waded across the mire. He reached the tall reed bank and by clutching on to the reeds he climbed up hand over hand above the marsh and broke a path through the dense vegetation to reach the far side of the bank. He gasped and stared open-mouthed across the last wide stretch of marsh to the sheer, dark walls of the dyke and the steep terraces that rose beyond them. He could not understand what had caused this change in the land and he turned back and shouted and waved to urge Pinvey and his army of marshmen to join him on the reed bank.

"This must be some of Erek's magic," Pinvey muttered thoughtfully. She had dismounted from Andzey's shoulders and had roughly pushed him and Alea away as she stood looking across the bubbling mud of the marsh at the dark wall of the dyke.

"Look, I can see figures with torches moving through the Hurlers' Gate and out along the top of that wall," exclaimed Mertzork.

"And look there, silhouetted between the gates in those yellow robes, I think it is that mumbler Erek was so fond of. She must have sent him to look out from the city and welcome us," Pinvey cried. She lifted her hands and cupped them to her mouth and shouted and then waved at the growing crowds on top of the wall.

"They are armed with spears and strange long bows. I can see them reflecting in the torch light," warned Mertzork.

"There is nothing to fear. Erek must have armed them to kill anyone foolish enough to follow my cursed sister," Pinvey answered, breathless with the excitement of seeing the city and the sheer, towering walls of Glitterspike Hall. Suddenly she grasped Mertzork's arm and pointed up to the light that shone in the tall crystal windows of the hall. "How can we get across the marsh? Where is the path? I must reach the city now!"

Mertzork frowned and shook his head. He sniffed the evening wind. "This stretch of marsh has changed completely. There may be paths beneath the mud but I don't know them nor could I guess where they might lie. The night wind may freeze the marshes but I don't think it will be strong enough to bear our weight for another night or two. It is too early in the new season yet."

Andzey listened closely and caught the rising note of impatience in Pinvey's voice as she demanded that Mertzork search for a way across the marsh. "Stay very close to me," he whispered to Alea and, loosening the hedgehog from where he had hidden it beneath his jerkin, he moved quietly away from Mertzork and Pinvey, through the dense cover of reeds to the edge of the bank.

"What are you going to do?" Alea asked, brushing her lips against his ear as she heard the army of marshmen clambering up on the reed bank behind them press closer.

Andzey put his finger on her lips. "I am listening for the crackle of the rime ice forming across the marshes, for that is the moment when it will be strong enough to support the hedgehog's weight. Now go to your sister and distract her so that she does not notice I am missing."

Alea frowned, at a loss to understand, and she would have pressed him again for an explanation but she heard Pinvey's voice rise to a shout of impatient anger. She rose and moved quietly through the reeds toward Pinvey just as she heard the first faint, almost whispering, soft crackle of the rime ice spreading its fingers across the marsh.

"There are at least a thousand torches on that wall. Look at their reflections on the freezing marsh!" Pinvey screamed, stamping her foot on the thick mat of broken reeds, shattering their brittle stems as she trampled them impatiently. "Even a blind man could find a way across in their light."

Andzey slipped silently down the reed bank and pushed his fingers into the freezing mud. It creaked and fractured but it did not break. He leaned forward and reached out as far as he dared without being seen and still the ice held the weight of his hand. Gently he put the hedgehog on the ice and pointed it toward where he could hear Mertzork and Pinvey arguing only a dozen paces away. "You are our only hope," he whispered, giving the hedgehog a gentle push.

The hedgehog squealed and scrabbled at the hardening rime ice with its tiny claws and it tried to turn around. "No, don't come back to me," Andzey hissed, turning the hedgehog around and pushing it more forcefully out across the ice. It squealed again and ran in a small circle. Andzey cursed it under his breath and, brushing away the cold beads of sweat that had formed on his forehead, he caught it as it scuttled past him. "Go. You are our only hope, go to my brother," he pleaded, giving it a forceful push.

Mertzork could hear murmurs of discontent amongst the army of marshmen crowding the reed bank behind him and he knew that he would have to do something to quell Pinvey's impatience. He looked down through the reeds at the frozen edges of the marsh and caught sight of the hedgehog. Clapping his hands, he shouted with laughter. "You shall be in the city before you have time to draw breath," he cried over his shoulder to Pinvey and he slid down the steep bank and shattered the thin layer of freezing mud. As he sank into the marsh up to his knees he reached out and caught the scuttling hedgehog in his hands.

"Look, Erek has sent me a guide," he laughed, holding up the tiny creature. "All I have to do is unravel the loose end of the thread and the hedgehog will find me the path. It rescued me before when I fell through the ice crust and it showed me the way up through the city and into Glitterspike Hall. I will be across in less than a moment, just follow my footsteps."

Andzey crawled silently up the bank and brushed the freezing mud from his fingers before he beckoned Alea to move closer to him. "Now you will see my brother's downfall," he whispered. "He believes that the healing woman has sent that hedgehog to show him a way across the marsh, that is the mistake that will kill him."

Alea turned her head as she heard Mertzork coax the hedgehog out on the ice. "He'll never believe it.

The hedgehog won't cross the marsh," she gasped.

"Watch," whispered Andzey. The hedgehog tired of Mertzork's rough hands as it repeatedly tried to scramble up to the safety of the reed bank. It sniffed the chill in the air and caught the scent of the terraces beyond the dyke before it set off scrabbling on its way across the ice, running in a zigzag path between the clumps of broken reed stems and rotting branches that protruded through the frozen marsh crust.

"There is our path!" shouted Mertzork, striding out, then rushing heedlessly after the hedgehog.

Pinvey frowned. She opened her mouth to call after him, to remind him that he had crushed the life out of the magical hedgehog that the healing woman had given to him in Glitterspike Hall, but her voice was lost beneath the sound of the freezing ice crust shattering under Mertzork's weight. He took another dozen floundering strides and sank deeper and deeper. Clutching at the fragile thread, he cursed the hedgehog, then the thread snapped between his fingers. He thrashed his legs in the clinging mud as he reached out for a half-submerged branch that snapped as he grabbed it. He was sinking faster now with each desperate movement.

"Come back, you fool, come back!" screamed Pinvey.

"The path! Where is the path?" he shouted at the hedgehog as it scuttled away from him.

"There is no path," shouted a familiar voice from

the bank. "There is nothing there but a bottomless marsh."

Mertzork recognized Andzey's voice and he struggled to turn back, clawing at the thin covering of ice as he tried to reach the reed bank. As he sank deeper and deeper into the swallowing mud he realized there was nothing, no spine of rock or hidden tree root, to rescue him. Nothing but the soft, ice-cold mud beneath his feet. Pinvey was screaming, white-faced, shouting at the marshmen on the reed bank to go and rescue him. The marshmen, fearing her rage, were scrambling down the steep banks and throwing out their nets and ropes, but they all fell short.

"Help me! Help me!" Mertzork screamed, flailing his arms in the mud as it reached his chest.

"I cannot help you, brother. This is your punishment for murdering our father," Andzey called, making Mertzork stop struggling for a moment and stare up at the silhouette on the reed bank.

"Punishment!" Mertzork sneered. "Our father was a fool and he deserved to die. He had discovered the beast Gallengab and would have shared that secret with every marshman from Fenmire. By murdering him and claiming the beast as my own I almost seized the throne of Gnarlsmyre."

Andzey laughed and waved a handful of gossamer threads at him. "I would help you, brother, despite your crimes, but I have wound all the spider's thread I had around that hedgehog."

"*You* made that spindle of thread?" Mertzork screamed. "*You*—not the healing woman?" He was now fighting desperately to keep his head above the mud.

Andzey nodded gravely and there was a hint of tears in his eyes as he watched his brother sinking into the mud. "Your belief in her treacherous magic has been your undoing, brother."

"I'll strangle . . . I'll kill . . . I'll . . ." Mertzork screamed but his words ended in a choking gasp as with a final swallowing gulp the marsh sucked him down, filling his mouth with black, drowning mud. His clenched fist shook briefly above the bubbling surface and then disappeared from sight.

Pinvey turned on Andzey and Alea, her teeth bared, her eyes burning with murderous hatred. "Kill them! Kill them both!" she hissed at the swarm of venomous spiders that Erek had set upon them.

Andzey laughed at her and tossed a handful of the spiders at the closest marsh hunter. He caught Pinvey in his strong hands before she could attack them, took her dagger from her and gave it to Alea. "The spiders are harmless," he called to the panicking marshmen. "We secretly milked their venom before the rains began."

The marshmen fell back in an unsettled silence as they stared at Andzey. Slowly he stepped toward them, breaking the gossamer threads away from his face and casting them carelessly into the marsh. "My brother is dead. He murdered our father and stole the title of marshlord from me," he said quietly. "Now I claim my title back and I take his Queen as my prisoner unless there is any among

you who would challenge my right and take her from me."

"You can keep her. Cast her into the marsh," called some voices in the crowd and throughout the reed beds heads nodded in agreement.

"How will you punish her?" shouted a voice as Pinvey fought and struggled against Andzey's grasp. "Will you stake her out for the mudbeasts?"

Andzey frowned and shook his head as he pointed across the frozen marsh crust toward the steeply rising roofs of the city that stood in the shadows of Glitterspike Hall. He watched the string of bright torches that now lined the high rim of the dyke and said, "It was the rumor of the woman, the one who tamed the mudbeasts and walked unharmed through the circle of beasts chained around the Glitterspike, that first brought me here. The marshes were full of wild tales of a princess who claimed the throne and all Gnarlsmyre as her own and it was her story that drew me to the city." He held Pinvey's murderous gaze as he added, "But your healing woman snared me with her magic in the shadows of that gateway and forced me through her evil spell to be your beast of burden, Pinvey, so that you could falsely claim to be the beast-rider and pretend to be the one who had rightfully won the throne. If this real Queen still rules, despite the treachery of the evil magic that you plotted against her, then she and she alone must be the one to judge your fate."

Pinvey threw her head back and shrieked with wild laughter. "She's long dead. Erek promised me that she would kill her the moment the rains began.

Look to the city walls. There her child, Naul, waits below the Hurlers' Gate to welcome me."

"You would kill us all, wouldn't you?" gasped Alea in horror. "To possess Mertzork would never have been enough for you, would it? You would have killed him in time and devoured everything in your insatiable lust for power."

Pinvey twisted in Andzey's strong grip, her face a rigid mask of hatred, and she spat in Alea's face. "The crones will swallow you, sister, they will suffocate you in their smothering riddle of rags. They'll suck the breath out of your body gasp by gasp," Pinvey shouted, her lips frothing with bright yellow flecks of spittle.

Alea staggered backwards away from such hatred, her face blanched in the torchlight, and she looked out across the marsh to the black wall of the dyke. Suddenly she caught her breath, bent forward and stared at two figures passing beneath the archway of the Hurlers' Gate. "No!" she breathed, blinking and looking again. Behind her she heard Pinvey's voice shriek with madness as Andzey and two of the strongest marshmen bound her wrists behind her back.

"Erek will pour swarms of spiders over you! The crones will chant evil spells!" she cursed, biting and scratching.

"Oh no!" called Alea firmly as she turned back toward her sister and pointed at the city. "Look again, look at who waits beside the master mumbler, look and see who stands beneath the Hurlers' Gate."

Pinvey twisted her head and stared across the marsh and her lips trembled in her twitching face as her teeth ground together. "Marrimian!" she hissed.

The great crowds parted to let Marrimian and Krann move along the dyke and they bowed and curtsied to them as they passed by, their movements mirrored in the shimmering surface of the frozen marsh.

"No!" Pinvey screamed, struggling to break free and almost throwing herself into the rime ice as she realized her bitter defeat. "Not you, Marrimian, not you, the cursed firstborn, and that frost-haired stranger," and she struggled in a frenzy against the ropes around her wrist until the knots screamed and creaked.

"Be still," ordered Andzey. "Meet the judgment you deserve with dignity."

"Andzey, look," cried Alea. "Some of those torch bearers near the Hurlers' Gate are moving across the marsh."

"There is the way across," shouted Pinvey, twisting toward the great army of marshmen that crowded along the reed banks behind them and stretched for as far as she could see before vanishing into the growing darkness. "I command you to swarm across the marsh and kill that cursed firstborn Marrimian who has stolen my throne. Kill everyone who raises a hand to stop you. Seize the city, take anything you want, rampage through every house, take their food, take their women . . ." Pinvey's voice began to weaken and she looked desperately from face to face. "Why? Why don't you attack the city?" she cried, sinking down on her knees and clawing at the broken reeds with her bound hands. "All you have to do is to kill Marrimian and the city and everything in it will be yours."

The marshmen closest to her looked down with rigid faces and their eyes glittered hard and cold in the flickering torchlight. They fiercely drove the butts of their spears and their iron spikes deep into the soft earth of the reed bank and knotted their sharpwires tightly around the barbed blades before they stepped back away from her. Andzey looked down at her for a long moment and then sadly shook his head. "You do not understand, do you?" he said quietly his voice breaking through her weeping and making her look up.

"The people of the marshes will never lift a finger to harm Marrimian now that your falsehoods have been unmasked, now that they know that she is the one who tamed and rode upon the mudbeast. Many of them caught a brief glimpse of her as she rode across the marshes but until tonight they were not sure which of you to worship and call their Queen . . ."

"It was me . . . *I* was the one . . ." Pinvey cried but the sea of unmoving faces that stared down at her made her hesitate and swallow her words.

"There will be no more bloodshed," Andzey called to the rows of waiting marshmen. "We will go in peace to the city to kneel before our rightful Queen and beg her forgiveness for following this false ruler," and he smiled at Alea and took her arm as two of the marshmen brought Pinvey along behind them and led her along the top of the reed bank toward the flickering torchlight.

For a moment Andzey hesitated and looked back to the broken ice crust where new fingers of ice were already beginning to form across the marsh. He stared at the place where Mertzork had floundered and sunk beneath the mud. "You were too impatient, brother, to take what was not yours. The path you sought was but a dozen paces away and clear to see if you had taken the time to look."

15

The Council of Voices

V OICES whispered and echoed throughout the great hall; the sound rose up in the shafts of morning sunlight that flooded down through the tall crystal windows and vanished amongst the darkened rafters overhead. Everywhere there was an air of hushed excitement in the densely packed crowds of craftsmen from each guild in the city, people from every marshery across the length and breadth of Gnarlsmyre. The hall folk had been given pride of place and were packed in the high galleries until they were overflowing, but still the scuttles were muttering and pushing and barging and craning their necks for a glimpse of the hall below. They were trying to catch sight of the two new thrones, beautifully carved with all the carpenters' skill. They had been fashioned from the heartwood of two black ebonies with an arch of solid marshoak inlaid across, joining the headrests, on which Ankana's name was written in scrolls and figurines cut from the wood of the pink-barked trees. The thrones had been set upon a high dais beside the Glitterspike.

Tall ragmen hissed at the scuttles, commanding them to be still. They twisted and turned their scrawny necks as they passed on the latest snatches of gossip rippling through the crowds.

"They say that Marrimian will cut off Pinvey's head," exclaimed a knowledgeable duster, drawing a long finger brutally across his throat.

"No, no," whispered one of the scullions who had found a place nearer the balustrade. "I heard Ansel say that she would be chained to the base of the Glitterspike in Yaloor's place in punishment for her crimes, and Ansel should know: she is always at the Queen's side."

A marshman overheard the scullion's whispers and looked up and shook his head. "Word says that she is to be hung beside one of the great causeways that are being built across the marshes, as a warning to anyone who might think of raising a treacherous finger against our Queen."

The scullion frowned, glaring down at the marshman, and was about to tell him how mistaken he had been to listen to such gossip when she caught sight of Ansel and Vetchim and the marsh-girl, Treasel, beneath the kitchen archway. "The Council of Voices is gathering!" she cried, and her words were taken up in ripple of excitement that spread across the hall.

Ansel hesitated for a moment as she stood in the shadow of the archway and the noise of the whispering died away. She glared darkly at the crowds that thronged the hall. Being a member of this council was far from her liking and she had been against meddling in the affairs of her betters, but her mistress and Krann had insisted and that had been the end of it. She was much happier bustling about her kitchens and overwatching the daily feeding of the great gangs of workers who were building those strange causeways across the marshes. Krann had said they would help to drain away the floods of the wet seasons. He had told her they would give more land to grow food and perhaps even to graze the ravine sheep and hill goats. Taking a deep breath Ansel gripped Vetchim's hand tightly in hers and strode forward to murmurs of approval, smiles and nods from everyone. She refused to look either to the left or right, feeling her cheeks flush hotly as they crossed the hall and took their places upon the dais on the right-hand side of the thrones.

Alca and Andzey both entered through the high archway and left their traveling cloaks with the waiting dressers. Everywhere throughout the hall the marsh people smiled and raised their hands to salute and welcome them as they too crossed to their places on the right-hand side of the dais. Syrenea and Treyster, laughing and talking noisily, excited by all the hustle and bustle that now ruled their daily lives, hurried beneath the archway that led down from their chambers above the daughtery and took their places on the dais.

Naul suddenly appeared from the narrow mumblers' corridor and swept through the hall in a blaze of bright saffron. The crowds shrank back with fear in their eyes as he smiled and called out, "I predict a good harvest and many children born in the city before the wet seasons begin." People started to smile as they surged back into their places and remembered that they had no reason to fear the mumbler or his magic.

Suddenly the hall fell silent and all eyes turned toward the wide, ornately carved archway that led up to the royal chambers. There was a light footstep on the spiral stairway and the rustling of a silk gown in the shadows beneath the archway. The crowd held its breath and leaned forward. The only sound that broke the silence was the rattling clatter of pindafalls' wings as they soared and glided between the towers of the hall, rising on the warm draughts of morning air.

A single hallwarden stepped forward and struck the floorstone beside the Glitterspike. Twice he struck it with his long-handled cane and cried out, "Enter Marrimian, Queen of all Gnarlsmyre, and enter Lord Krann, who rules beside her."

The crowd shouted their names and stamped and clapped, the sound erupting into thunderous applause as Krann led Marrimian out from beneath the archway into the sunlight that now streamed across the hall. Everyone they passed bowed or curtsied but the marshmen and women brought their hands up to their foreheads as they kneeled and twisted their fingers into horn shapes to salute the Queen, their Beast Lady, as she settled on to her throne.

Marrimian called the hallwardens to her and bid them bring Pinvey before them from the daughtery. She lifted her hand and quickly the hall fell silent once again. She turned her head and smiled at Krann before sweeping her gaze across the sea of expectant faces below her.

"You have all labored tirelessly here in the hall and in the lanes and alleyways of the city and in every marshery to bring about the peace and order that we now have in this, our land of Gnarlsmyre. You have built new dykes under Krann's direction and high causeways that stretch for leagues across the marshes and drain them. There are new terraces and broad fields that reach out far beyond those first hurried beginnings before the last wet seasons, but . . ." Marrimian paused as she heard the doors of the daughtery slam shut and the dragging, clattering sound of Pinvey's chains on the floorstones as the wardens led her toward the hall. ". . . but there is one thing that I have left undone, one matter that must be settled by the Council of Voices here in the shadow of the Glitterspike before the dry seasons come to an end. Pinvey has been my prisoner for too long. It is time to judge her and settle her fate."

A shriek of wild laughter erupted from the low archway that led from the daughtery. The crowd in the hall caught their breath and shrank back as Pinvey lifted the heavy loops of chain that bound her wrists and let them drop noisily on the floorstones, struggling to be free of the hallwardens leading her into the hall and forcing her to the edge of the dais.

"How dare you judge me," she hissed, spitting at

Marrimian and raking her hands through her disheveled, raven-dark hair. "I'll set the spiders on you all. Mertzork will wring your necks one by one . . ." She began to laugh, the sound rising in shrieks of madness as she spun round, tripping on the loops of the chains, and stabbed a long, thin finger at the crowds. "Erek will cast spells on you all. The crones will swallow you up in their riddle of rags if you dare to cross me . . ."

"Sister," Marrimian cried forcefully. "Erek is dead. The crones have lost their powers."

Pinvey turned sharply back toward Marrimian and lunged forward but the hallwardens restrained her. Marrimian shuddered as she looked into her sister's mad eyes. Pinvey had grown thin and haggard by refusing almost everything that was sent to her to eat, and her once startling beauty had drawn into a tight, fleshless mask that stretched across the bones of her face.

"Mertzork is dead," Marrimian said gently, but Pinvey just stared blindly through her, muttering and cursing. Marrimian looked helplessly at her for a moment and then turned to the members of the Council of Voices, who had gathered on either side of the throne. "What can I do with her? The madness grips her more forcefully with every day that I keep her locked away in the daughtery. I have tried to reason with her, I have offered to pardon her crimes and to let her begin again but she refuses to listen. You must help me decide her fate."

Ansel coughed and looked away. Vetchim watched Pinvey through narrow eyes and Treasel spread her hands helplessly, not knowing what she should say. Syrenea and Treyster remembered how they had both suffered at Pinvey's hands and glared at her with tight lips. They all feared her and dreaded Marrimian unlocking the chains that bound her wrists and allowing her to leave the daughtery unguarded.

"Mertzork will be here in a moment," Pinvey suddenly sneered, breaking the heavy silence. "He's searching for a path in those reed beds but when he comes back into the marshery he'll drop a sharpwire over your heads."

Andzey blinked at Pinvey's words and leaned down and whispered in Alea's ear. Alea frowned and violently shook her head in disagreement but Andzey, undeterred, stepped forward. "What are you Queen of?" he asked Pinvey.

She turned her head and stared at him, then frowned, as if trying to remember who he was. "Queen?" she cried. "Why, I am Queen of the Marsheries, any fool must know that. Look up there, those are my royal chambers!"

Marrimian frowned and leaned forward as Pinvey, wrapped in her belief that she was the Queen of the Marsheries, laughed and talked to herself.

"Andzey has touched on the center of her madness," Krann whispered. "Look how her face softens as she talks of the marshery."

Andzey moved closer to Marrimian and Krann. "The Fenmire Marshery is exactly as we left it but deserted, my Lady, none of my father's people has ever returned to it; they say it is cursed because of

Mertzork's and Pinvey's treacheries. You could give it to Pinvey and she would be safe there; she would never be able to discover the secret paths that lead back to the city and there is not a marshman in all Gnarlsmyre who would show them to her."

"But who would guard her?" cried Syrenea in dismay. "None of us would be safe in our beds."

"I am against it, completely against it, after what she did to us," cried Alea with Treyster nodding in agreement.

Marrimian looked from face to face, her eyes coming to rest on Ansel just as Andzey swept his hand across the marsh people who crowded the hall and said, "It shall be our task to overwatch her, to leave her food on the edge of the marshery. It will be our penance for ever doubting that you were our true Queen."

"What would you say to this, Ansel?" Marrimian asked quietly. "You have known us, the daughters of the hall, better than anyone else. How would you judge Pinvey?"

Ansel muttered with confusion, her oven-scarred cheeks flushing bright red. "Well, mistress," she said at last. "If that Fenmire Marshery is anything like the awful mires and swamps we struggled through in our long journey across the marshes I'd say she's welcome to it and good riddance to her."

"It is settled then," cried Marrimian. "We will deliver you, sister, into the Fenmire Marshery, *your* marshery, in the light of tomorrow's sun."

Amidst the roar of approval that echoed through

the hall and the shouts of delight to be rid of Pinvey's shadow Marrimian stole a fleeting glance at Krann where he sat beside her, knowing that it was also time to face the other shadow that lay across all her triumphs. She had not forgotten Krann's yearnings to return to Elundium, nor had she missed the way his gaze would wander out across the marshes toward Rainbows' End as the sunset. Gathering her courage, she took his hand and whispered, "After we have delivered Pinvey to Fenmire Marshery we will travel together across the marshes and you will show me all the wonders of these dykes and causeways that you have built from the Hurlers' Gate toward those bright, shining arcs of color at Rainbows' End."

For a moment he held her gaze and the roar of the crowds that filled the hall seemed to muffle and fade to nothing as he realized the true meaning in her words.

"But there is still so much left to do, so many fields to level and dams to build. So . . ." Krann fell silent as she shook her head and blinked at the tears that brimmed in her eyes.

"It has been settled by the Council of Voices. We begin the journey tomorrow," and she rose from the throne before the tears could flow down her cheeks and fled from the hall.

The roar of the great waterfalls was getting closer. The air was full of stinging droplets of icy water. Ansel planted her fat legs firmly on the huge spire of rock that jutted out above the falls and pointed proudly at the shimmering rainbows crisscrossing above their heads.

"There, it is just as I told you," she shouted to Vetchim above the thundering roar of water.

Just ahead of them Krann was pointing down into one of the waterfalls that boiled with white, frothing water. He was explaining to Marrimian that the ferocity of the floods had dammed and choked the channel leading to the waterfalls with hundreds of trees and bushes and had blocked it with mud until no more than a trickle of water flowed toward the lip of the falls. That had enabled the hoemasters and stonemasons to reach the edge of the falls and cut deep channels into the rock. "Twenty men high!" he shouted.

Marrimian nodded and looked out beyond the falls to the herds of mudbeasts that were now roaming across the water meadows. "Is that the beginning of your road home?" she asked quietly, pointing beyond the white spray of the waterfalls toward the distant line of mountains.

Krann laughed and shook his head, afraid to follow her pointing finger and for a brief moment she saw that haunted, faraway look come into his eyes.

"I never look beyond these bright rainbows. I have no wish to leave you. I love you," he cried.

But she had touched that hidden nerve deep down inside, that yearning to return to his home in Elundium. His love for her had stifled it for many seasons and for the first time in all the daylights that he had labored with the people of Gnarlsmyre, cutting drainage channels and building causeways, he let his eyes wander out across the mud flats where the silver-gray windflower heads swayed in the breeze and the glistening streams and rivers meandered through the rich water meadows toward the menacing wall of shifting fog that forever hid Elundium.

"The fog banks!" he shouted, seizing her hands. "Look, they have vanished, melted away!" And he stared spellbound at the distant line of tall, snow-capped mountain peaks that marched away beyond the edge of sight.

"It is winter in Elundium," he whispered longingly as all those hidden memories welled up and tear drops blurred his eyes, but he fiercely shook his head and turned his back to stare out across the marshes of Gnarlsmyre. "Elundium was long ago. It is here where I belong, here in Gnarlsmyre with you, Marrimian, because I love you."

Marrimian looked into his eyes and saw the strength of the love that flowed between them. She gathered her courage and drew him to her. "Krann," she whispered. "You must return to Elundium. You must search out the truth and lay the ghosts that shadowed your beginnings. You must finish the journey that you began before we met, then we can truly be together. If you don't I shall always feel that in some way I have held you with my love against your will." Krann drew back from her and saw that there were tears in her eyes. "You must, although my heart cries against it, you must go."

Krann shook his head and began to search for words to tell her that he could not find his way, he had used up his power of foresight searching for the secret paths while they built the dykes and causeways. He swept his hand out behind him across the water meadows in a hopeless gesture when Ansel suddenly shouted, "Look out—a pindafall bird!"

Marrimian broke free from Krann, snatched the bow from her shoulder and reached back into her quiver for an arrow. Krann spun round and his look of fear turned to a shout of laughter. "No, do not loose the arrow," he shouted. He knocked sharply against Marrimian's arm and sent the arrow spinning harmlessly down into the waterfall as a huge bird, the likes of which Marrimian had never seen before, slowly circled the spire of rocks. It shrieked once as it searched the rocks with unblinking eyes before it feathered its wings and stooped silently on to Krann's shoulder. Marrimian cried out in fear and staggered backwards beside Vetchim and the scullion. Krann reached up and gently caressed the aged Battle Owl's chest feathers and ran his fingers over the smooth, shiny talons.

"This is Mulcade, he is King Thane's Battle Owl and he perches beside the throne. He is the oldest and greatest bird of war in all Elundium."

"I don't know anything about Battle Owls," grumbled Ansel fearfully as the bird stared at her.

Krann paused, then turned and looked out across the water meadows toward the distant mountains and his lips trembled as he whispered, "He must have been searching for me for all the daylights since I fled from the Rising. He must have soared over every hidden valley, every rock and stone . . ."

"If your King and your sister, Elionbel, love you enough to send this great bird searching for you you must return and end their worry, you know you must," Marrimian urged.

Krann hesitated. He knew that Mulcade could find him a safe route through the quickmarshes, and only a few paces away a ladder of woven creepers that the channel diggers had used led down to the water meadows and the start of his long journey back into Elundium, yet he hesitated. He did not want to leave; his love for Marrimian still burned strongly in him and held him back.

"Come with me," he cried, reaching out and clutching her hand, and for a moment she clung to him, pressing herself against him, but slowly she pulled away.

"No, you must make this journey alone and put an end to all your doubts and fears. I cannot come with you, I must stay and rule over my people. But I will count the days until you return. Remember, my heart will be with you always and . . ." She hesitated, touching the pleats of her gown just above the embroidered belt buckle. "Part of you will always be with me here in Gnarlsmyre watching and waiting."

"You are with child," Krann gasped, staring at her.

Marrimian tried to laugh through her tears. "You

must hurry back for both our sakes. Now go, go quickly."

"No, I must stay with you."

Marrimian frowned and pushed her mist-wet hair out of her eyes. "Now it is even more important to know all your beginnings, for the child's sake."

"Mulcade will lead me back again, he will bring me safely back to Gnarlsmyre, I know he will," Krann cried, caressing the Battle Owl's chest feathers, and the great bird of war spread his wings, rose and flew high over the waterfalls, in and out of the shimmering rainbows, then gently stooped back and alighted on Marrimian's shoulder. She laughed, with tears flowing down her cheeks, and kissed Krann fiercely on the lips.

Mulcade rose from Marrimian's shoulder to lead Krann on his long journey back to Elundium and she cried out against the thunder of the falls, "I shall build a tower here between the rainbows and watch through every long day for your return."

MIKE JEFFERIES was born in Kent but spent his early years in Australia. He attended the Goldsmiths School of Art and then taught art in schools and in prisons. He now lives in Norfolk with his wife and three stepchildren, where he works, among other things, as an illustrator.

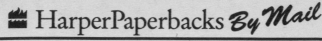